Praise for Liu

"Government fear of chaos is omnipresent in this expertly translated political farce . . . an intimate portrait of the local politics that matter so greatly in China."

—*The New York Times*

"A masterful tale that will make you laugh even as you despair . . . Wickedly subtle satire."

—*Kirkus Reviews* (starred review)

"A satirical tale that nimbly examines political corruption in China."

—*Publishers Weekly*

"Readers will enjoy this immersion in urban China and Liu's rollicking-good send-up of modern-day predatory capitalism."

—*Booklist*

"Those who enjoy Chinese literature will appreciate how the novel openly provides commentary on the disparity between the economic social classes and unscrupulous corruption found in almost any society."

—*Library Journal*

"The power of this novel is derived, partly, from the sharp glance the author casts at the modern Chinese society, plagued by corruption, poverty, and injustice. The dark tale is lightened by the author's delicious humor. Liu Zhenyun is an outstanding storyteller."

—Lijia Zhang, author of *Socialism is Great!*

REMEMBERING 1942

AND OTHER CHINESE STORIES

LIU ZHENYUN

TRANSLATED BY
SYLVIA LI-CHUN LIN
AND
HOWARD GOLDBLATT

Arcade Publishing • New York

Arcade Publishing books may be purchased in bulk at special discounts for sales
promotion, corporate gifts, fund-raising, or educational purposes. Special editions can
also be created to specifications. For details, contact the Special Sales Department,
Arcade Publishing, 307 West 36th Street, 11th Floor, New York, NY 10018 or
info@skyhorsepublishing.com.

Arcade® and Skyhorse Publishing® are registered trademarks of Skyhorse Publishing, Inc.®,
a Delaware corporation.

Visit our website at www.skyhorsepublishing.com.

10 9 8 7 6 5 4 3 2 1

Library of Congress Cataloging-in-Publication Data is available on file.

Cover design by Laura Klynstra
Cover image credit: iStock

Paperback ISBN: 978-1-64821-094-5
Hardcover ISBN: 978-1-62872-712-8
Ebook ISBN: 978-1-62872-715-9

Printed in the United States of America

Table of Contents

REMEMBERING
1942

Tofu

1

A half kilo of tofu at Lin's house went bad.

At the state-run grocery store, half a kilo of tofu came in five squares at a hundred grams apiece. At the private market, half a kilo of tofu came in one watery, mushy piece, impossible to stir-fry. So he rose at six every morning to line up outside the state-run grocery store to buy tofu, but that did not always mean he'd get any. The line was long and the tofu might run out before his turn came; or it might be seven o'clock before he reached the counter and he had to get out of line to catch the office bus. The new section head, Guan, worked doubly hard to parade his efficiency, watching like a hawk for anyone who came in late or left early. What Lin found most depressing was having to leave for work just before he reached the counter. He would curse the long line as he walked off:

"Damn it. Too many poor people is bad for the world!"

But he managed to buy some that day. He lined up till seven-fifteen and missed the bus, but that didn't matter since Guan was off at a meeting at the ministry and the deputy section head, He, was on a business trip. A new arrival, a college graduate, was in charge of attendance that day, so Lin kept his place in line until he got the tofu. After taking his prized purchase home, he then forgot to put it in the fridge before hurrying off to catch a public bus. He came home after work that evening to find the tofu still in the hallway, still secure in its plastic bag. It had been a hot day, so naturally it had gone bad.

His wife had come home before him, aggravating the problem of the spoiled tofu. She reproached the nanny for not opening the plastic bag and putting the tofu in the fridge. But the nanny would have none of that. She was ready to quit, since the pay was low and the food wasn't up to par, and Lin and his wife did their best to talk her into staying. The spoiled tofu did not bother the nanny one bit; she placed the blame squarely on Lin for not telling her to put it away before leaving for work. So when he walked in the door, his wife turned on him.

"I could have dealt with it if you hadn't managed to buy any tofu. But you did, so why did you leave it in the bag to spoil? What were you thinking?"

Lin had had a bad day at work. He'd thought he could be late for work that morning, but the college grad took his job too seriously and wrote him up for being "late." Lin went and changed it to "on time," but that just about ruined his day, for he worried that the new guy might report him. Now that he was home, the spoiled tofu made it worse. He was mad at the nanny for not putting it in the fridge just because he hadn't told her to. *Would it have killed you to put it away?* Then there was his wife, making a big deal out of nothing. *It's only half a kilo of tofu. So what if it spoiled? I didn't mean for it go bad, did I? Why go on and on about it? We're both tired after a day's work and we have to make dinner and take care of the baby. Are you trying to make me more tired than I already am?*

"All right, all right. It was my fault. We won't have tofu tonight, and I'll be more careful from now on."

It would have blown over if he'd stopped there, but he couldn't hold back:

"It's just half a kilo of tofu. Why raise such a stink? Did anyone complain that time you broke a vacuum bottle that cost almost eight Yuan?"

She blew her top at the mention of the vacuum bottle.

"Why must you bring that up all the time? Was it really my fault? It was in the wrong place, and anyone could have knocked it over. But forget about that and let's talk about the flower vase. What happened to that last month? It was sitting next to the wardrobe when you broke it while you were dusting. You have no right to criticize me."

With tears in her eyes, she blocked his path, her chest heaving and her face ashen. Experience told him that a bloodless face was a sign of a bad day at the office. Her work made her unhappy most of the time, just like him. But it wasn't right to vent work-related frustrations at home, and that thought caused another flare-up. He was fully prepared to continue the discussion of the flower vase if they didn't stop there. They would bring up more misadventures, talk that would degenerate into a vicious cycle, which, this time anyway, would likely result in her throwing the tofu at him. The nanny, by now used to their fights, stood nearby clipping her nails as if nothing were wrong. Her indifference stoked the fires of the argument, and Lin was ready to ratchet it up a level; luckily, a knock at the door stopped them both. His wife dried her tears while he fought to keep his anger in check, as the nanny opened the door. It was the old man who checked their water meter.

He walked with a limp, so stairs made for hard work, and he was usually bathed in sweat when he entered the apartment on his monthly rounds. He'd have to take a breather before checking the meter. A conscientious worker, he came even when the meters did not need to be checked, saying he wanted to see if they were operating properly. On this day he was there to check the meter, so husband and wife put on tranquil faces as the nanny led the old man over to the meter. But instead of leaving right away, he sat down on their bed, sending fear into Lin's heart—whenever the old man sat down, he would launch into a reminiscence of his younger days, when he fed horses belonging to a (now-deceased) government leader. The first time he heard the story, Lin was actually interested enough to ask questions, intrigued by the fact that the gimpy old man had worked for someone that important. But he lost patience as one repetition followed another. *So what if you fed a big shot's horses? Didn't you wind up a meter reader anyhow? What's the point of prattling on about a dead leader?* But Lin knew better than to offend the old man, who could shut off the water for the whole building if someone got on his bad side. *That wrench he's holding controls the water valve and dictates that I have to listen to him talk about feeding horses.* On this day, Lin was definitely not in the mood for more horse stories. It was clear that the old man had arrived during a fight, so why must he sit down without being asked? Pulling a long face, Lin stayed put instead of going over to chat with the man, as he usually did.

Oblivious to all that, the old man lit a cigarette and sent streams of smoke through his nostrils into the room. Lin was ready to be bored with horse feeding tales again, but this time, instead of bringing up the horses, the old man said he wanted to talk about something serious: the masses had complained that someone in the building was stealing water. Instead of turning the faucet all the way off at night, the thief was letting water drip slowly into a bucket, not quite enough to engage the meter. It was stolen water, and that had to stop. Could the water company stay in business if everyone did that?

Lin turned red, his wife went white. They were the guilty parties. They had indeed stolen water a couple of times the previous week, using a scam she'd heard from someone at work. She had instructed the nanny to try it, until he found it unseemly. *How much does a ton of water cost? Why stoop to stealing?* Besides, the drip-drip-drip kept them awake at night, so two days later they stopped. How had the old man found out about it? Who had ratted on them? Lin and his wife immediately zeroed in on the overweight neighbors across the hall. Claiming she looked Indian, the woman often dabbed a red mark between her brows. They had a child, about the same age as the Lin's daughter. The two girls often played together, which meant they also fought a lot. Because of the children, Lin's wife and the Indian wannabe were cordial only on the surface. Their nannies, however, had struck up a friendship and often put their heads together to find ways to deal with their employers. When the Indian wannabe heard the nannies talking about the theft of water, she went to the old man, who in turn had come to talk to them. But that was not something they could deal with openly, since it would make them lose standing with their neighbors. Lin rushed over to the meter man and declared that he did not know if anyone was stealing water, but that they would never do something like that; they might be poor, but they had integrity. His wife jumped in to add that whoever made the complaint must be the water thief. If not, how would they know the trick? It was the old scheme of a thief diverting attention from himself. The old man flicked the ash off his cigarette.

"No problem. Let's let this be the end of it. No matter who did it, it's in the past. We just have to make sure no one does it again."

He stood up and, with a magnanimous gesture, limped out of the apartment, leaving Lin and his wife standing there in embarrassment.

Compared to the meter man's visit and the theft issue, the spoiled tofu no longer seemed so significant. Lin grumbled about his college-educated wife: when had she become so petty? How much were two buckets of water worth? Now see what happened? Scolded by a meter man! Ashamed of her actions, his wife felt she had no right to abuse him over the tofu, so she went in to make dinner after one last searing glare. An imminent domestic skirmish had been preempted by the old man's visit, for which Lin was grateful.

Their dinner that night consisted of stir-fried green beans, stir-fried bean sprouts, sausage links, and a vegetable medley from the night before. The sausage links were for the girl, the other three for the adults, but the nanny refused to eat leftovers, claiming they upset her stomach. Lin's wife had argued with the nanny over leftovers in the past.

"So you're an aristocrat, and I have to eat leftovers, is that it? They give you stomach trouble, you say? What did you eat in the countryside?" Lin's wife fumed while the nanny cried and caused a scene, threatening to quit. In the end, Lin had to step in and talk her into staying, which gave her all the leverage she needed to never eat leftovers again. Left with no choice, Lin and his wife finished the leftovers before starting in on the new dishes. The child acted up during the meal, grabbing at one thing and throwing away another, and she was sniffling, the sign of a cold. Dinner did not end till nearly eight o'clock, when the nanny was to do the dishes, Lin to give the child her bath, and his wife was off to bed. Her office was farther than his, so she needed to get up earlier. Turning in early made perfect sense. But not this night. Without even washing her feet, she sat on the edge of the bed, lost in thought, a sight that always made Lin nervous. He was worried she might bring up something he'd rather not talk about, but luckily she went to bed after a quick wash of her feet. She could be a nag, but never in bed, and, in fact, would be asleep and sawing logs in three minutes, faster than their daughter. During the first few years of their marriage, Lin had been miffed by this trait. How could she fall asleep so fast?

"How can you fall asleep the moment you lie down? If this is how it's going to be, what do you expect me to do?"

"I work all day, and I'm out on my feet when I get home," she explained sheepishly. "Why wouldn't I fall asleep right away?"

The simple pleasures of life departed with the arrival of a baby. Besides moving several times, they had their jobs and their concerns over daily necessities, plus all the other things that involved the three of them. So, of course they were tired much of the time, and his wife became a nag, which was why he now considered her sleeping habit a plus in their relationship. Whenever they fought, he had something to look forward to—a cease-fire the moment her head touched the. pillow. Lin now realized that virtues and flaws were not absolute, for one could easily turn into the other.

After his wife, their child, and the nanny were asleep and had begun to snore, Lin made sure everything—lights, stove, water—was turned off in the apartment before going to bed himself. In the past he'd read a book or the paper at bedtime, sometimes even get up to write something down. But now, after all the household chores were done, his eyelids would be so heavy he abandoned his earlier habits. He went to bed as early as possible, since he had to get up at the crack of dawn to queue up for tofu. The thought reminded him that the spoiled tofu was still lying in the hallway. It could be the fuse for another domestic scrap, setting off his wife when she saw it the next morning. So he got out of bed, went into the hallway, and turned on the light so he could get rid of the spoiled tofu.

2

Lin's wife was a Li. She'd been a quiet, attractive young woman before marriage. On the slight side, she was cute and well proportioned, with small, bright eyes that everyone found endearing. Back then she wasn't much of a talker. Though she was always neat and tidy, with nice, long hair, she was not particularly fashionable. After a college friend made the introduction, they started dating. She was shy at first, but he could relax and feel serene around her. There was a sort of poetic quality about her. She got him to start paying attention to language and hygiene. How in the world had that serene, almost poetic girl turned into a petty nag who rarely combed her hair and had even learned to steal water at night in only a few years? Being college graduates, they'd both been ambitious; working hard and studying late into the night, they were determined to succeed. Back then they had sneered at positions such as section head or bureau chief at a government office, and held private companies, big or small, in contempt. They never expected that in a few years they would end up just like everyone else. Life consisted of buying tofu, going to and coming from work, doing the laundry, the daily routine of eating and sleeping, dealing with the nanny, and caring for their child. By nightfall, no one was in the mood to read, not even a page. Ambition and grand plans for life, like their ideals and dreams for an impressive career, were nothing but rubbish now, something only the young can indulge in. Everyone plodded along and life went on. So what if you had ambition or a grand plan for life? So what if you had ideals or dreams for an impressive career? *Dream of the Red Chamber* said it best: "Where have all the generals and ministers gone? Rotting in tombs overgrown with weeds." Who will remember you after you're gone?

And yet, when he mulled over his situation, Lin was generally content. He'd gone through some tough times at work, but the experience had turned him into a mature man who knew how to deal with things. You could have what others had so long as you were patient enough to wait and avoid anxiety and panic attacks. Take housing. They'd started out sharing a flat, then moved to the slums in Niujie; when they were slated to be torn down, it was off to relocation housing; finally, after several moves over the years, they landed a one-bedroom unit. When other families were buying refrigerators and color TVs, he did not have the money, and was ashamed. But eventually they saved enough to join them. Admittedly, they could not consider buying a set of modular furniture or a stereo system, but there was no need pursue material comfort anyway. As they say, don't be in a hurry; wait patiently and communism will be here soon. What he found trying were in fact daily trivialities—spoiled tofu, for instance. In the past, he had always considered "having a wife and children sleeping in their own warm beds" a sort of peasant mentality, but in the end, that's what real life boils down to. What else is there? Was it really that easy to manage a wife, a child, *and* a warm bed? The wife turns into a different woman, the child is too young to know anything, and the workload never lessens. Who can guarantee that the bed will stay warm forever? At first you complain about office politics, but domestic life turns out to be just as taxing. You can be forgiven for harboring grand ideals, since you were too young and immature to understand the natural course of development in life. As the ancient saying has it, a journey of a thousand leagues starts with a single step. For Lin everything started with spoiled tofu.

So, he got up at the six the next morning, as usual, to queue up outside the state-run grocery store. His wife, who was already awake, lay there staring at the ceiling. She fell asleep fast and woke up clearheaded, unlike Lin, who needed half an hour to get out of his dazed state. It took her a mere five minutes to be completely awake and continue her thoughts from the previous night. That was a virtue; it was also a flaw. Whenever they had an argument, she would wake up and immediately pick up where she'd left off the night before. His heart sank when he saw her sitting there, lost in thought, looking just like she had the night before. He wondered what she'd do or say next. To his relief, she simply ignored him, so he hurried off to brush his teeth and wash his face, before picking up another plastic bag to slink out the door. She spoke up just as he reached for the door handle.

"Forget the tofu today."

So she hadn't forgiven him, and the curtain was about to rise on act two of the tofu incident. The flames of anger were kindled. He'd already thrown away the spoiled tofu, but she wouldn't let it go, even after a night's sleep.

"Is a bit of spoiled tofu such a big deal that we won't buy any more from now on? I'll put it in the fridge and that will be the end of it. How long do you expect to go on about it?"

"I wasn't going to talk to you about tofu." She waved him off. "I did some thinking last night and have decided I've had it with that office. I'm thinking of quitting my job, and I'd like you to be on my side for a change. That's what I want to talk to you about."

Though Lin was relieved to hear that it wasn't about the tofu, the subject of changing jobs was even more annoying and more complicated. For a college graduate, she had a pretty good job, summarizing official documents and writing work reports, with enough free time to read the paper and enjoy a cup of tea. The problem was a lack of tact, which had led to problems in her personal relationships, very much like Lin himself when he started out. She'd learned her lesson and changed her ways, but scars from the previous encounters hadn't gone away, and friction was unavoidable. Whenever she had a bad day at the office, she came home and complained to him, threatening to look for another job. Then he'd counter with his own experience, saying that things would get better over time, once she abandoned her juvenile attitude and naiveté. What did she have in mind? All offices are the same, he'd say. Besides, did she think that finding a new job was going to be easy?

"Neither of us has power or status, and we don't know a thing about the job market, so how do you expect to find an office that'll take you?"

"You really are worthless," she'd complain. "Here your own wife is suffering, and you can't do a thing to help her out."

"I can't help you with a new job, but I can still be helpful. I try to explain things to you; doesn't that count as help?" That would calm her down, and after venting her frustration, she'd drop the subject and go back to work the next day. If that could have continued over time, she would have adapted to the office environment and he would not have had to deal with the headache of her desire to find a new job. But each time they moved, they lived farther and farther from her workplace. In their first place together in Beijing, she'd been happy about their improved living conditions. She'd thrown herself into decorating the place, from window coverings to furniture arrangement, even the placement of the refrigerator and TV. She'd focused on all the things they'd need to complete their apartment. But once everything was pretty much set, her happiness was compromised by the distance she had to travel to work. The office bus did not stop in their area, which forced her to spend three or four hours each way on crowded public buses. She got up at six a.m. and wasn't back home until seven or eight at night, leaving while stars still sparkled in the sky and returning after the moon was up. Over time, she set her heart on a job change. From her exhausted look when she came home, he knew this was different from problems at work, which could be tolerated. But no human effort could shorten the distance between home and work; that could only be accomplished by finding an office closer to home. They had no idea how difficult it would be until they decided to try. Like a blind cat trying to catch a dead mouse, they inquired at several offices, and each time they were turned down outright, with no room for further discussion. Naturally they were deflated.

"Forget it," he said. "It's hopeless. Why keep trying? You'll just have to put up with the way things are. There are people in Beijing with a longer commute than yours. And don't just focus on the distance. Think about all those women in textile mills. They're on their feet all day, while you get to read the paper and drink tea. You should be happy with what you have."

"You want me to put up with it because you can't do a damned thing. You get to ride the office bus, so what do *you* know about how *I* feel on a crowded public bus four hours a day? If I can't find another job, I'll quit outright tomorrow. Then you can support us all by yourself."

And she did stay home the next day, which threw him into a panic. It worked. He put his brain to work and eventually came up with an idea. He heard that the head of an office on Qiansanmen Street had gone to school with Deputy Bureau Chief Zhang at Lin's office. He had worked hard helping Zhang move to a new apartment, which had left a very good impression. Later, after Zhang had a lifestyle issue with a woman named Qiao, he began showing concern for those who worked for him; he was always happy to lend a helping hand, rarely refusing any request for help. So Lin figured that Zhang would not say no if he went to see him regarding his wife's job hunt. With Zhang's connections, she stood a chance of finding a position in the Qiansanmen office. Admittedly, it was still quite a distance. But it was on the subway line, making it a forty-minute commute; besides, the subway was never as crowded as a bus and there were sometimes open seats. She was pleased to hear his idea and agreed to the transfer. He went to see Zhang and laid out the difficulties his wife faced before mentioning the Qiansanmen office.

"I've heard that our esteemed boss knows someone there, and I'm wondering if you could help us out."

"No problem." Zhang said unhesitatingly, as expected. "With such a long commute, she really should get a different job. I don't know much about that office," he continued, "but the man in charge of personnel matters is an old school pal. I'll write to him. Then you can go see what he can do for you."

"Perhaps our esteemed boss could phone him first." Lin knew he was pushing it a bit.

Rubbing his big head, Zhang laughed heartily and tapped Lin on the head.

"You young people these days are much smarter than we were. Very well, I'll phone him."

Zhang made the call and wrote a letter for Lin to take with him. That letter was like an imperial edict to Lin and to his wife, who was delighted to see it. It worked wonders. When the head of personnel read it, he said:

"Yes, Zhang and I were schoolmates. In college, we were on the track-and-field team."

Lin, who was sitting on the edge of his chair across from the desk, quickly picked up the thread of the conversation:

"I can see that. He still loves to exercise."

After a quick glance, the man changed the subject and asked about the scandal. He wanted details, which put Lin in an awkward spot. Knowing he had to tell the man something, he focused on the important parts. Zhang and the woman, Qiao, he said, had just sat alone in his office and hadn't really done anything. Everything beyond that was strictly rumor. The man laughed.

"That old Zhang is still quite the character," he said.

Finally it was time to bring up the transfer. The man was in a good mood.

"Sure," he said, "can do. Zhang has asked me to help, so leave it to me. I'll check to see where there's a vacancy."

That sounded like a promise to Lin, who went home and said so to his wife. She was so overjoyed she put her arms around him and planted kissed all over his face. They had a pleasant evening.

She would have gotten the job and could have started riding the subway to Qiansanmen if only they'd left it at that. But they were too clever for their own good and ended up ruining her chances. The head of personnel was already working on their behalf, but that somehow didn't seem enough for Lin and his wife. So she asked around and learned that the husband of a close friend worked at that office, and was a section head, no less. Relying solely on the head of personnel office might not be enough to get the job done, she told her husband. Maybe they ought to go see the section head too. Without thinking it through, Lin agreed that one more person meant more clout, so he went to talk to the section head. The head of personnel stopped working for them as soon as he heard about Lin's visit to the section head. The next time Lin went to see him, he was decidedly cooler.

"Didn't you go see so-and-so? Why not wait to see what he can do?"

Lin was alarmed, realizing he'd made a strategic error. Asking someone for a favor was not all that different from succeeding in an office environment; you can only have one patron. Seek out too many people, and none of them will go out of their way to help. Besides, seeking help from multiple persons implies that you know lots of people, which in turn shows you are well connected. Why do you need my help, they wonder, if you already have someone in your corner? You can count yourself lucky if they merely decide to stand aside; they could be so offended they'll try to undercut your plan to show that they were the one you should have stuck with.

It was too late by the time Lin and his wife understood how it had all played out. After first blaming each other, they put their heads together to find a way to repair the damage. But what could they do? All he could come up with was to go see Zhang and ask him to call his friend again. On the other hand, he couldn't keep running to a deputy bureau chief. Lin and his wife had to put aside her job hunt for now, and he forgot all about it as time passed and got busy with other things. But she did not forget, in fact thought about it a great deal of the time. And that was exactly what she had been doing the night before, after the spoiled tofu incident, when she sat on the edge of the bed without washing her feet, deep in thought. She brought the subject up with Lin that morning as soon as she woke up. Convinced she wanted him to talk to Zhang again, which he dreaded, he said:

"We've already torpedoed our chances, so what's the point of going to see him?"

"Go talk to the head of personnel again instead."

He dreaded that even more.

"He was cool with me after you talked to your friend's husband. I don't have the guts to go see him again. Besides, it won't work anyway."

"And what makes you think it won't work? I've given it some more thought. You don't need to blame me for seeing my friend's husband, because that's not the key. The key is we haven't done enough. These days, when you want something done, talk is useless. I think we have to offer him something. A fly has to see blood before it makes a move. He won't be serious until he sees blood. So blood is what he'll get!"

"I've barely met him. I don't even know where he lives, so how are we going to send him the gift?"

"Just listen to you! I know you don't care a whit about me." She blew up. "What did you give Qiao that time you wanted to join the party? We were barely making it back then and could hardly afford milk for the baby, but did I say no when you wanted to buy her a gift? Why all these excuses when it's my turn? What's going on in that head of yours?"

Her face had turned white with anger, prompting a quick capitulation.

"All right. We'll give him something. Don't worry. We'll send a gift and see what happens."

That marked the end of their discussion. They went to work. When they returned in the evening, they had a quick dinner and told the nanny to take care of the child before heading out to buy a gift. But what? After wandering through a store for half an hour they still hadn't decided. Something cheap wouldn't do, but they couldn't bring themselves to spend too much either. In the end she found a handicraft item that fit the bill: a glass case etched with flowers, birds, and fish. It was attractive, presentable, and, under forty Yuan, affordable. But after talking it over, they decided against it. Would a head of personnel be partial to flowers and birds? If the man thought they were trying buy his help with a cheap curio, that could work against them. So they went back to browsing; his eyes lit up when they reached the soft drink counter.

"I've got it."

"What have you got?"

He pointed to a sign above cases of Coca-Cola. "Big Sale: 1.9 Yuan a can." A case of Coke normally cost three fifty. A highly desirable gift and, at 1.9 a can, a twenty-four-can case would cost them less than fifty. A famous-brand soft drink with enough bulk, it would be practical and smart looking; the man had to like it. But why was it on sale?

"What if it's passed the expiration date? That would be even worse."

But no, it hadn't, the shop clerk told them. How strange; it was as if it had gone on sale that day just so they could buy a gift.

"Well, it looks like we're in luck today, and that spells success."

Her spirits lifted, she took out her purse and bought a case. Then with Lin carrying it over his shoulder, they crowded onto a bus for their gift-delivery trip. It was eight thirty, an ideal time, when they reached the man's building in high spirits. They had just reached the bottom of the staircase as a man was coming down the stairs. It was none other than the head of personnel. Lin's greeting took the man by surprise. When he saw who it was, he was friendlier than he'd been back in his office.

"Ah, it's you," he stopped and said with a smile.

"This is my wife, Uncle Wang. Chief Zhang told us to come see you again about her job request."

"I know. No problem on my end. The hang-up is in the receiving office. If you can find an office that will take her on, have them contact me. I need to go out on business and the car is waiting, so excuse me for not asking you in."

Their hearts sank. It was an out-and-out refusal that made Lin forget all about the Coke until the man was already outside the building.

"Oh, I brought you a case of soft drinks, Uncle Wang."

"That's one thing we're not short of," the man replied with a laugh. "Take it home and enjoy it yourselves."

Then the car started and drove off. They froze in the hallway, embarrassed and feeling awkward for a long moment before finally snapping out of it. Lin threw the case onto the stairs.

"That fuck-head didn't even want our gift."

Then he turned to his wife. "Didn't I say no gift? But you wouldn't listen, so now see what happened? It's humiliating."

"What a terrible man," his wife said. "So petty."

They carried the case home, having failed to give it away, and feeling foolish about paying so much—forty Yuan—for something they'd end up keeping. Needless to say, their hearts ached over the expenditure. What were they going to do with a whole case of Coke? Anything edible was not returnable, so they'd have to drink it. But they couldn't just shut the door and drink a Coke anytime they felt like it. It took them two days to solve the problem; his clever wife opened the case and gave a can to their child every now and then for her to drink out in the yard. They had gained a reputation for being dirt poor, since they'd never before bought soft drinks or ribbonfish, and their child was practically in rags. They did buy a ribbonfish once, but it was on sale and hadn't smelled so good. The stink had spread into the hallway, which gave the Indian wannabe something more to talk about. Now giving their daughter a can of Coke to walk around with would improve their reputation, and they wouldn't have spent the money for nothing. Her job transfer, however, remained a nettlesome issue.

3

They had houseguests. He knew that the moment he walked into the hallway that evening after work. The sound of two men coughing issued from their open apartment door. People from his hometown. He was right. Two men with sunbaked skin and blue veins on their heads were sitting on the edge of their bed. Canvas bags that were popular in the seventies, with quotations from Chairman Mao stamped on the sides, were on the floor by their feet. They were puffing on cigarettes and coughing, spitting and flicking ashes on the floor. Pungent clouds made his little girl cough as she ran through the thick smoke.

He'd come home in a good mood. Guan, the new section head, still walked around with a stern expression, but he didn't have a bone to pick with the people who worked for him. For the quarterly evaluation, he gave Lin a top rating, which meant a bonus of fifty Yuan. While that wasn't much, fifty Yuan more was a lot better than fifty Yuan less, and it would surely make his wife happy. The arrival of the two visitors was a damper on what would have been a triumphant return. His wife wasn't home yet. As if hit with a bucket of cold water, he felt his high spirits vanish into thin air. The arrival of hometown visitors should have been something to celebrate, an opportunity to recall the past with people he hadn't seen for years. The problem was, they took all the joy out of it by dropping by so often; it had, in fact, become a burden. The guests had to be fed, which cost at least fifty Yuan each time, and the frequency made it a serious drain on family finances. These hometown guests were different from old friends or schoolmates. They might be sunburnt peasants with blue veins, but they cared much more about conventions. Old friends and schoolmates would forgive him if he didn't treat them like royalty, but not those from the countryside. They would be upset and complain about him back home, assuming that they were entitled to a grand reception, since he lived in Beijing. They had no idea that he fell into the lowest social stratum in Beijing and that he had to get up early to line up for tofu. Two additional dishes were added at the meal purely for their sake. Sometimes he had to laugh at their arrogant airs, even though he was unhappy with them. *What do you eat back home, anyway?*

It wouldn't have been so bad if they could have been sent off after a meal, but no such luck. Oftentimes after they ate their fill, they gave him a long list of tasks they needed done—getting supplies or chemical fertilizer, buying a car, or filing a lawsuit. And he had to shell out for their train tickets when they finally left. What made them think he was capable of accomplishing all those tasks, when he couldn't even manage to get his wife a new job? Hell, he even failed at giving a man a gift! How was he going to sue someone or buy a car? As for the train tickets, he had to queue up at the train station to do that.

At first, concerned about face, he tried accommodating them, since they'd have looked down him if he'd told them there was nothing he could do. But his efforts were usually wasted. He did have college friends assigned to various government offices, but they were too new to the job to enjoy any authority or power. Coming home to face his hometown guests was the height of embarrassment. Over time he smartened up and learned to say, "No, I don't think I can help you with that." Sure, they looked down on him, but they would have sooner or later anyway. Better to get that over with early—saves trouble. Yet they kept showing up and each visit at minimum cost him a meal. What complicated matters was the fact that his wife was from the city, with much simpler interpersonal relationships, and rarely had visitors. Her people seldom visited; his never stopped visiting, and they had to be fed. On top of that, the country folk were always carelessly dropping cigarette ashes or spitting wherever they felt like it, which embarrassed him. His wife had started out being okay about that, and said nothing, but that changed when the visits turned into a constant chore. She frowned when they arrived, refused to go grocery shopping, and stayed clear of the kitchen. Lin was unhappy that she made him look bad, but he had to admit that she was right to be upset, and it didn't take long for him to join her in that. Besides complaining about his wife, he found fault with the country folk, who let him down and showed him in a bad light. His hometown was like a bushy tail that would, from time to time, rear up to show his private parts, reminding everyone that he came from the countryside. As the fake Indian woman once said, his family was too coarse to look urban, a comment that made his wife cross. Which was why he was often on edge when the workday ended, worried that someone from his hometown might choose that day to pop in for a visit. He jumped whenever he heard someone speaking with an out-of-town accent in the yard and ran over to the balcony to see if that accent was walking into his building. Only after watching the person move on was he able to relax. Though he never looked forward to visitors from his hometown, he was always eager to entertain guests from his wife's side. When that happened, he welcomed them enthusiastically to make it up to his wife by balancing out the visits from his side. But they seldom came, which meant he was constantly plagued by guilty feelings. Oblivious of those feelings, his parents liked to brag about their son who lived in Beijing and often said to the neighbors, "My son's in Beijing. Go look him up." After a while he realized that his hospitality only invited more houseguests. That taught him a lesson, and hometown visitors began to receive a chilly reception, which naturally upset them. They would return home and tell everyone that he had forgotten his roots. *Well, let them talk! What's there to remember about roots?* He even wrote his parents to say stop the flow.

"I'm busy and money's tight. So please stop sending people here just so you can look good to your neighbors." He showed the letter to his wife, who wasn't fooled by his attempt to appease her.

"I wouldn't have married you if I'd known what your family was like." She spit on the floor.

That did not sit well with him.

"I told you about my family and you said you didn't care. Now you're making it sound as if I deceived you."

They could fight all they wanted, but that did not stanch the flow. Over time she took the visits more calmly, but always with a frown. Whenever they showed up, he had the good sense to add only two dishes, maybe fish or chicken, and never offered liquor. If that made them unhappy, so be it. Better to upset them than upset his wife.

But this particular visit called for more than a couple of added dishes. He didn't know who the two visitors—one old and one young—were at first and had to ask which village they'd came from. The old man's accent reminded Lin of his elementary school teacher, a Mr. Du, who had taught math and language for five years. One winter Lin had played hooky to go outside and play on the ice during study hall. The ice cracked and he fell into the water. Instead of giving him a hard time after he was rescued, the teacher stripped off Lin's wet clothes and draped his own padded jacket over the boy. Seeing his teacher again after more than a decade, Lin could not hide his emotions. He went up, grabbed the old man's hands, and said: "Teacher!"

His emotions sparked a similar reaction from the old man. "I wouldn't have recognized you on the street, Little Lin," he said before introducing the young man, his son.

Once they both had calmed down, Lin asked the purpose of the visit. He tensed up when the old man explained that he had emphysema, but the hospital in their hometown wasn't advanced enough to see whether he had lung cancer. He recalled that his most accomplished student had made it to Beijing, so he came with his son for Lin's help in finding a hospital for a diagnosis. If it turned out to be cancer, it would be best stay in a hospital for treatment; if not, he'd like an operation.

"We'll talk it over," Lin said, while racking his brain for a solution. He didn't know anyone at any Beijing hospital. The door opened and in walked his wife. Lin checked his watch; it was seven thirty. He tensed up again, observing the look on her face as he made the introductions. As expected, she did not appear happy to see the visitors, who had obviously fouled up the air and floor with their cigarettes and spittle. She nodded before ducking into the kitchen, from where the sound of her scolding the nanny for not having their daughter's dinner ready emerged. Lin knew that the outburst was aimed at him. It was his fault; he'd been chatting his teacher and forgot to tell the nanny to get the child something to eat. Besides, with the addition of two guests, there'd be six to feed that night and nothing was ready.

He excused himself and went in to explain to his wife. But first he took out the fifty Yuan as a token of good will before telling her that he had no choice, since the old man was his teacher, not just anyone from home. We'll throw something together and it will be over soon. To his surprise, she smacked his hand, sending sent the five ten-Yuan bills flying.

"To hell with you. You're not the only one with a teacher. My child is hungry and I have no time to think about your teacher."

"Not so loud." He reached out for her. "They could hear us."

"So what if they do?" She raised her voice. "With all these people coming and going, it's like I'm running a hotel. I can't take it anymore." She sat on the edge of the sink and wept.

He felt his anger rising, but it was pointless to be mad at a moment like this. His guests were still in the other room, so he had to entertain them. He could tell that his teacher had heard their argument. Being an educated man, he did not display arrogance over the less-than-cordial reception from Lin's wife; instead, he said in a loud voice:

"Don't worry, Little Lin. We ate before we came. We're staying in a hotel in Jinsongdi. We're just here to say hello and bring you some local things from back home. We need to go soon so we won't miss our train."

He had his son take two containers of sesame oil out of his canvas bag and take them into the kitchen.

That made Lin feel even worse. He was sure his teacher hadn't eaten, and had only said so for the benefit of Lin's wife. Maybe it was the sesame oil, and maybe she was using better judgment, but in any case she cooked dinner. It was a nice meal, with four dishes, including a stir-fry with shrimp reserved for the child. Finally the meal was over and he walked the old man and his son out.

"I've caused you trouble by coming here," his teacher apologized. "I didn't want to come, but your *shimu* said I should, so I did."

Lin's heart ached when he noticed how the gray-headed, wrinkled old man hobbled along. He hadn't even given him a chance to wash his face at home.

"You need to get a checkup in Beijing. Let me find you a cheap place to stay, and I'll ask around about hospitals tomorrow."

"Don't worry about me. I know what to do." The old man waved him off and took off his hat to retrieve a piece of paper.

"I was worried I might not find you, so I went to see Mr. Li, the section chief at the county education bureau. He has an old school friend who's now a director at a big government office. See, he even wrote him a letter on my behalf. As a high-ranking cadre, his friend ought to be a big help."

Lin let his offer drop after what the man said, since he couldn't possibly find a good hospital for his teacher anyway. He'd only be delaying the old man's treatment, so it would be better for him to get help from the director. He walked father and son to a bus stop, where they said their good-byes. As the bus pulled out, his teacher was still waving at him and smiling, his body rocking back and forth each time the bus stopped and started up again. Tears welled up in Lin's eyes when he saw the old man wave. Hadn't his teacher smiled just like that when Lin was in elementary school? He didn't turn to go home until the bus was out of sight. A great weight descended on him after he took only a few steps; like a mountain, it made him feel it could crush him at any moment.

At the office the next day he read a commemorative essay about a major figure who had died some years before. It mentioned how the great man had revered educators, even once bringing the last two surviving teachers from his childhood to Beijing, where he'd put them up in the finest hotel and shown them all around the capital. Lin had had a favorable impression of the great figure until he read the piece.

"Everyone wants to show respect to his teachers. I'd like to put mine up at the finest hotel and give him a tour of the city. But where do I get the money to do that?" He grumbled and threw the paper into the wastepaper basket.

4

Their daughter was sniffling and coughing, obviously coming down with something.

"Your teacher has emphysema. Could he have given it to the kid when he visited?" his wife asked.

Lin was just as worried. Everything changed when their daughter was sick. They couldn't leave her with just the nanny, so one of them had to stay home. He was incensed by his wife's preposterous faultfinding and blaming his teacher. He'd given her the cold shoulder for two days after his teacher left, as she had put him in a bad light and made him lose face in front of his teacher. The father and son had gotten a free meal, but they'd brought with them two containers of sesame oil that weighed five kilos altogether. In the open market a kilo of sesame oil cost sixteen Yuan, so it came to eighty Yuan for the oil. Had they eaten eighty Yuan worth of food that night? Knowing she'd gone too far, she did have a contrite look whenever she used the oil from his teacher. But now her worries over the sick child needed an outlet, and she wanted to regain an upper hand in the family, so the teacher became the best target.

"What she needs now is a checkup. If that shows no connection to emphysema, laying the blame on him before the results are in would be utterly shameful." He did not mince words.

So they both asked for a day off to take her to the hospital for a checkup. But what it all came down to was—money. These days it cost twenty to thirty Yuan each time the child saw a doctor, since a lab test would be ordered, needed or not, and always a prescription to be filled. Lin didn't mind that people in general weren't honest, but doctors too? How were they supposed to survive with doctors like that? It once cost them seventy-five Yuan when the child had diarrhea. His wife had to laugh despite her outrage. "Imagine, seventy-five Yuan for a loose bowel movement!" She shook her head.

They both felt they made trips with their daughter to the hospital just so they could be scammed. But what choice did they have if she ran a fever? Take this time, for example. They could tell she was running a fever as they headed out to see the doctor. Focusing all their energy on the girl, they forgot the blame game; they also put aside the knowledge that they'd be scammed again. They hurried out the door and squeezed their way onto a bus for the hospital, where a test showed she had nothing but a common cold. But at the pharmacy, the cashier wrote on the prescription the grand total of a little over forty-five Yuan.

"You see, they're skinning us again. Are we going to fill it?" she asked as she flicked the prescription.

He ignored her. He'd been worried earlier, not knowing what had caused the fever and wondering if she'd caught something from his teacher. Now that it had turned out to be only a cold, he felt better. But then his temper flared up again. *You were so sure she got it from my teacher, but the exam showed it was just a cold. What do you have to say to that?* He wanted to clear that up with her before moving on to her question. But with a long line at the pharmacy cashier window and the throng of patients around them, this was obviously not the right place to have an argument, so he said gruffly:

"Don't come here if you don't want to be skinned. Who says you have to get the medicine?"

"All right, I won't, if that's what you think." She picked up the girl and walked off. Now it was his turn to be worried, since he knew her well enough to realize that nothing could change her mind once she began to sulk. What would that mean for the child if they didn't fill the prescription? He tried to stop her:

"Don't sulk over something like this. Here, give me the prescription."

But she wasn't sulking.

"Let's not fill it this time." She looked at him. "It's just a cold. I still have some cold medicine from my office clinic that time I caught cold. We can give it to her. It's some powder and Xianfeng tablets to bring down the temperature. That's what we'd get no matter how much we spent."

"But that's for adults; it's not the same for children."

"Not the same? We'll just give her less. Don't worry. I'll have her feeling better in three days without spending forty-five Yuan. I can get more at the office if she needs it."

She made sense. He touched the girl's forehead. She was no longer running a fever, either because she'd just awakened or detected the smell of the hospital. Life had returned to her eyes, as she pointed at the melons across the street. Since she was feeling well enough to want a melon, he agreed to try his wife's solution. They walked out the hospital to buy a slice of melon, which made the girl even livelier. No longer coughing, she jumped down, took Lin's hand, and walked on her own. That cheered up both Lin and his wife, so he magnanimously dropped the subject of his wife's accusation. She hadn't meant it; she'd just blurted it out because she was worried sick. They were both in high spirits now that the sore subject had been dropped, they'd learned the cause of the child's illness, and his wife had found a way to save them forty-five Yuan, found money. Warming to her as they passed a street with snacking stalls, he said:

"You love pork-liver soup, don't you? Go get a bowl."

She smacked her lips. "It's one and half Yuan a bowlful. That seems a lot for a snack."

He took out the money and handed it to the stall owner.

"Give us a bowl of pork-liver soup."

When the food came, she sat down sheepishly to eat. From the way she savored each bite, he knew she truly enjoyed it. She picked up two pieces of pig intestines for the girl, who found them too tough and spat them out. His wife picked them up and ate them herself. Then she insisted that he try the soup. Pig's intestines had never agreed with him, and he was sure the soup would be awful. But she wouldn't give up, pleading with him, the loving gaze transporting him back to when they were dating. He had to take a sip. There was cilantro in the steaming hot soup and it wasn't too bad. She asked if he liked it and he said it was pretty good, earning him another loving gaze. Who knew that a bowl of pork-liver soup would give them a chance to relive tender moments from their past? Their high spirits lasted into the night.

Back home, his wife gave the child some medicine and she went off to play. She slept soundly that night without coughing. When husband and wife heard the nanny snoring in her room, they got into action, like a couple of newlyweds. When it was over, without being asked, his wife admitted her mistake. She'd blamed it on Lin's teacher because she was worried.

"Then it has to be ours. We weren't attentive enough, and the girl kicked the blanket off her at night."

But his wife said it wasn't their fault either—it was someone else. Lin's heart skipped a beat as he asked who could that be. She pointed to the other room, in other words, the nanny. She then rattled off a list of complaints: the girl was petty, lazy, and a gossip who talked about them to her nanny friends and revealed family secrets; she put on a show about caring for the child, but when they were at work, she let the child play with water, sleep, and watch TV alone. Of course the girl would catch cold. In September, his wife said, they'd send the child to day care and fire the nanny, who was paid forty Yuan a month. They spent another sixty to feed her, while she helped herself to their things. Taken together, she cost them more than a hundred Yuan a month, about the same each of them earned. No wonder they were always short of money. Once the child was in day care, their lives would get better, their future brighter!

The conversation buoyed Lin, who added his complaints about the nanny, whom he had never really liked. It felt good to vent. They kissed good night and turned over to go to sleep. She was asleep in three minutes, as usual, but he couldn't sleep, somewhat ashamed of what they'd said. They'd enjoyed a wonderful day, and it felt petty to blame all their problems on the nanny. The girl wasn't even twenty, and so far away from home, working as a nanny. Feeling small-minded, Lin sighed as fatigue overtook him. He shut his eyes and went to sleep. No more thoughts about the nanny.

But when morning came, he felt justified in those complaints. After his wife left early for work, Lin went out for his customary tofu purchase. It was drizzling and the line was shorter, so it didn't take long to make the purchase. He should have gone to work after dropping off the tofu, but he looked at his watch and saw that he had plenty of time. Still worried about the child's cold, he decided to double back and check up on the kid. When he got home, he saw that neither the beds nor the child's breakfast was made, and the little girl had yet to take her medicine. The nanny had given her a basin of water to play with while she busied herself with her own breakfast. Lin and his wife had eaten leftovers that morning, adding hot water to some rice to eat with pickled vegetables. They knew the nanny didn't eat leftovers, and it would have been fine with him if she were to make some congee for herself. Instead, she was making noodles in the pot reserved for making food for their daughter. A terrific smell greeted him as he walked in. She had put cilantro and baked tofu in the soup, had even added an egg. The nanny was startled when he walked in on her and quickly pushed the egg under the noodles, but too late. He felt his anger rising. What did she think she was doing? She should have taken care of the child first, but she was too busy stealing food for herself. *Life is hard for all of us. We shouldn't have talked about you behind your back and blamed you for everything, but you are unworthy of our respect and consideration.* But he refrained from criticizing her. She was caught in the act, and he could have yelled at her, but with a nanny like her, how was he to know she wouldn't take it out on the child after he left? The little girl was too young to suffer the consequences of her parents' actions. So he walked over, took the basin away and dumped the water in the toilet. The child was sniffling again after playing with cold water. And now with her "toy" taken away, she plopped down on the floor and began to cry. Doing his best to ignore her, he slammed the door shut and went out to take a walk. As he raced down the stairs, he cursed inwardly,

"Damn you. Come September, we're going to fire you!"

The child's cold seemed to be worse when he came home that evening. She had a stuffy nose, she coughed, and she had a bit of a fever. He knew it was the nanny's fault, but decided not to tell his wife about it, for that would cause another uproar. His wife, for some reason, wore a happy face and didn't appear to be too worried about the child's cold; instead, she sat by the bed lost in her cheerful thoughts. That expression told him that something good was up, so he went to the kitchen, where, sure enough, she'd brought back some sausage, and, more importantly, a bottle of Yanjing Beer, which he was sure was for him. Back in his bachelor's days, he'd loved drinking beer, a habit he'd slowly given up after getting married. Why spend that kind of money? Even if he didn't care about the expense, when would he find the mood for beer anyway? Baffled by what his wife had in mind, he went into their bedroom.

"Hey, what's with you today?"

She just giggled.

"What's so funny? Tell me." That really confused him.

"All right, I'll tell you. No more job problem."

"What? No more? Are you going to the Qiansanmen office? Did the personnel guy agree to a transfer?"

She shook her head.

"You found a new office?"

She shook her head again.

"Then what?" He was getting frustrated.

"I'm not going to ask for a transfer."

"Why not? Are you feeling sentimental about your current job? Are you okay with the bus ride all of a sudden?"

"Nothing sentimental about the job, but no more bus ride. My boss said a new bus route is being created for our area in September. Just think, with the commuter bus, there'll be no more public transportation and the commute will only take forty minutes. And on an office bus there will be empty seats. Isn't that better than taking the subway to a Qiansanmen office? I decided I'll stay if the bus starts running in September. It's not the best working environment around, with all the complicated interpersonal relationships, but who can guarantee that the one at Qiansanmen would be any better? Remember the personnel guy's face that day? You've convinced me that crows are black all over the world. If there's a bus, I won't ask for a transfer and just try to get through each day. See, problem solved."

He was pleased. That had been hanging over their heads for some time, causing friction between them. Now the problem was solved. She was happy, which meant she'd be in a good mood and worry free—no more arguments. It was so easy it was hard to believe. They'd gone asking for help, only to have their gift turned down, and in the end it had taken a mere new bus route to take care of everything. Who cared how the problem was solved? He cheered up.

"That's wonderful. No more problems and no more arguments."

"No more problems," she said before adding sweetly, "And who's been starting arguments? You couldn't help, so why wouldn't I argue with you? But I took care of things myself. Now we'll just wait until September."

"Right. You took care of things, and we'll wait till September."

They were in a very good mood, making their daughter's illness pale in comparison; they even shared the bottle of beer at dinner. After the child and the nanny were asleep, they enjoyed another round of conjugal bliss, another passion-filled round. But they were red-faced afterward—two nights in a row, when was the last time they'd been that eager? Then they talked some more. September. September would be a good month. Her problem would be solved, the child would be in day care, and the nanny would be gone, saving them a major expense. The future seemed rosy, and they looked forward to the happy days to come. They talked about what to do with the extra money.

"The child's still young," she said. "Maybe we should keep the nanny on another year, until our daughter can go to preschool."

"Absolutely not!" Lin replied vehemently, reminded of the incident that morning. "We do it this year, not because of the child, but because the nanny. We need to fire her."

His wife, who had major issues with the nanny, was so happy to hear his decisive response she gave him a kiss before rolling over to go to sleep.

5

September rolled around.

As expected, two things happened: his wife got to ride the commuter bus, and they sent the child to preschool after firing the nanny. The first change went smoothly. On September first, a bus showed up to take her to and back from work; life immediately took a turn for the better now that she did not have to leave before the sun was up. No more getting up at six in order to catch public transportation; now she could stay in bed till seven, get ready, have breakfast, and wait on her doorstep for a bus that would take her to her office, seated the whole way. It was no longer a wearying commute. She got off work at five and was home forty minutes later, before it turned dark, which gave her time to rest before making dinner.

She was pleased, of course, but her happiness was soon knocked down a few notches, no longer as complete as when she'd first heard about the bus. Originally she'd thought the route had been added because her boss cared about people in the office, but it turned out to have nothing do with them. His wife had a sister who had recently moved to Lin's neighborhood, prompting her to pester him into adding a route. It was deflating news, and the commuter bus suffered an instant drop in value. When she complained to Lin, he also felt let down, as if dealt a major insult. But this insult was nothing compared to the humiliation they'd suffered when the personnel guy had turned down their gift. So he told her it didn't matter who was married to whom or why she got the bus route. The most important thing was that she could ride the bus.

"I thought the route was created to be fair to everyone at the office," she said, "because the boss cared about us. But no, we are simply accidental beneficiaries. I won't be able to avoid thinking about the sister-in-law when I ride the bus now, will I?"

"What can we do? Just think, you wouldn't be able to ride if not for her."

"It feels weird, like I'm a second-class citizen."

"Don't be silly. Second class, third class, what difference does it make? Be thankful for the ride. Let me ask you, is it better to be an accidental beneficiary or to crowd onto a city bus?"

"You're right."

"Besides, you're not the only, are you? Is the bus full every day?"

"Yes. A bunch of spineless riders."

"So you're the only who isn't. Then, go back to public transportation. No one's forcing you to take that bus. Didn't we beg for help to get you a transfer? Weren't we left standing in the hallway with our gift?"

She laughed.

"I was just talking. You're taking it too seriously. But you're right. What is backbone worth in our situation? Who has backbone these days anyway? What good does it do? Who cares who's married to whom? I'll just keep riding the bus."

"Now you're talking." Lin clapped his approval.

So now she was in a permanent good mood.

But the child's preschool was a huge headache. Lin's office did not have one, while his wife's office did, but it was too far from home, and the child couldn't take the bus with her. They had to find a neighborhood center, of which there were quite a few. A government office ran one, the district office ran another, the neighborhood and residents' committees each ran them, and an old lady ran a private center. The first was the best, for the teachers had degrees in childhood education, and the children learned things. Except for the district center, the others were inferior, since the children learned nothing but how to line up, form a circle, or walk down the street.

The worst were the one run by the neighborhood committee and the private center, both staffed by old women who were in it to earn a little spending money, and didn't teach the children anything but games. Their future was tied up with their daughter's education, so his wife treated it more seriously than her own job situation. He, on the other hand, was indifferent, at least at first. Why was preschool such a big deal? The girl would only be there for two years, so no harm done. But he learned his lesson after his wife chided him for being overconfident.

"I'll talk to some people. I don't have any influence and can't be sure they'll help us out, so don't be inflexible."

The fake Indian woman across the way had a child, about the same age as Lin's daughter. Lin's wife told him that they had found a preschool for their kid, the one run by the government office, which she used to make her demand.

"What do you mean inflexible?" she said. "We must focus on the center run by the government office. That's where their kid is going and that's where ours is going to go. No need to look into the one run by the district."

Marching orders in hand, he got started, and quickly realized that placing their daughter in a preschool would be harder than finding a new job for his wife. Preliminary research showed that the government center was indeed well run and rated at the top each year in the city. Some district officials preferred it over centers in their own districts for their children. But there was a quota, and without solid connections, getting in would be harder than going to heaven. The director had exclusive control over the application forms and even the deputy director had no say in whom to admit. But getting a form from the director required a memo from a bureau chief or someone in a higher position. Lin went through the names of all his college friends in the city, but could not come up with anyone who might fit the bill. As the saying goes, any doctor will do when you're really sick. He could not think of a single college friend, but recalled the old bicycle repairman at his building entrance. As a frequent customer,

Lin called the old man Grandpa, and they had become friendly. Sometimes, when Lin forgot his wallet, the old man would let him walk off with his bike first. In one of their chats, Lin learned that the old man's daughter worked at a nearby preschool. It might have been this one. He was animated by the thought and hopped on his bike to go him. If it was the top center, the old man's daughter could serve as an opening and help forge a connection, even though she was just a teacher, whose word might not carry much weight. After hearing what Lin had to say, the old man was happy to do what he could. He agreed to enlist his daughter's help. A word from him was all he needed to enroll Lin's daughter in the center, if it was the one Lin wanted. It wasn't. She worked at the one run by the residents' committee. Disheartened, Lin went home to tell his wife, who first complained about his inability to come up with any connections, before adding:

"Let's spend seventy or eighty Yuan to buy the director a hefty gift and see if that works. How do you think the Indian girl across the way got in? Her father doesn't seem to be much of a hotshot, so they must have sent a gift."

"We don't even know the woman, so how are we going to send a gift?" Lin said with a wave of his hands. "Didn't we learn our lesson when we tried to give a gift to the personnel guy?"

"If you have no connections, and we can't even give the director a gift, what do you say we do?" she demanded angrily.

"Why not just send her to the center where the old man's daughter works? She's only three years old, so how much education are we talking about anyway? Didn't the impoverished Shaoshan area produce our Chairman Mao? It's all up to the child herself."

That did not go down well with his wife.

"She'd only know how to fix a bicycle when she grew up if she spent all her time with a bike repairman's daughter!" she said. "You haven't even met the director, so how do you know she won't take our daughter?"

She was right. Lin decided to go see the director without an introduction or a gift; he'd explain their situation, which he hoped would elicit the director's sympathy. On the way he tried to reassure himself that he was making the right move; things were always complex in China, so it might turn out all right. Connections can sometimes get complicated, since jealousy can rear its ugly head. So what if he didn't know the director? Maybe she'd be more sympathetic that way. He believed there had to be some good people in this world, and he might just run into one there.

He realized his naiveté when he got there. The director, a woman in her fifties, was quite pleasant but said that her preschool did not admit children whose parents worked for other government offices. What would parents from their office say if their children weren't admitted? There was one exception: the preschool wanted to expand, but could not get a permit. Since Lin worked at a government office, if he could help them get one, they would take his child. Lin was deflated. How was he going to help them when he couldn't help himself? If he could get a building permit, he'd be able to send his child to any preschool he wanted. He wouldn't have to work so hard on this one.

When he arrived home with the news, a storm was brewing. The nanny, who had learned that they were looking for day care, knew she'd lose her job the moment they found a place and decided to strike first. Upset that Lin's wife had said nothing to her, she wanted to quit immediately. Lin's wife found the nanny unreasonable. *Why should I talk to you about my daughter's day care? You say you want to leave before we find a day care, and that can only mean you want to make things tough on us.* An argument ensued. Unwilling to pacify the nanny, Lin's wife said:

"Go ahead, quit. You can leave right this minute."

Undaunted, the nanny started packing. By the time Lin walked in, she was about to leave with her belongings. Since he had failed to find a day care, the nanny's imminent departure caught him unprepared. He tried to get her to stay.

"Don't," his wife said. "Let her go. The sky won't fall just because she's leaving."

There was nothing he could do, but their daughter was sad to see the nanny go, after spending so much time with her. She rolled around on the floor. The young woman, who had fond feelings for the kid, picked her up, but in the end, she put her back down and ran down the stairs. With the nanny gone, Lin's wife started to cry, feeling sorry that the nanny was leaving after spending more than two years caring for their child. She told Lin to run over to the balcony and toss down another month's pay for her.

After that—chaos. With no place to send the child, the couple had to take turns asking for leave so one of them could stay home with her. His wife railed against the nanny for causing such a hardship and then against Lin for being so worthless he couldn't land a place for their daughter.

"They wanted me to get them a building permit. Not even our section head could manage that," Lin defended himself. "Besides, let's not complicate matters and just accept the fact that we have no means to send her to that day care center. Why don't we just go with the one where the bike repairman's daughter works?"

Given the way things were, his wife had a change of heart, since they couldn't keep asking for leave. They went to check out the center and came away with a favorable impression. Though it couldn't compare with the government-run day care, it was clean, with dozens of children in a number of rooms. There was even a piano in one of them. And it wasn't too close to any busy streets. Lin was relieved when his wife didn't say anything, a sign of no objections.

They went home to start getting ready, packing clothes, a pillow, a rice bowl, a spoon, a drinking cup, and a handkerchief, as if they were sending their child off to war. Tears filled his wife's eyes.

"Mom and Dad can only let you go to a day care run by the residents' committee, so do the best you can."

But the situation took a turn for the better right after their child passed the physical exam. The top preschool actually agreed to take her, though naturally that was not due to anything Lin had done. It was, surprisingly, the fake Indian woman's husband who came to their aid.

Someone knocked at their door the night before the child started school. Lin opened the door to find the fake Indian woman's husband. They could never figure out what the man did, except that he was always dressed neatly, shirt and tie, and rode a motorcycle to work. With a well-to-do neighbor whose home was so much nicer than theirs, Lin and his wife always felt inferior and had only limited interactions with them. The two wives met from time to time, but had never really gotten along, which was why they went on high alert when the husband showed up out of the blue. What did he want? To their surprise, the man sat down on the edge of their bed with a relaxed manner and said:

"I hear you've run into a snag trying to find a preschool."

Lin blushed. Was the man trying to rub it in? He began to stammer a response.

"I want to talk to you about something," the man said. "I have a spot if you want to send your child there. We were given two, one for my kid and one for my sister's child, but she changed her mind. If you think this one will do for your child, you can have the spot. We're neighbors, after all."

What a pleasant surprise. He looked quite sincere. So Lin's wife replied with a smile:

"That's wonderful. Thank you so much. We tried our best, but couldn't manage to get in and we were ready to send our daughter to the school run by the residents' committee."

Lin, on the other hand, felt awkward. He was so feckless they had to rely on someone else. Their neighbor would surely look down on him, which was why he didn't look as happy as his wife.

"I couldn't have done it myself if not for the fact that the father of one of my colleagues happens to be a bureau chief at that office," the neighbor said. "We went to him for help and got two spots. It's how things work these days, you know."

That made Lin feel better. The fake Indian woman was a troublemaker, but her husband was a nice guy. Lin took out a pack of cigarettes and offered one to the man. It was Changle, not one of the better brands, and it had been open for a few days, so the cigarettes were stale, but that didn't bother the man, who lit up and began smoking with Lin.

Now that their daughter was going to the school of their choice, Lin and his wife felt much better, and their relationship with the neighbors improved, while the two kids went to school together. But a few days later, his wife came home with a long face. When Lin asked her what was wrong, she said:

"We've been tricked. We shouldn't have sent our child to that place."

"What do you mean, tricked? And what's the problem?"

"On the surface it looks like they helped us, but I couldn't help thinking that something wasn't quite right. Well, they were actually helping themselves, not us. Their child was making a fuss about going to school alone, so they decided to get ours to go with her. The two kids are playmates, so it works out nicely for them when the kids go together. I also asked around, and found out that the husband doesn't have a sister. We're totally useless, so our child suffers. I ride the bus thanks to someone's sister-in-law and now our child goes to school as someone's companion."

She began to sob. Her words sent a chill up his spine. Damn it! So the fake Indian family had designs on them all along. But this was nothing they could talk about openly, and he couldn't argue with his neighbors, even though it felt sordid to him, as if they'd rubbed his nose in horse dung. What really got to him was the fact that, when all was said and done, their daughter still had to go to school as the other girl's companion. Still, being someone's companion at a good pre-school was better than muddling through at an inferior place, just as riding the commuter bus because of someone else's sister-in-law was more comfortable than crowding onto a public bus. Lin shed tears for the first time that night, after his wife and child fell asleep, even slapped himself in the dark.

"How could you be so worthless? Why don't you know how to get things done?"

But it was a gentle slap—he didn't want to wake up his wife.

6

There was a great cabbage harvest that year.

Lin sucked in cold air, as he stood in the long line with other residents of the city to buy cabbage for the winter, holding a piece of paper in his hand, like everyone else. Some of them were already wearing padded caps. After a while, they got to know each other. A middle-aged man in front of Lin gave him a cigarette and they got to talking after lighting up. Every year, when it came time to buy winter cabbage, Lin was besieged by anxiety and conflicting thoughts. He was anxious when he saw other people transporting cabbage home on bicycles, three-wheelers, and in large baskets, littering the streets with detached leaves in their wake, anxious that the cabbage would be sold out and his family would have nothing to eat that winter. He felt cheated each time he squeezed into a line, year after year after year. A few dozen heads of cheap cabbage would bring so much trouble, laying them out to dry and turning them over daily and bringing them back inside every evening, until they dried nicely to a smaller size. When they finally decided to eat it, the cabbage would be dry and shriveled. Each head would have only a tiny heart left under the layers; sometimes it would have a sour taste after being frozen. Every spring, when they were confronted by the remaining cabbages, he and his wife vowed not to buy any in the fall. But when fall came around, with piles of cheap cabbage subsidized by the government, they'd see people taking cartloads of the stuff home and feel they ought to buy some. The anxiety and conflicting thoughts were a torment, exacting a far higher price mentally than the actual cost of the cabbage. Which was why he made up his mind at the onset of fall: be resolute and do not buy a single head of cabbage. His wife agreed with him, saying it wasn't that much cheaper than buying cabbage in the market, after they removed the bad parts in the cabbage they'd stored up. So they didn't buy any, not at first, anyway. But after three days, Lin put on his cap and joined the line, but not because he wavered in his decision. There was a surplus of that year, and every government office rallied their employees to buy "patriotic cabbage," for which they would be reimbursed at the office. Lin and his wife couldn't pass up such a good deal, so he lined up to buy the maximum amount that would be reimbursed. He had a one hundred and fifty kilo quota at his workplace, his wife a hundred at hers, so two-fifty it was, much more than they usually bought. Lin even borrowed a three-wheeler from He, the deputy section head in his office.

"Since we can get reimbursed, we're forced to go through all the trouble once again."

The trouble was in the reimbursement, which was why he felt so put upon as he stood in line. He sighed and gave the cabbage a savage kick, absent-mindedly watching them weigh the cabbage up front, before he regained his focus. The "free" cabbage brought on a fierce competition—people were afraid there'd be none left when their turn came. Everyone was staring, which made Lin nervous despite himself; he rolled up the flaps on his cap to hear better.

The smell of two hundred and fifty kilos of cabbage that permeated their apartment soured his mood. But the free cabbages motivated his wife as she went about laying them out to dry. He knew the results by heart: they would turn into seventy or eighty hard heads. He lost his appetite just thinking of finishing that pile of cabbages in one winter. The only thing saving his mood was his wife's high spirits, and a heavy weight seemed to have been lifted in their home. They had visitors from his hometown again the day after he brought the cabbage home, six of them no less, making him tense and changing the expression on his wife's face. But the guests left soon after arriving without staying for dinner, heading northeast on business, they said. He felt better and his wife's face relaxed. They sent off their visitors with a great show of feelings, to everyone's satisfaction.

On this day, he left work early and went to the market, where he bought some sweet red peppers and exchanged some meal coupons for a kilo of eggs (the food situation at their house had improved since the nanny left, so they could use meal coupons for eggs now). When he was about to leave, he spotted a cart selling dried salted ducks from Anhui and a line of shoppers in front of it. He went over to take a look. The ducks were too expensive, costing more than four Yuan for half a kilo; but the entrails were only three Yuan. His daughter loved animal innards, so he lined up to buy some. Two people were working there, one with an Anhui accent who chopped up the ducks, while the other collected money, acting like the owner. When Lin went up and handed over the money, the owner took a look at him. Their eyes met.

"Little Lin!"

"Little Li Bai!"

Throwing down the duck entrails and money they were holding, the two men laughed as they embraced. Li Bai had been a college classmate and a close friend back then, when, as poetry lovers, they joined the literature club. They had gotten caught up in struggle, with energy that could open up a new world. Talented and diligent, Li Bai produced three poems a day on average, some of which were published. He was a carefree soul who knew everything under the sun, from early Chinese history to the modern era. Lots of girls at school had their eye on him. Lin and Li had gone their separate ways after graduation; Li was assigned to a government office. Later Lin heard that he tired of office work and took a job at a private company. How had he ended up selling dried salted duck? With this chance encounter, Li handed the stall over to the Anhui guy and went with Lin over to a tree nearby to have a smoke and catch up.

"I thought you were working at a private company? How'd you wind up selling ducks?"

Li laughed.

"The fucking company went bust, so now I'm my own boss, selling ducks. It's not bad, not all that different from owning a company. I take in eighty to a hundred Yuan a day."

That was a staggering amount to Lin. "Do you still write poetry?"

Li spat on the ground.

"Shit. I was too young to know anything. Poetry? Poetry is for posers full of hot air. I'd have starved to death if I still wrote poetry. Now I'm just trying to get by, that's all. You married yet?"

"I've got a three-year old kid."

Li clapped his hands. "You see? And you were asking me about poetry. Poetry, my ass. I got it all figured out. Don't indulge in fanciful thoughts or try to rise above the others. Instead, just muddle through and don't think about anything else, and you'll have a good life. What do you think?"

Lin couldn't agree more. He nodded.

"Any kids?" he asked.

Li raised three figures, another staggering number.

"What about family planning?"

"Married three times and divorced three times. I'm on my fourth now," Li said with a laugh. "Each marriage produced one and none of the women wanted the kid during the divorce, so I ended up with three. That's why I have to sell ducks here; I've got five mouths to feed."

Lin had to laugh too. His friend was still the Li Bai he used to know. He might have stopped writing poetry, but he was still as carefree as ever. They chatted until it started to get dark, when Li Bai slapped Lin on the shoulder.

"That's it!"

"That's what?" Lin was startled.

"I have to be out of town for a couple of weeks to get more ducks. I was worried that no one could be here to collect the money. Why don't you come do that for me after you get off work?"

"No way." Lin waved him off. "I have to go to work. Besides, I know nothing about selling ducks."

"I know you're thinking about face. Still naïve and immature, aren't you? Who needs face these days? If you care about face, you'll be just another poor pedant, but if you don't, you can be rich and powerful. You think you're taking the moral high ground, don't you? But look at you and what you're wearing. You have poverty written all over you. Come collect the money after work for ten days and I'll pay you twenty Yuan a day."

Without waiting for Lin's response, Li shoved a large duck into his hands and sent him off.

Shaking his head, but smiling, Lin walked home with the duck. His wife scolded him for coming home so late and not picking up the child on time. The duck he was holding upset her over the expense.

"Have you become a nobleman?" She shouted. "Are we supposed to be eating a big duck like that?"

He tossed the duck onto their dining table and glared at her.

"It was a gift."

"Have you been promoted?" she asked in amazement. "And now people are giving you gifts?"

He told her what had happened at the market, and was delighted over the news that Li had asked him to collect the money for him.

"Two hours a day and you still go to work as usual. Twenty Yuan for two hours is more than you'd earn as a waiter for big-shot capitalists. So why not? Starting tomorrow, I'll pick up the child after work and you go sell ducks. You can do it."

Lin was sprawled on the bed with his hands folded behind his head.

"Sure I can do it, but selling ducks would be a great loss of face."

"So what! Saving face is why we've been poor all these years. You're not looking for a wife and I don't care if you lose face, so what are you afraid of?"

Lin began selling ducks every afternoon after work. He was shy at first, unable to look the customers in the eye once he put on his white apron, afraid he'd run into someone he knew. And when he got home, he headed straight for the shower to wash off the smell of duck. But it took him only two days, two ten-Yuan bills in hand each day, for him to look up at the customers, acquaintance or not, and he no longer felt he needed a shower. Habit breeds acceptance. He began to think it wouldn't be bad to keep selling ducks, which would bring in six hundred Yuan a month. Wouldn't they be rich in a year? Too bad Li Bai was only away for ten days, putting him out of a job when his friend returned. Why couldn't he have met Li earlier?

On the ninth day, someone he knew showed up. He'd gotten used to seeing people he knew, but this one was different. It was the new section head, Guan, and that scared him a bit. Guan didn't live anywhere near the market, so Lin was puzzled why he was here. When Guan spotted his own clerk sitting behind a duck cart, his eyes bulged from the surprise, which embarrassed Lin. At work the next day, he was prepared to be summoned for a talk with the boss. Sure enough, Guan asked to have an "airing out" with him. But by that time Lin was no longer afraid. Everyone had to make a living, so there was nothing wrong with earning a little extra after work, as long as he didn't sell ducks at the office. Money made everything easier. He earned a hundred and eighty Yuan in nine days, which he used to buy a trench coat for his wife and a melon that weighed two and half kilos for his daughter, bringing smiles to everyone's face. Compared with that, face and a few words of criticism from his boss was nothing. But Lin had worked at the office long enough to shed his naiveté and the failing of candor; he'd learned to mixed the true with the false, since liars got promoted while truth-tellers always suffered. When Guan asked for an explanation, Lin flashed a guileless smile and said the duck cart belonged to an old college friend. He'd put on his friend's apron and shouted a few times, just for fun. He hadn't expected to run into his boss, and wasn't about to ruin the office's reputation by moonlighting as a duck vendor. Guan was relieved.

"That's what I thought. You work for the government so you couldn't be out selling ducks. I'll let this go since it was just for fun, but don't do it again."

The airing-out ended with Lin's promise to stop. After Guan walked off, Lin spat on the ground. *Why can't I sell ducks? For your infor-*

mation, I did it for nine days. Too bad this is the last day. If I could keep doing it, I would.

Too bad. Li came back that afternoon, bringing Lin's stint at the duck cart to an end. Telling him to come for a duck any time he wanted, Li gave him the last twenty-Yuan, adding that he'd ask for Lin's help again whenever he had to go away. No longer abashed, Lin replied loudly:

"You bet. Just give me a holler."

7

Three months had passed since their child started preschool. Lin or his wife dropped her off and picked her up each day. In all fairness, they had more household chores now that the child was in preschool. With the nanny gone, they had to do the dishes, mop the floor, and do the laundry. They had to be punctual when dropping off and picking up the child also, unlike before, when the nanny's presence made it possible for them to come home late. On the other hand, without the nanny and with the child away, life was easier, despite the increase of housework. Even when they brought their daughter home, there would only be the three of them, no more outsiders. On top of that, they saved more than a hundred a month from the nanny's wage and still had fifty or sixty left over after paying the preschool tuition. His wife was willing to spend more on food now that they didn't have to worry so much about it; she occasionally bought a sausage, sometimes even a roasted chicken. When they talked about their overall situation, they agreed that it was so much better without a nanny, and had plenty to say about their nanny's shortcomings. Eventually, they realized that it was petty to criticize the departed girl while enjoying a roasted chicken, so no more of that talk.

They were pleased that the child was in a good preschool, but they had yet to get over the psychological hurdle that their child got in simply to serve as a companion for their neighbors' child. They were reminded of that fact every morning when they dropped her off and every evening when they picked her up, and that was never pleasant. Besides, they often ran into the fake Indian woman or her husband and, after the obligatory greetings, felt mortified and awkward. Unaware of her parents' feelings, their daughter sometimes walked out of the school holding hands with the neighbors' child, like the best of friends. Everything is a process, and after a while, it no longer bothered Lin and his wife so much; occasionally, they even told themselves that nothing mattered as long as their child was happy and was enrolled in a good school. It wasn't all that different from selling ducks, which was a loss of face and brought on criticism from his boss, but they came away with two hundred Yuan in the process. Yet the irritation never completely vanished, and they sometimes silently cursed their neighbors:

"We don't owe you just because you helped us with the preschool."

Their daughter also went through a process. She threw a tantrum and refused to go the first few days, crying when they dropped her off and crying when they picked her up. She was just a kid who didn't know better, and simply did what her parents wanted. But she soon got used to the new arrangement and stopped crying once she got to know the teachers and other kids. Sometimes, it made his heart ache when Lin thought about how a little child had no choice but to learn to adjust. He also knew they couldn't keep her around forever. She'd grow up and learn to adjust to the world outside. He tried to ignore his heartache.

Then came another World Cup. As an avid soccer fan, Lin got caught up in the matches. They were great fun to watch, and he knew the names of the major soccer stars. Back then, he'd believed that watching soccer matches was one of life's main goals. The World Cup only came around every four years, and how many four years does one have in a lifetime? Later, once he started working and got married, he stopped watching the matches. What was the point? No matter how well the teams played, he still had tons of problems to solve—housing, childcare, coal briquettes, and hometown visitors.

He began tuning out the clamor around the World Cup matches. But now, feeling more relaxed with the child in preschool, he couldn't resist the draw of the final match. The live broadcasts came on at midnight, so he needed to talk his wife into letting him watch. To that end, he threw himself into the housework after picking up the child. Suspicious of his unusual behavior, his wife asked him what was going on. He told her with a sheepish look, adding for good measure that Maradona was playing that night. His wife was impervious to reason, as usual, and unmoved, as always.

"We're out of coal briquettes, and you're thinking about watching a game at midnight?" She threw her apron on the table. "I guess you're not so tired. Well, you can watch at midnight if you can get Maradona to bring us some coal briquettes."

He lost interest.

"Forget it then. I won't watch, okay? I'll go get coal briquettes tomorrow."

He stopped what he was doing and sat down on the bed to stare blankly, like his wife did when she had trouble at work. He couldn't sleep that night. When she woke up at midnight, she was alarmed by the look on his face.

"Go ahead and watch the match if you really want to. Just don't forget the coal tomorrow."

But he'd lost interest in the match. Ignoring her concession, he snapped:

"Did I say I want to watch it? First you wouldn't let me watch, and now you won't even let me lie here and think."

The next morning, he took half a day off to cart briquettes, then went to the office that afternoon. When the new college graduate asked him what he thought about the game the night before, Lin spat out:

"It's just some shitty game. What's there to see? I never watch soccer."

He began flipping through the newspaper so truculently he frightened the college grad.

When she got home that night, his wife experienced guilt feelings when she saw the coal in the kitchen and the unhappy look on her husband's face. So she busied herself with housework and the child, watching his face when she spoke to him. That in turn bothered him enough to vent a bit of anger.

The lame old meter reader showed up just as they were about to eat dinner. It wasn't the regular day for reading the meter but he was there and they had to stop to let him check their meter. In addition to the wrench in his hand, the old man also carried a large backpack, which must have been heavy, since his face was prickled with sweat. The large backpack put Lin on alert, wondering what the old man had in mind this time. Sure enough, after reading the meter, he sat down on their bed without saying anything. Standing in front of the old man, Lin wondered what he wanted to talk about, feeding horses as a youngster or stealing water. Neither. Instead, the old man smiled broadly and said to Lin:

"I have a favor to ask."

"What do you mean, a favor?" Lin was taken aback. "I'm the one who's always asking for favors."

"I need your help. You work in the ministry section where an out-of-town report is being held up, I think."

Lin seemed to recall a document in his section, probably held up by Peng, who had been too busy learning qigong at the Sun Temple Park to take care of it.

"You may be right."

"I knew it!" The old man clapped. "That's my hometown. They're in such a hurry to get an approval that the county party secretary came to me for help."

Lin was astounded that a party secretary would ask a meter man for help when he came to Beijing. But then, the old man had been a big shot's stable hand, so no surprise there.

"What help could I give him?" the old man said. "I could only advise him to find out where it was being held up, and he did. Imagine my surprise when I heard it was your office. So I thought that since we know each other, I might as well come to you for help. Could you do something?"

Having worked at the government office for more than five years, Lin knew how things worked. It could be easily accomplished. He could talk to Peng, and it would take only the time she needed to put on some lipstick for the document to be released. But it could also be hard. If he went to see her about a stranger's document while she was doing her qigong or when she was in a bad mood, it was hard to say what would happen. She might find problems with the document and troop out all sorts of government rules and regulations to show how she could not give her stamp of approval. She could even convince you that she was right. It all depended on Lin. If he was willing to help, the approval would be released the day after, but if not, then it would be held up for a few more days. But the meter man wasn't just any old timer; he was in charge of their meter, so Lin had to lend a hand. But he was a different person now, more sensible and levelheaded. If this had been in the past, he'd have agreed to help right off if he thought he could; that was a naïve approach. A mature Lin would say he couldn't help even though he could, and he'd tell the man it was a challenge even if it wasn't, which would ensure gratitude from the meter man once it was done. If he agreed right off, but a problem arose and he failed to carry it through, he'd earn nothing but complaints. So he put his hands behind his head and leaned back against the blanket.

"It's not going to be easy. There is one such document waiting for approval, but I've heard it has problems and might not be approved right away."

Many years had gone by since the old man had fed the horses and now, as a meter man, he was clueless about the ins and outs of office politics. He could only give Lin an ingratiating smile.

"That's true. I told the party secretary the same thing. Things are done differently here in the capital and rules are strictly followed. But no matter what, you have to help us out."

Lin's wife sensed there was something more to this, so she said:

"Gramps, he's only good for stealing water. He can't help you with this."

"That was a misunderstanding." The old man seemed embarrassed. "Just a misunderstanding. I shouldn't have listened to unfounded accusations. Water is so cheap, who would bother to steal it?"

He took out a large cardboard box from his backpack and said, "A small token of my gratitude. Please take it."

Then he got up, and, with a wink to Lin, limped his way out. The moment the man was gone, his wife said, "I have a feeling our life will improve."

"What do you mean?"

"See that?" she pointed at the box. "We're getting gifts now!"

She opened the box and what she took out stunned them. It was a small microwave oven, something that would cost seven or eight hundred Yuan.

"This is highly inappropriate. We could accept a cloth doll but not something worth seven or eight hundred. I'm giving it back to him tomorrow."

His wife concurred, and they finished their dinner with a heavy heart.

"Let me ask," she said at bedtime. "Can that document be approved easily?"

"It's not hard. I'll talk to Peng tomorrow, and try to get it approved."

She clapped and said, "Then I'm keeping the microwave."

"Are you sure?" He was concerned. "A microwave oven for getting an approval. Won't it look like I'm exploiting my office for personal gain? Besides, that would give the old man something on us."

"What could he say if you got it done for him? And what do you mean, personal gain? Have you seen anything happen to officials who pocket tens of thousand of RMB? A microwave oven is nothing compared to that."

He had to agree with her, so he stopped objecting. She plugged in the microwave oven and put in a few pieces of sweet potatoes to try it out. The aroma of baked sweet potatoes permeated the room within minutes. They opened the oven door to reveal steamy hot sweet potatoes. They dug in, all three of them, baring their teeth and smacking their lips. Delighted, his wife told him the microwave oven had many uses other than baking sweet potatoes, including baking cakes, toasting buns, and roasting chickens and ducks. Lin happily ate his sweet potato, inspired by the revelation that an improvement in life was not beyond their reach. All he had to do was be part of the system. That night the couple enjoyed more intimacy; the microwave oven made her more passionate and diminished the impact of the soccer incident from the night before.

Lin talked to Peng the next day and, sure enough, they chatted amiably until she approved the document.

Something was up with their daughter after they'd enjoyed using the microwave oven two weeks. She'd gotten used to going to school and stopped crying at drop-off and pickup; sometimes she even bounded into the place. But for two days straight she cried in the morning, refusing to go, claiming a bellyache or needing a bathroom visit, though she produced nothing when they gave her a bedpan. When they scolded her and forced her to leave the house, she stopped crying along the way, but had a dazed look. Lin and his wife suspected that something had happened at school; either she was being bullied by another child or one of the nannies had picked on her, making her stand in the corner or look bad in front of other kids, so injuring the child's self-esteem she was afraid to see the nanny again. When they asked her what happened, she started crying again.

"I'm fine. Nothing's wrong."

So they asked around when they picked her up that afternoon and discovered that they were the cause; they'd been neglectful over New Year's. Before the holiday, every other parent had sent gifts to the nannies, big or small, as a token of appreciation, all but Lin and his wife. The consequence of their carelessness was manifested in the child.

"What's the matter with you? You can't even remember New Year's now that our daughter is in preschool? Who knows how much the nannies laughed at us? They were probably all saying we're cheapskates, poor slobs, even."

"You're right. We should have paid more attention. But after our gifts were rejected, I've been so afraid of giving gifts I forgot when it was time to send one."

They talked about how to make up for their mistake, but they had trouble coming up with an appropriate gift. It would be too miserly to give a New Year's card or a wall calendar, not to mention the fact that the holiday had passed. Blankets or clothes were too lavish for the women to accept.

"Should we ask our daughter?" Lin said.

"What for? What does she know?"

But Lin called the child over anyway to ask her what other parents had given to her teachers. She actually knew and answered crisply:

"Charcoal."

Lin was flabbergasted. "Charcoal? Why charcoal? What do the teachers need charcoal for?"

So his wife conducted another round of inquiry the next day. The girl was telling the truth; many parents had given the teachers charcoal for the new year, a good gift during Beijing's winter, when everyone enjoyed mutton hot pots.

"That's easy. Since everyone else gave charcoal, we'll do the same."

But when they set out to buy charcoal, they found that there was none for sale in Beijing. Stumped for a solution, Lin said to his wife that they should give something else, particularly because the other parents all sent charcoal and what charcoal they could manage to find would be superfluous. But the word charcoal had stuck with the child, who asked every morning as soon as she woke up:

"Papa, did you buy some charcoal for my teachers?"

Despite his annoyance, he had to laugh when his three-year-old girl insisted upon giving charcoal. He patted the edge of the bed and told her:

"It's only charcoal, so I'll get some if I have to search every corner of the city."

At last he bought some charcoal at a tiny, out-of-the-way shop in a suburb; he had to pay an exorbitant price for it, but at least he got what they needed. He told his wife to take it along to the school, and sure enough, their daughter returned to her normal self the next day and went back with a smile. When the girl was happy, the whole family was happy. For dinner that night, his wife roasted half a chicken in the microwave oven and even got a bottle of beer for Lin. The beer made him dizzy and, seemingly, get bigger.

"Actually everything under the sun is easy," he said to his wife. "You just have to understand the logic and follow it. Then life will go smoothly day after day like flowing water. There's nothing wrong with that. When the world runs smoothly, the globe turns on its axis."

Knowing he was getting tipsy, she snatched the beer bottle from him. He was giddy even without the beer and slept like a log that night. He dreamed about sleeping under a blanket of chicken feathers on a mattress of human dandruff. It was soft and comfortable, and a year passed in a single day. Then he dreamed of a vast crowd surging forward before changing into thickets of ants praying for rain. It was daybreak when he awoke, but he could no longer recall his dreams in any detail. His wife woke up and told him to go line up for tofu, when she saw his dreamy look. That cleared his head. Pushing his dreams aside, he jumped out of bed to line up for tofu, after which he went to work.

A letter was waiting for him at the office. It was from the son of his former teacher, who had come to visit him. The son told Lin that his father had passed away three months after they returned from his visit to the hospital in Beijing. Before his father died, the old teacher told his son to write to Lin and express his gratitude for Lin's hospitality during their visit. Lin felt bad all day after reading the letter. He had failed to find a hospital for his teacher when he came to Beijing, and now he was dead. He hadn't even managed to get his teacher to wash up, while his teacher had given him his own padded jacket back when he'd fallen through the ice in elementary school. But his sadness lasted only a day. By the time he boarded the commuter bus, his thoughts had turned to the cabbages. They would be heating up, so he had to go home to air them out by dividing them into smaller piles. Soon the teacher's death was pushed aside; what was the point of thinking about the dead anyway? In the meantime, the living had cabbages to worry about. Once that was taken care of, he said to himself, if his wife would roast a chicken and let him drink another bottle of beer, he'd have everything he could want in life.

College

1

I was discharged from the army and returned home nine years ago. In my father's words, I wasted the four years away from home, since I hadn't managed to join the Communist party or get promoted as a cadre. Except for the stubble on my cheeks, I showed no visible change from the day I'd left home. On the other hand, not much had changed at home either, except for my two younger brothers, who were now as tall as me, whose faces were covered with acne, and who reeked like young horses. At night I heard my father sighing in his room. All three of his sons had grown to six feet tall and reached the age of needing a wife, enough worries for him to drown himself in a pot of liquor. That was 1978, the second year after the college entrance examinations resumed. I wanted to try my luck, but father disagreed.

"You weren't much of a soldier, so what makes you think you'll pass the entrance exam? Besides . . ."

Besides, it would cost a hundred yuan to enroll in the review sessions at the middle school in town. My mother supported me. "But if he . . ."

"How much separation pay did you get?" Father asked.

"A hundred fifty."

"Go ahead and do what you want, it's your money." He spat a thick gob of phlegm onto the door frame. "We don't want your money, but won't give you any either. If you pass, you're in luck; if you fail, you've got no one to blame but yourself."

And that was how I showed up at the middle school in town, where I enrolled in review sessions to prepare for the college entrance exam.

The sessions were offered specifically for older adults who had missed the opportunity to go to college because of the Cultural Revolution. I took a look at the students in the class, and saw many familiar faces, some of whom were my high-school friends from four years earlier. We were back together after a period of dislocation and hardship, which instantly brought us closer. There were a few younger ones too, those who had failed the exam the year before upon graduation from high school. The teacher called us over to the athletic field, where we squatted down for a brief meeting. He checked our bedrolls and sacks of steamed buns before announcing the formal opening of the review session. When it came time to select a class leader, a *banzhang*, to collect homework and enforce rules, the teacher's eye fell on me. He said I should be the class leader since I'd been a deputy squad leader in the army. I hastened to explain that I had been in a feeding squad in charge of fattening up pigs. He waved me off. "We'll make do, won't we?"

Next came dorm assignments, men in one large room and women in another. There was a small room for the *banzhang*, but so many people had showed up for the review session that three more students were put in the room with me. Then we went to the production brigade drying ground for some dried wheat stalks to put on the floor before spreading out our bedrolls. An argument erupted in the men's dorm over the corner spot. But not in the small room, where the other three let me take the corner, since I was the *banzhang*. We were good friends by bedtime. Thirty-something Wang Quan was my classmate in middle school; back then he'd been the dumbest kid in the class, always at the bottom. I had no idea what had gotten into him to get him to show up here. My second roommate, a short fellow nicknamed "Mozhuo" (a localism for a short person), wore a wide belt. My third roommate, nicknamed "Haozi" (rat), was quite good looking.

We got into bed but were too excited to sleep, so we told each other our motivation for enrolling. Wang said he hadn't planned to enroll, since he was married with two kids, and shouldn't be thinking about going back to school. But the local society was rife with problems, with corrupt officials taking advantage of the powerless, and he thought he'd join the review so he could punish those officials if he passed the exam, got into college, and became a county magistrate or something like that. Mozhuo said he had no ambition to be an official; he just didn't want to stay on the farm harvesting wheat under a scorching sun that would end up killing him. Haozi, who was reading a filthy book with curled edges under the kerosene lamp, told us he was the son of a cadre (his father was a commune civil administrator). He loved literature, hated math and science. His father had forced him to come, but he didn't mind, since the girl he was chasing, Yueyue (the prettiest in the class, with a bow tied to her braids), had turned up here. He didn't care if he passed the exam, but he had to win the girl's heart. When it was my turn, I told them I wouldn't be here if I were married, like Wang Quan, nor would I have shown up if I'd been in love with a girl. I only came because I had nothing to show for my years on earth.

We talked about what we'd just learned and concluded that Wang had the noblest motivation; we fell asleep after someone said we'd wake up to a new life.

2

The school was located in a town called Tapu, a name originating from a twisted brick tower on a hillock to the west of a village behind the town. The tower had seven tiers, but no roof, which, legend had it, was brushed off when a traveling immortal flicked his sleeve. The top of the tower afforded a nice vista, but no one was in the mood to go up for a look. Situated below the tower, the school had no wall and bordered a cornfield. To the west of the field was a creek. When the male students got up to relieve themselves at night, they irrigated the crops.

Our first class was language and literature. After the bell sounded a few times, the classroom quieted down. Haozi, who shared a desk with me, nudged me to draw my attention to his girlfriend, Yueyue, who sat in the second row. With a bow at the tip of her braid and a small, rosy face, she was definitely a pretty girl. He asked me to find a way for them to sit together. I nodded, as the teacher walked up to the rostrum. Ma Zhong, a man in his forties, had a long, gourd-shaped face. Everyone knew he was small-minded and had sarcastic tendencies. He didn't say a word as he stood on the rostrum, scrutinizing each student below. When he spotted the ones who had failed the previous year, he pointed with his long face and said with an impassive grin:

"Good, excellent. You're back. By not passing the exam last year, you've ensured my job another year. I hope you'll continue to support me."

He held his hands together in mock salute, and no one knew how to react to that. His sarcasm was directed at the younger students, but everyone suffered. Instead of starting the lesson right away, he told me to take attendance. Each time I called out a name, the student answered, "Here," and Ma nodded. When that was over with, he concluded,

"You all have very nice names."

Then he started, by writing on the blackboard "The Donkey of Qin." To show off his knowledge of literature, Haozi said aloud, "The Donkey of Jin," immediately getting a laugh from the class. I saw Yueyue blush, which was evidence that they were an item. Wang Quan piped up to say we don't have a textbook or any review material, angering the teacher:

"Did you bring your nanny with you?"

When the classroom went quiet, Ma began reading the text in a drawn-out voice: "A busybody shipped a donkey in." By the time he reached the part where the donkey fought a tiger, we heard snores from the back. Naturally, Ma stopped to trace the source of the sound; we followed him with our eyes to Mozhuo, who was fast asleep with his head on the concrete board. We thought Ma would blow his top again, but he just stood calmly in front of Mozhuo's desk to watch, until Mozhuo woke up with a start and, like a frightened rabbit, stared red-eyed at the teacher, clearly embarrassed. Ma bent over and said in a soothing voice,

"Go ahead, sleep. Chairman Mao said that students are allowed to sleep if the teacher isn't teaching well." Then he straightened up and continued, "So you are free to sleep, and, of course, I'm free to stop teaching. I admit I'm not qualified to be your teacher, so I'll stop. I'm off now."

He returned to the rostrum, picked up his folder and textbook, and stormed off.

The classroom erupted: some jeered, some laughed and some complained about Mozhuo. Looking shamefaced, he explained that he never slept well the first three nights in a new place, so he was tired after a sleepless night.

"That's just the beginning of your problems," Haozi said. Someone jeered. I stood to keep order, but no one paid any attention.

That was when I noticed a girl who shared Yueyue's desk. Instead of joining in with others, she was bent over her concrete board, studying diligently. She looked to be in her early twenties, with short hair and dressed in a red padded jacket with buttons down the middle. Like a meditating monk, she fixed her eyes on the book she was holding, softly reading the text. I was impressed—the only good student in a class of people who were croaking like toads.

Mozhuo was in the dumps at lunchtime. He took out a cold steamed corn muffin from his sack but didn't finish it. That evening, back in the dorm, he threw himself down on his bedding and began to sob. I tried to comfort him, but he wouldn't listen. Haozi, who was writing something next to him, groused, "Stop crying as if someone in your family has died. Damn you, I'm writing a love letter."

That made it worse for Mozhuo, whose sobs turned into loud wails. I walked out after failing to get him to stop. With no destination in mind, I walked through the cornfield, until I reached the creek.

The setting sun hung precariously over the creek, in which the water was tinted a bloody red by the dying sunlight as it flowed along slowly. On the bank in a distance, a farm girl was raking grass. I was downcast when I thought about my situation; nearly twenty-seven, I was too old to be hanging out with these kids. And yet I had nothing to show for my life so far and couldn't claim a future in this vast world. I could only sigh and turn back. The farm girl had gathered a large stack of dried grass by then. I was surprised when I looked closer, for it was none other than the girl who had been reading the text by herself. I walked over to greet her. She was short and stocky, on the heavy side, but her fair face had a rosy hue, not bad looking at all. I told her I was impressed by her in class earlier; she didn't reply. So I asked her what she was doing with the grass. She blushed before telling me that her family was poor, her father was sickly and she had two younger brothers and one younger sister. She had to cut grass to sell in order to pay her tuition. I sighed and said life was hard. She looked at me and said, "It's better now. We were much worse off before. I went with my father to Jiaozuo to get some coal when I was fifteen. It was just before New Year's. We had a flat tire when we got to Jiazuo, and it was midnight by the time we found someone to fix the tire. We pulled the cart down the street, where people in the neighborhood were setting off firecrackers to welcome the new year. We felt terrible. Now I'm back in school, and I have to study hard so I won't let him down."

I nodded silently, as many things seemed to make sense all of a sudden.

Mozhuo was no longer crying when I returned to the dorm. He was quietly putting something together, while Haozi was humming a tune as he read the same filthy book by the kerosene light. I guessed

he must have sent off his love letter. Wang Quan raced in to say he'd
been looking all over for me. I asked him what was up. He said my
father had come with some steamed buns but couldn't wait to see me
so he got on the road to return home that night. He handed me a sack.
When I opened it, I was surprised to see some wheat rolls, which we
only ate over New Year's. A warm current coursed through my heart.
Reminded of the girl by the creek, I asked Wang about her. He said
he knew her. Her name was Li Ailian and she was from Guo Village.
Her family was dirt poor and her father was a drunk; she'd fought
with him three times before she could come to the review sessions.
I nodded without saying anything but Haozi piped up, "What, does
our *banzhang* have his eye on her? You have to act right away. Here,
I'll lend you this *Complete Collection of Love Letters,* so you can get a
move on her. Seize the opportunity, pal. There's no more after this,
and you'll never get anything so good—"

"Screw you!" I threw the sack at his head.

I'd obviously shocked everyone in the room, for even the
dejected Mozhuo looked up at me, his tiny eyes staring in surprise.

3

Winter arrived. A cold wind blew in and out of the classroom and
our dorm, so we were cold day and night, with no place to hide. As if
that weren't bad enough, snow fell and quickly turned everything icy,
making it even colder. We were often awoken by the cold at night.
Finally we decided to form two sleeping teams, rolling up two blankets together for two people to sleep under.

No fire burned in the classroom either. At night, we each lit a
small oil lamp and slumped over our cement boards to review our les-
sons. The flames flickered each time a cold gust slipped in through
cracks in the wall. Sitting in rows, we tucked our hands into our
sleeves as we read, our shadowy figures like those of temple demons.
When I looked out the window, the black tower shook in the wind,
seemingly on the verge of toppling over.

The flu arrived and began to spread, causing everyone to cough, and claiming the two younger students sitting in the front rows as its first victims. Spiking a high fever that had them spouting delirious speech, they were forced to withdraw and go home with their parents.

By then I was sharing a desk with Li Ailian, after Haozi had moved to sit with Yueyue. We got to know each other pretty well. I told her about life in the army, when I had to feed the pigs. She talked about how she had climbed elm trees as a kid. One morning she climbed eight elms to collect enough pods to cook a meal. Her mother was nice, but her father had a temper and liked to drink. He often hit them when he was drunk. Once, when her mother was pregnant, he kicked her and sent her rolling down a slope.

The food was really awful at the school. Most of us were from poor families, so we brought cold corn muffins from home, which we ate with a piece of pickled vegetable and cornmeal gruel that we bought in the galley. Anyone who could afford fifty fen could buy a bowl of cabbage soup, and that would count as a major dietary improvement. Haozi's family was better off than the rest of us, so his parents often sent him some good food. But none of us was invited to share with him, only his girlfriend. Occasionally Wang and I would get a taste, but never Mozhuo, whom he didn't like. At such moments, Mozhuo would sit stiffly to the side, a hungry, hurt look in his eyes. It was heartbreaking to see. He was never again caught dozing in class, and threw himself into his studies, which exhausted him so much he became visibly thinner and seemingly smaller.

Finally spring arrived and green buds sprouted on willow trees. When I was eating dinner in the classroom one day, Li Ailian quietly handed me a bowl. I looked down to see a few vegetable rolls made of fresh, tender willow leaves. After giving her a grateful look, I took a hasty bite; it was a rare delicacy. I could not bring myself to finish them all; instead, I saved one to give to Mozhuo behind everyone's back. But he looked at me and shook his head; he would not take handouts.

Wang's wife came to see him one day. A big woman with a shrew-ish look and a swarthy face, she started cursing him the moment she walked in, saying they had nothing to eat at home and that their chil-dren were crying from hunger. She wanted him to go home and do something.

"The three of us are suffering at home while you're having a great time here. How nice for you."

Without responding, Wang found a stick and drove her out. Like a couple of kids, they chased one another around the athletic field, until he finally got her to bound off. Everyone else was laughing at the sight, as he spun around and returned to the dorm.

Wang's older child came the next day with a sack of steamed buns. He held the swarthy kid's hand and sighed.

"You and Mama will have a better life when Papa passes the exam and becomes a big official."

Something quite strange occurred. A red glow appeared on the face of Mozhuo, who had been reduced to skin and bones. One night he came in late, with an oily sheen on his lips. When I asked him where he'd been, he wouldn't say and went straight to bed. After he fell asleep, Wang Quan and I figured the guy must have found a place to eat. Why else would his lips be greasy? But where did he get the money?

"He must have been stealing," Haozi cut in. I glared at him and we all went quiet.

Eventually I found out. One night I returned to the dorm after a study session, but Mozhuo wasn't there. So I stole out of the room to look for him. He was nowhere to be seen. Then I went to the toilet, where I saw a flickering flame behind the wall like a will-o'-the-wisp. Someone was sprawled on the ground. What the hell? It was Mozhuo. I tiptoed over and saw burning scraps of paper in which newly hatched cicadas were crawling. Mozhuo was licking his lips, his eyes fixed on the fire, as he tossed in more cicadas. The fire died out after a while, but it was unclear whether the cicadas were dead or cooked through. He picked them up one after the other and stuffed them into his mouth. He chewed noisily. It gave me a bad feeling, so I backed off, but made a noise as I did. Startled, he stopped chewing and turned to see who it was. When he realized it was me, the fearful look turned to embarrassment, as he stammered, "Want one, *banzhang?*" he stammered. "They're delicious."

I didn't reply, nor did I take one, as a sadness welled up inside me. In the dim moonlight, he looked like a squat little animal. There were tears in my eyes as I went up and took his arm, as if he were my own brother.

"Let's go back, Mozhuo."

"*Banzhang,*" he pleaded tearfully. "Please don't tell anyone else."

"I won't."

The school finally offered us something better to eat when Labor Day came around. Stewed turnips with pork, fifty fen a portion. You can be poor all year round, but never skimp on holidays, as the saying goes. So everyone bought a bowl and was immediately slurping away; an occasional shout signaled that an extra piece of pork had been spotted in someone's bowl. When I returned with my food to the classroom, I saw Li Ailian sitting alone at her desk with her head down. She must not have any money, I said to myself. So I took a few bites and pushed the bowl to her. She looked up at me; her eyes reddened when she took it. I was touched but sad, suddenly feeling protective and somehow noble. Tears welled up in my eyes as I spun around and left the room. She was gone when I returned that evening.

Something's not right, I thought. I asked Wang to come out with me to see if he knew what was wrong. With a sigh, he said, "I heard her father is sick."

"Serious?"

"Pretty bad, I heard."

I raced back inside to borrow Haozi's bicycle and rode off to her village after buying some pastries.

The family really was dirt poor, with three dilapidated, rammed-earth rooms under a thatched roof; the yard was pitch black, as was everywhere else, except for the central room. I saw movement inside when I called out "Li Ailian." The curtain parted and she came out.

"Ah, it's you!" She was surprised to see me.

"I heard your father was sick, so I came to see."

I noticed a grateful look in her eyes.

A kerosene lamp on the wall gave off a dim yellow light to reveal a gaunt matchstick of a middle-aged man on a bed against the wall. Straw was strewn all over the bed, around which stood several sniffing children. At the head of the bed stood a middle-aged woman with a disheveled bun at the back of her head; Li Ailian's mother. They all looked at me when I walked in.

"I'm a classmate of Li Ailian," I explained. "At school, when we heard that Uncle Li was sick, they asked me to come see him." I handed the pastries to her mother, who snapped out of her daze and offered me a seat.

"Ai-ya! You didn't have to do that. And there was no need to bring such expensive treats."

Her father sat up and coughed, while offering me the pipe on a table. I waved to say I wasn't a smoker.

"This is our *banzhang*. A very nice person. He brought you this bowl of meat and vegetables."

I spotted the half-finished bowl of food on the rickety bedside table. She hadn't eaten it, but had brought it home for her father. My heart ached at the sight of her younger siblings staring greedily at the pork in the bowl.

After spending a bit more time there and finishing a bowl of water Ailian handed me, I learned about her father's illness. It turned out that he had gotten drunk again, which brought on his usual stomach problems. I told him to take care of himself and stood to leave.

"I'll head back now. Why don't you spend the night at home and come back to school tomorrow?"

"You're such a nice person." Li's mother took my hand. "We have nothing in the house. I just wish I could offer you something to eat." She turned to her daughter. "Go back with him. There are enough of us here to take care of your father. Go back with the young man, and be sure to work hard at your studies."

The road on the dark night meandered like a serpent. I rode along with her on the back of the bicycle, but we couldn't find anything to say to each other, until I realized that she was sobbing. Wrapping her arms around my waist, she pressed her face against my back and called out,

"Ge—"

A warm current filled my chest and my eyes began to well up. "Be careful. Don't fall off," I said, while silently vowing to myself that I must study hard and pass the exam this year to be a worthy "*ge*," a big brother.

4

Only two months until the exam, we heard we'd also be tested on world geography. That was news to all of us, including our teachers, who had thought we only had to study Chinese geography. It threw everyone into a panic, for we were nearing the breaking point of our focus and energy. Wang Quan had been suffering from insomnia; Mozhuo suffered from headaches and his eyes glazed over each time he opened a textbook. Cursing the school for not getting it right, everyone complained about a crippling hardship. But the biggest problem facing us was the absence of review material for world geography. Everyone got into action searching for the materials, everyone but Haozi, who remained cheerful despite the chaos. We heard that his love life was thriving, like crops sprouting in the spring.

After a few days of commotion, some found review materials, while others continued to search. People turned selfish as the exam drew near, and those who had gotten what they needed kept it a secret from others, hoping to eliminate competition. In our room, Mozhuo was the only who managed to get hold of a yellowed copy of *World Geography*, but he was adamant in his denial while furtively memorizing the contents on the hillock behind the school, a reprise of the time when he ate roasted cicadas. Unable to get a copy, Wang Quan, Li Ailian, and I were as anxious as ants in a hot wok. When my father came with more steamed buns, he noticed the distracted look on my sallow face and asked me what was going on. I told him and he clapped his hands. "Your aunt's son teaches at Ji County Normal School. Maybe he has something."

My spirits soared as I was reminded of the cousin. Father stood up, tightened his blue cloth belt, and volunteered to head to Ji without delay.

"Why don't you go home and tell mother first? Or she may be worried."

"We can't worry about something like that at a time like this."

"But you don't know how to ride a bike. It's ninety kilometers round trip."

"When I was young, I could cover a hundred and fifteen in a day," he replied confidently before tottering off. I ran after him and handed him the sack. He looked at me and a smile escaped from the stubble that circled his lips as he took out four buns. "Don't worry. I'll be back tomorrow evening."

Tear welled up in my eyes again.

I whispered the news to Li that night during study session; she was elated also.

On the following evening, she and I stole out of the school and met up at the hillock to then walk a kilometer to the main road just outside the village to meet up with my father. We started out in high spirits, talking and laughing, but soon it grew dark and my heart sank when no one but an old man collecting animal droppings came into view.

"Maybe your father's feet hurt and he had to slow down." She tried to make me feel better.

"What if he couldn't find anything?"

We waited quietly, until the crescent moon was dipping west. There was no point in staying, so we walked back dejectedly. But we agreed that we'd meet up again just before dawn the next day.

I got out of bed at the first crow of a rooster, and went back to the same spot. A figure appeared in the distance so I ran up, thinking it must be my father, but it turned out to be her.

"You're earlier than me!"

"I just got here."

An early morning frost had turned the green fields white. Roosters were crowing here and there in a nearby village. I felt a sudden chill and looked at Ailian; she was trembling, so I took off my overcoat and draped it over her shoulders. She didn't turn down my offer, and instead looked at me with emotion-filled eyes, while slowly pressing up against me. Feeling hot all over, with a tingling sensation coursing through my body, I had an urge to kiss her, but I didn't.

It was getting light, the eastern sky was tinted red from the early morning sun. Suddenly we spotted a figure stumbling toward us from the distance. She squirmed out of my arms and pointed.

"Is that him?"

I perked up after taking a look. "Yes, that's him. That's how my father walks."

We took off running. I waved my arms and shouted, "Father!"

"Ai!" A reply came from the end of the road.

"Did you get it?"

"I did, son!"

I was so happy I yelled like a madman as I raced ahead. I didn't stop when Li fell. I kept running until I reached the tottering old man.

"You got it?"

"I got it."

"Where is it?"

"Don't worry. I'll show you."

He was equally excited as he sat on the ground. By then Li had caught up and watched as my father carefully undid the blue cloth around his waist and unbuttoned his padded jacket and the shirt underneath to retrieve a thin, well-worn volume. I snatched it out of his hands. It still had his body warmth, but I was concerned only about the title, *World Geography*. Li took it from me and one look so thrilled her that even her ears turned red.

"Yes, that's it. It's *World Geography*."

Father laughed at our ecstatic state. Then I noticed the tip of one of his shoes had cracked open and something bright red was oozing out. I took off his shoe and saw that his wrinkled, dirt-splattered foot was covered in blisters, some of which had already burst to turn his foot bloody.

"Father!"

"It's all right. Nothing serious." He was still smiling as he pulled his foot out of my hand.

"Thank you so much, Uncle." Ailian was on the verge of tears.

"You're sixty-five years old," I said.

"It's all right. It's nothing." He was still acting tough. "This book is in high demand and hard to find. It took your cousin a whole day to get a copy, or I'd have made it back last night."

Ailian and I exchanged a look, and I saw she was all dusty. I asked if she'd hurt herself when she fell. She pulled up her sleeve to show a bruise on her arm, but that only made us laugh.

"Your cousin said it wasn't easy to get a copy. In fact he pretty much took it away from its owner," Father said somberly. "We have to return it in ten days."

We nodded solemnly.

"You do your best," he continued, "But we won't give it back if ten days isn't enough for you. I'll tell him I was careless and lost it on the way home."

"Ten days will be enough," we said together.

By then we'd recovered from the excitement enough for Father to size her up with a quizzical look, so I hastened to explain, "This is Li Ailian, a classmate."

She blushed.

"A classmate. I see," Father said with a cunning glint in his eyes. "Go ahead and start studying." He stood up to walk home.

"Rest a while, Father. Don't be in a hurry to go home."

"I have to go. Your mother must be worried sick."

He walked off and soon disappeared down another road. Book in hand, Ailian and I felt buoyed again as we looked at each other before turning back. We agreed to sneak out and meet up by the creek to memorize the contents together.

I left early the following morning with the book, and walked through the cornfield to reach the spot where she'd been cutting grass that day. Sure that she would be there before me, I planned to creep out of the field to scare her. But I stopped in my tracks when I parted the corn stalks and gazed at the riverbank. The picture in front of me froze me on the spot.

She was sitting serenely on the riverbank in front of a small round mirror propped up on the grass. With her eyes on the mirror, she was brushing her hair leisurely with a plastic comb with broken teeth. She worked methodically, slowly, and carefully, one side of her face painted a golden yellow by the rosy rays of an early morning sun.

It dawned on me that she was a girl, a very pretty girl.

I was distracted that day, unable to focus on the book that had taken so much trouble to secure. I kept thinking about something else, and I discovered that she was a little flustered too. We avoided each other's eyes as if we were upset with ourselves.

That night we came to the main road, where we worked on memorizing the text with the help of a flashlight. It could have been the dark night or the tranquility, but we had exceptional concentration and made great progress. We'd memorized a third of the book by the time the lights-out bell sounded on campus. Surprised and thrilled, we put the book aside and lay down in the grass, not willing to return just yet.

The stars were bright in the dark, impossibly deep and distant sky. I'd never before noticed how lofty, vast, kind, and delightful the sky could be. I could hear her breathing beside me and I knew she too was gazing at the sky.

But she lay there silently.

A wind started to blow, a chilly gust of wind. We remained motionless.

"Do you think we'll pass the exam?" she whispered to break the silence.

"Of course," I replied firmly. "We will."

"How do you know?"

"The stars and sky tell me so."

"That's nonsense." She laughed.

We fell silent again as we continued gazing at the evening sky.

She spoke up again, this time with a tremor in her voice. "What if you pass, but I fail?"

I shuddered when I gave the question some thought, but I replied firmly, "I'll never forget you if that happens."

She let out of long sigh and said, "I won't forget you either if I pass and you fail."

I could feel her hand next to mine so I took it, the rough hand of a farm girl, a warm hand on a chilly night.

"I'm getting cold," she said.

Something stirred in my heart and I put my arms around her. Staying in my arms, she gazed up at me with a docile look in her serene, dark eyes. I bent down to kiss her damp lips, nose, and moist eyes.

It was my first kiss.

5

Exhaustion. Sheer exhaustion and nothing else.

Wang's insomnia was getting worse; he couldn't sleep, his eyes were bloodshot, and his hair was all rumpled. Looking more demon than human, he had developed a temper, and was no longer his kind old self. One night, when Mozhuo was snored loudly, Wang punched him twice. Mozhuo woke up, buried his head in his blanket, and sobbed, while Wang sucked on his lips.

"This can't go on," he grumbled.

Mozhou's headaches had gotten so bad he could no longer read. He spent twenty fen on a tin of menthol balm to rub on his temples, infusing the room with a menthol smell. One night I saw him crying when I got back.

"Did Wang Quan hit you again?"

He shook his head. "This is too hard. It's awful, *banzhang*. Can I just aim for a junior college instead?"

Cuckoo birds were calling in fields where wheat was ready for harvesting. Our teachers stopped tutoring us and went to work in the school's fields, leaving us to our own devices, like horses let loose in the mountains. I went to talk about it with the principal, who said the only solution was to help bring in the wheat so the teachers could be free to resume tutoring. I was upset by how heartless that sounded; we had only a month left, and he had to exploit us. Yet when I passed this on my classmates, they were enthusiastic. Apparently, everyone's nerves were so frayed, they weren't making much progress in their studies. The principal's plan gave them time to rest their brains, so with a shout, they stormed out of the classroom and headed to the wheat field, west of the creek. Taking the scythes from the teachers, we spread out horizontally, and, with the intense rhythm of "ka-cha," cut sheaves of wheat speedily and methodically. After finishing a large section, we were soaked in sweat and our taut nerves relaxed for a while. We laughed and horsed around like typical farm boys and girls, while the teachers watched approvingly from the edge of the field.

"I don't know how they'll do on the exam but they're good at harvesting wheat," Ma Zhong said. "They'd all pass if that were on the college exam."

As I wiped the sweat from my face and looked at the field and the people in it, I felt, for the first time in my life, that manual labor was satisfying.

It didn't take even an afternoon to finish bringing in the wheat, which so impressed the principal that he told the kitchen to prepare a special meal for us, free of charge. It was pork stewed with turnips again, but this time there would be plenty. We washed our hands and faces before going into the dining hall, where we enjoyed a good meal.

But some unhappy events occurred over the next few days.

The first was Wang Quan dropping out. The exam was barely a month away, but he decided to give up. It was the first year after the land-lease system was implemented and villages parceled out land along with wheat seedlings to families, including Wang's. Now the wheat was ripening and ready for harvest. Wang's towering wife made another visit to school, but this time she didn't rail at him. Instead, she talked to him in a serious tone.

"The wheat is drying up in the field. Are you coming back to harvest? If you are, I'll get started, and if not, well, the damned wheat will just have to die out there."

She turned and walked off, without waiting for a reply, leaving Wang to his own thoughts.

That night he got me out of the classroom. He took out a pack of cigarettes, the first time for that, and offered me one. We lit up and smoked.

"We were classmates back then and now we've shared a dorm room for more than six months. Are we good friends?"

"Do you really have to ask?"

He took another puff. "Then I'm going to ask you a question and you have to be honest with me."

"Sure."

"With what I've got, do you think I can pass the exam?"

That caught me by surprise, and I didn't know what to say. To be frank, Wang wasn't all that smart. It didn't matter how hard he tried to memorize something, nothing stayed with him after two days; he might even say that the Yellow River was thirty-three kilometers long. Worse yet, he hadn't been sleeping well since he got here, which affected his ability to remember what he learned. But everyone could see that he worked hard.

"You've made it this far, and you only have to keep at it for one more month."

He nodded and took another drag, before blurting out emotionally, "But it's been hard on her and the kids. I never told you this, but I took our oldest out of school so I could prepare for the exam. What will I say to him if I don't pass?"

"What if you do? No one can tell how it will turn out."

He nodded again and continued, "And then there's the wheat. We won't have anything to eat if the wheat goes to ruin."

"I'll get some classmates to help you."

"I can't ask for anyone's help at a moment like this." He shook his head.

"Don't worry so much. It would only be this season if the wheat went to waste, but the exam could mean a lifetime of difference."

He nodded.

But we woke up in the morning to find his spot empty; only the yellow wheat stalks remained. Obviously he'd made up his mind to leave without saying good-bye. Then we noticed how he had stuffed his tattered summer mat under Mozhuo's pillow. We were saddened by the sight. Mozhuo lost control and began to cry.

"Would you look at that? Wang Quan didn't say a word. He just up and left like that."

I was emotional myself, but I tried to console him. I never expected him to cry openly.

"I feel terrible. I had a copy of *World Geography*, but wouldn't share it with him."

Another unpleasant incident took place a few days later. Yueyue broke up with Haozi. He wouldn't tell us why, except to complain that she was "heartless." Apparently, he wasn't good enough for her, so she decided to cut off all ties with him, even threatening to tell the teachers if he didn't leave her alone. Throwing his copy of *A*

Complete Collection of Love Letters to the floor, he spread out his hands and wept, a first for him.

"That's so vile!"

I tried to make him feel better by telling him that with his family background and his looks, he'd have no trouble finding another girlfriend. He was somewhat consoled as he uttered a somber vow, "She thinks I'm not good enough for her. I'm going to start over, and I'll see the look on her face when I get into a college in Beijing."

He put on his shoes and went to the classroom to go over his notes and textbooks. But it was clear to us that, no matter how smart he was, it was too late to start over two weeks before the exam.

The third piece of bad news was Ailian's father falling ill again. I went to the classroom one night and saw a note she'd stuck in one of my books.

"Ge,

My father is ill again, so I have to go home. I'll be back soon, don't worry.

Ailian."

But she was still not back in two days, which worried me so much I borrowed Haozi's bike and rode out to her village again. Neither she nor her father was home. Her mother, who was sowing wheat seedlings in the field, told me that her father was so ill this time that he was taken to Xinxiang. Ailian had gone with him.

I pushed the bike and turned around dejectedly. When I reached the village entrance, I stopped to look at the paved road to Xinxiang and the tall poplar trees on both sides. *I wonder how serious his illness is this time*, I said to myself. *We only have two weeks left; I hope she won't miss the exam.*

6

Finally it was time for the college entrance exam.

It was held in our classroom, but the place felt completely different. The walls were covered in warnings in different colors:

"Observe the rules of the exam site," "No talking," "Violators till be banned from the exam," etc. On the door was "Rules for the exam": we needed admission cards, our photos would be checked before the exam papers were distributed, anyone more than half an hour late would be barred from entering, etc. Five teachers were assigned to the small room to proctor the exam, one of whom was Ma Zhong, who stood at the rostrum and announced with a swagger, "I'll be watching all of you. It will be a loss of face if you fail, but it will be scandalous if you violate the rules and get thrown out."

The warning was followed by the appearance of policemen with insignias on their caps and collars, nearly taking our breath away and making our hearts race. Outside were several three-wheeled motorcycles from the public security office to deliver and collect our exam papers. A white warning line was drawn thirty meters away and guarded by a policeman.

Students' families gathered beyond the line, waiting anxiously for us to finish. My father was among them; he had brought along a sack of hard-boiled eggs. Mother had cooked them for me, all thirty-six of them: six times six makes thirty-six and two sixes brings good luck, he said. He added that eggs were easier to eat, so I wouldn't waste any time. He was oblivious to the dense layers of beady sweat on his forehead, nor did he realize that he was covered from head to toe in dust kicked up by people around him. It made me sad to look at the exam site, the families beyond the line, and my father sitting on a broken brick.

The first two hours of the exam were devoted to politics. I felt a sudden dizziness and nausea, but I gritted my teeth and kept at it. Finally, I felt better, but then was overtaken by an unprecedented sense of fatigue. *I'm finished*, I said to myself. *I'm going to fail.*

Besides, I couldn't concentrate, for I kept thinking about Ailian and the note she'd sent two days before.

"Ge,

The exam will start soon, and whether or not we've wasted six months of hard work will be revealed over the next two days. I can't take it in town because I must stay here to care for my father, but I'll go to the exam site in Xinxiang. Ge, my dear, we can't sit in the same room but I know our hearts are together. I think I'll pass, and with all my heart I wish you the best of luck. Ailian."

That was all she wrote. I'd gazed in the direction of Xinxiang, letter in hand, as a tremor stirred in my heart.

Now as I sat in exam room, I couldn't stop wondering about her: has she made it in time to the Xinxiang site? Is she exhausted from taking care of her father in the hospital? Is she intimidated by the exam paper? Does she know the answers? And then a sudden vision of her stern face appeared in my head; she was saying to me,

"Stop those wild thoughts, for my sake, and focus on the exam."

That enabled me to close my eyes and concentrate on the questions. Now I knew what they were and how to answer them. They weren't too hard; in fact, I'd memorized them all. Feeling more self-assured, I was no longer afraid as I started writing after shaking my fountain pen a few times. As soon as I began, I was able to recall everything I'd memorized. I was happy about my change of mentality and grateful for the timely appearance of Ailian's stern face. I kept writing, constantly checking the time on a borrowed wristwatch, and finished just as the bell rang.

I got up, surprised to see that I was drenched in sweat, beads of water dripping from the tips of my hair. Ma Zhong's menacing voice sounded from the rostrum: "Time's up. Stop now. Turn your paper upside down on your desk. This one minute isn't going to decide whether you pass or not. You are now like ants on a hot wok; it's, useless no matter how hard you race against time."

I wasn't worried, as I put the paper on my desk and walked out.

Father was already on his feet, standing on his tiptoes, looking in the direction of the classroom like everyone around him. He walked up when he spotted me and asked anxiously,

"How did you do?"

"Not bad."

He smiled, a relieved smile after a long, worried wait. It looked a little forced to me, a pained and fatigued smile. There were tears in his eyes when he looked at me. I was surprised to see a glint of gratitude in those aging eyes.

"Good, very good," he said while taking out six eggs for me. But I didn't feel like eating anything; all I wanted was some water.

"No, no water. You have to go back inside and you'll want to pee if you drink water."

I couldn't follow his advice, and ran over to a faucet where I gulped down as much water as I could.

We had ten minutes before the next session, so I returned to the dorm. Mozhuo and Haozi were both there, the former flipping through a book with great urgency. When he saw me, he said in a trembling voice verging on tears, "I'm finished, *banzhang*. I was so stupid. I memorized every one of the questions, but I mixed them all up. I put down 'General guidelines for socialism' for 'the party's basic guidelines.'"

"What about the other five questions?"

"I messed up two of those too." He was almost crying now. "Oh, no. I'm going to fail the politics part."

"It's over, so stop thinking about it," I said. "Now just try to focus on the next one, Math."

"That's easy for you to say. You did well on the first part, so you're not worried." He still sounded worried. "I knew all the answers but I messed them up. It's so unfair. I'm so stupid, just stupid." With a pained look, he began to bang his fists against his head.

Haozi wasn't looking much better, as he sprawled on his bed without saying a word.

"What about you, Haozi?"

"None of your business." He actually glared at me before putting his head in his hands and crying out in agony. "Fuck. I knew all the questions but they didn't know me. It was easy for me, because I didn't write anything. I managed to write a few words when the bell rang. Do you think the damned readers will give me a few points for "Long Live the Chinese Communist party'?"

The bell sounded for the next session. All the students returned to the room, some looking happy, some worried, and some utterly downcast. The families gathered again to wait beyond the line, including my father, who was back on the broken brick under a scorching sun. Ma Zhong gave us another lecture: "Some students did not behave in the previous session. Obey the rules this time or don't blame me if I throw you out."

We were all on edge as we waited for him to finish, because that took away eight minutes of our time. Finally the exam papers were handed out; the noise of everyone spreading them out filled the room before silence returned as we read the questions, followed by the sound of pens scratching paper.

Suddenly I heard a "thud" behind me and the room was thrown into chaos. I turned to look; I was shocked to see Mozhuo passed out on the floor. The proctoring teachers raced over to him, giving some students the opportunity to whisper or sneak a peek at others' paper. The teachers had to forget about Mozhou to maintain order, while Ma Zhong repeated his threats. Mozhuo was carried out only after the room quieted down.

I took a look at him as he was carried past me. His eyes were closed, he was shaking uncontrollably, even his teeth were clattering; sweat dripped from his hair onto his ghostly white face. The sight pained me so much I began to tear up. *Mozhuo, my good pal, is it over for you? Where's your menthol balm? Why didn't you put a thick layer around your temples? Why did you have to pass out like that? Six months' hard work wasted. How terrible for you, my good pal!*

Another commotion broke out before this one was over. It was Haozi. Ma Zhong, who was standing in front of him watching him answer questions, abruptly snatched the exam paper away from him.

"What are you doing?" Ma's eyes bulged in anger. "What kind of equations are these? Are you trying to be a troublemaker?"

The other teachers were startled.

"What's going on? Did he write an antirevolutionary slogan?"

"No, he didn't, but he's caused plenty of trouble. Let me read it to you." Ma began in a singsong voice, "'Party Central Committee and Ministry of Education, I'm very emotional as I write this letter to you. I don't know the answers to the questions, but my heart is devoted to you, so please let me into a college. I promise I will do my best to serve the people.' What's this all about? The times have changed and you can no longer get into college by writing a letter like Zhang Tiesheng did."

Ma Zhong ranted on and on until the principal came in to stop him and allow the students the peace and quiet to continue.

The two days passed like that, and the exam was over.

7

The exam was over.

I thought I did pretty well and would likely get into a college, if not the best one. When I told father, who had waited for two days beyond the line, about my feelings, for the first time in this old farmer's life, he hugged his son tightly, like a Westerner, so excited he was incoherent.

"Are you kidding me? That's great."

He let go and, with a happy laugh, walked out of the school holding my hand. "Let's go home," he said. I had to remind him that my stuff was still in the dorm. So he left on his own, saying he'd take the good news to my mother and younger brother.

Now that the review sessions were over, the students would soon go their separate ways. Some did well, others did badly, which made some laugh and others cry. But we were about to say good-bye, so everyone suppressed their emotions and gathered in the big dorm, where we chatted like brothers and sisters. The only one missing was Mozhuo, who was still in the hospital. Pooling our money together to hold a farewell party, we bought two bottles of liquor and a pack of peanuts, and we each had a couple of peanuts as we took turns sipping the liquor. Some were so moved they began to weep, and a few girls sobbed openly. We continued chatting when the liquor was gone, vowing we wouldn't forget each other whether or not we passed the exam, whether we made it big or remained a farmer. Someone cited a line from the classics: "Never forget others, even in fame and wealth." We continued until sunset, when everyone packed and returned to their village homes.

I lingered after everyone left, as I searched for a place to relax by myself. Eventually I ran five kilometers and arrived at a bridge, where, not seeing anyone around, I stripped naked and jumped into the river to wash myself clean of the dirt I'd accumulated over the past six months. After that, I swam downstream and then upstream; when I was tired, I floated on my back to gaze at the blue sky. Before long, I was reminded of Wang Quan, Mozhuo, and Haozi, and that dampened my spirits. I was happy now, but they must be suffering. Like someone who has committed a shameful act, I quickly got out of the water and put my clothes back on.

As I walked down a path, my mind was in a mixture of joy and sadness. I thought about my parents and younger brother, who had scrimped on everything over these months so I could attend the study sessions. I should go pack up and return home right away. Then my thoughts turned to Ailian, as I wondered if her father had recovered and how she'd done in the exam. I had a sudden attack of anxiety, and made a decision to go to Xinxiang the next day.

Experiencing a jumble of thoughts, I walked on and suddenly saw, directly ahead, a donkey cart carrying manure. The carter looked like Wang Quan, so I ran forward to catch up, and it was indeed him. With a shout, I threw my arms around him.

It had been barely a month since I'd last seen him, but he was already a different person; retaining no trace of his student days, he looked like a typical farmer, with a tattered straw hat, a soiled jacket, a stubbled face, and a whip.

He was glad to see me as he returned the hug, asking me about the exam, while I inquired about his wheat harvest, his wife and children. We laughed, not knowing who should answer first.

We walked together for a while and said all the things we wanted to say to each other, when I was reminded of Li Ailian.

"Do you have any news of Li Ailian? How's her father's illness? She told me she'd take the exam in Xinxiang. Do you know how she did?"

Instead of answering, he looked at me with searching eyes.

"Don't you know what happened to her?"

"What happened? She wrote to say she'd take the exam in Xinxiang."

He sighed. "She never took it."

I was stunned; my mouth hung open, for I didn't know what to say. He was quiet, keeping his head down.

"What?" I finally found my voice. "She didn't take the exam? Impossible. She told me in her letter that she would."

"She didn't." He sighed again.

"What did she do then?"

He stopped and squatted down, holding his head in his hands. It took him a moment to continue. "You really don't know? She got married."

"Ah!" The news came like a thunderclap. I didn't know how to react. When I finally recovered, I grabbed him.

"You're lying. That's nonsense. How could it be? She wrote to me. How could she be married? We're good friends, Wang Quan, so please be serious."

He began to sob. "So you really didn't know? We're good friends and I know how you feel about her, so why would I lie to you? Her father was seriously ill and began coughing up blood when they reached Xinxiang. The hospital demanded five hundred before they would admit him for a lifesaving operation. But where would her family find the money? Her whole family was worried sick when Lü

Qi, a man who had recently struck it rich in her village, offered to pay for them, if Ailian would marry him. With her father's life hanging in the balance, they had no choice but to agree."

I let go of him and stood up in a daze. It felt so unreal.

"But, but what about the letter?"

"She was trying to make you feel better so you could focus on the exam. Did you ever wonder how she could take an exam in Xinxiang without being a local resident?"

That came as another thunderclap. Of course, she couldn't. Why hadn't I thought of that? I was so stupid, so selfish. I was thinking only about myself.

"When was the wedding?"

"Yesterday."

"Yesterday? I was taking the exam yesterday."

My teeth were clattering. I must have presented a terrifying sight, for he stopped crying to comfort me.

"Don't take it so hard. It's over, so don't feel bad. It won't do any good."

"She's married?" I asked.

"Yes."

"Why didn't she wait till after the exam? Why be in such a hurry?"

"The man was afraid she'd change her mind if she passed the exam. That's why."

I gave my head a savage thump. "Which village?"

"The Wang Village."

"What's the guy's name again?"

"Lü Qi."

"I'm going to go see him."

Ignoring his shouts, I took off running as if my life depended on it, while he came after me. When I reached the edge of the village, I realized I'd been heading toward Guo Village, where her parents lived. I turned and ran toward Wang Village.

I slowed down when I got there, as my head cleared up. I was reminded of what Wang had said: "What's the point of looking her up now that she's married?" I squatted down by the entrance of the village and began to sob.

After crying for a while, I dried my tears and walked into the village, where I asked directions to Lü's house. I was greeted by a large red character for double happiness when I reached his door. Another explosion went off in my head, as if struck by a thick log. All I could do was stand there like an idiot, not moving, for a long time.

Finally the door opened with a creak and out walked a woman dressed in a bright red blouse over a pair of green Dacron pants, a red velveteen flower in her hair. Was that the girl who had put her arms around me and called me "ge"? Was that the girl I'd held in my arms and kissed? The one who'd said we'd never forget each other?

But she'd been married the day before, instead of taking the exam, and was now someone else's wife.

I stared at her. I couldn't move.

Finally she saw me and she quaked, as if struck by lighting. She froze.

I remained motionless, not even shedding a tear. I opened my mouth to say something, but it was parched and something was stuck in my chest to make my tongue stiff. I couldn't utter a word.

She was quiet too; leaning her head weakly against the door frame, she gazed at me until tears began to stream down her face.

"Ge—"

I managed to muster enough energy to call out to her, in a tiny voice.

"Meimei—"

"Come inside. This is my house."

"Your house?"

I turned and ran off; I ran until I reached a riverbank outside the village, where I threw myself down and began to cry.

She caught up with me.

I told her to go home after we'd walked a while.

"Go on back home."

She caught me off guard by resting her head on my shoulder and crying uncontrollably. Then she turned my face toward her to kiss and touch me, abandoning all reason and common sense.

"Don't forget me, Ge."

I held back tears and nodded.

"Don't be mad at me. I know I've let you down."

"Ailian!" I took her into my arms.

"When you go to college, Ge, remember you're there for both of us."

I nodded again.

"Don't forget there are two of us, no matter where you are, what you do, or how your life turns out."

I could only keep nodding.

Dusk had descended, with the last rays of bloody sun lingering on the western sky.

I left.

After a while, I turned back to look. She was still on the river-bank gazing in my direction. A wind raised her lapel, as she stood by a small willow tree, against an evening sky with a hint of blue and the blood-red sunset. It looked like a paper-cut.

Office

1

May First, China's Labor Day, was just around the corner. The government office had a truckload of pears delivered for the employees. When it was time to divvy them up, a platform scale was set up outside the building, where straw was strewn across the ground. Two men, Lao [old] He and Xiao [young] Lin, carried a large basket of pears into their office, where their co-workers began scrounging for means to transport their pears home. One found a mesh bag in his desk drawer, another came up with a ripped paper bag, and the third took possession of the wastepaper basket. Xiao Peng went for the carrying basket, saying she could use it for coal briquettes at home. Then Xiao Lin was sent to borrow a steelyard and a scale pan for the second round of dividing up the pears. Lao Qiao, who'd been to see a doctor earlier (Xiao Peng said it had something to do with her uterus, but no one felt comfortable asking), made it back in time to see that every type of container had been claimed. Not letting on how displeased she was, she went instead to check on the pears and cried out the moment she removed the lid.

"Hey, why did you guys bring rotten pears?"

Her officemates stopped what they were doing and rushed over to see. Sure enough, all rotten, the edible portions running from one-third to two-thirds of each pear. Even the best of them had coin-sized bad spots. Discontent rained down on He and Lin. *We trusted you two when we sent you for the pears, so why did you bring back nothing but rotten fruit?* Lao Sun, the deputy section head, told Lao He, "Go check the other offices and see what their pears look like."

He explained to everyone that the general manager's office had said they had to pick baskets without examining what was inside and take them back to their own offices. A while later he returned looking greatly relieved.

"It's the same for everybody. Section One, Section Two, and Section Seven all got rotten pears."

Now the complaints targeted their unit.

"Labor Day, the one day a year we're sent a truckload of pears. Just our luck to get nothing but rotten ones."

Xiao Lin walked in with the scale at the moment.

"Hold on," someone said. "They're all rotten, so why weigh them? Just divide them into piles."

Laying down the scale, he began putting the pears into piles, then rubbed off the mush stuck to his hands and told everyone to choose a pile. In the past there'd always been big and small pears, which got people interested in picking a pile; now they just took the pile closest to their desks and let that be the end of it. They cut out the rotten spots, starting with the worst looking ones, and soon the sound of people eating pears filled the office, unlike previous times, when they saved the fruit to take home. Only Lao He washed his pears before biting into them, as if savoring unspoiled fruit.

"Don't do that, Lao He. Skip the rotten spots. They could cause cancer."

"The rotten parts are edible, too," he said unashamedly. "Apple sauce is made from rotten apples, you know."

They all knew he had to support a large family, including his wife's grandparents, on what little he earned, so they said no more and let him eat his pears.

As they were eating, Lao Qiao went out to check around and returned to tell them why the pears were rotten: the truck had broken down on the road (the pears had come from Zhangjiakou) and it had taken two days to repair, hence the rotten pears. Why had the truck broken down? Well, during the previous round of housing assignment, Lao Diao, head of the drivers unit, had asked for a large three-room apartment, but had been given a small one instead. Upon hearing the news, everyone turned their anger on him.

"That's outrageous. How could he give us rotten pears just because he's unhappy?"

Later that afternoon, when everyone was gathering their pears in old newspaper before the commuter bus took off, they heard the latest news: there had been a few baskets with perfectly fine pears, but they were kept aside by the general management office for those in higher positions. This rekindled flames of outrage that had died down in the course of the day.

"Damn him. We got a truckload of rotten pears that still had enough good ones for *them*."

"The bus is about to leave," Deputy Section Chief Sun said. "Don't listen to rumors. All pears in the same truck will go bad together once there's even one bad one. Fruit does that. This is common knowledge, so how could they have good pears?"

Before he finished, Xiao Yu, an office clerk, walked in with a mesh bag filled with fine looking pears. They were for Lao Zhang, he said. Zhang hadn't come to work that day, so Xiao Yu wanted someone to take the pears to him. Lao Zhang, their one-time section chief, had recently been promoted to Deputy Bureau Chief. Everyone turned on Lao Sun.

"You see. One of the bosses is getting good pears. He was just promoted, and see what he gets?"

Sun looked down to gather up his pears.

"Enough of that talk. Whoever lives closest to Chief Zhang will take the pears to him."

Xiao Peng lived in the same building as Zhang, No. 5 and 6, so she was the one. Lao Qiao, still resentful over the basket Xiao Peng had taken, needled her, "Xiao Peng, you got rotten pears, but have to deliver good ones. Only a wimp would do that."

Xiao Peng didn't get along with Lao Zhang, who, as section chief, had written a review criticizing her for being "muddled-headed," and they had banged on each other's desk. Zhang might have been promoted, but she was too hotheaded to be bothered by consequences of her actions. Provoked by Lao Qiao (another one with whom she didn't get along), Xiao Peng glared at her and tossed the bag of pears into a corner.

"Whether I'm a wimp or not has nothing to do with delivering the pears."

They left the office with their rotten pears, leaving the good ones behind. Lao Sun was the last to leave. He and Lao Zhang were friendly only on the surface. He glanced at the bag of pears before locking the door with a loud click.

2

Deputy Bureau Chief Zhang walked into the office at eight o'clock the following morning, since his desk had not yet been moved to his new office. His promotion meant he could be driven to work, but he insisted on riding his bike. It took him an hour or more to cycle from his home in the Chongwen District to the office in the Chaoyang District, so he arrived in the office with sweat dripping from his thick, fleshy neck. But while limbering his neck, he liked to say, "It's not too tiring." Or, "Riding a bike is good exercise."

On this day, he spotted the pears the moment he walked in the door.

"Ah, I see we got pears, " he said happily. "That's nice. Pears are great."

By then the others had arrived.

"Don't talk about the pears, Lao Zhang," one of them said. "The rest of us all got rotten pears."

"I could only make stewed pears with my share," Lao Qiao commented.

"Really?" Zhang was surprised. "That wasn't nice." He picked up the mesh bag and put it on his desk. "Have some, everyone. My wife got some at work, so I won't take these home."

So everyone crowded around his desk to get a pear. As they ate, they started in what had happened the day before. Sun didn't take one; he smoked instead, saying it was a bad idea to eat cold food so early in the morning, that it could cause diarrhea. Xiao Peng stayed away too; she slammed her kidskin purse down on the desk and pouted. Earlier that morning she'd heard that someone had broadcast her refusal to deliver the pears the day before, turning it into a minor news item. Sooner or later, Zhang would get wind of it, which didn't bother her. What incensed her was the turncoat in her own office; she suspected Qiao or Sun as the traitor who had sold her out.

After they finished, Xiao Lin gathered up the skins to throw them away, as Lao Sun rapped his knuckles on his desk to share a central government document with everyone. He began reading aloud: "All autonomous regions in every city and province, every major military command . . ." When he finished the page, he passed the document to Lao He, who read the second page and then passed it to Lao Qiao for the third page, and then it went to Xiao Lin. It was Lao Zhang who, as section chief, had started the practice of taking turns reading the documents to stop people from ignoring him; he'd been so upset seeing them trim their nails or knit a sweater that he came up with the idea to get everyone's attention. Even that was not enough for him—he said they did not have to read it in Putonghua. Why not use their hometown dialects? After all, they'd come from all parts of China and it would be enjoyable to read the documents in a variety of dialects. After his promotion, he was no longer a member of the office and did not have to read, but he sat there listening with his hand over his vacuum mug.

When they were two-thirds into the document, two men from the general manager's office showed up to tell Zhang that his new office was ready and they were there to help him move his desk.

"Isn't it supposed to be next week?" he asked.

"The office is ready, so the bureau chief asked you to move now. It will be easier if he needs to talk to you."

"All right then. They're reading a document, so we'll wait till they're finished."

The men waited by the door.

Finally it was finished, and people got up to help move Zhang's desk.

"You've been promoted, Lao Zhang," someone said, "so you'll have to treat us to something."

"Didn't I treat you with some pears?" he said with a smile.

"That doesn't count. Pears don't mean anything. You have to treat us to a meal at the Furong Hotel."

Amid a flurry of activity, the desk was moved, the wastepaper basket was picked up, and desk drawers were removed. Everyone joined in except Xiao Peng, who was still pouting. She had handed the document to the next person earlier, saying, "My mouth is rotten." Obviously, she hadn't gotten over what had happened that morning.

After moving the desk to the second floor, they realized it was wasted effort, because Zhang had gotten a big desk, the same size as those for other deputy chiefs. The new desk had a large, spotless glass top, on which stood a programmable phone. A few potted plants were scattered in the office, which was also furnished with easy chairs and a large sofa, all draped with new cotton covers. The sparklingly clean room was as big as the whole office in the section he had formerly run.

"Lao Zhang has exchanged a fowling piece for a big gun," someone quipped.

"But I'll have to be here alone," he said with a smile. "I'd rather be there with all of you; it feels better that way."

"The old desk is useless here, Lao Zhang," one of the moving men said. "Should we put it in storage?"

"Sure, go ahead. Thanks for your hard work." He handed them each a cigarette, then handed them out to his former officemates.

They went back to their office, the men puffing on cigarettes, where they discovered that the empty spot left by the desk looked strange. Xiao Lin got a broom and swept the dusty outline. The reality that Zhang had truly been promoted to deputy bureau chief set in. Now, who should take the spot? Lao Sun, naturally.

"Hey, Lao Sun, you should move your desk here now that Lao Zhang has left," someone teased.

"Oh no, not so soon," Sun said, still puffing away.

As a senior member of the party, Lao Qiao didn't think much of Sun, so she said, "Stop pretending! Listen to you, you're obviously quite sure about it."

"How can I be that sure?"

After having some fun at Sun's expense, the others began to wonder who would replace him if he was promoted to be the section chief? That got everyone thinking about their own future, and they were no longer in a joking mood. Their talk turned to Zhang and the reason behind his promotion. Someone said he was decisive, someone else mentioned his amiable personality, while a third person focused on his competency at work. Then Xiao Peng piped up, "Rubbish. I saw him giving the bureau chief two whole fish on the first of the year."

Someone offered a dissenting view, saying that Zhang got promoted not because of the bureau chief but a particular deputy bureau chief. Yet another said it was neither, adding that Zhang was connected to someone high in the ministry. While they talked on, Zhang pushed open the door and came in to pick up a pair of office slippers he'd left behind. They clammed up, looking awkward, as they could tell that he'd heard everything. But he didn't seem to mind. Pointing at Xiao Peng with his slippers, he joked, "You're in charge of the two potted plants on the window sill now. Water them with some leftover tea in the afternoon before you go home."

That eased everyone's concern.

"Yes, water them with tea," they said in unison.

After he left with his slippers, someone said, "Maybe he didn't hear us."

"So what if he did?" Xiao Peng said.

They continued their speculation, while Zhang returned to his new office. He'd heard them gossiping about his promotion, but it hadn't upset him, since it was to be expected. Would he have joined in if one of them had been promoted instead? He put himself in their shoes and forgave them, since they had worked side by side. But he couldn't stop from cursing angrily as he leaned against the sofa after changing into his slippers and shutting the door.

"Damn you, assholes. What are you gossiping about? You don't know shit. I didn't rely on anything but my own luck."

He was fully aware that originally he hadn't been considered for the position that had remained unfilled since one of the deputy bureau chiefs died of cancer. The bureau chief had favored another section head, named Qin, while a deputy minister had wanted to promote a fellow named Guan who headed the Seventh Section. A tug-of-war broke out and lasted a year, angering the minister, who said, "For a whole year, you've been fighting over recommendations. Are you Communist party members or aren't you? Well, I'm not going to take either one. I'm picking one no one has recommended."

Which was how Lao Zhang ended up getting the promotion. It was a convergence of opportunity and good luck, which he concluded with the traditional Chinese saying, "The fisherman benefits when a snipe and a clam are locked in a fight." The chief and his deputy each had a talk with him, both claiming to have strongly recommended him, with the mistaken assumption that he was completely in the dark. Zhang nodded as he said to himself, "To hell with you both. You think I'm a fool? I owe nothing to anyone, only to the party."

On that particularly morning, he ran into Section One Chief Qin and Section Seven Chief Guan when he came to work. They were vocally jealous, so Zhang made a joke to smooth things over, but deep down he was gloating.

"What's the point of being jealous? Now that I'm sitting in that chair, all you people had better watch out. I have a vote on the bureau party committee."

He walked around with his hands behind his back, sizing up his office. It was spacious, clean and quiet, with lots of light. By nature he preferred being alone and had never enjoyed sharing an office with so many people. A sadness rose up at the thought that he'd had to work so hard to finally have his own office at the age of fifty. Time waits for no one. But a sense of gratification made its way in when he recalled that Qin and Guan still shared offices with the people who worked for them. It hadn't been easy. He'd never dreamed of becoming a deputy bureau chief, and had made preparations for his retirement. The promotion came as a total surprise; now that it had happened, he'd sit in this office for a few years. After lunch, he lay down on the sofa, draped a jacket over himself and dozed off. He could never have done that in the big office, where, in addition to having no sofa, he could not have fallen asleep with the noise of people washing their lunch boxes and knitting sweaters, plus the click-clack of Xiao Peng's high heels.

He was startled awaken by the sudden realization that he had yet to learn how to use the programmable phone. Jumping to his feet, he rushed over to his desk, where he read the instructions and punched in some numbers. He placed a call to his wife and then his daughter at work to tell them his new number and to make sure they didn't dial the old one. He even added an instruction for his wife—buy a roast chicken on her way home.

3

A luncheon for everyone in the building was held on April thirtieth; they were given meal coupons from the general manager's office. With them they could select two dishes, a preserved egg, and a bottle of beer, all free of charge in the dining hall. They would eat in their offices, selecting the dishes individually, then bringing the eggs and beer back to a large dining table formed by moving several desks together. They would also use money from selling scrap newspaper to buy a large packet of peanuts and set it in the middle of the table. By ten thirty, everyone began looking for bowls and platters and getting the desks ready, creating a sense of festivity. Even those who normally didn't get along were friendly enough that they could order each other around—you go buy some steamed buns, you go wash the cups, and so on. By eleven, they picked up the bowls and platters before heading to the dining hall, where they could get a spot at the head of the line to pick the food they liked. But then Lao He came up to Sun with his bowl.

"We're out of coal briquettes at home, Lao Sun, so I have to go home and get them some."

That dampened the mood, for everyone knew that was just an excuse; Lao He treasured the free food too much to share with them, and wanted to take it home for his family, especially his wife's grandparents. He was famously henpecked, and they heard that he never had more than fifty cents in his pocket. Naturally he didn't smoke.

"Don't do that, Lao He," Xiao Peng said. "There's no need to fight the crowds on the bus for the sake of two free dishes."

"Forget it then," one of the others said. "If Lao He isn't going to eat here, neither will we. We don't need a free lunch."

"We really did run out of coal briquettes." Red and white splotches appeared on He's anxiety-ridden face as tried to explain.

"Don't worry about it, Lao He." Sun waved him off. "Stay and eat with us. You can go get the coal this afternoon. I want to talk to you about something. We'll air it out downstairs."

He had to stick around now. He laid down his bowl and said again,

"We really did run out of coal briquettes."

While the others picked up their bowls and platters to line up in the dining hall, Sun took He down to get some fresh air beyond the metal fence. The so-called "airing-out" was a term unique to their office, meaning two people having a heart-to-heart talk, with no others around. They did a lot of that; sometimes after airing out, the two people would pretend they hadn't on their return to the office; they'd exchange a meaningful smile and say,

"We went out to buy something."

Sun never hid his intent from the others; he always announced openly that he wanted to have an airing-out with so-and-so.

Sun and He walked beside the fence. When they reached the far end they turned and walked back. Lao Sun, dressed in a steel blue suit, was a short, squat man with a belly. Lao He was tall and thin, wearing a tattered tunic jacket was a mass of wrinkles; on his sallow face sat a pair of glasses in a yellowed plastic frame. The two men had started work at the same time twenty years before and had even lived in the same dorm for a while. Sun had done much better, eventually being promoted to deputy section head, while He was still a clerk. After his promotion, Sun moved into a three-room apartment, while He remained in the slum area of Niujie, nine people from four generations crowded into a space of fifteen square meters.

When Sun was first promoted, they still treated each other like brothers, since they had started out together, but the distance between them grew over time. Seeing how He had grown diffident, Sun began ordering him around.

"Copy this document for me, Lao He."

"Lao He, get the stuff at the general manager's office."

One time, when they were all given tickets for a movie, Lao He went with his wife and Lao Sun went with his. They were sitting together. Sun pointed at He and said to his wife when they met, "This is Lao He from our section."

Lao He should have introduced Sun to his wife as "our deputy section head, Lao Sun," but the man's tone of voice irked him. They'd come to the office at the same time, and He didn't mind if Sun acted like the boss at the office, but why must he do that in front of their wives? He said nothing. But even without her husband's introduction, his wife knew who Sun was. On their way home after the movie, his wife said angrily, "See how well he's done, a deputy section head? Then look at you. You're still a foot soldier. I have no idea what you've been doing these twenty years."

To be sure, Sun was not the one who'd done the very best. Lao Zhang had also lived in the dorm, but he'd obviously fared better than Sun. That gave He a reason to rebuff his wife: "What's so great about him? He has to act like a grandson around 'Grandpa' Zhang."

"Then what about you, his great-grandson?" his wife retorted.

He went silent. *Damn it all. How did this happen? We came at the same time, so what happened to divide us into grandfather, grandson, and great-grandson? What's wrong with the world?* He sighed.

Sun did not normally have an airing-out with He; there was no need, since he was He's boss. So He felt anxious. *What does Sun want to talk to me about?*

Nothing special, it turned out. Sun began by shooting the breeze.

"Are you still living on Niujie?" he asked.

"Where else would I be living?" He tilted his glasses to glare at Sun. "I'd like to move to the leaders' compound at Zhongnanhai, but they won't let me."

Instead of getting upset, Sun smiled good-naturedly.

"Does the roof still leak?"

Lao He's temper flared at the mention of the leaky roof.

"You should have seen what happened on April fifteenth after that rainstorm. We even laid out the rinsing cups, and my wife and I got into a fistfight over it."

"Whose fault is it that your rank's so low?" Sun said unsympathetically. "You'd have moved out long ago if you were a section head."

Naturally that only made He angrier. "I'd like to be, but you won't recommend me."

Sun chortled. When he managed to control himself, he took out a cigarette, lit it, and continued, "Let's talk about something serous, Lao He. About the office. Lao Zhang has left, you know that."

What does that have to do with me? Lao He wondered.

"Lao Zhang is outrageous," Sun said as he looked at He. "Remember back when we were living in the dorm and how he got a two-room unit? He's a deputy bureau chief now, so they say . . . Lao He, I don't want to be section chief, but normally it's clear who should take over. But I heard something yesterday. The bureau wants an opinion poll on who should be the next section head. What kind of lousy idea is that? I suspect it was Lao Zhang's idea."

"But isn't that what the Central Government has been advocating lately?"

"You believe bullshit like that? Who was polled for Zhang's promotion? He should be doing something good after taking over as deputy bureau chief, but instead he tries to put people down. What a prick. You know that he and I had issues before."

Lao He stared at Lao Sun.

"Here's what I think, Lao He. Zhang is being difficult and obviously doesn't like me. I'm not afraid of him, and we shouldn't wait for other people to decide our fate. How's this? We'll work on those running the bureau and the ministry. We'll spend whatever is necessary, and if it works out we'll take over the section. You'll be my deputy section head."

Confused by what he was hearing, Lao He was quiet for a while before stammering, "That, um—can we do that?"

"You're so damned naïve. Who doesn't get promoted that way these days? I'm suggesting this because we once lived in the same dormitory. Let's stop pretending, all right? Let me ask you this. Do you want to move into a better place? Do you want to be the deputy section chief?"

Lao He gave the question some thought and said, "Of course I do."

"Well, that's it, then." Sun clapped his hands. "We don't have to be afraid of Lao Zhang if we join forces. He doesn't have any sway in the bureau party committee. They won't take him too seriously since he's just been promoted."

"I'll think about it."

Sun laughed. He knew that what Lao He really meant was he'd go home and talk it over with his wife; he also knew that Lao He's wife would definitely tell him to work with Lao Sun. That put Sun's mind at ease.

"That's all for today," he said. "Let's go back for lunch. I imagine the poll won't take place for a while yet, so we still have time. But this is just between us, so don't tell anyone else."

Lao He gave him a look of "You don't have to tell me that."

"After working in the same office for so long, Lao Zhang is a jerk to act the way he is," Sun added as they headed back inside.

So they had lunch together that day. Not knowing what kind of airing out Sun had with He, the others didn't give it much thought, and instead focused on the food and drinks, creating a festive air. What puzzled Lao He was that after badmouthing Lao Zhang, Sun had gone up to the second floor to invite Zhang to the luncheon. He even went so far as to suggest "a toast to our esteemed leader." Lao He realized that Sun was also a jerk.

The luncheon ended at two o'clock. They were given the afternoon off to hold a dance. Every one's face was bright red by then, though no one was drunk, no one but Lao Qiao, who had been feeling down recently and obviously had a bit too much to drink. But it seemed to help her get over whatever was bothering her and she felt good enough to go with her younger colleagues to dance in the second floor conference room.

Lao He did not join in. They really were out of coal briquettes, so he asked Lao Sun for leave and went looking for a three-wheeler to carry coal home.

4

Xiao Lin was twenty-nine. He had been working in the same office for four years after graduating from college. He felt he'd learned more in four years at the office than in college. When he first arrived, he still looked like a college student and, like most youngsters, didn't care much about anything. He was often late to work and knocked off early; he came to work in sandals; he never took the initiative in office cleaning; he frequently had parties with classmates who worked in other offices, and didn't bother to clean up after they left.

"Do you think you're still in college?" Lao Zhang reprimanded him. "Do you think you can just come and go as you please?"

The comment irritated Xiao Lin, who argued with Zhang.

Lin had another problem—he was careless with his words. For example, when he got together with college friends, they'd ask each other about work and the workplace. Lin's response to "how's your office" was,

"Our office suffers an imbalance of yin and yang, with four men and two women."

Somehow the comment made it back to the office and enraged everyone there.

Another case in point: back when he'd sat at the desk across from Lao Qiao, who had yet to suffer any female problems, she kindly helped him with things. Being the party's office leader, she had an airing-out with him to get him to apply for membership. Out of kindness, she let on that Lao He was also applying.

"Lao He may have been here for twenty years, but you can get in before him if you align yourself with the party."

She had issues with Lao He, but her advice to Lin was well intentioned, so it came as a surprise when he said, "Right now I'm not particularly interested in your illustrious party, so I'll let Lao He in first."

Later, when he'd come to his senses and wanted to join, it was too late, since the party organization had already begun grooming Lao He. Xiao Lin was told he needed more education and testing to raise his consciousness. Since then he'd been told to turn in monthly reports on his personal ideology, focusing on his understanding of the "illustrious party."

But he realized his mistake too late. It took him three years to rid himself of his childish attitude, something that occurred not as a result of self-reflection, but was imposed by others. It became a recurring issue every time he tried to join the party. Some of his college pals had already become party members; he had not. Some had been promoted to deputy principal section chief, some were even principal section chiefs; he was still a clerk. Now when they got together, they no longer felt at ease with each other, so no more joking around or acting childish. As for housing assignments, some received two-room units, some one-room units, while he, even as a married man, had to share an apartment with another family, all because of his low rank. The mere mention of apartment sharing had him on edge, for it was truly sharing—two newlywed couples lived in a two-room unit, sharing the living room, the kitchen, and the toilet. When he was first married, it hadn't bothered him; he was happy just to have a place for the two of them. As time went on, the families began fighting over the public spaces. Such as the kitchen. When they got off work, they were all hungry, so who got to cook dinner first? Or the living room. Whose stuff should be out there? Or the toilet. Every one needed to use it, but who would clean it? Who would empty the trash can? They all tried to be nice at first, but their patience began to wear thin. The men dealt with it better than their wives, who scowled when they met. In the end, each day was characterized by bad moods, from dinnertime to bedtime. Little by little, it affected them physically, as every few days a conflict—open or veiled—erupted over something trivial.

The other couple's wife was particularly hard to deal with; a shrew with a doughy face and fuzzy hair, she'd never let go of an issue if she didn't have to. Both families' coal briquettes were stored in the kitchen, and Lin's wife once accidently used one of theirs. Who knew that the wife kept track of hers? When she counted and realized that one was missing, she cursed the so-called thief, throwing things around, even tossing Lin's suit coat, which was drying on the balcony, into a muddy puddle on the ground.

Then there was the toilet. At first they agreed to take turns cleaning it, but at some point they lost track of the schedule. After a while, filth began to pile up. No one wanted to scrub the toilet either, and the seat and cover were often wet. Xiao Lin said, "It's okay. It won't kill us to clean the toilet. I'll do it if they won't."

But his wife grabbed his collar to stop him.

"Don't. We have to hold out. We can't let her intimidate us."

The toilet got dirtier as time went by. Once the blocked drain sent filth out to flood the floor, and neither family would clean it up even though they had to live with it for three days.

If anything, this was just the beginning of their troubles. After a lapse in birth control the previous year, Lin and his wife had a baby, which ushered in more trouble. Lin brought his mother out from the countryside to help care for the baby. She spent only one night in the living room, when the other couple came to talk to him, saying it was a public space that could not be used by one family alone. They were right, of course. So Lin moved his mother into his bedroom, where she shared the bed with his wife. A different kind of clash arose after that. The other woman could not have a child of her own and could not stand a baby's cries. Whenever Lin's child cried at night, she turned on their cassette player with the volume so high it was impossible for the baby to go back to sleep and made life a living hell for Lin and his family. They had to walk around the room with the baby in their arms.

"She's not human," Lin's wife said. "She's an animal."

Human or animal, either way they had to share the apartment. So Lin often said, "If we could get our own place, even a single room would be okay."

But he had to be a principal staff member for that. Who would promote him after he'd been so slapdash and carefree? And who would assign him a place of his own if he was still a clerk?

If that weren't bad enough, he had to deal with inflation. He had no idea why the damned prices kept going up. His and his wife's combined salaries were insufficient to support a family of four, so they could only afford discarded sweet peppers and cabbages, never meat or fish. Back when he was single, he could spend his money however he wanted, but now he had to line up with old women to buy discarded vegetables. They could eat discards or forgo fresh vegetables entirely, but what about the baby? Could he live without his baby formula, eggs, or meat? Once his wife picked up the baby and began to cry the moment she came home. He asked her what was wrong.

"When I talk to people in my office, I learn that their babies eat shrimp," his wife said. "And us? We're not doing the right thing for our baby. He's going to have shrimp even if I have to sell my sweater tomorrow. Look at his dull, yellow hair and the blotches on his head. That's a sign of calcium deficiency."

That brought tears to Lin's eyes. He sobbed as he said he'd let them down, and it was all because of his low salary. He had to be promoted to get more pay and to do that, he could not act as if he could not care less about his job.

Money, housing, food, sleep, the toilet, and everything else hinged on how well he fared at the office. He had to do better to provide for his wife and baby. So he developed the habit of staring blankly at Lao He, seeing his future self in He's gaunt, lusterless face. What would he say to his family if he ended up like him, still a clerk at fifty, with his kind of salary and living quarters? He shuddered each time he thought about it. What would he say if someone asked:

"What have you been doing all these years?"

That was how he turned a new leaf. He came to work on time, exchanging his sandals for cloth shoes; he stopped making jokes and got active in cleaning up the office and fetching hot water for everyone; he showed respect to the old-timers. When the pears came, he offered to bring them in and divide them up. He gathered up the skins when everyone was done eating; he got the desks ready before the luncheon without being told to. What was interesting was how the others viewed him. Back when he was an indifferent slacker, the others thought it was natural for him to be a slacker. Now that he'd turned over a new leaf, they took the change for granted. When the office needed cleaning or the vacuum bottle needed a refill of hot water, they'd say:

"What is it with Xiao Lin?"

Besides taking the initiative at work, Lin also turned proactive in other areas. He filled out an application to join the party, he wrote an ideological report once a month, and he had frequent chats with party members like Lao Qiao, Lao Zhang, and Lao He. Slowly he came to a new understanding: the world was big and China had a huge population, but what demanded one's immediate attention were simply the few people around you. That went for everyone, including the minister, the bureau chief, the section head, and Xiao Lin himself, of course, whether you were ambitious or not. He started by cleaning the office, bringing in hot water, and gathering fruit peels, in order to move up the ladder. Joining the party, like cleaning up, was a prerequisite for moving up. How could you be a deputy section head if you didn't join the "illustrious party"? But to do that, he had to fill out an application and write ideological reports to re-examine why it had been "your illustrious party" to him then and was now the party he wanted to join. *Come clean, Xiao Lin. Otherwise, you'll never be a party member, and that means you'll never do well enough to move up and never eat, sleep, and shit well! And don't be naïve. Do you honestly believe that what you've done is all you need to do to become a party member? Wrong. That only represents the first step in a long march, to be followed by more important steps—working on relationships with party members, who will then become backers.*

Everyone wanted to be a party member, so what would make Xiao Lin their first choice? Take Lao Qiao for example. She was the section's party leader, so he had to be on good terms with her, even though she was his least favorite officemate. In her fifties and nearing retirement, she was a nag who smelled bad. Back when he'd just arrived, with his devil-may-care attitude, he'd declared, "There should be a rule against anyone with BO working here, so as not to affect other people's mental balance."

When she heard his comment, she complained to Lao Zhang, saying the new college grad had launched a personal attack on her. Now Lin had to get to know her and her body odor, enduring both even in the hottest month; he had to sit next to her once a month when he gave his report and poured his heart out.

But even that wasn't enough. He made a few gestures at certain moments in the hope that she would lend him her support. Once, during a reunion with his college pals, someone brought up the number of young, single women who had slept with officials of various ranks. The others were saying that Chinese women had no moral integrity.

"Not true," Lin disagreed. "They are the epitome of that."

And so, on May 2, still a work holiday, he took the subway to call on Lao Qiao with two bags of preserved fruit and a bottle of sesame oil (brought back by his mother from her hometown), as well as a sack of walnuts (a gift for his son's one-month ceremony) and several soft drinks. His wife objected at first, saying they needed to save the money for milk for the baby. He explained to her that he was going to see Lao Qiao when they needed the money for milk precisely so that the baby could have more in the future. They went back and forth until he ran out of patience and called her "nearsighted," afflicted with peasant consciousness, before she let him go. He spent half an hour at Qiao's house, ate two apples, and was told that he had been doing well lately. The party group had deliberated his application, which would likely be approved during the first half of the year.

"I'm about to retire, so I ought to do something good for my colleagues," she added.

He was thrilled as he left; walking alongside Qiao, who saw him to the subway station, he did not detect her body odor. On the subway, he ran into Xiao Peng, who asked where he'd been. He told her he'd attended a college friend's wedding. Peng, who was dressed to the nines, told him about the forthcoming poll to select their future section head and deputy.

It'll be anyone but me, he said to himself. *All I need now is to join the party.*

He got off at the Chongwen Gate stop after saying "See you at the office tomorrow" to Xiao Peng. The sun was so bright when he came out he lost his sense of direction and took a long time finding the stop for the No. 9 bus to go home.

5

When they went back to work after the holiday, there was indeed a poll to see who would be the best deputy section head and deputy. The organization section sent two pollsters, who gave everyone a piece of paper to write down names, adding that they need not limit their choices to those in the same office. It was called an opinion poll, but there were only four workers to be polled: Lao He, Lao Qiao, Lao Peng, and Xiao Lin. Lao Sun recused himself and left the office.

"Go ahead and write with your backs to each other. Don't feel pressured," they were told.

In the meantime, Lao Sun paced the hallway, wondering what was going on inside, his heart aflutter as if pawed by a kitten. He'd known about the poll, but hadn't expected it to take place as soon as the holiday was over, so soon that he was caught off guard before he could make a move. Convinced that it was yet another scheme cooked up by Lao Zhang, he was outraged, cursing Zhang for being so relentless. He'd had issues with Zhang back when they'd been in the same office, but why couldn't Zhang let go of their former discord, now that he'd been promoted? Why make life hard on Sun? As a matter of fact, Sun's complaint was not justified. Sure, the poll had been Zhang's idea, but he'd had nothing to do with the speedy way it was conducted. It was the organization, though even they hadn't planned to hold it so soon either. On the last day of April, the head of the organization section had a major hemorrhoid flare-up, and arranged with a hospital for surgery, which would require recovery time in the hospital. Wanting to clear his desk before the surgery, he'd moved up the date. Not knowing the background information, Lao Sun blamed Lao Zhang. In fact, Zhang had been in such a good mood over his promotion that he had no time for messy personnel issue or for undermining others.

No matter how it had come about, Sun did not have time to carry out his scheme with Lao He to get the higher-ups to cancel the poll. Now he had to find the next best solution. After getting wind of the poll on the morning of May First, he went to inform Lao He that afternoon, adding that they could only work on those to be polled. They divided up the labor, with Sun going to see Qiao and He meeting with Peng and Lin. They would tell their colleagues to do the right thing, to be responsible at a critical moment like this, and not to fill in a name without careful consideration. Lao He, who had been hesitant at first, decided to go along after talking it over with his wife, who gave her full support and said that Sun wanted his help because he held He in high regard. But doubts crept back in when Sun had come to his home to inform him of the latest, complicated development, and it took some talking on Sun's part to rekindle He's interest.

On that night, Lao He went to see Xiao Peng, following Lao Sun's instruction not to be seen by Zhang, who lived in the same building. At work the next morning, Lao He took Xiao Lin downstairs for an airing-out, which took so long they missed breakfast in the dining hall. He failed to "clear the air" completely and Lin left with only a vague understanding that his application to join the party would be approved soon (something he'd already learned from Lao Qiao). When Lao He brought up the poll and asked him to be careful,

Lin had no idea what he meant by that, since He had trouble making his case. That did not matter, however—Lin unhesitatingly put down "Lao Sun for the section head and Lao He as his deputy" when he was handed the paper. He didn't really understand He's intention, nor did he particularly like his two senior colleagues, but he did not want any change in the office's party group to affect his imminent membership. If an outsider was brought in, altering the makeup of the group, that could change a man's fate, and that was something he did understand.

The men from the organization section left with the polling slips. It was now Lao Qiao's turn to have an airing-out with Xiao Lin.

"Whom did you pick?"

"Whom did *you* pick?" Lin knew exactly what he needed to say.

"Someone came to see me and asked me to pick him," she said with a sneer. "But I didn't. I filled in two outsiders."

"Me too."

"That's right. That was the right thing to do." She was pleased.

They went back inside, and now it was Xiao Peng's turn to have an airing-out with Lao Qiao. But, bearing a grudge from their earlier dispute, Peng would have none of Qiao's scheme; instead, she said loudly as she reapplied her lipstick at a mirror, "I picked the ones I wanted. Weren't we told it was a secret poll?"

Qiao's face turned bright red from the rebuff.

"I was just asking."

That was followed by a series of airing-outs, Sun with He, He with Lin, Sun with Peng, and Peng with Lin, and so on.

Three days later, Sun heard from someone in the organization section, a man from his hometown. He was visibly happy during his next airing-out with He.

"Good. It's all good, Lao He. Everyone did well except Lao Qiao."

"Good." He was pleased too. "It's all good."

"Xiao Lin's not bad. He's smart enough to take a hint and doesn't work behind the scenes. He was a bit careless and immature when he first came but he's shaped up lately. What do you say we take care of him the next time we have a group meeting?"

"Sure, we'll take care of him."

"Let's work separately on people in the bureau and the ministry. Things look good at the moment," Sun said. "Our only obstacle is Lao Zhang."

"As long as people in the bureau and ministry don't object, Lao Zhang may not be able to do us any harm, since we have the support of the masses," He offered.

"You're right. He's the proverbial mayfly trying to shake down a tree."

A week after the mayfly comment, the bureau sent someone over to say that Deputy Bureau Chief Zhang was making a business trip to Baotou and asked the section to send two people to accompany him as support staff. Sun was uncomfortable with the request. *You stopped caring about your old colleagues in the section after your promotion and only think of us now when you have a trying trip coming up? What's support staff but gofers to carry your suitcase, open the door, buy train tickets, and take care of lodging and receipts?* Sun grumbled, but was in no position to say no and decided to send Qiao and Lin. On the day before the trip, however, he changed his mind and replaced Qiao with himself. After a violent mental struggle with himself, he realized he couldn't afford to bicker with Zhang. Ruining their relationship would be a stupid move, and suffering the consequences would not be worth the chance to vent his displeasure. The smart move would be to turn an enemy into his friend by being proactive. Which was why he decided to go himself; he'd use this opportunity to resolve problems between them. If he could do that, perfect. If not, what did he have to lose?

Deputy Chief Zhang, Lao Sun, and Xiao Lin boarded the train for Baotou together but did not spend the night in the same car. A deputy bureau chief was entitled to a soft seat during the day, while the others were in a car with hard seats. At night, Lin got an upper bunk, Sun the bottom, with another man in between.

The moment the train started moving, Sun told Lin to watch their stuff while he went to see Zhang in his soft-seat car to be "proactive."

Truth be told, the dispute between Zhang and Sun was really nothing. They had come to office at the same time, lived in the same dorm, and worked in the same section all these years. They had actually been quite close and could talk about anything. At the time, their section head was old and frail, often missing work. Sun once said to Zhang,

"If he can't come to work then he ought to leave. Why occupy the toilet when you can't shit?"

His comment somehow made it to the old section head, who bore a serious grudge against Sun, who naturally suspected Zhang, for how else would the old man learn of a private comment? It wasn't something Sun chose to pursue, but he was silently unhappy about the betrayal. The old man eventually did retire, and was replaced by Zhang. Sun later received his own promotion, but the rift never disappeared. Sun had a problem with Zhang's ethics, while Zhang considered Sun petty. In addition, back when they were newlyweds and shared a two-room unit, their wives had fought over cleaning the toilet, which worsened the problem between the two men. Sun could do nothing but watch Zhang move up the ladder, while he remained in a subordinate position. Zhang might be a shabby individual, but Sun had to yield; as the saying goes, one must lower one's head when standing under someone else's eaves. After all these years, he had to take the initiative to make peace with Zhang, the thought of which made him sigh emotionally—Life is hard.

When he found Zhang's compartment and knocked on the door, Zhang pulled it open and beamed.

"Come in! Come on in." Zhang patted the bed. "Have a seat."

Zhang offered him a soft drink the moment he sat down.

"There was no need to make the trip yourself. You could have sent someone else."

"What would it look like if I didn't accompany the boss?"

"Don't use that word with me, Lao Sun. Don't forget, we sat across from each other for over a decade."

"Well. I'm happy to come along when Lao Zhang goes on a business trip. How does that sound?" Sun said with a laugh.

That brought a hearty laugh from Zhang.

The laugh was followed by an awkward silence. Zhang was not pleased to have Sun come on the trip with him. He would find it hard to give Sun orders, creating difficulties in getting the work done. And there was the unspoken rift, which, oddly, was precisely the reason why Zhang had to let Sun come along. What an absurd world we live in. Zhang knew that Sun had never forgotten about Zhang ratting on him years ago, though Sun was not aware of Zhang's predicament. Zhang had not ratted on Sun; he had merely mentioned it to his wife. Later on, when Zhang's wife and Sun's wife got into a fight, Zhang's wife was so mad she told the old section head when they visited him in the hospital. When they left, Zhang had actually reproached his wife for selling out his friend. But how was he supposed to explain the complicated backstory to his old friend? Since he couldn't do that, he turned and castigated Sun for being petty; to him, someone who bore a grudge like that was not cut out to be in a leadership position, and he slowly lost respect for Sun.

Sitting across from each other in the compartment, they still hadn't found anything to talk about when the train passed Nankou. In the end it was Sun who broke the silence by asking after Zhang's child. Zhang was relieved to hear that, and asked Sun the same thing. After talking about their children for a while, Sun said unexpectedly,

"There's something I want to talk to you about, Lao Zhang."

Surprised, Zhang pricked up his ears and said gravely, "What is it?"

"I've been wanting to do a self-reflection. You were so nice to me, like an older brother, when we started out in the same office. But I was so immature I did some things that were out of line—"

Zhang was touched by the unforeseen confession. "What are you talking about, Lao Sun? I wouldn't put it that way. I'd say we've had a damned good relationship."

"I'd like to ask your forgiveness."

"Don't say that. We're comrades, good comrades, actually."

"Please forget my past mistakes, Lao Zhang. I'll follow your orders from now on. I'd leap into a pit if you, the boss, told me to."

"Don't say that, Lao Sun, and please stop calling me boss. I don't think I'm the right person for this position. I've been telling myself I must make demands on myself like an ordinary clerk, even though the party trusted me enough to give me the job."

"That's true. Everyone in the unit has remarked on how you still ride your bike to work even after your promotion."

"It's exercise for me. Just look at my neck."

And so they carried on an animated conversation until the railway staff came to invite them to dine. When they got to the dining car, they fought over the check, each holding the other man's hand before it reached into a pocket. It was as if they'd returned to the days when they first started working together and shared a dorm room.

But after they ate and returned to their compartment, they calmed down enough to sense that it had just been a performance, and they hadn't said what they were really thinking. As he sat in his hard seat compartment, Sun began to feel that he had accomplished nothing but paying for a meal. Lying on his soft-seat bed, Zhang began to rue his actions, which now seemed ridiculous and improper. A mild case of chagrin produced a silent curse:

"That old Sun was out to irritate me again. Damn him."

Both men forgot all about Xiao Lin when they went to the dining car, which did not stop Lin from taking care of his own stomach. In fact, he'd already made some instant noodles in a tea mug out of fear that the two bosses might ask him to join them in the dining car. His wife had packed the noodles for him so they could save the travel allowance to order milk for their baby the following month. It was a girl, nearly three months old. *It was hard on you last month, my little girl,* he thought, as he ate the noodles. Then he was comforted by the prospect of a brighter future when he considered that his boss had trusted him enough to pick him for the trip.

The three men returned from Baotou two weeks later.

6

At fifty-four, Lao Qiao was slated for retirement in a year. She'd been mild-mannered and easy to get along before her ailment, though she was afflicted with the terrible habit of rummaging through co-workers' desk drawers.

"Why did you do that?" they'd ask her.

"To see if there's anything of mine in there," she'd reply.

Everyone knew about her habit after a while, and began to lock their drawers when they could and dump unimportant objects in the drawers that couldn't be locked. Let her rummage.

But Qiao would never touch Xiao Peng's drawer. A rather simple-minded woman, Peng was also hot tempered, which made her hard to deal with. To quote Qiao, Xiao Peng was a housewife, pure and simple, devoid of aspirations or career goals. Just look at her. She never once asked to join the party nor did she seek to better herself; she didn't care about mending fences and no one could do anything about her. What irked Qiao the most was the existence of people who didn't care about order, no matter what anyone else did or said. So the sight of Peng could easily set her off, but she shied from getting Peng to lose her temper. They were like a wolf and a dog, fearful of each other and yet, once provoked, would not think twice about nipping at the other's heel. The pear incident before Labor Day was a case in point. Peng was not bothered by the spat. But Qiao was, which had her stewing privately, and created more soreness between them.

The three men returned and were back at work. Before they left, Peng had asked Lin to bring back a pair of dog-skin socks from Baotou. He had seen some in a shop, but hesitated to buy because Peng hadn't given him any money. He wouldn't splurge on a pair for his own wife, so why buy one for someone else? Besides, Peng wasn't even a party member and couldn't do him any good. So he didn't buy any. When they were on the train home, however, regret began to set in. They shared an office and yet he couldn't even bring back a pair socks for her. She must think he was a miserly person. The more he ruminated, the more intense his regret. Later when the train made a stop at Xia-huayuan, he saw a peasant selling crickets on the platform. Fifty cents a cricket in a cage made of sorghum stalks. Quite affordable. So he bought one for his daughter and was inspired to buy another one for Peng as compensation for not getting her the socks. When he came back, he was worried that Peng would not appreciate the cricket and would be upset over the socks. Imagine his surprise when she was so pleased she jumped up and down, tossing away her compact case to grab the cricket out of his hand. Then she twirled round and round in the office, playing with the cricket, touching its antennae and pinching a piece of the flowers left by Lao Zhang to feed the insect.

"You're really nice, Xiao Lin," she said.

The sight of a delighted Peng only irritated Qiao, who was sitting coolly off to one side. Peng accidently knocked over Qiao's wastebasket, littering the floor with trash. Yet she didn't even bother to help Qiao clean up, which aggravated the older woman even more. Qiao banged on the basket as she picked up the trash, knowing full well she shouldn't lose her temper over something like that. Peng ignored her completely, so Qiao could only glare at Peng's back. Now, since Peng's glee over the noisy cricket had been brought on by Xiao Lin, Qiao's annoyance was extended to him. When Peng went to the toilet, leaving her cricket to sing in the office, Qiao went up to Sun and complained angrily,

"Why don't you do something, Lao Sun? Our office is turning into a zoo."

Sun was smoking a cigarette, engrossed in his own thoughts. Qiao's unwelcome interruption annoyed him; coupled with his dislike for the woman, he reacted by waving impatiently and saying,

"Let it go. Don't exaggerate. It's an insect, not a zoo denizen."

The rebuff really upset Qiao, who walked over to Lin and complained,

"Try to be serious at work, Xiao Lin. Don't be a loafer and stop bringing animals to the office."

He could not afford to antagonize Qiao, the party leader, so he mumbled with a red face,

"Sure. Sure. It'll never happen again."

That made Qiao feel a little better.

Everything would have been fine if it had ended there and would soon be forgotten. As luck would have it, something else happened at noon. Qiao, Peng, and Lin were eating in the office when Peng, out of good intentions and to show her appreciation for the cricket, said to Lin while spooning food into her mouth,

"Congratulations, Xiao Lin."

"What for?" Lin was baffled.

"When you were away, Lao He and I had an airing-out." Peng leaned over and whispered. "He said he'd talked to Lao Sun about approving your application to join the party."

It was old news to Lin, who had heard it from Qiao earlier and from Sun during the trip. So what Peng just said meant that it was really going to happen. Naturally Lin was thrilled, but he was annoyed by Peng's lack of tact and failure to take the intricate interpersonal relationships into consideration, since Qiao was sitting nearby. So he signaled to Peng with his eyes and twitched the corner of his mouth in Qiao's direction. But Peng did not understand what he was getting at; instead she thought he was trying to make her watch out for Qiao. Looking as if she didn't give a damn about Qiao, Peng raised her voice,

"Lao He told me to learn from you." She followed that with a loud laugh. "But I don't want to join the party, so I don't care who's guarding the party's gate."

Sure enough, her outburst touched a nerve again and Qiao fumed over the younger woman's smug look: *You're not a party member*

*so what gives you the right to discuss an application? Xiao Lin doesn't need
an airing-out with you to apply.* Qiao's wrath then turned on Lin: *With
your eagerness to join the party, you should be burying your head in work, but
instead you're forming a little clique, hooking up with Xiao Peng. You brought
back a cricket and had an airing-out with her. If that's weren't enough, you've
also linked up with Lao He behind my back to help with your application. You
don't need me anymore now that you have others to help you, so you and Peng
can gang up on me. All right, then. We'll see if you can get your application
approved so easily with them on your side. I didn't know that behind that nice
appearance lies a schemer. You even gave me gifts at Labor Day, but now you're
tossing me aside after a junket with the bosses, who will obviously help you.
But don't you forget, I'm the party-group leader and we'll see how you make it
without me.* Qiao was carried away by her own thoughts, and that further fueled her rage. So when Peng went to the toilet, Qiao, without
thinking, went to sit in Peng's chair and began rummaging through
her desk drawers as a way to vent her anger. Peng walked in and blew
her stack when she saw Qiao going through her drawers.

"Stop right there, Lao Qiao. How dare you go through my
things!"

Qiao wasn't even conscious of what she was doing, and froze at
the realization when Peng screamed at her. She was tongue-tied.

Walking up to Qiao, Peng went on the attack, feeling fully justified.

"What do you think you're doing? Just what are you doing?
Have you lost your mind? You're old enough to know what's right
and what's wrong. Why are you so sneaky, always going through people's stuff?"

Her mouth agape, Qiao still could not come up with a reply, as
Sun and He came in and, along with Lin, tried to smooth things over.
Qiao cocked her head and let her eyes sweep over everyone.

"You all think you're better than me, don't you?" she erupted. It
seemed directed at them all.

She stood up and, with her face in her hands, ran out of the
office, sobbing and kicking over her own wastebasket in the process.

Peng laughed, cackling like an old hen.

"Now let's see if she dares do that again."

Still engrossed in his own thoughts, Sun frowned and banged on his desk, annoyed by something.

"Let it go, Xiao Peng. This is, after all, an office."

Lao He, who had just gotten a new pair of glasses with metal frames, took off his glasses for the hundredth time to wipe the lenses.

"Yes, let it go. Lao Qiao has health problem, so we need to be nice to her."

Lin kept quiet. He knew the fight between the two women was a bad sign; Peng would come out unscathed, but he would not escape the consequence of what just happened. Qiao would surely blame it on him, since he was partially the cause of their spat. His apprehension grew when Qiao returned to the office in the afternoon, her eyes red from crying, with a hand over her belly. He cursed Peng for being rash and tactless and sought an opportunity to comfort the older woman and minimize the damage. But with everyone in the office and Qiao seemingly glued to her chair, he couldn't find the right moment. Finally, it was time to knock off for the day. Lin hurried to walk out with Qiao to the bus stop. After making sure no one was around, he edged close to her and said,

"Are you all right?"

The words were barely out of his mouth when he realized it was the wrong thing to ask. What had he meant by "all right"? Was he asking after her health or was he making sure she was "all right" after the fight? As expected, she ignored his good intentions and turned to glare at him.

"Stay away from me from now on, Xiao Lin. Where did a young man like you learn to be so two-faced?"

He stopped in his tracks. By the time he recovered, Qiao was long gone. All he could do was let out a dispirited sigh as he walked down the stairs alone. He couldn't stop wondering, unhappily, how he ended up in the same office with people like them. If he had been sent to a difference office during the postgraduation job assignment, he would never have run into these crazy people. But it was just his luck to be sent here. But then on second thought, he probably wouldn't fare much better if he were at a different office anyway. As they say, crows are black all over the world. He was disheartened as he went home.

Life at home was tough too. The drain was stopped up again. The neighbor's wife was fuming on the other side of the wall, while on this side his daughter was wailing, his mother had a cold, and his wife was sitting on the edge of the bed in tears.

"When will this ever end?" he asked himself.

7

Deputy Bureau Chief Lao Zhang stopped riding his bike to work, while a Volga began delivering him to and from work every day, against his wishes. He'd wanted to keep riding to work, since he needed the exercise to get rid of that thick neck of his. So he'd continued to ride to the office after the business trip, until the head of the administrative section came to see him.

"I need to get your instruction on something, Chief Zhang," the man said as he sat on the edge of the sofa.

"Go ahead, Lao Cui, and please don't use the word instruction."

"Won't you stop riding your bike to work? We have a car for you."

"No need for a car," Zhang said, waving the man off. "No need at all. I love riding the bike. It's good exercise."

Without changing his position, Cui sat quietly, looking awkward.

"What's the matter, Lao Cui?" Zhang asked.

Cui stubbed out his cigarette and said with difficulty, "I should not be the one to tell you this, Lao Zhang, but please stop riding to work. We have enough cars and the other bureau chiefs and vice bureau chiefs all ride to and from work. Just think, what do they do if you insist on riding your bike?"

Zhang slapped his head as he saw exactly what the man was getting at. He'd just been promoted and hadn't learned how to look at things with greater care. He had only been cycling for the exercise, but to other chiefs, not riding in a chauffeured car was posturing and would make them look bad. Fortunately for him, Lao Cui had put him straight; otherwise, he'd have kept riding, oblivious of the perception that he was set on giving others a hard time. Obviously, he had a lot to learn.

"Of course, Lao Cui," he said gratefully. "I'll take your advice. Starting tomorrow I'll take the car."

Happy to hear it, Cui stood up.

"I'm glad Chief Zhang agrees with me. That will make our job easier."

Zhang offered Cui a cigarette. He accepted it and lit up, and then walked off in a good mood.

Starting on May 25, Lao Zhang was driven to and from work every day. It took some getting used to. Riding a bike was easier, for he could slow down or speed up whenever he felt like it, while the car zipped down the street like a whirlwind. But as time went by, he began to enjoy being driven; it was better than riding a bike, especially when he saw people moving down busy streets and passengers crowding onto packed buses. One day his driver could not restart the engine outside the residence, so Zhang hopped on his bike and rode to the office. It was hard work and farther than he recalled. He never rode his bike again.

At first people talked: "Lao Zhang settled into his chauffeured car the moment he was promoted." But soon they, too, got used to it and stopped gossiping; they thought it was only natural that he be chauffeured around. Only his neck suffered; without the bike to work on his flabby neck, he brought a dumbbell to the office so he could exercise each morning. He would work up a sweat and, after a while, began to see positive results. His wife, on the other hand, troubled him to hitch a ride to work, since her office was on the way. Zhang made it clear to her that it was an official car, assigned to him for his convenience, and that letting family members ride in it would incur criticism from his comrades. She grumbled, but he was adamant. She rode in the car only twice, both times on rainy days, and Zhang okayed it with his driver each time.

"It's raining today, Little Song. Okay for Lao Hu to hitch a ride?"

Touched by being asked, he said,

"Sure. Hop in!"

The news made it to his old office, fueling a new round of gossip.

"So he rode his bike to work after his promotion for show," someone said.

"Well, he's a deputy bureau chief now, so he deserves to be driven. Why waste the opportunity?"

Lao Sun was the only who offered no comment. He just smoked his cigarettes. He'd been feeling down of late; with so much on his mind, he had no time to worry about Zhang being driven to work. There were two reasons for his bad mood: one, he was not pleased with how his talk with Zhang during the trip had gone. It had been a tiring journey and he'd often paid for the meals but they could never settle their business. Zhang had been amiable throughout, and yet they were unable to untie the knot in their relationship after all these years. Political problems from the past could be redressed, but not personal issues. So it was a wasted trip. The second reason had to do with the poll. It had been carried out swiftly but no one had heard a word about the result since. After sounding out his hometown friend in the organization section, Sun learned the official reason—the section head was still in the hospital waiting for a repeat surgery following a partially failed operation. The man did not know the real reason, since he was only a clerk, and not privy to what was going on at higher levels. Based on his years of experience in the area, Sun knew that a promotion relied on speedy action; things could easily go south if nothing was moving, when there was no news. And once something went south, it would be hard for a promotion to go through. Sun also heard rumors that the bureau was leaning toward an outside section head. A name was even mentioned. Which meant the end for him.

When he revealed his concerns to Lao He, all the man did was take off his glasses and wipe the lenses.

"What else can we do? Just wait."

Sun fumed. *How did I ever form an alliance with a useless guy like that?* But he kept his anger in check, so as not to look tactless and make future maneuvering difficult. All he could do was sigh and say, "We need to work on it. We can't just sit on our hands."

Three days later, when Sun was alone in the office, Lao He came up to his desk with a gleeful look.

"Good news, Lao Sun."

Sun's heart skipped a beat at the sight of his spirited colleague. He took the cigarette out of his mouth.

"What is it? What's the good news?"

"Guess." Lao He was smiling.

Assuming that his promotion was moving forward, Sun brightened up. Normally he refused to play guessing games with He, but now he went along.

"News from the organization section?"

That first attempt was met with a shake of the head.

"News from the bureau?"

Again He shook his head.

"The ministry?"

More head shaking.

"I can't guess it. What is it?"

"I heard that Lao Zhang is moving to a new place next Sunday, and it's been confirmed."

What a letdown. Sun's temper flared.

"Why joke at a time like this? You call that news?"

"Why not? Just think. Wouldn't he be impressed if we helped him move?"

Sun gave He a contemptuous look.

"You don't know shit," he fumed. "Now I know why you'll be a clerk forever. Why did I ever try to team up with you? Do you think this is like children playing house and that he'll give you a boost after you help him move? You can go if you want, but not me. Who the hell is Lao Zhang? And you, your head is stuffed full of old ideas and a peasant mentality."

Xiao Lin walked in just as Lao He slunk back to his desk after the reprimand, and he could tell that something was wrong, but had no idea what. After losing Lao Qiao, he had doubled his efforts to get Sun and He on his side. It depressed him to see them have a falling out. He desperately wanted colleagues who were party members to get along and stand united because he was out of luck if they did not, and all his efforts—including taking the initiative, being conscientious, bringing water and cleaning desks, and aligning himself with the party organization—would be in vain.

Lao Zhang was indeed moving Sunday, from the same dorm building as Xiao Peng to one for bureau chiefs. Taking a lesson from his bike-riding experience, he agreed unhesitatingly when the general affairs office notified him of the planned move, and went home to tell his wife to pack and get ready.

A great many people showed up to help on the day of the move. The office sent two trucks and the general affairs office hired three migrant workers, while former colleagues from the office came to pitch in. Xiao Lin was there, so was Lao He, who was puzzled to see Lao Sun, who rode up halfway through the move, after cursing Zhang only days before. He greeted everyone with a laugh.

"Sorry I'm late."

Zhang rushed out while rubbing dust off his hands.

"Not you too, Lao Sun." Zhang was visibly touched. "The comrades from the section are all I need."

"I'm not here to help you move. I came to help with your new place. I love arranging furniture."

With a hearty laugh, Zhang said, "Great. I'll turn the new place over to you. Now sit down and have a cigarette."

Taking his cue, Sun sat on a truck tailgate, lit up, and chatted with Zhang as he watched Lin and He carry things out.

Lin had been the first to arrive. Before setting out, he'd changed into an old army uniform, the sight of which saddened his frail wife.

"Don't go, Xiao Lin. You don't have to demean yourself all the time. I feel terrible seeing you like this."

"I'd rather not help those jerks move, but I have to if we want to move out of here ourselves."

He worked harder than anyone else, quietly doing what needed to be done—carrying out a large wardrobe, moving potted plants, and lugging an armful of vats and jugs. He worked up such a sweat that even Zhang's wife, a woman with a pug nose, was somewhat guilt-ridden.

"Let's take a break. We're going to wear this young man out."

With two trucks and enough helpers, they were able to quickly load up everything and head to the new place. Zhang, Sun, and Zhang's wife and daughter sat in one of the cabs, while everyone else sat in the back. Lao He and Xiao Lin sat together.

"I didn't want to come, but I had nothing better to do at home, so here I am," said He.

Lin said nothing.

When they arrived at the new building, everyone got off to help unload and move the stuff up the stairs, all but Sun, who went up with Zhang's wife to work on the furniture arraignment. Lin followed them up to check out Zhang's new apartment. Wow, a five-room unit. The living room was big enough to race horses, and a telephone had already been installed. The bathroom came with a huge tub, and the kitchen was equipped with a gas line, making it unnecessary to lug coal briquettes. Lin was actually concerned—wasn't the place too big for a family of three? In any case, it was good to be a bureau chief. Xiao Lin knew he'd chosen wisely to come help.

By noontime, they'd moved everything inside and placed it where Sun told them. The place looked neat and orderly, which prompted a hearty laugh from Zhang, who said Lao Sun had untapped talent as an interior decorator.

"The place could use some vinyl flooring, which would make it look even better."

When they were done, Zhang's daughter had already cooked up a meal on the gas stove. Zhang invited everyone to sit down and have a drink, but Lao He clapped his hands to shake off the dust and said, "No need, Lao Zhang. We're happy to help you move. You don't have to feed us. We're off now."

Zhang held him back. "You can't leave like that, after you've been busy helping us all morning. Don't go." He made Sun go in and wash up.

The others followed suit before sitting down to eat. But first they drank—hard liquor and beer. Sun's red face was a sign that he was tipsy; his eyes watered.

"Would you like to lie down for a while, Lao Sun?" Zhang's wife asked.

"No need. I'm fine. I'm just happy to be here to help the boss move, and I've had a bit too much to drink. That's all."

"Not at all," Zhang said. "You haven't drunk that much."

When they finished eating, they got up to leave. Zhang told his driver to take everyone home. Sun, who had ridden over, hopped on his bicycle and left alone. After everyone was gone, Zhang went to the bathroom and, to his surprise, found Xiao Lin there. Apparently after lunch, Lin had noticed yellow stains on the toilet and had stayed behind to clean it, scrubbing the surface with a steel brush after pouring some cleaning solvent on the spots. Zhang was moved by the sight.

"Why are you still here, Xiao Lin? And what are you doing? Put it down. I'll do it."

Wiping his sweaty forehead with his sleeve, Lin said, "I'm almost done. Don't worry about it."

After cleaning the toilet, Lin emptied the wastepaper basket.

When he came back, Zhang had prepared a basin of water for him to wash up, and asked Lin to sit awhile. Zhang poured him tea,

peeled an apple, and unwrapped a piece of candy for him. Lin too
was touched.

"It's been a tiring day, Lao Zhang. You should take a break."

"This young man worked harder than anyone today." Zhang's
wife said to Lin, "You must be tired."

"He's a good kid," Zhang said to his wife, and he meant it. It
looked like the young man had grown up and learned a few things.
So Zhang asked him some questions while they were walking down
the stairs.

"Lao Sun brought up your situation a few days ago. Not bad. A
young man needs to work on moving ahead and not muddle through
life as if nothing mattered."

Lin nodded.

"Treat me like your own son, Lao Zhang, and don't hold back if
you have any criticisms."

"I won't. I'll definitely tell you," Zhang said. "Sad to say, that's
the way I am. The more I like a comrade, the more demanding I am
with him."

As Lin walked off, Zhang shouted, "Come see me any time."

"Go back inside, Lao Zhang," Lin shouted back.

8

Lao Qiao asked for a leave of absence and stopped coming to the
office. She also filed a complaint with the bureau, claiming that people were bullying her and she could not continue to work there. The
bureau sent someone to the office to see what was going on.

"She's nearing retirement, so don't bully her," the man advised.

The complaint set Sun on edge. This was a critical period, the
worst time for anything bad to happen in the office, since the organization section was watching them. Sun was already on pins and
needles over the generally cheerless days, and now Qiao had filed a
complaint; he could kill the woman. Yet he could not afford to show

his displeasure; instead he forced a smile and explained to the man that it was nothing serious.

"It was all over a cricket and going through someone's drawers. The two comrades had a spat, nothing serious." Sun added that, as the current head of the section, he was partially responsible for the discord. Promising to take care of the matter, he reassured the man that there was nothing to concern the bureau.

After walking him out, Sun came back and smashed a cup in anger.

"What's the cunt thinking? She should retire and go home to play with her grandchild. Why is she causing us trouble? Why hasn't a car run her over?" Then he turned on Xiao Peng:

"And why couldn't you leave her alone?"

"It's a lot better when she's not in. The office is nice and quiet."

"Quiet?"

After his angry outburst, Sun rode over to Qiao's place that afternoon, where he put on a smile and tried to talk her into coming back to work.

When he got there, she'd just had a blowup with her domestic helper, who became a punching bag because of Qiao's bad mood. She'd happened to count the eggs in the kitchen and found they were one short, which was just the evidence she needed to punish the girl by making her work nonstop. The helper normally wasn't cowed by Qiao, but sensing that her mistress was acting differently than before, she did not fight back, for if Qiao fell ill, as usually happened when she was angry and was laid up in bed, the helper would have to wait on her. Qiao felt better now that she'd vented her anger.

She led Sun into the living room.

"Don't be upset, Lao Qiao," Sun said as he set down his briefcase. "Come back to work."

Her temper flared again at the mention of being upset.

"I won't. The office has been turned into a zoo and people bully me whenever they feel like it. I can't work there."

"Let it go, Lao Qiao. You're their superior and a party member, so why get angry at the youngsters? Come back to work tomorrow morning, won't you?"

"I'm superfluous there. The office is like a marketplace, and I'm not going back. I'm going to apply for early retirement."

"That won't do, Lao Qiao. The section depends on you for too much."

She was feeling better, but continued to feign resistance:

"With all those capable people at the office, you don't need me."

"We need an old comrade like you to write reports on our office work and compose official documents for the provinces. An official document represents the ministry, and there's no room for error."

"You're right there. Xiao Peng made a mistake last time, which turned us into a laughingstock. She was resentful when Lao Zhang said her thoughts were all jumbled. She's nothing but a housewife."

"Put the office work aside and think about personal issues. Lao Zhang has just been transferred, leaving me to take care of everything in the section, so I need all the support an old comrade can give me. There's so much to do and I can't do it all by myself. I need the help of an old comrade like you."

Sun's plea finally brought a smile to Qiao's face, but she would not relent.

"I can go back to work, but on one condition."

"What is it, tell me." Sun puffed on his cigarette.

"I'll still be in charge of party matters."

"Of course. You are the party group leader, after all."

"If I'm in charge, then I want to reopen the issue we talked about last time. I don't want Xiao Lin to become a party member."

Sun was flabbergasted. Xiao Peng was the one who had fought with her, so why was she picking on him? That was preposterous.

"Xiao Peng was the one who quarreled with you, Lao Qiao. Xiao Lin didn't cause any problems."

"I'm not looking at it from a personal angle. After what happened, I could tell that he's two-faced, and we can't have someone like that in our party."

"What do you mean, two-faced?"

"He sings a different tune with different people, and he's gotten real tight with Xiao Peng. I can't stand people like him. I won't allow him to join."

"It's tough on him, you know," Sun said with a sigh.

"I won't go back to work if you're all keen on standing by him." Qiao flared up again. "We must have principles when we recruit party members."

"All right, all right," Sun conceded. "Come back to work and we'll talk about his application at our group meeting."

Qiao went back to work the next day, and everything seemed fine at the section office. Sure enough, she called a party group meeting soon afterward, where she launched an impassioned tirade against Xiao Lin, stressing the need to delay approving his membership in order to rid him of his shortcomings. Sun sat there smoking without saying a word. Lao He made a feeble attempt to speak up for Lin but didn't want to upset Qiao (strange how they felt they all owed her something when she refused to show up for work). In the end, Lin was the one who suffered the consequences—his application would not be approved for some time.

Revitalized by her victory, Lao Qiao came to work early every morning; no longer a slacker, she seemed to be more cheerful. She even chatted and laughed with the others, a stark contrast with Sun's low spirits. She talked and laughed with everyone, and sometimes even tried to chat Peng up, but she gave Lin the cold shoulder. Every time he tried to strike up a conversation with her, she would say, "Everyone should focus on doing his job well and nothing else."

Lin's face reddened at the rebuke.

He had already learned about the delay in his application approval, but was surprised to discover that the consequence of unintentionally offending Qiao could be so staggering. His diligence at the office was wasted effort, even helping Lao Zhang move. He sometimes felt like throwing everything away and adopting his former, nonchalant, college student attitude. He could rail against the woman enough that she might fall ill again, maybe even die. But he swallowed his anger when he got home and saw his baby girl. In the end it was Lao Sun, who came to his rescue out of pity.

"Didn't you impress Lao Zhang? Why don't you go see him?"

"But he's not the party group leader. What's the use of talking to him?"

"Do as I say and go see him. It will help."

So Lin went to see Zhang, and it worked.

"She should not have done that. Everyone has flaws, and she shouldn't focus only on yours. I'll talk to her."

Zhang went to see Qiao and asked her to correct her views of Lin. She actually listened.

"Don't mind me, Lao Zhang, I was just venting. We'll reopen the discussion at the next group meeting."

"Very good." Zhang was pleased. "I'm glad to hear that."

Why would Qiao listen to Zhang? All part of her plan. She had been a troublemaker at work, with erratic performance, even stopped coming to the office for a while, all because she was unhappy with her salary. She was a year from retirement, after a lifetime at the office, and was still a clerk, which she considered an affront. It was not that she wished to be the section head or the deputy; all she wanted was the title of associate research investigator, which would give her plenty of face and something to show her son. But that would require approval from those higher up in the bureau level, including Lao Zhang.

It was an effective move that raised Lin's spirits—for the moment. Lao Qiao did not reopen the discussion at the next meeting as promised; instead, she voiced another complaint, calling him a sneak. He had gone behind her back and complained to someone at the bureau level. *As I said, he's no good. I was going to reopen the discussion, but this new development shows that we shouldn't do that.* Lin's application was further delayed, which put him in a terrible mood. He continued to bring in hot water and sweep the floor, and he still talked and laughed with the others, but deep down he was in a funk.

"Don't look so dispirited, Xiao Lin," Lao He said. "I wasn't admitted into the party until I was forty-five."

"I'm not dispirited."

But of course he was, and that sometimes carried over at home. He began to lose sleep, as a jumble of thoughts filled his head. One day he was up until five in the morning (but he dared not toss and turn, with the whole family sleeping in the same room), making him so anxious he thought he was about to see stars. He loathed that woman. Yet at work the next day, he mustered the will to fetch water and sweep the floor. When he saw Lao Qiao, he tried hard to chat her up, hoping to smooth over the issues she had with him.

Xiao Peng was also in a bad mood, not over a party membership application, but over a leave of absence that would allow her to spend some time with her aunt at Shijiazhuang.

"What kind of office is this, with this one staying home and that one asking for a leave of absence?" Lao Sun complained. "We might as well shut down altogether."

"I don't care if someone else wants to stay home, but I want to take my annual twelve-day vacation."

"Why can't you take your vacation in July? Will your aunt be moving out of Shijiazhuang before then? I've been there; it's like a big village. There's nothing to do there."

"Yes, there is."

"No, I won't approve your leave."

She could not go without his approval, which put her in a very bad mood. When she saw Lao Qiao prance around in the office, intimidating even Lao Sun, she couldn't hold back:

"Even Lao Sun is a damned bully, always picking on the weak."

Nearsighted Lao He accidentally knocked over Peng's mug, spilling tea all over her desk and into the drawers. She jumped to her feet.

"Are you blind? Why the hell did you do that? Have you learned nothing after all these decades?"

Instead of getting mad at her, Lao He just chuckled as he picked up a rag to wipe her desk and drawers and flick water off her papers.

Peng's mood improved after this outburst; everyone returned to work and the office resumed an air of normalcy. On the following afternoon, when Peng and Lin were alone in the office, he was still engrossed in his own miserable thoughts. She sneaked up and smacked him on the shoulder. Startled, he was about to explode, but just smiled when he turned and saw it was her.

"What are you thinking about?"

"Nothing," he said, "nothing, really."

She changed the subject. "I've got two tickets for a three thirty movie. Do you dare come watch it with me?"

He looked around the deserted office. "Sure. Let's go."

They gathered their things, but he hesitated as they were leaving. "Will Lao Sun be coming back to the office?"

"Look what you've become, all because of party membership. Is it worth it? He went to the ministry for a report and won't be back today."

Feeling assured, Lin walked out, just as Lao Qiao returned. He hesitated, so irritating Peng that she demanded loudly, "Do you or don't you dare to go to the movie?"

Caught in a bind, Lin stood there and, after a glance at Qiao, finally said, "Sure. Let's go." He walked off with Peng.

Qiao went to see Sun the next morning as soon as he walked in.

"You see? I was right not to let him join the party. You were away yesterday, so he left hand-in-hand with Xiao Peng to a movie. He even had the gall to say, 'Sure. Let's go.'"

"I see. I'll talk to him," Sun said with a frown. When he called Lin over, Lin tried to explain what had happened.

"It was about the Sino-Vietnamese war. Boring," he said.

"I don't care if it was about the Sino-Vietnamese war or the Sino-Franco war. Just be careful next time, all right? How could you do that in front of her? Don't you realize the situation you're in?"

"I do." Lin nodded. "I'll be careful next time." He cursed silently. "What a bitch!" He decided not to divulge the conversation to Peng for fear of causing an argument between the two women, which would bring him nothing but grief.

9

It had been a month since Lao Zhang moved into the building for bureau chiefs. The apartment was nice, which made his wife and daughter happy; but not him, not at first. He felt awkward when he ran into his former superiors when he entered and left the building; life was easier in the old place. But he got used to it as time went by; they were bureau-level chiefs and so was he. Why should he feel awkward? They greeted him, "Have you eaten yet, Lao Zhang?"

In the past he'd put on a smile and say, "Have you, Mr. Bureau Chief?" But now he said offhandedly, "Have you, Old Xu?"

When the others ducked into their chauffeured cars, he did the same. As his car fell in behind theirs, he leaned back and sized up their cars, no longer feeling out of place. The others, on the other hand, were jealous of his good luck, since they all knew how he'd gotten to where he was. It took them some time to get used to the fact that he was now their equal. They were, in fact, a bit put off by the way he acted as their equal and talked among themselves about how he had become conceited and brassy. One day, when he went to visited Bureau Chief Xiong, after some small talk, Xiong said with some hesitation, "Be a bit more humble, Lao Zhang, since you've just been promoted."

Caught off guard, Zhang could only nod, as he broke out in a cold sweat. But when he got home and the cold sweat had dried, his indignation rose to the surface:

"Damn you people! I'm a deputy bureau chief, but you want me to be as humble as a section head. Well, I can be humble, but what about you?"

After venting his anger, he put the whole business out of his mind, took off his clothes, and lay down beside his wife. When he got up the next day, he greeted people and climbed into his car the same as always. After a while the others stopped saying he wasn't humble enough and accepted the way he was. They began addressing one another as equals, and once they got used to that, it felt natural, which signaled a tacit agreement that he was one of them.

"I'll be damned. That Lao Zhang isn't as worthless as we thought. He might have a pig's neck, but he has interesting qualities and quite a personality."

Day in and day out, Zhang led a normal life, traveling between the office and his apartment, like everyone else, until August 2, when something happened, quite by accident, that did not look good for him. Initially, it was known only to a small circle of people, but somehow the news got out and everyone at the bureau heard about it.

Xiao Lin went to work as usual, but something felt different the moment he walked into the building. People were rushing in and out, wearing mysterious looks of excitement. Assuming that pears or chickens were being distributed again that day, he did not give it much thought at first. But when he went to fill his vacuum bottle with water after sweeping the floor, he ran into Xiao Hu from Section 7. "Have you heard?" Hu asked enigmatically.

"Heard what?"

"You really don't know? Something happened to Lao Zhang. Two days ago. And you still don't know?"

"Lao Zhang?" Lin was understandably surprised. "What happened?"

"I can't believe you don't know." Hu was unhappy that Lin was so ill informed. "It's a lifestyle problem."

"What?" Lin was so flustered he put the vacuum bottle stopper in wrong, and sent it bouncing off the ceiling. When he retrieved it and put it back in the bottle, he'd recovered enough to shake his head.

"Lao Zhang with a lifestyle problem? Impossible. I don't believe you."

"You see." Hu clapped his hands. "I knew you wouldn't believe me."

Lin began to waver.

"Who with?"

"Guess."

Lin went through the list of women who might be involved in affairs. "Zhang Xiaoli?"

Hu shook his head.

"Wang Hong?"

Hu shook his head again.

"Sun Yuling?"

More head shaking.

"That's it then. I knew he didn't have a problem. Even if he did, it would never be something you say. With that pig's neck of his, he couldn't find anyone to be involved with if he wanted to."

"But he did," Hu said with a broad grin. "I'll narrow the possibilities for you. It's someone in your office."

"Our office?" Lin was confounded. "Xiao Peng?"

"No."

"That was it." Lin clapped his hands. "There's no one else, unless we're talking about a homosexual liaison."

"You forgot the other woman." Hu giggled as he continued. "I won't make you guess any more. It's Lao Qiao."

"Lao Qiao? How is that possible?" Lin was so stunned he nearly bounced off the ceiling. "They're old. Besides, how in the world did they get together? Impossible."

"What do you know? So what if they're old? Old age translates into experience. Want to know where they did it? In Lao Zhang's office. I hear they were trying something new and were caught in the act. You see, older people know lots of tricks."

Lin stood there blankly while Hu walked off with his vacuum bottle, but turned back when he reached the door.

"Want to know who caught them? It was none other than his wife. I heard she'd been on his track for several days."

Lin was too amazed to move. *This is crazy. How could that be possible? Lao Zhang and Lao Qiao both seem so upright. How come I didn't notice anything?* As Lin thought about it, he realized that Lao Qiao had been absent for two days, but no one knew why. At noon the previous day, he also saw Sun and He whispering animatedly, but they clammed up the moment they saw him. They pretended to be talking about something else, so something must have happened. He recalled seeing Zhang's wife walk out of Chief Xiong's office, her eyes red. Lin had wondered why she hadn't bothered to say hello, after he'd helped them move. *Ingrate*, he thought. Now it all made sense. Something had happened to Zhang. Damn!

He shook his head and sighed his way back to the office. Unlike the day before, when Zhang's incident had been secret, no one at the office felt the need to suppress the news and guard against each other. Now an open discussion took over the office. Sun cheered visibly, with a reddish glow on his face. When Lin came in with the water, it meant everyone was present, so Sun announced, as if relaying documents from the central government, "I have something to say before we start work today. You may feel as unprepared for the news as you were years ago when Lin Biao defected and people were shocked, wondering how Chairman Mao's closest comrade in arms could defect. But he did. So I'm going to tell you something, and you'll be just as shocked. I won't blame you if you are. But you won't be any longer, once we analyze the situation. I too was shocked when I heard, but I soon recovered from the shock. Nothing happens overnight; there is always a process. We were too careless and insensitive to notice the process. It's not a major incident, but neither is it trivial. It's like this: Lao Zhang, originally from our office, and Lao Qiao, currently from our office, have committed a lifestyle problem. They were caught in the act. In theory, our section does not deal with sordid issues like this. Comrade Zhang's wife caught the adulterers in the act and filed a complaint with the bureau. Some of you may ask why I'm telling you this, since it's not our concern. Well, after some thought, it seemed necessary, since it could involve our work. That is why I'm bringing it up today. After he was found out, Comrade Zhang was put on leave to write a self-criticism. He was in charge of our section, along with Sections 6 and 7, wasn't he? Well, we've been notified by the bureau that Deputy Bureau Chief Xu will take over Sections 6 and 7, while Bureau Chief Xiong himself will be in charge of our section."

When he was finished, the office was abuzz over what had happened; the talk would likely continue for some time. Xiao Lin took the opportunity to make a quick tour of the building; everyone in the other sections was talking about the same thing, supplementing details that he hadn't heard, such as how Zhang and Qiao first got hooked up, how many times they had done it, what the room looked like, how his wife found out about it, how she stormed the door, how they were stark naked, but she would not let them get dressed before calling Chief Xiong over to have a good look, and so on. The matter occupied everyone's mind and time, from morning to afternoon, from the time they boarded the bus till they got off. Naturally, they relayed what they'd heard to their spouses.

In fact, it wasn't as complicated as everyone thought. Here is how it happened: one day, Zhang was picking his teeth after finishing his lunch (rice with stir-fried celery and a small dish of pork belly) and was about to lie down on the sofa for a nap when Qiao pushed open the door and entered with a work report. He was displeased that she'd come at naptime, but, reminded that he was a deputy bureau chief, he decided to take the high road. So, patting the sofa, he invited her to sit down. Using the work report as a pretense to request a promotion to associate research investigator, Qiao talked a blue streak; asking him to consider her case. She reminded him that she was about to retire and would not come see him again after this. Zhang wanted to get rid of her quickly, so he said, "Sure, all right. I'll bring it up at our next meeting."

Unexpectedly worked up by his quick agreement, like a young girl, she patted the back of his hand, which was as thick as a toad's belly.

"You are, after all, from our section, Lao Zhang. You're the only one who cares about me, when every one else bullies me."

She began to sob, even wiping her eyes with a handkerchief. When she first put her hand on his, Zhang felt his heart stirring; no one except his wife ever showed any interest in him, a man in his fifties with a pig's neck. Now seeing her cry, he was somewhat aroused. He turned and saw she was sobbing like a girl. They had come to the section at about the same time, when she had been quite a looker, prettier even than Xiao Peng. So he patted her on the shoulder and said, "Don't cry, Xiao Qiao. You can count on me."

The term, "Young" Qiao, for a young woman, gave her the illusion that she had returned to her younger self, and a momentary lapse of judgment had her press her shoulder in his arms. Zhang, too, suffered a momentary lapse of judgment, and began to grope her, clumsily. His wife pushed open the door right at that moment. She rarely showed up at the office, so it was just his luck that she wasn't feeling well and had asked for a sick leave, but then forgot her key. She could not believe her eyes when she walked in on them. Being in a bad mood from her physical discomfort to begin with, she flew into a jealous rage at witnessing her husband fooling around with another woman in his office. Leaping into action, first she gave Qiao two vicious slaps and then wailed her way out and into Chief Xiong's office next door. *Go take a look. Go see what Lao Zhang is doing.* In the meantime, Zhang was stupefied. He and Qiao had always acted properly, yet after several decades of proper behavior, they did what they did, and when they were old, no less! He could not get over his puzzlement, which was why his hand remained between her legs (outside her pants) when Xiong walked in.

"Look at you, Lao Zhang. What do you think you're doing?"

Once things calmed down and everyone—Qiao, Zhang's wife, and Xiong—had left, Zhang went limp, as it finally dawned on him what he had done that day. Regret set in. Damn it all! It was like trying to shoot a fox but getting only the foul odor. He stayed in his office all afternoon, not even going out when his bladder was so full it hurt. Naturally he couldn't come to work the next day, and the bureau told him to stay home and write a self-criticism. Qiao decided to stay away also, even without notification from the bureau. Separately in their respective homes, Zhang and Qiao calmed down and, as regret welled up, found fault with the other.

"You're no good, Lao Zhang, you sneaky old man. How dare you take advantage of me in a moment of weakness!"

"What a bitch, that Lao Qiao. How could she not know that her seduction could ruin me?"

But Zhang was, after all, in a leadership position, a better person than Qiao, who blamed Zhang as if she were faultless. She cried her eyes out.

"No doubt about it, she was wrong, but I'm not totally blameless." Zhang was able to admit that to himself at least.

When he stopped going to work, so did his wife, who pushed a sofa up against their front door to keep him from going out. She wanted an explanation from him before she'd let him write his self-criticism; she wanted to know how many times they'd done it, how many others there were before Qiao, and how many times he had done it with each, and so on. Being in the wrong, Zhang had to control his temper and could only repeat himself, "I told you we did not do it. Honest, we didn't do anything. Why wouldn't we lock the door if we had?"

"I don't give a damn about the door. Why would she let you touch her that way if you weren't doing anything?" his wife cried. "I might as well electrocute myself or drink pesticide."

He had to keep an eye on her so she wouldn't do that.

The office building was alive with excitement. Zhang's promotion had been a compromise in a fight between the ministry and the bureau. When he fell from favor, each side blamed the other for promoting such a despicable person. While condemning the other side, they ganged up on Zhang to prove they hadn't been the ones who had promoted him. They reached an agreement in the end: Zhang was to stay home to write a self-criticism, he was relieved of his duties, and the administrative affairs office would conduct an investigation at his previous office.

Sun was elated at the news, so happy he nearly danced a jig. He worked day and night, even sacrificing his Sunday, to prepare his own version.

Fuck you, Lao Zhang. You probably never thought this day would come. You've been screwing me for over twenty years and now it's my turn to return the favor, Sun said to himself. Then he went to see Lao He.

"The administrative affairs office is investigating Lao Zhang, so you need to be prepared."

"But he worked with us." Lao He wasn't conflicted. "It doesn't seem right to me."

"Why are you so spineless? Yes, we worked together, but what has he done for us, his former colleagues, following his promotion? I wouldn't mind if he didn't want to help us out, but he went all out to make things hard for us. Why has neither of us has been promoted yet? He was messing with us. Now he's on his way down. If you don't help push him all the way, he could come back up again, and we'd be the losers. You're not getting any younger, and yet you don't know a thing."

Lao He finally figured it out.

"You're right, Lao Sun. You're absolutely right. I'll follow your advice and put some materials together. Back when he was working here, he loved to flirt with Wang Hong, from Section 7."

"Now you're talking! Go see Xiao Lin and get him moving on it too."

Lao He went to see Xiao Lin, who had lost interest in the incident. In his view, the office was a mess, and even Lao Zhang and Lao Qiao were having an affair. He had helped Zhang move, given them his reflections, sent Qiao gifts on Labor Day, and acted obsequiously around them. What could he do now that they were mired in a sexual scandal? His former actions seemed utterly absurd, and he decided to go passive. He wanted to return to his old self, unafraid of anyone, so he began coming to work late and stopped fetching water and sweeping the floor. He frequently sneaked out to play Ping-Pong after spending a few minutes at his desk. Owing to the recent excitement in the office, Sun and He failed to notice anything different about Lin. When they found the vacuum bottle empty, they just thought they'd finished the water; it never occurred to them that Lin hadn't brought in hot water that day. When Lao He came to ask Lin to help expose Zhang, Lin had just finished playing Ping-Pong. He was getting dressed to go home and see his daughter.

"You go ahead and expose him," he said in an offhanded manner. "It's got nothing to do with me. I'm not even a party member."

His response confounded He, who didn't quite understand what the younger man meant.

"How could it have nothing to do with you, Xiao Lin? Isn't it because of Qiao that you're not a party member? You'll be able to join now that she's been taken down. It's as simple as that. Why can't you see that?" Lao He instructed Lin the same way Sun had talked to him.

Lin saw the light. He'd come close to missing an opportunity, with no one to blame but himself. Lao He was right about Qiao being the stumbling block. With the obstacle gone, he would likely make it, wouldn't he? At a moment like this, he mustn't lose confidence; if he did, he'd be a complete fool, wasting years of hard work. Due to a momentary lapse in mental clarity, he had foolishly been about to give it all up. He had to become proactive and not throw everything to the wind. Slapping himself on the forehead, he said to Lao He, "You're right, Lao He. I'll take your advice."

He got into action immediately, sweeping the floor and getting the water.

"I didn't mean for you to sweep the floor or get the water," Lao He said from behind him. "We want you to help expose Lao Qiao and Lao Zhang."

"Right, that's what I'll do," said a sweaty Lin.

He came to work on time the next day. After finishing his chores, he got together with others in the office to gather information on Zhang and Qiao.

Xiao Peng joined them out of spite for Qiao, but would only go halfway, stopping at attacking Zhang. Lao He wiped his glasses while trying to enlighten her. "Have you forgotten that Lao Zhang once said your thoughts were chaotic?"

"I haven't, but I'll only focus on Lao Qiao, because I'm sure he was blameless. It was all Qiao's fault. That old fox, I knew all along she was up to no good. Back when she refused to come to work, Lao Sun was so cowed by her he even went to her house and begged her to come back. See what happened? If he hadn't gone to her, we wouldn't have this incident to deal with. I'm going to expose her and Lao Sun. He's partially responsible for this."

"All right, all right." Sun spoke up. "Go ahead, expose anyone you want, or just Lao Qiao if it suits you."

That afternoon someone came from the administrative affairs office, accompanied by the section head, who had recovered from his hemorrhoid surgery. Everyone in the section spoke up eagerly, to the satisfaction of the administrators.

10

Lao Qiao's husband came to the office to apply for her early retirement. Rumor had it that she had raised hell at home for several days, which affected her health. She'd vented her anger on the maid, who vowed to quit. Lao Qiao slapped her and ran her out of the house, then turned her wrath on her husband.

"What do you plan to do now? Separate or divorce?" She was forcing him too choose. A diminutive fair-skinned man, he'd been henpecked all their married life. He wasn't happy about what had happened, but had to force himself to comfort her, with her acting up the way she was.

"Don't worry. I believe you." That wasn't good enough for her.
"I can't keep going like this. What do I do?"

"Don't go back to the office. That place is bad for you. We'll apply for early retirement. I'll go take care of the paperwork."

So he went to the administrative affairs office, wrapped up his business, and then came to the office to get her things. To everyone's amusement, the fair-skinned old man did not seem embarrassed by Lao Qiao's incident. Instead, he acted like an interoffice liaison, politely nodding at everyone before gathering up her things. After denouncing the disliked Qiao a few days before, they felt compelled to be nice to her husband, so they nodded in return. Lao He and Xiao Lin even went over to help him bundle up the contents of Qiao's drawers. Xiao Peng was the exception, turning away when he greeted her. When he left, the others criticized her pettiness.

"Disgusting!" she retorted, before taking out of a mirror to check her face.

Lao Zhang returned to work after ten days. The ministry and the bureau had originally wanted him to stay away a bit longer, while they reconsidered his job assignment, but Deputy Bureau Chief Xu was hospitalized after another bout of heart trouble. Lao Zhang was told to come back to pick up the slack. After the incident Zhang should have been demoted, since the bureau and the ministry wanted him out, but they got into another fight over his replacement. When the minister heard about it he was naturally displeased.

"Does this even look like a government office?" he fumed. "Why do you people fight all the time? I'm going to give the job to someone who isn't fighting."

With an upcoming trip abroad before the National Holiday, he decided to act quickly and decisively by keeping Lao Zhang on as a deputy bureau chief. Zhang and Qiao hadn't gone that far, so the situation wasn't particularly serious, and punishment by the party would suffice. So Zhang once again benefited from the internal struggle, with a warning from the party, but no disciplinary action against him. Understandably grateful to the minister for getting his old job back,

Zhang decided to turn over a new leaf and work especially hard. His determination notwithstanding, the incident still cost him the respect of other bureau chiefs, who stopped considering him their equal. Being cognizant of the situation, Zhang knew he had to act cautiously and humbly. Whenever he ran into neighbors in the building, they would continue to greet him, "Have you eaten yet, Lao Zhang?"

But he no longer returned the greeting casually; instead, he bowed and said, for instance, "Have you eaten yet, Mr. Kong?"

And he stopped rivaling others in banging the car door shut when he was picked up. Now he shut it softly and fell in behind the other cars. He also stopped looking around and adopted an amiable attitude toward his chauffeur. Instead of visiting friends at various offices, he stayed at his desk and worked all day. After a while people were saying, "That incident was a blessing in disguise for Lao Zhang. He's more cautious and humbler now."

His wife stopped pestering him at home. The whole process felt like a gunshot wound that healed by itself as time went by. She turned her back to him in bed, but he didn't mind that, as long as there was peace and quiet. In any case, their family life resumed its natural rhythm. He did, however, feel bad when he heard about Qiao's early retirement.

"It's my fault," he said with a private sigh.

With his guilty conscience, he treated the people who worked for him more considerately. But the women were hard to please; they avoided him, almost as if anyone who had contact with him would be corrupted. Even the girl who delivered documents scurried off the moment she dropped a file on his desk, no longer stopping to chat.

"What a bunch of hypocrites!" He was irate. "Like I'd screw any woman who came into sight!"

About ten days later there were developments at the section office. The bureau announced that Lao He would be promoted to deputy section chief. Obviously thrilled, he wore a big smile all day long and could not stop taking off his glasses to wipe the lenses. Sun did not fare so well; he was still a deputy section chief. Sun should have been on the promotion list and felt he'd had a good shot at it, since he'd worked on all the important people. But he'd been passed over, wasting months of hard work. It came as a big blow, and he felt terrible. Worse yet, the newly promoted He could not hide his joy, the sight of which irritated Sun even more. After forming an alliance with He, Sun had helped him with all the necessary maneuvering and yet He, not Sun, had been promoted in the end. Mulling it over, Sun looked for a reason why he'd been passed over; ultimately, he blamed Lao Zhang. Sun was sure he'd been on the list until Lao Zhang came back to work, and must have read the documents supplied by He. He decided to avenge himself by bypassing Zhang. To him, the punishment the bureau meted out to Zhang was too light. As a deputy bureau chief, he should have been working in his office instead of using the place for personal pleasure. And yet all he received was a warning. That wasn't nearly tough enough. That in itself was a terrible practice, and was the cause of his suffering a vengeful slight.

In fact, Lao Sun was wrong—his being passed over had nothing to do with Lao Zhang; it was the administrative affairs chief who stopped the promotion. The bureau had planned for Sun to be the section head and He his deputy. While they were drawing up the document, the administrative affairs chief came to their office while they were denouncing Zhang and Qiao. On that day, Sun was outspoken, filled with indignation, nearly foaming at the mouth, which left a negative impression on the administrative chief. It was important to expose problems, but it was not necessary to go overboard. He went back and reported to Xiong, with the recommendation that they promote only He this time and "table" Sun so they could observe his work performance. Following the suggestion, Xiong brought up the case for discussion at the bureau meeting. Zhang, who had returned to work, was present but said nothing damaging to Sun. As a matter of fact, after his recent setback, he had decided to act with a clear conscience and endorse Sun for promotion. Zhang even praised him as highly competent; even though he'd heard how eagerly Sun had denounced him, he brushed it off as part of a difficult task facing every comrade. With someone speaking up on Sun's behalf at the bureau meeting, Sun should have been promoted despite the objection of the administrative affairs chief. But the issue was complicated by the very fact that his advocate was Zhang, not anyone else. In the others' view, Zhang himself had committed a transgression and should not consider himself their equal, which he completely understood and tried to conform to their expectations by being humble. But when he spoke up at the meeting, he sounded like their equal again, and that made everyone unhappy.

"Table him!" someone said.

"Use your head, not your heart, Lao Zhang. We must be cautious when promoting a cadre. We cannot demote him later. We've learned our lesson."

"Let's observe him for a while."

And just like that, Sun was "tabled" for further observation, to ensure a flawless promotion. In the end, he would have fared better had Zhang not spoken up for him. Naturally, Sun knew nothing about what transpired at the meeting, and was convinced that Zhang had been the spoiler. He fumed; there were times when he was able to see that it was just an official position, not worth getting upset over, but he simply could not get past the fact that he was as capable as the next man and yet had been stabbed in the back. He was more or less able to accept the outcome when he wasn't at work, but could not stomach the sight of a beaming He, his shallow colleague and former ally. Soon the anger, disappointment, and resentment piled up to affect his health and caused liver problems that put him in the hospital.

With Qiao retired and Sun on sick leave, Lao He took charge at the office, which was little more than supervising Lin and Peng, the only two left. But he was content with that, even opened his heart to his junior colleagues.

"There are only the three of us now, but our section will look as good as the others if we work hard. Numbers don't mean a thing. More people doesn't mean greater strength."

After his promotion, Lao He was among those who received a new housing assignment at the end of the year. He would be moving from Niujie to a two-room unit in a building by You'anmen. The non-stop good news had the tall, slight man squatting down in the office and sobbing, wetting his new lenses in the process. He blurted out to Xiao Lin, the only other person around, "Don't worry, Xiao Lin. I'm not the type to forget former colleagues after a promotion. Rest assured of that. This is not the office where Lao Qiao used to work, and there will be no more delay of your party membership. I'll fight for you at the next group meeting."

It had been a long time since Lin had received any good news of his own, so he was naturally happy to hear this.

"We've worked together for several years now, Lao He, and we know each other well. You haven't changed a bit since your promotion. I'll work hard and do my job well so you'll be proud of me."

They talked on like bosom pals. After work, when Lao He bought a roast chicken to celebrate with his family. So did Lin. But his wife was unhappy when she saw the chicken, a waste of money. When he excitedly related the good news, she grumbled, "Still, there's no need to buy a roast chicken. Is party membership worth that much? A sausage would have been enough!"

11

It was New Year's Day. Another truckload of pears was delivered from Zhangjiakou for everyone in the building. This time the truck did not break down, and the fruit was in fine shape. Once again, straw littered the area around the building. And once again Lao He and Xiao Lin brought the pears into the section office before borrowing a scale to divide them up and searching for containers to transport the fruit home. The pears were so nice they all wanted to take them home, which meant fewer discarded skins for Lin to sweep up.

Lao Sun was discharged from the hospital, but was still in poor shape, with a sallow face. He was often seen smoking quietly by himself, and turned over most of the office work to Lao He, who ran up and down the stairs to carry out his duties. But sometimes his eagerness was misapplied, leading to mistakes. Once, when the bureau asked their section to draft a document, Lao He decided to do it himself. He handed in more than thirty pages, for which Xiong rewarded him with the comment, "Wide of the mark." Xiong even went so far as to summon the administrative affairs chief, demanding to know how someone like that could have been promoted. The section chief was so nervous he began to sweat, eventually admitting that a mistake had been made. But now that He had been promoted and had already moved into the two-room unit, it would be hard to demote him. Xiong decided to let it go.

"Be careful next time," was all he could say.

The bureau wanted Sun to take charge of office operations, but he refused, unable to get over the fact that he was passed over, which convinced the higher-ups in the bureau that this particular section office could use a stronger leader. Sun, who began to act up after being "tabled," was definitely not the right person for the job. They decided to send a section head from outside when the time was right, news that Sun greeted with even less enthusiasm. He started to slack off at work, sometimes arriving late and leaving early, leaving his desk a mess and covered with dust. He appeared to have given up, the same immature behavior Xiao Lin had adopted when he first came to work, and that thrilled the chief of administrative affairs. He might have been wrong to promote Lao He, but at least he made the right decision not to promote Lao Sun, who was petty and buckled too easily under pressure. If Sun had been given the job of section head, Xiong would likely have criticized him again, he told himself.

Xiao Lin, on the other hand, was doing well. Lao He did work hard on his behalf and brought up his membership at a branch meeting, after promising to help with Lin's application. But no one at the meeting thought much of Lao He, despite his recent promotion, owing to his tendency to be long-winded and somewhat effeminate. As his words carried little weight and, with Lao Sun still hospitalized,

Lao He had been Lin's sole advocate, so no one gave much thought to his application. On the contrary, party members from the other sections made strong cases for their own colleagues, and in the end Lin was not among those whose applications were accepted.

He was, to be sure, dejected over the news, but that only lasted a few days before something good came his way. After Lao He and his family moved into the two-room unit, his old place on Niujie was vacant, and no one wanted to move in, because it was so remote. After a prolonged deliberation, Lin was given the place. He was overjoyed, even happier than he'd have been with a party membership. To him, the whole point of becoming a party member was a promotion that would make his life easier, not something ideologically lofty. The new place was on Niujie and not spacious, but it would be their own, not shared with the shrew. He wasn't sure if it would meet his wife's expectations, so he went home bearing good news, but with apprehension. In light of her complaint the previous time, he bought only a sausage to celebrate. To his delight, his wife was happy about the change.

"Niujie is good. It's great. I love the mutton there. Besides, I'd happily move to a dump so long as I didn't have to be around that shrew."

Then she demanded to know why he hadn't bought a roast chicken.

"You gave me hell for buying a roast chicken last time."

"That was for party membership. We deserve a chicken this time."

Which was why Lin had been feeling better than others.

As for Xiao Peng, she changed little. After Lao Qiao's early retirement, her life was better, now that her antagonist was gone, and she was often seen knitting sweaters in the office. Yet someone like her could not live without an antagonist for long. Being the newly promoted deputy section head, Lao He showed great enthusiasm in everything, frequently telling Peng to do this or that, and he became her antagonist after a while, frequently confronting him with choice words. Luckily Lao He was a softie who could deal with people who were submissive, but not get angry with anyone who dared talk back. In fact, he would brood over how that person felt, and as a result, they got along fine.

Lao Zhang continued to be chauffeured back and forth to work. After two months, bored with talk of the incident with Lao Qiao, people resumed their former relationship with him. The girls, too, were no longer intimidated. As for Zhang himself, he finally managed to put the tough, obsequious days behind him, and his wife not only stopped railing at him, but even joked about the incident occasionally. When he met other residents, he began to feel like their equal again and greeted them that way; he banged his car door as loud as ever. Once he ran into Lao Sun in the men's room at work. The partition between the two stalls had been taken down for repair, so they squatted in the same open space, a trying experience for them both. Sun recalled all his unhappy experiences with Zhang, while Zhang, after the baptism of his recent setback, could be forthright enough to break down the barrier between them. Knowing that Sun was resentful over the failed promotion, he said, "I want to say something to you, Lao Sun."

"Sure, go ahead." Sun knew he couldn't turn him down.

"You're a terrific comrade in every aspect but one, and that is the ability to get through hard times. Learning that would give you a boost."

Lao Sun held his tongue, but as he was walking out the door, he really let Lao Zhang have it: "You've got the heart of a beast. How dare you criticize me when you were involved in a sex scandal!"

He followed that up with a complaint about an unfair world. After committing such a major offense, Zhang not only suffered no disciplinary action, but was even allowed to remain in his position during the immediate aftermath of his error. As for Sun himself, though he'd worked hard for the party, he was dismissed like a rider thrown from his horse. How could they expect him to be proactive?

The pears were parceled out on the morning of the thirtieth, followed by a section luncheon. They ate in low spirits. Sun said nothing, while Xiao Peng busied herself with her knitting. Xiao Lin had his eye on the basket, which would be perfect for moving. Lao He tried to try to liven the mood by telling jokes. But he was so bad at it that no one laughed, which only made the atmosphere worse. They hastily finished their lunch and picked up their pears to head home.

Lin was the last to leave the office, wanting to wait for the basket. When he came downstairs, he ran into Lao Qiao, whose appearance in the office came as a surprise. She'd lost weight over the past few months, and there were bags under her eyes. Although she'd been the roadblock to his application to the party and had found fault with him whenever possible, Lin thought he ought to be nice to her now after what he'd said. In fact, he felt guilty when he noticed how thin she'd gotten, so he went up to greet her.

"You're back, Lao Qiao."

She was just as surprised to see him and was touched when he came up to talk to her. She had indeed tried to block his application, but he hadn't let that bother him. He wasn't so bad (a while earlier she'd run into Peng, who looked surprised but didn't say a word to her).

"Off work, Xiao Lin?"

"Yes. You're not busy today, I see."

"No, I'm free all day. Say, Xiao Lin, I won't be living in Beijing starting tomorrow."

"Really? Where are you going to live?"

"I'm moving to Shijiazhuang with my husband. I thought I'd come take another look at this place before I leave town. I started working here at the age of twenty-two, and before I leave I want to have one more look at the office where I spent thirty-two years of my life."

Lin knew what she meant and it make him feel bad. He wanted to say something to her, but the bus was about to take off, so he hurried off with a bag of pears in one hand and a basket in the other.

"So long, Lao Qiao."

"So long."

Officials

1

The eight county party secretaries were on their own when they came to a meeting in the provincial capital, like an ordinary production team leader coming to town from the countryside. They slept four to a room, and had to line up to buy food in the massive dining hall. They had all they could take of it after three days.

"Damn it. We wine and dine them when they come to our counties," Lao Zhou of Pi County complained. "But they make us eat out of the same pot when we come for a meeting."

"You said it!" The others agreed.

A discussion followed about eating out that night, but that involved the question of who would pay.

"Let's draw lots," someone suggested.

Lao Hu, a fair-skinned man from Nanxian County, sprawled on his bed to make four batches of lots, one each for liquor, vegetables, pork noodles, and egg drop soup. The idea was to have them draw lots from the four batches, so they'd each pay for one item, which seemed fair. But Jin Quanli of Chungong County would up with all four. Amid cheers from the other three, he tossed the lots out the window.

"That doesn't count," he said. "Let's do it again."

They ignored his protest and walked out with him.

"Of course it counts," Lao Bai from Wujiang County said. "It was just your luck. You'd have gotten a free meal if you hadn't drawn any lots, so with all four in your hand, you pay."

It was ten o'clock by the time they left the restaurant. They were arguing about whether the liquor was "up to par" when they spotted someone standing in the guesthouse entrance. It was Lu Hongwu, the district party secretary who headed their delegation.

"Where have you been?"

"We were dying for a decent meal, so we went to a restaurant, Mr. Lu."

Lao Zhou, from Pi County, took out a paper bag.

"Here, some leftover chicken giblets for you."

Lu laughed and said as he munched on the giblets:

"I couldn't find any of you when Director Shen of the Provincial party Organization Department wanted to talk to you."

They sobered up at the mention of Director Shen. They washed their feet and climbed into bed, but couldn't sleep that night. County secretaries were intimidated by the organization director, the way a production brigade branch secretary was cowed by a county secretary. Their future was in his hands. The position of deputy commissioner was vacant and they'd heard that it would likely be filled by one of the secretaries from the eight counties, though no one knew which. They had all undergone reviews recently, and since the director wanted to talk to them, maybe there was news. They'd been drinking together earlier; now one of them might be on the verge of a promotion. That was the only thing on their minds, and it drove away all thoughts of sleep. Zhou kept going out to use the toilet, while Bai couldn't stop spitting out the window. The next morning they got out of bed with dark circles under their eyes, and acted awkwardly with each other when they went out to wash up.

That day's agenda was a morning report by the new provincial party secretary, followed by a discussion in the afternoon. The discussion did not go well, for they had had trouble concentrating on the report; then the organization director had one-on-one meetings with each of them. They were summoned to Lu Hongwu's room, which was a step up, for it slept only two, with a private bathroom. Each emerged from the meeting with a sweaty forehead. The conversation consisted of nothing but harmless questions about their age, family situation, performance in their county, and future plans; they forgot everything they'd prepared and looked rattled. They were mortified and displeased with their performance as they emerged from Lu's room.

The matter seemed settled three days before the meeting ended. They heard that the organization director had sent a report to the provincial party secretary in which, based on cadre reviews and comments from the district party secretary, he recommended Jin Quanli for the position of deputy commissioner. The provincial party secretary happened to be holding a standing committee meeting that evening, so the recommendation was speedily approved. The organization director informed secretary Lu that the formal appointment would come down from provincial authorities the next month. The passed-over secretaries lost sleep again that night when they heard the news, but on the surface they reacted to the decision with high spirits and clamored for Jin to treat them to another meal.

"You've been promoted, Lao Jin. You'd better treat us to a good meal."

"No more drawing the lots this time."

"Who says I've been promoted?" Jin tried to fend them off. "I haven't seen the paperwork. Have you?"

"Come off it. We all know how it works. It's your treat."

So Jin treated them to another meal, but not everyone went this time. Zhou, Bai, and Hu stayed behind, and only Lao Cong from Zhu county and three others went. With fewer people this time, the atmosphere at the dinner table was strained. Cong, who had had worked with Jin on a socialist education campaign in the early 1960s, tried to console his old friend:

"Don't feel bad, Lao Jin. Something unexpected came up for Lao Zhou and others."

"We've known each other a long time, Lao Cong. I know my promotion has to have a negative effect on everyone else."

"Don't talk like that. No one would be that petty, not after so many years in the party."

"What is it then, if not pettiness?" Jin was clearly irritated. "The food is ready, but they're not here. They're obviously trying to embarrass me. We've worked together for years and I've treated them well whenever they visited my county. Besides, the decision was made at the provincial level. It's not up to me, so what can I say? To be honest with you, I don't care one bit about the position. We already have the use of a car and a guesthouse in the county, which is as good as a district office. I'm a party secretary now, but will only be a deputy commissioner in the district. Who knows what kind of abuse I'll suffer? They can have it if they want it. How about that?"

"Don't be upset," Cong said. "We have to work together in the future."

"I'm not upset. I know that everyone feels bad after working so hard all these years."

"Feeling bad accomplishes nothing. It won't change the decision."

"Drink up," a couple of the men at the table said. "No more talk about that."

They ran into Zhou, Hu, and Bai on their way back to the guesthouse. Jin was still peeved, while Zhou and the other two, feeling sheepish for missing the dinner, came over to talk to him. The incident blew over after some bantering.

Zhou and the others were uncomfortable with Jin not simply because they had stayed away from the dinner. While Jin was ranting about them at the restaurant, they had learned that Jin was promoted because he was an old school chum of the new provincial party secretary, Xiong Qingquan. They felt better now, because, with a connection like that, Jin was entitled to the promotion. Zhou or Hu would have been promoted instead if they'd been a school chum of the provincial party secretary. They realized that they shouldn't be unhappy with Jin, once the logic was clear to them; besides, his promotion was settled, so what was the point of being resentful? Jin was a decent man and they got along well. So they went up to chat with him when he came back from the restaurant, and the incident blew over quickly. On his part, Jin forgave Zhou and others after seeing the change in their attitude; he even reproached himself for being petty. They were permitted to be upset when they first heard about his promotion, weren't they? The former amicable feelings returned to their shared room. When it was time to turn off the light and go to sleep, Hu went over to the door in his baggy underpants.

"Let's get this settled first, Lao Jin," he said. "Don't lord it over us after you become our boss. We won't take it if you do."

The others joined in with their friendly threats.

"That's right."

"Right, we won't take it."

"We'll treat him with standard meals at our counties if he does."

"How can I lord it over anyone, with a chickenshit position like that?" Jin said. "I'll just go to a restaurant if you refuse to feed me."

"Right!" The others laughed. "We'll let him pay for his own food."

On the day the meeting ended, each county sent a car to pick up their party secretary. They shook hands, inviting each other to visit before getting into their cars. Zhou pointed at his Nissan Bluebird when he saw Jin's old Shanghai.

"Come on, Lao Jin. I'll give you a ride back."

Jin told his driver to go back on his own and got into Zhou's car. When they reached Zhou's county, Zhou had the driver take them to the guesthouse, where he ordered a hot pot, some crab, and a turtle soup, plus a bottle of liquor, *Wuliangye*. They ate and drank their fill before Zhou had his driver take Jin home.

2

In fact, Xiong Qingquan and Jin Quanli were not school chums; they had just met ten years earlier when they'd shared a room at a conference for deputy county party secretaries in Dazhai. Both were given to drink, but had only a moderate capacity for liquor, which brought them together. During the day, they went on tours, while at night they shared drinks at a local diner, where they vied to pay. One night Xiong got drunk and threw up in the room. Jin got dressed and went out to find some coal cinders to sweep the mess up. They were young and could talk about anything, chatting in bed about pretty girls in their counties and giving each other a "quota" if they were to visit the other's county. By the time they parted two weeks later, they had become good friends, and were teary-eyed when they invited each other to visit.

They lost contact after that, however, and never made the visits. When Xiong showed up ten years later, he had done very well for himself, having been promoted to provincial secretary general. Before then, Jin had come across Xiong's name in the paper, chronicling his promotion to secretary for the planning commission, to director of an agriculture committee, secretary-general of the provincial party committee, vice governor, member of the provincial standing committee, to governor. But Jin never made the connection, since so many people shared names. Not until this meeting, when he sat in the meeting hall and listened to a report by the provincial secretary general, did he learn that the Xiong in the newspaper was none other than the man he'd met ten years before. Except for a fuller face, a thicker waist, and grayer hair, he was the same as always. But he was a different man once he opened his mouth. Xiong could really talk, going on for four hours without notes, and he knew everything, from the central government down to administrative villages, with the international production modes thrown in. He was, clearly, no longer the man who had talked about women in a guesthouse.

Jin realized how much he lagged behind Xiong in knowledge of the world and leadership qualities, not only in the area of career advancement. He'd wanted to go up and chat with his old friend, but changed his mind and walked out of the hall with the others. What would he say to him? What would he look like in the midst of all the provincial cadres surrounding Xiong? Jin blushed at the thought of seeking out his old friend. Imagine his surprise when Xiong not only remembered him, but helped him out behind the scenes soon after he arrived in the provincial office. Jin knew he would never have been promoted without Xiong's help, for Zhou and the others were equally competent, with similarly fine performance records in their counties. Why couldn't any of them have been chosen to fill the vacancy? Jin was also impressed by Xiong, who, as the provincial party secretary general, must have known countless people, and yet still remembered someone he'd had a few drinks with ten years earlier. Someone who cherished friendships was rare among ordinary people, let alone provincial cadres. Those in the central government had been wise to promote Xiong, an outstanding individual.

Jin was filled with admiration for Xiong, though he hadn't felt comfortable seeking him out at the meeting. The next time they met, he told himself, he would not greet him as an old friend, but would act according to his position as a subordinate, showing Xiong the respect he deserved and following his instructions. He would never brag about his connection with the provincial party secretary general, unlike some shallow people he knew, who were notorious name-droppers. If anyone were to ask him if he knew Xiong Qingquan, he would say, "I heard him give a report once," which was the right response to show his own humility while protecting Xiong's reputation.

He vowed that he would, after assuming the position of deputy commissioner, devote himself to his work to show the party how he appreciated the nurturing. His wife and child would stay behind at first so he could concentrate on doing his job well and have something to show for it.

As these thoughts swirled in his head, Jin returned to his county seat, a less affluent place than the one headed by Zhou or Hu.

Not all the roads were lit at night, dead piglets were often seen floating in the two open sewer lines, and sugarcane peels littered the streets. These were the sights that had always bothered him, but now he found them endearing. The town did have unlit areas, but the sparkling stars were a joy to behold. No matter what, it was a place where he had worked for more than a decade.

As they entered the county seat, he told Zhou's driver to take him to the guesthouse, where he got a room to take a bath. Soon his office manager arrived to give him updates. After telling the man to give Zhou's driver two cartons of cigarettes and send him home, Jin went to take his bath while the director gave his report from outside the bathroom. The updates were merely about what had happened during his absence over the past few days, but the director tried to pry out some news when he was done with the report,

"There's a rumor going around the county town, Mr. Jin."

"What is it this time?"

"People are saying you'll be leaving us soon to work at the district office."

Jin came out, wrapped in a towel.

"I didn't know that. How come I never heard of that? Who's saying I'm leaving? Do you want me to leave?"

"It would be wonderful for you, Mr. Jin." The director laughed as he handed Jin a cup of hot tea. "But we don't want you to leave."

A bowl of noodles was delivered. Jin ate while the director said from across the table, "There's something else, Mr. Jin."

"What is it?"

"There's a township chief meeting tomorrow."

Jin's mood soured and he dropped his chopsticks onto the table with a frown. He did not get along with the county chief, Xiao Mao, a young cadre who had been recently promoted to the position as a college graduate, at a time when emphasis was being placed on youth and knowledge. Mao had done well in the past, but his promotion had gone to his head; now he talked big at county meetings and during reports to higher-ups, as if he could change the county overnight. Jin was supposed to give the report when Lu Hongwu made a visit to the county, but Mao often interrupted him, as if he knew better than Jin. Naturally that ticked Jin off. *Who is No. 1 in this county anyway? How long have you been here? You were nursing at your mother's breast when I became a county level cadre.* Jin grumbled silently, and gradually formed an impression of the young man as fickle and showy, with little substance. Mao, on the other hand, complained that Jin was stubborn, conservative, rigid, and uninterested in progress. Once Jin heard that Mao had said to a group of young clerks at a dinner, "We need a personnel change in Chungong County; otherwise nothing will get better."

Jin was so outraged that he smashed a cup.

"Why not make him party secretary and everything will get better? He was saying the provincial and district leaders are blind to the fact that I've been bringing harm to the people. So he's better than them, I guess. If that's case, why isn't he working at central government headquarters?"

To be sure, their clashes were veiled at first, limited to complaints behind each other's back, and they remained cordial when they met. They did what was required of them when they sat together at a speakers' table. Jin would have to say, "I totally agree with what Chief Mao has just said, and would like to add a few things."

For his part, Mao had to respond with, "What Secretary Jin said was absolutely right and necessary. We must follow his suggestion thoroughly."

But that did not last long, as they began to disagree in public. Once, after Jin had told Mao to attend a county-party committee, Mao chose to accompany a section chief from the provincial government office on a tour of the county. Jin was incensed over the young man's impertinence.

"Does he still consider himself a party member? Why didn't he send his deputy and attend the meeting? Why go himself? He may be young, but he already knows how to suck up to the higher-ups." Jin was not done with his angry outburst. "He thinks he's hot shit, but I can't see anything special about him except that he has the same last name as Chairman Mao."

Mao was naturally unhappy when told about Jin's comment, and made a point of staying away from the next county meeting. Jin then returned the lack of courtesy by not attending meetings at the county office.

"There's no need for me to give a speech. Chief Mao can do it. Aren't we supposed to keep party and government separate?"

A pattern gradually formed: Mao was absent at the meetings of the county party committee while Jin stayed away from those held by the county chief. Which was why Jin frowned when his office manager mentioned a county meeting. He frowned again and dropped the noodles he had just picked up.

"He can have all the meetings he wants. Why tell me?"

"Of course, Mr. Jin, I would have ignored it if this were an ordinary meeting. But Chief Mao was driven over to our office to say that he wanted to know the moment you returned and he asked you to speak at the meeting. So, I'd like to know whether I should let him know."

"No, don't tell him." Jin was adamant. "Arrange for a car for tomorrow so I can check on the people in Dachun Village. I'll be with the masses while he has his meeting!"

"All right, I won't tell him," the director continued. "And I'll go get the car ready now."

"Go have your meeting," Jin mumbled to himself as he walked out of the guesthouse. "I won't be there." He experienced a surge of pride.

"You think so highly of yourself that you can treat me with contempt, but now realities prove that the party trusts me, not you. Why weren't you promoted to be the deputy commissioner if you're so hot? They wouldn't have picked me if I didn't know a thing or two. You'd better not be so arrogant, because I'll be your direct superior once I start work for the district. You'll do what I ask you to do; you'll give me a report on your performance in the county when I come down to Chungong County. You think you're the Monkey King with all sorts of magic tricks? Well, we'll see how you fare in the palm of my hand."

Jin was enjoying these fanciful thoughts as he walked down the street on his way home. He was eager to see his family after a two-week absence. A VW Santana coming toward him stopped and a man stepped out. It was Mao, dressed in his usual suit but wearing a cap.

"I see you're back, Secretary Jin," Mao greeted him.

Jin was surprised to hear himself addressed that way. Mao had shown him respect when the young man first arrived, always calling him Mr. Jin; later he changed it Lao Jin, when his disrespect caused problems between them. Jin thought he must have misheard, but Mao came up and took his hands.

"Comrades at the office told me you were back, so I rushed over to welcome you home, Secretary Jin."

With self-restraint learned from years of experience as a cadre, Jin said with a smile, "I was on my way to see you at your home."

"Hop in and we'll go together." Mao was pleased by what he heard. "I have a bottle of Gujing."

Jin could not say no, so he went along. When they got there, Mao told his wife to prepare some food while the men began drinking.

"Please come give a speech at tomorrow's county meeting, Secretary Jin," Mao said after three rounds.

"There's no need for me to go." Not letting the alcohol go to his head, Jin stuck to his principles and bottom line. "You can give the speech. After being away for two weeks, I'm not up to date on what's been happening."

"You have to go, Secretary Jin. Two weeks isn't such a long time, and I'm sure you know everything. Besides, I'd like you to share what you learned at the provincial meeting."

"I'm not prepared for that. I'm actually thinking about calling a meeting for township party secretaries, and that's when I'll pass on what transpired at the provincial meeting."

"Then let's do this. I'll move my meeting back, and we'll hold the two meetings at the same time."

"I don't think it's a good idea, mixing the two."

"Why not?" Mao asked, while picking up the phone to call his office.

"Notify the townships that the meeting will be postponed a day." Mao put down the phone and refilled Jin's glass.

"I have something to tell you, Secretary. Jin."

"Go ahead."

"I've heard, Secretary Jin, that you'll be leaving Chungong County soon. I've been working under you for three years, and, to tell you the truth, I've learned a lot from you. But as I was too young and too inexperienced, I was out of line in many instances after first taking up my position here. I wasn't aware of how badly I behaved until a couple of days ago, when I heard about your imminent departure, and then it hit me. I'm young, so please forgive my transgressions, Secretary Jin."

The young man's words were heartwarming, and Jin was moved, for Mao had never said anything quite like that before. Jin was so touched, his mood lightened and he felt magnanimous. There was no need to be petty with Mao, now that he would soon be an assistant commissioner. It was only normal for a young man to be arrogant when he first got the job; Jin felt partially responsible for not being a mentor to him. He was reminded of Xiong, a generous man who recalled a casual acquaintance from ten years before, and reproached himself for bearing grudges.

"Don't talk like that, Chief Mao," Jin said after downing another glass. "We worked well together."

"Please call me Xiao Mao."

"All right, Xiao Mao," Jin said with a laugh. "If we had some issues, it was my fault, since I'm older."

"No, it was my fault," Mao said with an earnest nod, before picking up the phone and handing it to Jin. "Please call your office."

Jin had no choice but to have the operator connect him to his office. "Notify the townships that we'll have a party secretary meeting the day after tomorrow," he said to the office manager.

"Perfect!" Mao laughed heartily. "That's great. You'll be the main speaker, and I'll lend moral support."

"We'll both speak."

Mao presided over the joint meetings two days later. He tapped the microphone on the speakers' table to get everyone's attention.

"We have two tasks today, comrades. One, Secretary Jin will pass on what he learned at the provincial party secretary meeting, and two, we'll have a farewell party for Secretary Jin, who will be leaving Chungong County in a few days. Commissioner Jin has been here for more than a decade and has made tremendous contributions to our county. I'm sure he feels an emotional attachment to this place, and we hope he will make frequent visits to a place where he lived and worked. The eight hundred thousand residents of Chungong County will always welcome him. Now, I'd like to invite Secretary Jin to speak."

Thunderous applause erupted in the hall.

Touched by Mao's words and the applause, Jin stood up and bowed emotionally, prompting another round of applause. He waited until it was quiet again before relaying what Secretary Xiong had said at the meeting.

The warm feeling lingered as he was driven home after the meeting. He said to his office manager, who was sitting next to the driver, that the cadres in their county were not bad, adding that he felt strongly about them, including those he had criticized before.

"Xiao Mao isn't bad, either."

"I want to tell you something, Secretary Jin, and please don't be upset," the officer manager said.

"Go ahead."

"The comrades at the county party committee are all saying you must not be deceived by Little Mao. You know what he's been like. He's showering you with respect now purely for personal reasons. You'll be the deputy commissioner soon, which will affect him directly. Besides, he wants your job. Do you think he'd be so respectful if you were demoted, instead of being promoted?"

Jin felt a chill on his back. What his office manager said probably wasn't wide of the mark. The ceremonious scene at the meeting lost its some of its luster, but, feeling disheartened, he glared at the office manager.

"What sort of nonsense is that, making Chief Mao look bad? I don't believe a word of it. We're all party members and we must treat each other with respect. We must not be petty. As a standing member of the county party committee, how can you say something like that?"

"I knew you wouldn't believe me," the office manager said, clearly stung by the unfair rebuke.

3

Jin Quanli had been in office a month.

He arrived at the commission with enthusiasm; the promotion delighted his family. In fact, his wife had a toothache the day of the announcement, and the good news drove away the pain. He had strong ties with party cadres and ordinary residents of Chungong County, most of whom were decent people; he wasn't quite sure if Chief Mao was scheming or not. On the day he left for the new job, many people showed up at the county building to see him off, surrounding his car and delaying his departure; some female comrades even wept. So as he was being driven away, he vowed not to disappoint them and do a good job as the deputy commissioner. But he was barely a month into the new job before he began to realize that it would be a challenge.

For one thing, his approach to work needed some adjustment. As county party secretary, he loved driving around the county to check things out, something he could not do in his new position. He spent all his time in the administrative office building, pushing paper. Once when Lu Hongwu showed up at his office and asked, "How's it going, Lao Jin? Gotten used to everything here?"

"Not yet, Secretary Lu." He decided to be frank. "I feel so constrained."

"You'll get used to it," Lu said with a laugh.

Then there was the change in status. He'd been the man at the top in the county, where everyone did what he wanted, but now all that changed. Being a deputy commissioner meant he had to seek instructions from his immediate superior, the commissioner, and the district party secretary. It had been a long time since he'd had to ask for instructions, so he had to learn that all over. Luckily, Secretary Lu was an old friend and Commissioner Wu was easy to get along with. Still, it annoyed him that he couldn't make a single decision on his own and must run everything by his superiors, which led him to grumble in private that the promotion wasn't worth it. It was a demotion in disguise.

In his daily life, he also encountered problems. For instance, he loved a hot bath whenever possible. Back at the county office, he simply headed to the guesthouse and told the staff to run some hot water. It wasn't that easy at the new place. Sure, there was a guesthouse, and it was better appointed than the county one, but in today's China a damned deputy anything was a nobody. In fact, there were dozens of deputy district cadres, including retirees, and the guesthouse could not handle them all at the same time. Once, when he went for a bath and told the staff to run hot water, as he had used to do, one of them said,

"There's no hot water."

"How come?" He was surprised.

"Where am I supposed to get hot water when they stop working in the boiler room?"

The nonchalant attitude infuriated Jin.

"Do you know who I am?"

For that question, Jin got a sideways glance. "Aren't you Mr. Jin, the *deputy* commissioner? We wouldn't have hot water even if Commissioner Wu himself showed up."

If that had happened back at the county, Jin would have barked:

"Where's the manager? I want this man fired, and tell the boiler room to get hot water ready."

But he couldn't say that here. It might not work in the first place, and would make him look bad. So he had to swallow his pride and, with a sigh, go for a soak at a public bathhouse.

Meals were another problem. With frequent visitors to the county, he had been able to eat anything anywhere, but now, with his wife still back at the old place, he had to line up in the dining hall to buy food, which reminded him of the meeting at the provincial capital. He was rarely asked to join the district secretary or commissioner when they hosted a visitor from the provincial office. His palate needed something better after a month, so he went to a restaurant one day and treated himself to some good food and drink. The next time he had something decent to eat was when he visited Zhu County, where he enjoyed Lao Cong's hospitality. Cong, a dependable hard worker, came to report on work progress the moment he arrived. After the report, Cong asked, "What would you like for lunch, Mr. Commissioner?"

"I'll have whatever is good. I haven't had a good meal in a month."

Then there was the matter of transportation, another inconvenience. He'd had a car and driver in the county, which meant he could go anywhere any time he wanted. At the district office, only the party secretary and commissioner had their own cars; deputies had to request the use of a car when they needed one.

He could always get a car when he wanted, but he hated having to ask, and he never got the same one. It didn't feel quite right to keep switching from Bluebird, to Volga, to Shanghai, to a tiny Lada. In the past, he could stop on a whim; now he had to watch what he said to the driver.

But all these unpleasant changes paled in comparison with the nature of his work. Before he started, Lu and Wu had wanted to place him in charge of rural and small town enterprises as well as urban construction, areas familiar to him, and that pleased him. Then another deputy commissioner, Chen Erdai, started giving him a hard time. A stumpy man with an upturned nose, Chen had little regard for his peers because he had once worked in the organization section of the provincial party committee. He was a bully through and through. For instance, he managed to monopolize a Toyota Crown, even though none of the district deputies had a private car and driver; behind his back everyone else called him "Two-fifty," slang for an idiot, from the last three digits of the license plate. Two-fifty was contemptuous of Jin, who had just been promoted from the county level. Originally in charge of disciplinary investigation and family planning, he declared he didn't want to do that anymore the day after Jin's arrival, even though it was his kind of work; instead, he wanted Jin's job. A perennial bully, he had cowed Lu and Wu into asking Jin to switch with Chen. He was pissed. He liked rural and small town enterprises and urban construction, which could be seen by everyone and easily showed results. In contrast, disciplinary investigation and family planning was a thankless portfolio that antagonized people. Chen was clearly bullying Jin, the newcomer.

"I don't want disciplinary investigation and family planning, Secretary Lu," Jin said. "I want to work on what I know best."

"Let it go, Lao Jin. What difference does it make what you do? That's the way he is, so don't mind him."

"I'll do what you ask, but he shouldn't push me around like that. If that's how things work here I'd rather go back to the county office."

"Don't say that. Couldn't you just take on the job for my sake?"

Which was how Jin came to be in charge of discipline investigation and family planning.

After stumbling along for a month, he slowly made adjustments and, once he knew more about what it entailed, the work became easier. Sitting behind a desk was no longer a problem and, in fact, he started to see how exhausting it had been to run around all the time. Now he could even go to a movie in the evening if he was free. Transportation was no longer an issue, for it made no difference to him what kind of car it was, as long as it ran well. He would treat himself to a good meal at a restaurant or visit a neighboring county if he was bored with the dining hall food. The bathing problem was also solved. The tourist board had a guesthouse on Zhengfu Street; the manager, who was originally from Chungong County, showed Jin the respect he deserved and let him have a bath any time he wanted. He even managed to earn admiration from Two-fifty, who was impressed when he displayed no sign of displeasure in their interactions, after he had wrestled the portfolio from Jin. He began to treat him with deference after learning that Xiong Qingquan was an old friend of Jin's, and asked Jin to join him at a banquet for the director of the provincial planning committee.

Once he became familiar with the place and the people, Jin had room to maneuver, which improved his mood and in turn convinced him that his current position was better than his former one. He was addressed as "Commissioner," not "Secretary," and he outranked his former peers when he visited their counties, giving him a sense of superiority. Xiao Mao made a point of paying him a visit when he came to a meeting at the district office, bringing along a basket of apples for his pleasure. As he bit into an apple, Jin was pleased with himself, so much so that he forgave Mao for all his faults. As a result, he did not object when Lu Hongwu recommended Mao as Jin's successor. Everyone else at the meeting with the district party secretary and Commissioner Lu raised their hands in support, and Mao became the new party secretary of Chungong County. Jin Quanli raised no objection.

4

A call came from the provincial party committee to say that the general secretary, Xiong Qingquan, would be visiting their district on an inspection tour in two days. This was the new general secretary's first visit, which put Lu and Wu on edge, for neither of them knew the man. Feeling the pressure, everyone shifted into high gear, preparing presentation material for their bosses.

Jin heard the news the day after the call. Excited at the prospect of seeing an old friend after ten years, he quickly went to the guesthouse for a bath and a shave and did his laundry. As he scrubbed his clothes, his excitement turned into anxiety when he recalled how his old friend, now the general secretary, talked. Ignoring his laundry, he returned to his office to write out answers to questions Xiong might ask. Then Jin had second thoughts; Lu and Wu would surely accompany Xiong, while the deputies might not get a chance to meet him. Wouldn't he be wasting his time and energy preparing notes if none of the deputies was included in the retinue? He was laughing at his earlier jitters when Lu opened his office door and walked in.

"Comrade Xiong will be here tomorrow, Lao Jin. You're an old friend of his, so come along with us."

Jin was pleased to be asked along, but he had to show humility: "With the two of you accompanying him, I'll stay behind."

"No, you have to come with us," Lu insisted. "He's an old friend of yours, so you have to meet him. Besides, I don't know much about him, and we'll feel better with you around."

Jin had to suppress his self-satisfaction before saying, "Comrade Xiong is actually quite approachable."

"Is that so? He looked so serious when he gave a report at the provincial committee."

"Of course he had to look serious on that occasion."

"You're right. That was a different occasion." Lu nodded. "I wonder what kind of questions he'll ask," he continued.

"Most likely about agriculture, industries, and rural and small enterprises, and maybe with cultural and ideological progress thrown in. What else could he want to know?"

"We're prepared for those. We're just worried he might ask some unusual questions, and it will be awkward if we don't know what to say."

"I doubt he'll do that. He's new, so I don't think he wants to make things hard on us."

"You're right, but I do want to work on it some more. I'm going to have some numbers verified at the statistics section." He hurried off.

After Lu left, Jin continued with his own notes. In addition to questions from Lu, he also worked on questions he might be asked, just in case.

A contingent of people from the district and administrative offices went to greet Xiong at the guesthouse the following morning. A call was placed to the provincial secretary's office to see if Xiong had left. They were told he'd left at eight that morning, right on time; everyone's nerves were on edge at half past nine, since the drive normally took two hours.

Lu sought out Jin.

"Tell me what Comrade Qingquan is like, Lao Jin."

"What do you mean?"

"For instance, does he like to drink? Is he picky about what he eats? Should we have the kitchen make him something special or will simple fare be better?"

"He used to love to drink," Jin said based on what he knew. "But I have no idea if that has changed."

"That makes it tough," Lu said with a sigh. "It's already nine thirty. What shall I tell the kitchen?"

Seeing that Lu was in a jam, Jin felt sorry for him.

"He's not a difficult man and he's not picky."

"It's just that this is the first time for us. How's this? Since you're an old friend of his, why don't you ask him in private what he likes. We could offer something fancy if it suits his taste and of course we'll do what he wants if he insists on simple fare. You couldn't know, but when Governor Ma visited the Quyang area, the district office put on a feast for him. The old man loves to eat, but he decided to be righteous that day and gave them hell. He pointed at the table and demanded something simple, making the comrades at the district office look really bad."

"Sure. I'll ask him."

"Great. I'll have the kitchen prepare two meals and we'll bring out whatever he likes." Lu raced over to the dining hall.

Jin was besieged by uneasiness after Lu left, feeling the weight of the onerous burden. He felt like kicking himself for talking big. He hadn't seen Xiong for ten years and really had no idea whether he should ask him or not.

Everyone crowded around the guesthouse entrance at ten to welcome Xiong's motorcade, but by ten thirty, there was still no sign of him.

They were getting anxious, which worsened when Xiong still had not shown at eleven.

"Could he have taken a turn and stopped along the way?" Wu asked Lu. "Should we have everyone go back to work?"

"Let's wait in the conference room," Lu said before turning to the director of the district office. "You wait here and let us know when you see his car."

They went into the conference room, where some shared their comments while others smoked. Before long, the office director ran in.

"They're here!" He was breathless. "They've arrived."

Everyone stopped talking and surged into the courtyard as Xiong's three-car motorcade reached the entrance. Xiong's secretary and assistants got out first, followed by a smiling Xiong, who shook hands with those waiting for him.

"Was the traffic bad, Comrade Xiong?" someone asked.

"No, it was fine. We just stopped briefly along the way. I'm sorry to have made you wait so long."

"We ran into a peasant cutting down cotton stalks and Comrade Xiong stopped to chat with him," his assistant said.

After Xiong shook hands all around, Lu said,

"It's twelve thirty already, Comrade Xiong, so why don't we have lunch first?"

"Sure. Let's get something to eat."

As they headed to the guesthouse restaurant, Lu poked Jin in the waist, signaling him to ask Xiong what he'd like for lunch. But Jin was in the dumps, for Xiong had treated him, an old friend, just like everyone else when they shook hands; he didn't even show a sign of recognition. Maybe he'd forgotten him now that it had been ten years and he was a big shot. But then Jin was reminded of his own promotion; why would Xiong help him out? Unable to find an answer, Jin was confused and conflicted; he couldn't bring himself to ask Xiong when Lu poked at him. Luckily, Xiong spoke up and unintentionally solved Jin's dilemma.

"What are we having for lunch? How about a bowl of noodles each and we'll talk after lunch."

"Yes, right. Noodles it is," Lu said, poking his office manager to alert the kitchen staff, since he hadn't asked them to prepare noodles, either as part of a fancy or a simple meal. A car had to be sent out to buy noodles, so they all had to wait. It was one in the afternoon by the time noodles were brought in.

"Comrade Xiong must be starving," Wu said.

"I am hungry, but I wasn't about to say so unless you did."

Everyone had a good laugh over his response, especially Wu, whose face turned bright red. The laughter died down, replaced by the sound of everyone slurping noodles.

They went into the conference room when lunch was over. Earlier, when Lu learned of Xiong's lunch choice, he told his office manager to bring out cups of green tea, replacing the club soda and Coca-Cola that had been laid out for the meeting. A cup of tea in hand, they listened as Lu and Wu gave reports on their progress in industry, agriculture, and rural and small town enterprises.

Xiong spoke up midway through the reports:

"Can you hurry this up, Lao Lu? I heard about your famous Mount Lang, with its temple and monks. Are you trying to stop me from visiting the place?"

Everyone laughed again.

"Of course not." Lu raced through his report. "Now for your instructions, Comrade Xiong."

"I just got here, so what do I know?" He pointed to Wu. "Mr. Wu here is a veteran comrade, so why don't you say something?"

"You're being too modest, Comrade Xiong." Wu's face turned red from the attention. "You needn't be so modest. I'm here to give you a report and we await your instructions."

Xiong threw off a few comments, which could be summarized as one, be practical and realistic, and two, be sure to consult with experienced comrades, such as Mr. Wu. Wu was naturally flattered again as everyone applauded. Then they all climbed into cars heading out to Mount Lang to see the temple and monks.

Xiong did not exchange a word with Jin the whole time. He was stung by the slight, as he noticed Two-fifty glancing at him constantly, as if doubting his relationship with the secretary general. It was obvious that Xiong had forgotten him; it was also clear from Xiong's behavior that of all the people in the district office, he thought highly of Wu only, mentioning the latter whenever possible. He asked Wu, not Lu, to ride in his Mercedes before they left for Mount Lang. Wu would soon step down from his leadership position, so why would Xiong value him so much? Jin could not understand, nor could anyone else, it seemed.

They returned to the guesthouse for dinner after the outing. When they finished, Xiong was invited to rest for the day.

"Sure, we'll call it a day. There's a match tonight. You can watch it on TV."

Everyone dispersed after shaking hands with him. When they walked out of the guesthouse to go their separate ways, Xiong's assistant ran out to Jin.

"You must be Comrade Jin Quanli."

"Yes, I am."

"Comrade Xiong would like to invite you in for a chat."

Feeling the blood rush to his head, Jin said repeatedly, "Sure." The unhappiness from the perceived slight that had been building all afternoon vanished. The old friend from ten years before hadn't forgotten him after all. He cast a meaningful glance at Two-fifty before following Xiong's assistant inside.

Xiong was taking a bath when they walked in, so the assistant said to Jin, "I hope you don't mind waiting awhile."

He walked out, leaving Jin standing in the room.

Twenty minutes later, Xiong walked out, draped in a towel, drying his hair along the way. He chortled when he saw Jin before thumping him in the belly.

"Why are you standing there?"

Jin took a seat.

"Look at you. Do you still remember me?"

"Of course I do, Secretary Xiong." Jin stood up.

"Do you still drink?"

"No more."

"Bullshit. You did ten years ago, and now you don't?"

"All right, I do."

"Don't be so uptight." Xiong had a big laugh. "You weren't like this back in Dazhai. Sit down."

Feeling more at ease at the mention of Dazhai, Jin sat down and laughed with him.

"Tell me, why are you acting this way? Like a bashful young girl."

"I'm terrified of you, now that you're the secretary general." Jin had to tell the truth.

Xiong laughed again before taking a bottle of Yanghe from his briefcase.

"Will you join me?"

"Of course."

Xiong opened the bottle and took a swig before handing it over to Jin, as they'd done back at Dazhai. Jin took a drink.

"Your district is terrible. No one offered me a drink."

"We wanted to. We had something ready for you, but didn't bring it out because we didn't want you to criticize us." Jin offered the truth.

Xiong got dressed and took a seat across from Jin.

"You're right," Xiong said with a sigh. "I'm not free to do anything since the promotion. I can't even drink now."

Reminded of Xiong's help with his promotion, Jin felt compelled to show his gratitude, so he said, "I heard the moment you arrived in the provincial office. I wanted to go see you, General Secretary, but didn't because I knew how busy you must be. You have so much to do and yet you remembered me and looked into my advancement—"

Jin waved him off.

"No more of that, Lao Jin. I didn't help you with anything. As a new arrival, I don't know much about the situation here, so I treat everyone the same whether I know them or not, and I don't care for crass maneuvering. You have absolutely no reason to thank me if you're referring to your promotion, because I had nothing to do with it. You were nominated by the organization section at the provincial party and the district party committee levels, and your promotion was discussed and passed at the provincial standing committee. You just do a good job and don't think about anything else. You can thank the party if you want."

Jin nodded. His admiration for Xiong mounted.

"You've made tremendous progress over the years, Secretary Xiong."

It sounded off to him, but Xiong didn't seem to mind as he lit a cigarette.

"It's all due to the training and encouragement of the party. Without it, I wouldn't have been able to go anywhere or made any improvement."

Xiong changed the subject and started talking about other things before asking Jin about his work. Jin told him he had finally gotten used to working at the district office, to which Xiong responded with a nod.

"Since you're new, you ought to ask the senior comrades for advice if you aren't sure of something. You must learn to respect them, particularly Lao Wu, here in this district office."

Jin nodded rigorously to show he understood.

They talked until nine o'clock, time for the match to begin. Xiong turned on the TV, so Jin got up to leave.

"All right. Call me if you need anything. The people at the district office aren't bad. Lao Wu and Lao Lu are good people."

The implication wasn't lost on Jin, who nodded again with gratitude.

"I won't forget what you said, Secretary Xiong. I'll be going now, so you can rest."

Xiong insisted on walking him out.

Early the next morning, as Xiong was leaving to visit another district, everyone came out to see him off. Xiong shook hands with them, again treating Jin like everyone else, with no extra words to him. Knowing enough not to feel slighted by then, Jin was even more impressed by how Xiong conducted himself.

5

Jin Quanli was a completely different person after Xiong's visit. No longer bothered by advantages or disadvantages at the office, he threw himself into his work, sitting at his desk reading documents or traveling out to the counties; he didn't care which car he got and always treated the driver cordially; he ignored Two-fifty and showed old Mr. Wu his utmost respect by consulting with the old man whenever he wasn't sure how to proceed. On weekends, he visited the old man at home and wrote down everything he said. Wu was impressed.

"I have some advice for you, Lao Jin," Wu said to him once.

"By all means, Mr. Wu. As my elder, your criticism of me is a sign of concern."

"Expand the scope of your work," he said with a nod. "Don't limit your focus to disciplinary investigations and family planning. You should keep your eyes on other areas as well. But of course, just keep an eye out, don't interfere. I'll be stepping down in a couple of years and you young people will have to take over."

Jin was so touched he was nearly in tears.

"Please don't talk like that, Mr. Wu," Jin said earnestly. "It makes me feel terrible to hear you talk about stepping down. The district cadres and masses wouldn't let you do that. As for me, I've learned so much from you."

"This is just between us. Don't mention it to anyone else. I rode with Comrade Xiong when he was here and he shared some of his thoughts with me in the car. He's a good man and the central government was right to promote him. He has my utmost respect."

"He has nothing but respect for you, too," Jin said.

"I just felt bad that we offered him nothing but noodles."

"He's from Henan and loves the stuff."

Wu laughed.

Jin worked even harder after this conversation.

An assistant from the administrative office opened his door one Thursday when he was reading files.

"Someone's here to see you, Commissioner Jin. Will you meet with him?"

"Who is it?"

"He just said he wants to file a complaint."

"Sure, send him in." Jin thought it was another exposé against a cadre. "He's come a long way to see me."

Jin was surprised when the assistant showed the visitor in; it was the officer manager from the Chungong county party office.

"What are you up to, Lao Zhong?" Jin laughed. "You know you can come see me directly. Why did you say you're here to lodge a complaint?"

"This isn't a personal visit, Commissioner Jin," Zhong said, clearly angry. "I am here to file a complaint. You're in charge of discipline investigations, aren't you?"

Jin poured Zhong a cup of tea after the assistant left the office.

"Who's the offender? What's your complaint?"

"It's Xiao Mao. I'll go to the provincial office if you won't do something, and to the central government office if they do nothing. I'd go all the way to the United Nations if necessary."

"All right, I hear you. Get hold of yourself. Didn't I tell you all to work with him before I left? You must think of the eight hundred thousand residents and not make things hard on him."

"It's not us." Zhong scowled. "He's the one who's making it tough for us. He removed me from my position." Zhong crouched down and began to sob, holding his head in his hands.

"Really?" Jin was stunned.

"Yes, really." Zhong dried his tears. "You're a big official now, so you must not care about us little people anymore. Why don't you come see for yourself what he's doing? He hasn't done anything but bully people since he became the party secretary. With all that power, he wants to replace everyone in the office with his own people. Actually, I wasn't the first to suffer his axe."

"Is it really that bad? He came to see me when he attended a meeting at the district office."

"He's two-faced; he must have lied to you. Why else would he remove me but for the simple reason that I used to work for you?"

That comment stung. What was Mao up to? He hadn't objected to the man's promotion, so how could he be so insolent? Jin maintained his composure and asked with a smile, "So you're out of work now?"

"He wanted to transfer me to the science commission. You know what kind of office that is. You have to take care of this, Commissioner. I'm going to sleep in your office until it's done. People used to tell me how I made the wrong choice by working for you. They said I should have gone to work in the county government office. You glided away for your new position, leaving us behind to be persecuted. You were our boss, so you must help us." Zhong began to weep again.

"That's enough. Take my lunch box and meal coupons to the dining hall and get lunch for two."

Zhong got to his feet, dried his red-rimmed eyes, and went off with the lunch box.

Jin angrily smashed a cup when he was alone in the office. *Damn you, Xiao Mao. Getting rid of my people? What gall!* He grabbed the phone and told the operator to connect him to Chungong. But he thought about Xiong before he was put through; reminded of how the general secreary handled personnel issues, he felt his anger subside, and told the operator to disconnect the line.

They sat down across from each other to eat when Zhong came back with the food.

"Tell you what, Lao Zhong. Go see Secretary Lu at the district party office when we're done here. Tell him what's going on and ask for his advice. The district party office is the right place for county party affairs."

"No way, Mr. Jin." Zhong glared at him. "You can't send me away like that. You're our old boss, so why would Secretary Lu step in if you won't? I'm not going to see him. I want *you* to take care of this."

Jin lost his temper.

"You'll do what I say and go see him. What do you expect me to do? Have a fight with Little Mao? There are proper channels in the organization, and for this you're supposed to see Secretary Lu. Why can't you understand that?"

Zhong looked down and scratched his head through the thick hair with a chopstick. He seemed to see the light, but then maybe not.

"All right. I'll go see him."

Zhong went to see Lu after lunch. But Jin felt bad after he left. He sighed as he wondered if he had been selfish, turning away his old colleague for his own future. But looking at the big picture, he knew he couldn't afford a confrontation with Mao at the moment. It would be detrimental to the whole situation. Yet, he was uncomfortable sacrificing old friend for his own sake. Distracted by these conflicting thoughts, he couldn't concentrate on work the entire afternoon.

About a week later he ran into Secretary Lu.

"Someone from Chungong came to lodge a complaint against Xiao Mao, Lao Jin. Do you know anything about that?"

"No, I don't. What was the complaint about?"

"It was the county party office manager, saying that Mao had retaliated against him for personal reasons and removed him from his position. I placed a call to Mao, and that turned out to be quite not the case. The office manager had a lifestyle issue. He spent too much time at the county guesthouse, fooling around with the girls there."

"Is that so? Well, he shouldn't be working at the county office if that's the case."

"It's over now. Nothing serious. He's just an office manager. I thought you knew, so I wanted to tell you what's been done. I agreed with how Xiao Mao dealt with it."

"He did the right thing," Jin said. "I agree too."

Jin's anger flared as he walked away. That damned Mao. A lifestyle issue was just an excuse; he needed to find a cause to fire someone. Jin had known that Zhong loved to hang out with women; it was nothing new and hadn't bothered Mao before. He started firing people once he was promoted, which could only mean he wanted a sort of regime change. No one was blame-free. You can always find something against someone you want to fire. Besides, who doesn't like women? It's all a matter of what you do. Jin had a guilty conscience when he thought about how he'd refused to help an old friend out, until he convinced himself that he couldn't have done anything, since Zhong worked for Mao.

Why didn't you watch your step? Lifestyle issues are easy to prove. I can't go telling people you didn't do anything wrong, can I? I didn't help you because I couldn't, not because I wouldn't. Besides, I'd suffer if I even tried. Jin felt better, but these thoughts continued to plague him and kept him awake that night. He was reminded of Xiong again just before dawn, when morning clouds began to appear in the east. Everything was clear to him again and his confidence in his work was restored, so he ate a couple of slices of cake, put the matter behind him, and went to work in high spirits.

6

Commissioner Wu suffered a stroke shortly before the end of the year.

As he did every morning, he'd gone to the open market with a basket to buy fish. He picked a big one and a small one, but after the fishmonger put them in his basket, the large one leaped out and flapped around on the ground. Wu passed out when he bent down to pick it up. Unaware of his status, the fishmonger took his time getting him to the hospital, which delayed treatment. Wu was awake when his family rushed to the hospital, but was paralyzed and could no longer speak.

"I told you not to go buy fish, but you wouldn't listen," his wife sobbed. "You thought you could do it. Now see what happened?"

Holding up as best he could, Wu merely smiled.

Secretary Lu Hongwu arrived and took the commissioner's hands.

"You should have sent someone to buy fish, Lao Wu. Why did you have to go to the market yourself?"

Wu held on to Lu's hand and smiled.

No one was aware of Wu's conundrum, which involved having fish for each meal, a live one, no less; a dead fish would lead to a stomachache and diarrhea. Before mealtime, he'd go into the kitchen to make sure the fish was still flapping, and replace it with live one if it wasn't, even if it had been leaping shortly before being put in the pot. Going to the market had not been necessary when he was promoted to commissioner. But, being young and energetic, he made frequent visits to the counties under his jurisdiction, where this quirk was well known. Before he departed, the county secretary would usually put a bucket of live fish in the trunk of his car or have someone deliver fish to him. That had changed in recent years, when old age and a lack of energy prevented him from making so many trips. Besides, everyone knew he'd be stepping down soon and rarely felt the need to curry favor. Which was why he'd gone to the market himself.

Jin Quanli, who was overseeing family planning in one of the counties, raced back when he heard the news. He had an emotional attachment to Wu, a decent man, even though he hadn't worked for the old man for a year. Wu was asleep when Jin got to the hospital. His wife was dozing at his bedside. Jin tiptoed inside once he caught his breath. Wu's wife got up to find him a chair when she saw him walk in. Jin took her hand to stop her from waking Wu up.

"Don't. Let him sleep," he whispered before sitting down to watch Wu silently.

Wu was still asleep an hour later, so his wife said, "Go get some rest, Deputy Commissioner. I'll tell him you came to see him when he wakes up."

"I won't be able to sleep, so I'll sit here and wait."

It was three in the morning when Wu opened his eyes. As his wife helped him sit up for a few sips of orange juice, he noticed Jin. An unusual glint shone in his eyes. He pointed at Jin, then at his wife and finally the clock on the wall.

"He's been here most of the night," his wife said.

Wu's eyes were moist, as were Jin's when went up to take his hands.

"What happened, Commissioner?" Jin was choking up.

Wu, who had acted tough with other visitors, let tears stream down his face in front of Jin. Grabbing Jin's hands, Wu wrote on his palm:

"You get live fish from now on."

Jin nodded before choking up again.

"I've let you down."

Wu patted Jin's hands with surprising force.

"Should I give Comrade Xiong a call and have him take you to the provincial capital?"

With a shake of his head, Wu wrote:

"Better here."

Jin nodded again to show he knew what the old man meant.

Jin went to see Wu every day. Whenever he needed to visit one of the counties, he would race over as soon as he returned. Lu went too, but not as frequently as Jin, due to the press of work at the office. Two-fifty, not keen on hospital visits, came only once. The other deputy secretaries and commissioners also made it over. Xiong sent his personal assistant when he heard, making Wu cry again as he held the assistant's hands.

Everyone knew that Wu could not return to work after they saw him. He himself had no illusions about his health, and wrote on Lu's palm during one of his visits:

"Early retirement. Please consider."

"Just keep getting better, and don't worry about this," Lu said.

On his way out, however, Lu realized that the district office could not function long without a commissioner. He sent a report to the organization section to suggest that Wu's position be filled by a deputy commissioner.

Lu's report spread quickly, surpassing Wu's illness as the news of the day and turning everyone's attention to the question of Wu's replacement. Visits to the district hospital grew farther and farther apart as palpable tension seized the administrative building, with its five anxious deputy commissioners—Two-fifty, Jin, Sha, Guan and Liu. Sha and Guan, who had moved up because of their seniority, had mediocre work performance. Liu, a recently installed college graduate, was still studying at the central party school. None of the three was a serious contender; Jin and Two-fifty were the only two who could be considered. Jin, who had a solid record and worked day and night, without putting on airs, had the popular support. Two-fifty had made the right choice in swapping with Jin, and had performed well with rural and small town enterprises and urban construction. Naturally the two men became the focus of everyone's attention. All things considered, Two-fifty had the upper hand, since he had been there for five years, while Jin was finishing up his first. Two-fifty was in charge of tasks with visible results, the enterprises showing concrete yields and large-scale urban structures under way. In contrast, Jin spent all his time dealing with strayed cadres and pregnant women, which meant less-noticeable job performance. The difference did not escape the attention of Two-fifty, who was thrilled by Wu's illness, convinced that he would be the logical replacement. After learning about Lu's report to the provincial organization office, where he had once worked, Two-fifty got into his car and went to the provincial capital to work on his connections. He returned after three days with haughty airs, as if he had the job in hand.

Naturally, Jin wanted to be Wu's replacement, something Wu seemed to have suggested himself. But Jin had not expected Wu to fall ill so suddenly, which sped up the process. Affairs of the world are complicated; it can be unfavorable to have things happen too slowly but it can also have an adverse effect if they occur too soon, like Wu's retirement. Having been on the job for under a year put him at a disadvantage. In all fairness, Jin had not been in a hurry to become a commissioner and knew he needed to work for Wu to build up his credentials. Yet he was unwilling to give way to Two-fifty now that they were competing for the position, because Jin believed he was more competent than the bully Two-fifty. The five million residents of the district would suffer if someone like that became commissioner. Besides, if he were promoted, then Jin would have to work *for* him, something he found distasteful. But the decision had to come from the provincial office, so all he could do was worry. His anxiety intensified when Two-fifty returned confidently. Jin then recalled his old friend, Xiong, and decided to copy his rival by going to the provincial capital to see him. But as luck would have it, Xiong had gone to Beijing for a meeting with the central committee. Jin returned unhappily to await his fate, since he knew no one else in the capital.

Two comrades from the organization section came a week later with the express plan to promote Two-fifty and sought the views of the district party committee. If no one objected, the provincial standing committee would hold a meeting to discuss the nomination and eventually move ahead with the promotion. Lu settled for asking one question:

"Should we ask Mr. Wu's views?"

"We can do that," they said.

Lu went to the hospital and told Wu about it.

"What do you think, Mr. Wu?"

Wu put his hand out to his wife, who knew what he wanted and brought him a pen and paper.

"Please tell the provincial committee," Wu wrote in a shaky hand, "that I object to appointing that man." He tossed down the pen and paper in such anger that Lu was startled.

"So who would you like?"

"Jin Quanli," he wrote.

Lu nodded to show he understood. "I'll relay your view to the committee."

The two men from the organization office shrugged when he told them.

"We'll report what we've heard," one of them said.

And that was what the committee members heard at their meeting, causing a minor argument. The head of the organization section leaned toward Two-fifty, while the governor said, "He's obviously not good enough, since even his own boss objected. Let's choose Jin Quanli instead."

"All right. Jin Quanli it is." They all sided with the governor, when Xiong spoke up.

"Jin Quanli has been a deputy commissioner for barely a year, so it may not be a good idea to promote him so soon. In my view, he should remain a deputy and build up his résumé. Since we don't have a suitable candidate at the moment, why don't we keep it vacant? We can ask Comrade Lu Hongwu to serve as interim commissioner for a year or two, and then find a replacement."

His idea was met with unanimous support and the decision was made. A heavy burden fell on Lu, who had to divide his attention between the district committee and the administrative office. Two-fifty was disappointed; clearly the provincial committee didn't trust him, especially after his maneuvering. He knew that Wu had played a role in blocking him, but he focused his displeasure on the committee, which, in his view, lacked conviction and had listened to the wrong person. Lu also incurred his ire, now that he had taken over as commissioner.

"The central government is advocating the separation of government and party, but they ignored that and gave him two hats," Two-fifty ranted in his office.

Jin wasn't unhappy when he saw the document from the provincial party committee, for he was in no hurry to be the commissioner, so long as Two-fifty wasn't promoted over him. He didn't mind waiting; in fact, the longer it dragged on, the better his chances. He felt even better when he heard of Two-fifty's rage.

"What an idiot," Jin said to himself. "The more he acts up the less likely he'll ever become the commissioner."

It seemed a cinch that the position would be his sooner or later, now that Two-fifty was out of the picture, so Jin threw himself into his work. Wu was impressed when he heard about Jin's diligence, which reassured him that he had keen eyes and had picked the right person.

"Must believe in party," he wrote on Jin's palm when he came to see him at the hospital one day.

Jin knew what the old man meant and also how Wu had done his best to veto Two-fifty in favor of him. He gripped Wu's hand and shook it as a wave of gratitude welled up inside.

7

The central government began a campaign of reporting on official malfeasance, incurring a huge increase of workload for Jin, who received calls or letters nearly daily. He handled the caseload by taking turns with a deputy party secretary from the district office. Eventually, the growing caseload prompted Lu to recommend that Jin be in charge only of disciplinary investigations and turn family planning over to Sha, another of the deputy commissioners.

One day Jin received a letter charging four county secretaries of building houses with yards or multi-story residences; they were Cong from Zhu county, Zhou from Pi county, Hu from Nancheng county, and Bai from Wujiang. Zhou and Bai even took women to their county guesthouses for dalliances. The letter shocked Jin, for they were all friends from the past.

He didn't feel comfortable questioning them, since he couldn't be sure of the report's veracity, and couldn't investigate them even if the charges were true. Besides, they knew him too well to be honest with him, and he was well aware of what Zhou and Hu were like. Jin cursed Two-fifty once again for shoving this thankless job onto him. The earlier reports had all been on shop managers and village or county chiefs, which were so easy to deal with: he simply wrote "Investigate" on the accusations for his team of investigators to look into the complaints. How could he to do that when it involved former peers? It was not unthinkable that they would rip up his order when the team went to their counties to carry it an investigation. Jin's displeasure turned on these county secretaries, who had been nurtured for years by the party. They had been doing well enough in their jobs, and it was not out of line for them to be wined and dined. But why go and build houses like that? Why get themselves into trouble? Jin mulled the complaint for a while, unable to make a decision. When he recalled how he'd dealt with Xiao Mao's dispute with his office manager, he wrote on the letter:

"Submit to Comrade Lu for further deliberation."

Jin felt relieved. But the letter was returned that same afternoon, with Lu's comment:

"I suggest that Comrade Jin personally investigate."

Jin felt cold all over. This was his first setback since starting working at the office, and he had only himself to blame. He shouldn't have kicked the ball to Lu, who kicked it right back and put him in an awkward position. If he hadn't done that, he could have simply turned the task over to his team of investigators. But now he had to go himself. He had been too clever for his own good. Not wanting to antagonize his old peers, he couldn't afford to ignore Lu's order either. He had to go. As the saying goes, a petty functionary has no free will.

In the end, he decided to go talk to Zhou and others, but had misgivings when he got up the next morning. The allegation had to be looked into, but he needed to determine who to investigate first. Both Zhou and Hu had bad tempers, and, as he recalled, they had refused to join him at dinner after his promotion. What would they do if he showed up to investigate them? It would probably be better to see Cong first. They had a decent relationship after having worked on a socialist education campaign together; besides, Cong was not as ill-tempered, so it would be easier to get a sense of the situation from him.

He went with his investigators that morning to the county party office in two cars. They were greeted by the office manager.

"Where's Lao Cong?"

"He, um, went to a meeting, I think," the director stammered. "I'll go find him."

Jin knew exactly what the man was doing.

"What meeting? Where? In the district or the provincial office?" He didn't let up with his questions. "Maybe the central government sent a private plane to pick him up? Be honest with me. Where is he?"

"Mr. Cong is building a house in Beiguan, the county seat." The office manager gave Jin an uneasy smile. "He hasn't been to the office for two days. I'll go get him."

"No need." Jin climbed back into the car and said to the driver, "Beiguan."

The report was legitimate. Cong was building a house for himself, and had even arranged for a crane to work on a two-story structure in the palace style, with glazed tiles and a jade white color scheme. When Jin arrived at the half-acre site, Cong was waiting for him with a broad smile. It was obvious he'd been informed of the visit.

"How did you know I was coming?"

"I could tell." Cong changed his tone and told him the truth. "The office manager called."

They lit up as Cong looked at the contingent Jin had brought with him.

"What are you doing here? Why bring so many people along?"

"To investigate you." Jin decided to be frank also. "Look at the house you're building here."

"Go ahead." Cong smiled, putting his hands together for Jin to put on handcuffs. Jin smiled.

Cong got into Jin's car and they drove to the county guesthouse.

"I've got some lamb from Inner Mongolia. Let's share a hot pot. What do you say?"

"Why do you have to ask?" Jin added, "Get someone to find some live fish and put them in my car."

"What for?"

"For Commissioner Wu."

Cong knew of Wu's circumstances, so he turned to his office manager, who had rushed over to the guesthouse. "Go to the reservoir."

With a nod, the office manager walked out.

For lunch that day, Jin and Cong had their hot pot in one room, while the others had theirs in another room with the office manager as their host.

"We're friends, so I'm going to be frank with you," Jin said after a few bites of mutton. "We've been nurtured by the party for years and are both cadres in leadership positions. So I really don't understand why you, Lao Zhou, Lao Hu, and Lao Bai have suddenly decided to build your own houses."

"Do you know how old I am?" Cong asked.

Jin was caught off guard by the question. "Fifty-four?"

"Fifty-six. What about Lao Zhou and the others?"

"They must all be in their late fifties."

"That's right." Cong downed a cup of liquor. "We're in our late fifties, about to retire. You've gotten your promotion, but unlike you, we're not going anywhere. When we reach that age, we'll have to retire. We have to be prepared. We need to have a place to live, don't we? After working for the party for years, who will even give us a second glance once we're retired? Just look at Lao Wu. He was a commissioner, but wouldn't be able to eat live fish now if not for you. That's how people are these days. You can't tell me to go live in a hovel after retirement. Would you visit me there? Where would you get mutton hot pot then? You've been promoted, Lao Jin, so you don't understand how those of us down below feel. Let me ask you this: If you were still working in the county office, would you or would you not build a house for yourself before retirement? Of course you would. I'm saying this to you only because we know each other so well, and you mustn't take offense. Sure, people talk about party consciousness. But your position determines the level of your consciousness. You can't be at a high level if you live in a hovel."

Jin smoked and looked at Cong quietly. They ate in silence for a while before Jin spoke up again.

"Of course you should and that isn't the problem. The people are allowed to build a house, so are county party secretaries. But you picked the wrong time and went against the trend."

"What trend is that? I'm not afraid, and I don't think the others are either. So what if we build a house? There's nothing in the constitution that says we can't. I spent my own money on the house, paying out of my own pocket for the bricks, wood, cement, sand, and land. Why should I be afraid? You're here to investigate, right? Well, go ahead. Do your job. I'm not afraid."

"Of course I have to investigate. You paid for the land and the building materials, but no one else could get what you got for the little money you spent. How big is your property? Half an acre, wouldn't you say? You must have taken over farmland."

"So I took over farmland. What about you people at the district office? Do you live in the air? Where does Lu Hongwu live? And what about old Mr. Wu? Their houses are better than mine. You should investigate those further up. The higher up, the bigger the offense. You should work for the central committee for disciplinary investigation. This place is too small for you."

"Nothing wrong with the central committee." Jin laughed at the last comment. "I'd love to work there, but they don't want me."

Cong finished his cup and laughed also when his office manager walked up and said, "You're scheduled to speak at the party education meeting this afternoon, Secretary Cong. It's about to start."

"Can't you see that Commissioner Jin is here?" Cong gave the man a displeased look. "Send a deputy secretary over."

"Right," the man said as he walked out.

"You go ahead with your work, Lao Cong. I have to head back anyway."

"Whatever work I have will get done by the others," Cong said with a dismissive wave. "I'm building my house."

After lunch they got a room with two beds and lay down to chat about families. Jin took out a magnetic therapy device for Cong's wife, who suffered back pain. Around two o'clock, Jin got up off the bed and said, "How do I deal with this, Lao Cong? To be honest with you, it's better here than at the district office. I've run up against this guy Two-fifty, who shoved this thankless job onto me. Damn, this is tough."

"Don't worry about it and go on back." Cong sat up. "I'll tell the county disciplinary committee to write a report, along with a detailed account of the land and materials, and you'll have done your job."

Jin nodded.

"What about the other three? Should I go see them?"

"You'd better not," Cong said after some thought. "We're good friends, so I don't mind your coming to see me. But how do you think they'll react if you show up? How would you do your job if you lost the support of these counties over a trifling matter like this? It would be hard for you as commissioner. Let me give them a heads-up and tell them to do the same as I'm doing."

Jin nodded again, filled with gratitude to his old friend.

"There's another thing about Lao Zhou and Lao Bai. The report said they're fooling around with women."

Cong cackled like an old hen as he replied, "I'm not touching that. You can check it out yourself and see if they're a bunch of rapists."

Jin just smiled.

"The investigation won't go anywhere, because you won't find any evidence. No matter what you do, all you'll get in the end will be 'Unfounded accusation.'"

With a laugh, Jin got to his feet.

"I'll head back then, Lao Cong."

"This is a business trip, so I won't keep you." Cong walked him out.

"I went to Chungong a few days ago," Cong said.

"Did you drop by my house?"

"Of course I did. They're all fine, but I must tell you they're unhappy with you. They said you're selfish."

"I'm not selfish. Don't listen to them."

"They complained that you ignore them now that you're a big official. You should take them to live with you, if it's not too much trouble."

"I have to wait on that, but sooner or later it'll get done."

Cong nodded, but turned emotional again when they reached the bottom of the stairs. "I'm retiring soon, Lao Jin. I tell you the truth, Lu Hongwu talked to me last time he came."

"Talked to you? About what?" Jin was surprised.

"One more year." Cong raised a finger.

For the first time, Jin noticed his friend's gray hair, someone he'd known for more than two decades. Cong looked much older, and Jin felt a sudden pang as he grabbed the man's hand.

"I'll come by often."

"I always look forward to your visit. There isn't anyone else I can to talk to so frankly in this county."

"Anything I can do for you?"

"I can manage, for the moment anyway. I'll come see you if I can't get any help after retirement."

"Take care."

"Go on," Cong said.

As the car drove off, Jin put his hands behind his head and leaned back against the seat. He was feeling sentimental, a rarity for a political animal.

Two weeks later, the disciplinary committees at the five counties sent the files, which Jin took to report to Lu Hongwu.

"You can consider the case closed now that your investigation discovered no major problems. Write reports to the central and provincial committees; they received a copy of the complaint and passed it down to me last week."

Jin returned to his office and told his team to send the reports up.

8

Old Mr. Wu died after spending six months and three days in the hospital. He was said to have died alone, a terrible thing for anyone.

His wife was pretty much the only one caring for him during his illness. No matter how high one's status or accomplishment, one usually ends up dying with only family members around. The administrative office had sent someone to relieve her, but he was married with children, so he naturally was more concerned about his own family, which meant that Wu's wife was the only one who could and would be devoted to him. She stayed by his side day and night, except on this day, when she went home to fetch a blouse. Wu had breathed his last by the time she returned. She threw herself on him.

"How could you leave like that? Why couldn't you wait for me? What do I do now?"

Lu Hongwu, Jin Quanli, Two-fifty, and other officials from the district committee and the administrative office arrived. A gloom settled over them as they viewed the body of a man with whom they'd worked and dined for years. He was gone now. After recovering from their own sorrow, they turned to console Wu's wife before meeting in the hospital conference room to discuss funeral arrangements.

"After working in the district his whole life, Lao Wu has left his footprint in every corner of the district," said Sha, one of the deputy commissioners. "So we must do everything we can for his funeral."

"We're materialists, so don't talk about doing everything we can," Two-fifty interjected. "Whatever we do will be no more than sending his body to the crematorium. Besides, the central government is promoting simple funerals."

Jin, who felt strongly about the old man, knew he had to speak up. Wu had been good to him and he had treated the old man well, having made at least a hundred visits to the hospital over the past six months. Jin had managed to provide the old man with live fish, and he felt his conscience was clear. To be sure, he was sad to see Wu gone, and yet he was comforted by the fact that he had done his best for the old man. It mattered little to him how the funeral was conducted, but anger flared when he heard the tone adopted by Two-fifty, who was clearly a heartless man. Mr. Wu was dead now, but Two-fifty obviously still bore a grudge, which was unbefitting of a Communist. Jin had always tried to be nice to Two-fifty, but on this day he could not hold back.

"This will happen to every one of us here, whether our funeral is simple or not."

He regretted it immediately, for it affected not just Two-fifty but also Lu Hongwu and others. It was too late for regret, as Two-fifty reacted with a glare.

"What do you mean?"

Jin couldn't take his words back so he decided to go all out. "What do I mean? I mean some people lack the conscience of an average person, let alone a real Communist."

Veins bulged on Two-fifty's forehead as he stormed up to Jin.

"Who lacks a conscience? Go on, tell us. Who are you talking about?"

"Whoever has no conscience knows better than anyone else."

Lu Hongwu blew up at that moment. An ordinarily calm man who rarely betrayed his emotions, he lost his temper in a big way, pounding the table so hard its glass top cracked.

"Stop that and act like real deputy commissioners. What kind of talk is that? You should be ashamed of yourselves, acting like women on the street!"

He turned to Deputy Commissioner Sha and told him to follow precedent in forming a funeral committee. He was to inform the provincial committee and government office, and notify Wu's relatives. Lu stormed out of the hospital and got into his car to return to his office, leaving the others behind at a loss of words.

Mr. Wu's funeral was a respectable affair, dignified and formal. The provincial committee and government office each sent a wreath, as did every unit in the district office and counties. General Secretary Xiong sent a condolence telegram. Wu had been adept at connecting with the masses and had treated the people with kindness; some of them came to pay their respects. An old woman on special welfare whom Wu had once helped wept so hard she fainted.

"Such an honest official! Such an upright official!" she cried out before she lost consciousness.

Wu's wife, though sad over the loss of her husband, was pleased with the ceremony, which in turn helped console her. After hearing about the argument over funeral arrangements, she naturally attributed the dignified affair to Jin's effort. Seven days later, she came, wearing a scarf, to his office.

"Today's the seventh day rite, Lao Jin. I have to come thank you before going to the cemetery. I know you were good to him and now that he's gone, I'm here to thank you on his behalf."

She bowed and began to sob, covering her face with her hands.

Jin rushed out from behind his desk and took the old woman's hands.

"Please don't, Mrs. Wu. Old Mr. Wu gave me so much help, and I feel guilty for not taking better care of him," he said tearfully.

"Otherwise, he'd still be with us. We'll treat you the same as always even though he's gone," he continued. "Come see me if you need anything."

"You're a good man," Wu's wife sobbed. "It's rare to see someone like you these days, and those in the party were smart enough to promote you. I told him he was getting old and must let you take over his position. Now it's too late."

"Please don't talk like that, Mrs. Wu. Your husband was a noble man who deserved respect from everyone, and I will never forget what he did for me. Please do come see me if you need anything."

There was no more to be said, thus bringing their meeting to an end. Jin was moved by the occasion, which, to his surprise, actually brought him plenty of trouble. Taking his promise to heart, she treated Jin like a true friend, turning him into a substitute for her late husband. She came to see him all the time, for concerns major and minor—housing, the use of Wu's car, funeral expenses, even her son's job transfer and his daughter's admission to day care. Jin received her cordially at first, taking it upon himself to help her out, but some matters were simply outside his authority and fell into the domain of Lu Hongwu or Two-fifty, creating considerable difficulties. Death often exposes the inconstancy of human relationships. Back when Wu was alive, a government vehicle would be sent over whenever she needed a car, but now she was told the car was out of commission when she asked for it. Jin lost his temper over this several times. The office would have the car fixed, but it would break down again the next time she asked for it, and Jin knew he could not get angry each time, since he had no authority over those in charge of vehicle use. After the death of her husband, Wu's wife became increasingly sensitive, recalling how everything had been different when her husband was alive each time her request went unmet. She would show up at Jin's office in tears. While he felt sorry for her, he had to kick himself for talking big and taking on such an impossible task.

His enthusiasm began to cool, which she noticed, and she stopped showing up at his office, going to see Lu Hongwu instead.

"I thought he was a decent man," she said privately. "It turns out he couldn't withstand the test of time."

Jin felt badly hurt when he heard her criticism.

"It's my fault, all my own fault," he muttered to himself. "I should have known the boundaries."

Someone knocked on Jin's door one day when he was reading documents. "Come in," he shouted casually and was surprised to see that his visitor was Xiao Mao from Chungong. Jin had been feeling low, and that was aggravated by Mao's presence. He had yet to deal with Mao over the man's provocative act of removing his former office manager, and now here he was. What kind of scheme did he have in mind this time, Jin wondered, and decided not to stand up or offer Mao a cigarette or tea.

"Have a seat," he said coldly.

Mao respectfully and sat down to wait until Jin looked up after signing the document.

"What can I do for you, Secretary Mao?"

Mao forced a smile, sensing the strained atmosphere.

"Nothing, really. It's just that General Secretary Xiong asked me to deliver a letter to you."

Jin was startled. What? Xiong asked him to deliver a letter? How could that be possible? When had Mao become an acquaintance of Secretary Xiong? How had he managed that kind of connection? Jin took the letter.

"When did you see Comrade Xiong?" Jin held his surprise in check.

"Secretary Xiong stopped by Chungong County for lunch on his way to inspect Chengyang. I gave him a report and he asked me to give you this letter."

That put Jin at ease. So Xiong had just been passing through and treated Mao as a messenger. He softened his tone:

"Have some water."

Mao walked up to the vacuum bottle and poured himself a cup, which he drank while Jin opened the letter. It was a brief note, nothing important.

"Long time no see. I've been thinking about you. Come visit me in the provincial capital, won't you? Xiong Qingquan."

The warm note made Jin feel better and, temporarily forgetting Wu's wife, he walked out from behind the desk to sit across from Mao and ask about Xiong's stop at Chungong. Mao grew animated as he relayed how Xiong was kind, not one to put on airs, how much the man knew, and how simply he lived, asking for nothing but a bowl of noodles for lunch.

"That's the way he is." Jin laughed heartily. "He's been like this since we met over a decade ago."

Mao had heard of Jin's relationship with Xiong, but hadn't expected them to be so close that Xiong would ask him to deliver a letter when he was just passing through. Wondering what was in the letter, Mao was puzzled by Jin's nonchalant reaction, especially the way he laughed, which nudged Mao into showing more deference. He even began to regret his behavior back when Jin was the county secretary, as well as his subsequent action against Jin's people.

"I have something else to talk to you about, Commissioner Jin," Mao said after they chatted for a moment.

"What is it?"

"I did a terrible job handling that earlier matter and I know I let you down. I've long wanted to come see you about it."

"What was that?" Jin's heart skipped a beat.

"It's about removing the office manager. He had worked for you for many years, and I shouldn't have fired him. But the investigation by the county disciplinary committee turned up problems and the woman confessed. So there was nothing I could do."

"I washed my hands of what happens in Chungong once I left." Jin waved him off. "There's no need for you to tell me this. Go see Mr. Lu if you want."

"Don't be angry with me, Commissioner." Mao stood up. "I was in a difficult position and I had to do it, but I'm planning to transfer him back once everything calms down. I came here today to tell you. I'd like to have him back."

Jin was mollified. He considered himself a magnanimous man who not only allowed others to make mistakes, but also permitted them to make amends. Jin had forgiven Mao in the past and he could do it again for the young man. Touched by his own magnanimity, Jin said to Mao genially, "That should be decided by the county party committee and I can't interfere. But based on my observation in the past, he is overall a good man, despite some flaws."

"That's true, and he's well liked. This is what I have in mind, and I'd like your opinion. Why don't we send him to the organization section, since the position of office manager has been filled. It's an office with real power and he'll be a member of the standing committee, comparable to his old job."

"Sure. The organization section or the office, either is fine."

"Then I'll be going," Mao said with a smile. "I brought a basket of apples. They're in the car. I'll have them sent to your room for your enjoyment."

"No need for that. I don't care for raw food."

Sure enough, the former office manager was transferred to the county party office to head the organization section a week after Mao's visit. Immediately after taking up his new post, he came running to the district administrative building, where he stormed into Jin's office and fell to his knees.

"Thank you, Commissioner Jin, for giving me a second chance in life." He sobbed, so startling Jin that he ran up to the man.

"What do you think you're doing, Lao Zhong? Get up."

"I knew it." Zhong wiped his tears as he got up. "I knew my old boss would never forget me."

"What do you mean, forget you? I had nothing do with that and you have only the party to thank. Go on back and do a good job."

"I will. I'll do a good job and make you proud, Commissioner Jin."

9

Lu Hongwu, the district party secretary, had been in a funk for a while, mainly because of health problems. He felt he might soon be following in Wu's footsteps, and had been badly stung when Jin had said that day would come for everyone shortly after Wu died. However, for the sake of his work, he kept his concerns to himself, not even telling his family. He avoided the district hospital and instead drove to the provincial capital, where a medical examination showed that there were problems with his heart, liver, and spleen. The results made him realize that, be it for his own health or for the party, he could not continue holding two positions at the same time. Having made up his mind to let someone take over as commissioner, he explained the situation in a report to the provincial party committee and asked the members to recommend a candidate. They had learned their lesson from the earlier argument over Jin and Two-fifty, so decided not to show their cards; instead they asked the district committee to give them a name, which they would send up to the provincial committee once the man passed a review. It was a hard task for Lu, who believed that there was no viable candidate in the district office. He for one would not choose Two-fifty, someone he did not respect. But he didn't think Jin would do either, though not because he had anything personal against Jin or because Jin had hit his sore spot with his comment. It was simply because Jin's job performance, from what Lu had heard, was not up to par. For instance, someone from the district committee once said that deep down Jin was not an upright official even though on the surface he looked solid, diligent, and hardworking. He had little to show after being in charge of disciplinary investigations for two years. He had done a perfunctory job investigating the county party secretaries who built private houses; in fact he had done nothing, because they were his old friends. And there was more. Jin had often asked the various county offices to send up live fish for him to butter up old Mr. Wu when he was ill. And recently he had agreed to let Little Mao reassign an errant cadre to a new position. All these added up to a case against promoting Jin, who would neither do the party nor Lu himself any good if he became the commissioner. Yet Lu was aware of the friendship between Jin and Xiong Qingquan, so he had to tread carefully; he turned the matter over in his head, only to end up feeling even more conflicted. In the end he found a compromise by recommending Lao Feng, a deputy secretary from the district office, and Jin, whom he placed in second on the list.

When Two-fifty heard the news he tossed caution to the wind and ran to the district building without waiting for his car. He stormed into Lu's office and blurted out, "What kind of trick are you playing, Lao Lu?"

Lu's liver was acting up so much his forehead was bathed in sweat and he had to press a fountain pen cap against his abdomen to ease the pain. But he did not lose his head as he replied, "Sit down! Lao Chen."

Chen refused to sit, choosing to stand in the middle of the room instead.

"You can tell me if you're unhappy with me. But why stab me in the back?"

"Who stabbed you in the back?" Lu was puzzled.

"You, of course. Why isn't my name on your recommendation list for commissioner? We've worked together a long time, Lao Lu, and you have to be fair. I've done a great job in rural and small enterprises and urban construction over the past two years. When the city couldn't force stubborn homeowners to move, I was the one who cleared them out. I'm sure you know how much this year's rural and small enterprises earned for us; how else would you be able to stay on as the district party secretary? But what has Jin Quanli done? Why is he on the list, and I'm not? This is unfair. He's recommended because he knows the provincial secretary general, is that it? Is this how our party works? Let me tell you, Lao Lu, I won't take this sitting down. I'm going to file a complaint at the provincial level. I'll go all the way to the central committee if that doesn't work."

Without waiting for an answer, he spun around and stormed out. Lu was shaking with rage as he pointed a finger at the open door.

"How, how dare he, talk to me like that?"

Yet once he calmed down he had to agree that the man wasn't entirely unreasonable, even if he didn't appreciate his rudeness and impertinence. Knowing he could not be angry with someone like that, he sighed and went back to work.

Jin was equally unhappy with Lu when he learned about the list. He had been so close to a promotion the last time, and would have been promoted if not that the provincial committee wanted him to serve as a deputy a while longer. Since then, old Mr. Wu had expressed an intention for Jin to replace him, so how did someone from the district office appear out of the blue to block his way this time? It could only mean that Lu Hongwu didn't think much of him. *I've been here for nearly three years now, and I've never taken even a Sunday off,* Jin fumed. *I've done my best, and took over a thankless job no one else wanted. I may not have dealt with everything in the best way possible, but minor issues should never overshadow the main aspects of my performance. Yes, the way I dealt with the personnel issues might not have been altogether appropriate, since I placed personal relationships ahead of party principles, but I'm sure you would have done the same if you were in my shoes. No one can ignore personal relationships. Do you think you made it all the way to district party secretary without personal connections? If you insist on principles, then why were you on edge for days before the provincial secretary's visit and even prepared two types of lunch? This is purely putting Marxism and Leninism into a flashlight—to shine on others but never on yourself! It's all right if you want to shine it on others, but have you any idea how it affects me? I may not get the commissioner's job this time and, at my age, if I don't I'll likely retire as a deputy. You'll have essentially destroyed my future, and that's just vile. I've treated you with the same respect I showed Mr. Wu, but you're not as magnanimous or generous as he was and you lack the tolerance befitting someone in a leadership position.*

Jin was weighed down by these unhappy thoughts for days. Lu Hongwu had sent his recommendation up and it could not be changed, so it would be too late for Jin to talk to him. As they say, the rice has already been cooked. Jin could only sigh over his lousy luck for running into someone like Lu. It was hard not to miss Mr. Wu, which brought on self-reproach for not treating Wu's wife better.

Someone walked in unannounced one day while Jin was sitting in his office feeling glum. It was Lao Cong, the party secretary from Zhu County, not an ideal visitor at the moment, for Jin knew that his promotion had been affected by the way he dealt with Cong and others. But he had to conceal his feelings, for the sake of the work they had done together.

"Have a seat," Jin said.

The mood in the office didn't seem right to Cong, who knew what was on Jin's mind, so he put on a smiling face.

"You don't look too happy."

"What do you mean?"

"We've heard. You're placed in second for promotion because of us, and we feel bad. Lao Zhou and others asked me to come take you to Zhou's county to get away from all the unhappiness."

Jin was moved. Cong hadn't forgotten and wanted him to feel better when he was in a funk, even though what he'd done for Cong was nothing major. Yet he knew this wasn't the time to go away, especially not to see Cong and others. That would be like putting his head in the noose. He smiled.

"Thank you," he said, "but I'm swamped these days. I'll come see you all when I'm free."

Cong didn't press Jin, for he understood what Jin was thinking. He got up with a smile.

"Well. I'll head over to the organization section."

"Something happened again?"

"Time's up for me, Lao Jin. I'm wrapping up my retirement paperwork. I'll be an ordinary citizen starting tomorrow."

"Ah, so you're retiring." Jin walked over and grabbed Cong's hands. So Cong was really leaving. Saddened by the news, Jin regretted his earlier displeasure. He was retiring while Jin would still be a deputy commissioner, which was a much better prospect. There was no need to be upset with Cong. He took hold of his arm.

"Come have lunch with me when you're finished."

"Thanks, but I have to hurry back. I need to pick up my wife from the countryside."

"I'll come see you in a few days."

"I'll be waiting for you."

"I promise."

They were both emotional.

"I have something to say to you but I don't know if I should say it, Lao Jin."

"Go ahead. Tell me."

"In all honesty, you're as good as Lao Feng, actually might have the edge over him. You know Secretary Xiong, don't you? Why don't you go see him. A connection like that should not be abused, but it would certainly come in handy at a moment like this."

A light went on in Jin's head. Cong was right. He could go see Xiong again, instead of waiting for his fate to be decided by others. Xiong had asked him to come visit in the note delivered by Xiao Mao. If he were willing to help, it would be child's play for someone in his position to get him promoted. He was buoyed by the possible solution, and grateful for the reminder from an old friend, though he knew he shouldn't advertise it.

"That won't do for me. You know how I am. I'll be fine whether I get it or not, so there's no need to work on someone like Secretary Xiong. Besides, I don't want to trouble him with a matter like this."

"Then just pretend I didn't say anything." Cong knew exactly what Jin was getting at, so he shook hands and walked out.

Jin went to see Xiong the following morning. He noticed a familiar car ahead when he was leaving the district office. When he got closer, he saw it was Two-fifty's car, with its plate number ending in "250." So he too was on his way to the provincial capital.

"Take a different route," Jin said to his driver.

"But this is how we get to the provincial capital." His driver was confused.

"Do it, I said. Take a different route. It'll get us there just the same."

Seeing Jin lose his temper for the first time, the driver turned off, away from "250."

10

Jin did not rush over to see Xiong when he got to the provincial capital; instead he checked into a hotel before placing a call to Xiong. He gave his name to Xiong's assistant, who had picked up the phone and asked him to wait. After a few minutes of anxious waiting, he heard Xiong's voice:

"Is that you, Lao Jin?"

"I'm taking care of some business at the provincial government office and would like to come see you, Mr. Xiong. Will you have time to meet?"

"Why are you so formal?" Xiong laughed. "I have a meeting this morning, so this afternoon will work. Come later in the day and I'll wait for you."

Jin was pleased when he hung up. He had to be in luck to find Xiong so easily and get to see him that same afternoon, which could be a good sign. He went back to his room and, feeling sorry for blowing up at the driver earlier, said, "Come, Xiao Wang. Let's get something to eat. My treat."

They went to the hotel restaurant, where Jin ordered food and chatted amiably with the driver, who laughed at his jokes. After lunch, he returned to his room, took a bath, and went to bed. He napped until one thirty before waking up the driver to take him to the provincial committee building. The guard stopped them at the gate, and they could go no further. Jin went to the reception room and placed a call to Xiong's assistant, who came down to escort him.

Xiong's office was located in a two-story building surrounded by green cypresses.

The assistant poured him a glass of water after they walked in.

"Please wait a little while, Commissioner Jin. Comrade Xiong was free to see you, but something came up. He has go to the train station to meet a senior official from Liberation Army Headquarters who is passing through the city. He asked you to wait and said he'll be back soon."

"Sure, I'll wait. I know how busy Comrade Xiong must be."

The assistant sat at his desk to do some paperwork. Jin felt awkward, sitting stiffly on a sofa, not moving except to take a drink of water or check the wall clock.

He waited for more than three hours, but Xiong was still not back by five thirty. It seemed pointless to wait any longer and, besides, Xiong's assistant might laugh at him. He was about to get up and leave when he heard a car outside.

"Comrade Xiong is back." The assistant stood up.

Jin stood up too. Xiong strode in when he spotted Jin. Poking him in the belly, Xiong said with a smile, "There you are. Sorry to make you wait so long. I had to see the old man off but the train was delayed for two hours."

"Secretary Xiong is a busy man and I don't mind waiting. I was just wondering if I shouldn't have come to bother you."

"Bothering me? You can go home now if that's how you feel." Xiong laughed, and so did Jin. "Let's have dinner. What do you say?"

The gloom Jin had felt while waiting for Xiong vanished.

"That would be great."

"And something to drink?"

"Of course."

Xiong looked at him and laughed again, before turning to his assistant.

"Come have a drink with us."

"I have to go pick up my kid." The man smiled while straightening a stack of paper.

"Very well, you go pick up your kid and we'll go have a drink. Let's go, Lao Jin."

Xiong put his arm around Jin's shoulder as they left the office. Instead of getting into Xiong's car, they walked out of the office compound and down the street.

"What shall we have, something fancy or a simple fare?" Xiong asked.

"Whatever you like."

"In that case, we'll have a simple dinner."

Xiong led Jin to a small diner on a quiet side street. They found a table and sat down. As usual, Xiong spread his arms out on the table and leaned forward to place his head on his hands while he talked, a gesture that immediately transported Jin back to a decade earlier. The dinner reminded him of the Dazhai Commune, and Xiong looked just like then; they'd fought over the bill.

The diner wasn't especially busy, so their food arrived quickly. Xiong took out a bottle of Yanghe from his coat pocket and gave it a shake.

"We'll polish this off today."

"Absolutely."

They toasted each other and Xiong asked after they'd each downed six glasses. "Why didn't you come see me earlier?"

"You're the secretary general and I don't want to look bad coming to see you all the time. I'll only come when something is up."

"So you're here to see me about something?"

"No, not really. Just to see you."

"You're contradicting yourself. I know why you came today," Xiong said with a smile.

Jin glanced at him and knew that Xiong had seen through him. He smiled awkwardly.

"But I have to tell you I can't help you this time. I hope you'll understand."

Jin's heart sank. Could Xiong have heard something, something negative about him? It would be helpless if that were the case. A chill rose inside and Jin felt drained of energy, but he tried not to show his disappointment.

"You must have been mistaken, Secretary Xiong. You've done more than enough for me."

"I really can't help this time, Lao Jin," Xiong said. "Not because I won't, but because I can't. I'll be transferred next month."

"What?" Jin was dumbfounded. "Transferred? You're leaving?" Xiong nodded.

"But, but how is that possible? Our province needs you. Where are you going?"

"To be the deputy director at a research center in Beijing."

Jin knew about the place, a flashy unit with no real power.

"Are you—is this a demotion? You're First Secretary here." It didn't sound right to his own ears, but Xiong didn't seem to mind.

"Demotion or not, it's still working for the party. That's all."

"That can't be!" A sudden rage had Jin pounding the table. "But why? Everything improved in the province after you came, and now they want to transfer you."

"I'm telling you this because we go way back. No one in the province knows about it yet. I've just been summoned to a meeting at Central Government headquarters."

"This isn't fair." Jin nodded before crying out again.

"It was my own fault." Xiong sighed. "I shouldn't have come to this province; it was like jumping into a cesspool. There are things I can't say to you, but you probably know some of them already. There are two factions in the provincial party committee. When the old secretary general retired, they had wanted to promote someone from inside the province, but the two factions fought so fiercely that I was transferred here to take over. I hadn't expected the place to be a cesspool. Think about it, how could anything get done in the province if the people in the committee can't work together? I don't mind the transfer; at least I'll be out of the filth. They can bring over someone better and see what he can do."

Jin was overwhelmed by what he'd just heard. He hadn't been aware of the difficulties Xiong faced at work every day. On the outside Xiong was the First Secretary of the Provincial party Committee, but he had his own troubles to deal with. Who knew? In Jin's view, Xiong deserved better than this. But the decision had been made and no one could change it. Feeling sorry for his old friend, Jin wanted to offer some comforting words but couldn't find the right thing to say.

"Why don't I go to Beijing with you then," Jin blurted out.

Xiong chortled. "Are you all right with a demotion?"

"Yes, I am."

"You should stay here. As a deputy commissioner, at least you have your own driver and a guesthouse. If you go to Beijing, you'd be a cadre at the bureau or the department level and will have to take the bus to work."

"It just gets me that things can be so unfair."

"Let's not say any more about it. We need to adhere to party principles no matter where we are and watch our words. I just wanted to tell you that I can't help you, so please accept my apology."

Jin realized that his own situation was nothing compared with Xiong's. The reflection made him so emotional that he reached out to take Xiong's hands.

"Please don't say that. You've given me more than enough help."

They left the diner and began walking down Xingzheng Street. It was a clear, starry night. Xiong took a deep breath of the fresh air and said, "It's been more than a decade since we visited Dazhai, hasn't it?"

"Yes, it has."

"Life has its cycles. Time really does fly."

"Don't feel too bad, Mr. Xiong."

Xiong laughed. "We're still Communists and we should never forget that, no matter what."

With his eyes on Xiong, Jin gave him an earnest nod.

Jin walked on, after saying good-bye to his old friend. It was getting late and he was the only one around. As emotions welled up in his mind, everything became clear: whoever wanted it could have the position of commissioner. He would be happy to be his deputy. His driver was fast asleep when he returned to the hotel. Jin got undressed and lay down on the bed, when his thoughts turned to his family. He hadn't been back to see them for a while.

The driver asked him after they washed up and breakfasted the following morning, "What are our activities today?"

"We're going back."

"To the administrative office?"

"No, back to Chungong. I'm going home to see my family."

Recruits

1

Lamb chops were our first meal as new recruits. The reddish meat looked fresh and tasty, but was stringy, some pieces even with blue veins. Everyone in the company came from Yanjin in Henan Province; having grown up in farming villages, we rarely got to eat meat at all, so we thought the lamb was done well. "The army's lamb chops are delicious," some were heard to say. Yet, being new recruits meant a change in status, so we knew we had to act with some dignity, which was why we pretended we couldn't care less. None of us finished the meat, intentionally leaving a bone or two with bits of meat on our plates, everyone but the platoon leader, Song Chang, that is; he ate it all. A man in his late twenties, he was the one who had brought us from our hometowns to this distant place. When he finished, he walked around the dining room, arms behind his back, to check our plates.

"Had enough to eat?"

"Yes, sir," we replied in unison.

"Then go take care of your internal affairs."

That meant to put our barracks in order. With the exception of the platoon leader, who had a bed by the window, we slept on the floor. A recruit from my village and a former classmate, a guy we called "Fatty," ran for a spot by the heater.

"I'm always cold, so this is for me."

Recruits from different villages weren't happy with that. "You're not the only one who's cold," one of them grumbled.

The platoon leader stopped going through the dirty clothes he had changed on the road and shouted, "Li Sheng'er." That was Fatty's legal name.

"Sir!" He put his hands along the seams of his pants and stood at attention, something we'd learned on the train ride over.

"Go sleep by the door."

"Not me," he said with a sulky look. "It's too drafty."

"Too drafty for you? Than who do you think should sleep there? Come on, give me a name."

Fatty couldn't do that, because whoever he named would be offended.

"You can't do that, so you should sleep there. Does that work for you?"

"Yes, it does, sir." Fatty's eyes reddened.

"Go on then, since you say it works for you."

After the platoon leader walked off, Fatty spread his bedroll by the door.

"You're a bunch of rats," he complained. "We're from the same area, so why pick on me in front of the platoon leader?"

We were having none of that. "Nobody's picking on you. You're the one who tried to grab the spot by the heater."

That afternoon we were divided into squads to check the area. Fatty came up to me, eyes red.

"I'm finished, Banfu." He used my title of assistant squad leader.

"What do you mean, finished? You haven't even been here a full day."

"The platoon leader hates me."

"Well, you shouldn't have peed on him," said Wang Di, a fair-skinned young man who was walking ahead of us.

That had happened in the boxcar that brought us from our hometown. There were no chamber pots on the train, so we had to open the door a crack to pee out. Fatty, who had a problem peeing while we were moving, stood by the door for a long time but couldn't go; others were waiting behind him.

"Move over if you can't go."

"I have to pee. I really have to, but I can't while the train's moving."

When the platoon leader saw us standing there, he shouted for us to move away from the door. Then he came over to drag Fatty away. "Go on," he said. "If you can't pee, that means you don't have to."

When Fatty turned around, the dam broke and soaked the platoon leader's pants.

"Now look what you've done, Li Sheng'er. You've left your mark on me."

What Wang said touched Fatty's sore spot, turning his eyes even redder.

"You worry too much. It was just a fluke, an accident."

"Wang Di is such a suck-up," Fatty whispered. "I saw him washing the platoon leader's clothes around noontime."

"Enough of that. No one told you not to do his laundry."

A group of Mongolians rode by. They were in long robes and short jackets, with thick layers of grease on their collars. We'd never seen anything quite like that back in Henan, so we stopped talking to gawk.

"How come there are no women?" Wang Di blurted out.

"There's one." A man we called Chief pointed. "Over there, the one in the red kerchief."

Sure enough, it was a woman with a kerchief over her head. But she was really ugly, with a dark, sunburned face.

"I guess a woman like that is good enough for the border regions," Wang said as he adjusted his cap.

The Mongolians rode off, leaving us to the vast, boundless Gobi. Pointing at the pebble-strewn ground, Wang said that the Gobi was an ocean in primitive times, which, according to him, was why there were pebbles all over the barren spot, where not even a blade of grass grew.

"What do you meant, barren? See those trees? And the river over there?" Fatty objected.

We looked where he was pointing and, sure enough, there was a stand of dark trees, beside a river, with watery mist shimmering above it.

But there was nothing else around it.

"Ocean or not, this is a desolate place," someone said.

"The platoon leader said he was once stationed in Lanzhou, but it turned out to be over five hundred miles from Lanzhou," Wang said.

"And you did his laundry," Fatty said.

"Says who?" Wang's face reddened.

They squared off, so I went over and separated them, just as the squad leader shouted from the barracks for us to return for a meeting.

The squad leader, who was in charge of our military drill, was Liu Jun, a veteran soldier. We held the meeting in the barracks, where we sat on our bedrolls. Liu gave a speech about respecting our superiors, being loyal to our comrades, observing discipline, and training hard to defeat the enemy. Then he criticized us for wasting food at lunch, since we'd left pieces of bone, which were dumped into the swill bucket. Never do that again, he said. Finish what's on your plates. Don't take too much if you can't finish it. We felt it was unfair for him to call us wasteful, because we hadn't cleaned our plates in order to seem more civilized. At dinner that evening, we ate till we were about to burst, even licking the bottom of our plates. Chief wolfed down eight big steamed buns. It was as if the more we ate the less wasteful we'd appear.

Fatty made a fool of himself yet again. Dinner that evening was stewed cabbage with pork, mostly fatty slices with a little lean meat floating on the surface. That was still better than what we ate at home, so we finished everything on our plates, all but for the platoon leader. With his plate still half full, he was picking up bits of bun and leisurely putting them in his mouth. Fatty, who thought the platoon leader wanted to savor his food slowly, dumped what he had been savoring onto the platoon leader's plate, as a way to make up for his misstep earlier.

"This is for you, sir."

He had no idea that the man hadn't finished because he didn't like fatty pork. He shook in rage at the sight of Fatty pouring the contents of his half-eaten plate into his.

"What—what do you think you're doing?" He smashed his plate on the floor, sending mushy cabbage flying.

Fatty was in a funk that night, sighing as he tossed and turned. When I woke up in the middle of the night to relieve myself, he was still thrashing in his spot by the door, holding his head in his hands. He followed me out.

"Banfu, I meant well," he said in a choking voice and spread his arms.

"I know you meant well, but what did that get you? Another tongue-lashing by the platoon leader."

"I don't mind that. What bothers me is Wang Di and the others sniggering when the platoon leader yelled at me."

"After what you've done, you can't stop them from laughing at you, can you?" I told him to go back to sleep.

"I need someone to talk to, Banfu."

"It's too late. Go back to bed. The drills start tomorrow morning."

He sighed and walked back inside with me. A crescent moon was dipping to the West and all was quiet. Two sentries were parading in the distance under the moonlight.

2

Our training began. Each squad formed a drill unit as we practiced quick march, parade march, double-time march, dropping to the ground and crawling on our bellies. We weren't allowed to use our feet, but were forced to pull ourselves forward with our arms.

The days were exhausting, but we had no peace at night either, with unannounced emergency musters. A shrill whistle would call for an emergency muster when we were fast asleep. The lights remained out, so we had to get dressed in ten minutes in the dark and muster with our backpacks and rifles on the parade ground. Training during the day was nothing compared with what happened at night. Mayhem reigned in the barracks during those dark ten minutes, as we snatched the wrong socks or put on someone's pants, anxious to leave but unable to. In the meantime, the company commander and the political instructor, pistols in hand, were counting heads on the parade ground to see which squad showed up last.

"Enemy agents were spotted several kilometers away. Be there in twenty minutes," one of them would say gruffly.

We'd then take off running with our rifles and return, panting and drenched in sweat, where they waited to see if our backpacks were intact or if we were dressed properly.

Each squad had at least one screw-up. In ours it was usually Fatty or Chief, a thin man with a serious face, who was taciturn and caught up in his own thoughts. He was forever screwing up one thing or another, putting his shoes on the wrong feet all the time. The company commander usually called him out and made him march in front of us. Mismatched shoes forced him to walk with his feet splayed like a lame duck, an uproarious sight. Once after we returned to the barracks, Wang Di said, "The company commander shouldn't have criticized Chief. They call us out in the middle of the night in order to catch enemy spies, don't they? His footprints will create confusion for them."

We laughed and looked over at Chief, who hadn't yet changed out of his shoes. He sat glumly, staring daggers at Wang.

Fatty's problem was putting his pants on backward, leaving the opening in the back to expose his rear end. It was not a sight the company commander wanted to parade in front of us, so he simply announced that someone had put his pants on backward. "How can someone like that be expected to catch a spy?"

After we were dismissed, Fatty pulled the opening behind him together with a dejected look, as if it had been his fault that we failed to catch a spy.

In addition to the nighttime muster, we were also required to stand sentry at night. A team of two, an hour each, with an alarm clock passed from team to team. Only seventeen or eighteen at the time, we were at the age where we'd be sleeping on the threshing ground back home. So after a whole day of training, we were sleepy and hungry. We'd eaten our fill at dinner, stuffing our faces with steamed buns, and yet hunger pangs struck when we were standing sentry.

And it was bitterly cold. Late December in the Gobi Desert is unlike winter anywhere else, with temperatures plummeting to twenty below all the time. When it was my turn, my favorite place was the boiler room, manned by an old-timer named Li Shangjin. Unlike other veterans, Li never bullied the new recruits, even called me "Eighth Banfu," deputy leader of the eighth squad. We got to know each other better as time went on. Working in the boiler room at night, he was entitled to an additional meal that consisted of seven or eight meaty buns he toasted on the boiler. He gave me a couple each time I showed up, before settling down on a bench and squinting as he watched me devour the buns. They were nicely toasted, brown and crisp on the outside, with a mouth-watering aroma. I never had enough, but knew better than to finish off his night snack. "That's enough. I'm full," I'd wipe my mouth and say, pushing back the buns he offered.

Li was given to smiling, guileless, friendly smiles.

"Have you applied for party membership?" he asked the first time we met.

"I just got here." I shook my head. "Isn't it too early?"

He gave his thigh a slap, displaying a sense of urgency. "Hurry up and apply. Do it as soon as you can. Tonight back in the barracks. Don't end up like me. I was late applying. It's been three years, and I'm still not a member."

But when I asked other old-timers, I learned that applying early wasn't the determining factor. The key was to have a heart-to-heart with someone in the organization section. Li's application had been rejected not because he hadn't turned it early but because there was a disciplinary action against him. Once, on a home visit, he had sneaked a bayonet along, for the sole purpose of impressing his wife-to-be. On the day he met her, he'd put on a brand-new army uniform, complete with a Sam Browne belt and a bayonet, cutting an awe-inspiring figure as he strode through the market with his parents. The girl was awed enough to marry him, but the army somehow learned about the bayonet, which was a black mark that affected his advancement.

"When will your application go through?" I asked the next time I saw him.

"Any day now, I think." He was holding a poker in one hand and rubbing his stubble with the other.

"Why's that?"

"They sent me here to work the boiler, didn't they?"

I was confused. How would working the boiler lead to party membership?

"It's a test."

I got it, and I was happy for him. "Sooner or later it will be approved. I heard that some veterans were decommissioned without becoming a member."

"That would be a great loss of face."

The first two weeks passed, and we had gotten used to army life, to the point that we even walked like real soldiers. We all actively sought advancement, as we began writing our applications for party membership. We fought over the brooms in the morning, and tension built among us, since we couldn't all become party members at the same time. Some would make it and some wouldn't. We were all on edge, waking up before daybreak, intent on running for the broom at the sound of reveille.

Then came the selection of squad "key cadres," who would shoulder more responsibilities, the first step in career advancement.

Understandably, everyone coveted the title. But the company stip-ulated that each squad could have only three, thus complicating the matter. Take our squad for example. I was the banfu, the deputy squad leader, which logically gave me one of the slots. The second one was to be Wang Di, to which no one objected, since he was a talented painter and calligrapher who had put out a wall newspaper and could sing to set pace for marches. The problem was with Chief and Fatty, two problematic candidates who had started out unfavorably but rec-tified their problems. For Chief, it was simply putting a brick on each shoe to avoid mixing them up in the middle of the night, while Fatty kept his pants on when he went to bed. With their problems solved, now they were usually the first to arrive on the parade ground and were standouts. They had both taken the initiative to carry out other "charitable acts." Without telling anyone, Chief began cleaning the company toilets, while Fatty went for the broom every morning and even stood sentry all night once so the others could rest. They tried to outdo each other, but neither came out ahead.

The problem was solved for the squad leader when he thought about the lamp cord, which could only be touched by a key cadre. The cord hung over the door, where Fatty slept. Chief would have to switch with Fatty if he was to be chosen. The squad leader didn't want to go through the trouble; besides, he was the one who had assigned Fatty the spot to begin with. In the end the squad leader said to me, "Just give it to Li Sheng'er."

Which was how Fatty became a key cadre in charge of the lamp cord. He had benefitted from an earlier misfortune, and smiled for days, exposing his big yellow teeth. Chief was naturally disap-pointed, but he knew he had to hide his feelings; he wrote a pledge to the squad leader, in which he said he hadn't worked hard enough, but vowed to learn from the key cadres and hoped to be selected next time. That started a trend, as the remaining soldiers in our squad all began to write their own pledge letters.

Company headquarters passed down an order for us to gather sheep droppings left in the wild by the nomadic Mongolians. We would cart the droppings back as fertilizer in the spring. Each squad was to send two soldiers to work a cart assigned to the squad by the company. Since it was a job for the company, each squad sent their key cadres. For us that was Wang Di and Fatty. But Wang had been working hard on the wall newspaper and I couldn't get away, so the squad leader decided to send Chief along.

Chief, who never dreamed of carting droppings, was heading to the drilling ground with his rifle. He was so happy he couldn't keep the smile off his face when he heard the order from the squad leader; putting his rifle aside, he smoothed down his uniform and took a look at himself in the mirror before running off cheerfully to cart sheep droppings, a job meant for a key cadre. When he returned at the end of the day, he was covered in dirt, with bits of dry droppings in his brows and hair. Still in high spirits, he splashed cold water over his face as he said, "The company leader said we'd go back in two days."

He washed his leather cap before putting it next to the heater to dry, when the whistle sounded for an emergency roll call. That threw him into a panic. The platoon leader blew his top when he stormed in and saw the wet cap.

"Time for a roll call. Did you think you could avoid it by wetting your cap? I don't care how but you have to dry it right now. Or come outside with it wet."

Poor Chief had to stand in the wind wearing his wet cap, which was covered in ice when roll call was over. But we weren't done yet, for another roll call in the platoon followed. The platoon leader launched into a speech, adding that a certain comrade had no sense of order and discipline, making his cap wet before roll call. Everyone turned to look at Chief, who stood still.

Chief disappeared after roll call. I found him sitting motionlessly in a windy spot behind the barracks, still wearing his cap. I thought he was crying and went up to nudge him. But he wasn't; he just looked up at me.

"Take off your cap, Chief. It's frozen stiff," I said.

"How could I be so stupid?" he cried out repeatedly.

"It's not your fault. You were carting sheep droppings earlier today."

"I'm just stupid, Banfu." He was sobbing now.

"No, you're not. No one could have anticipated the roll call."

He stopped sobbing long enough to tell me that he received a letter from his father that day. Someone had written it for his father, who told him to work hard in the army. "Now see what I did today," he said.

"It's nothing. Everyone stumbles. You just have to get up, that's all."

He nodded.

He handed our squad leader another pledge the next morning, saying the ideological origin of the wet cap was his lack of order and discipline. He had stumbled, but he was resolved to get up and start over.

3

We were told to fall in during one of our drills. A senior officer was coming for an inspection and all squads were to stop regular drills to focus on formations. We were keyed up by the news, since we had yet to see a ranking officer. We couldn't stop whispering among ourselves. How senior was he? Could he be a regiment commander? When I stood sentry with the squad leader that night, I asked him. He told me it was a military secret, which led me to suspect that he had no idea either.

After two weeks of formation training, we were notified that the inspection would take place the next day, with the added information that it was not a regiment commander nor a division commander, but an army commander. The barracks erupted excitedly. An army commander coming for an inspection! Some soldiers were about to sit down and write a letter home about the good news. Even our squad leader couldn't hide his excitement as he regaled us with a description of the army commander. Reminding us not to cough during the inspection, he made a rearrangement of the formation and assigned us new positions. When that was done, we cleaned our rifles and shined our bayonets.

Lights-out sounded shortly after eight; we were to go to bed early, get a good night's sleep, and wake up energized. But how could anyone sleep? Finally we dozed off, but soon we were awakened by a whistle.

"Another emergency muster?" Chief blurted out.

Thrown off balance, no one dared to turn on the light as we began to get dressed and collect our backpacks.

"An army commander is coming for an inspection tomorrow, so why are we falling in now?" some grumbled, echoing everyone's sentiment.

The company commander came in and snapped the light on. We weren't to fall in. We were to head over to the mess hall for an early breakfast, after which we would line up to board a truck. We were to reach the reviewing ground by eight.

We breathed a sigh of relief.

"I never thought we were supposed to fall in," a wiseass said.

Excitement returned, but it was still pitch-black outside.

Blood-red cloud clusters appeared in the eastern sky, a typical desert sunrise; we waited for the sun to roll out from behind the crimson sea of clouds, completely unprotected. It was nearly twenty below zero, but the cold didn't bother us, as we stood packed on the truck bed. The driver seemed to have been infected with our excitement as well, for he tore down the road like a whirlwind; when we drove over a ditch, we went *Aah* as we bounced up and down, holding our rifles in our arms with their well-oiled bayonets attached.

Finally we arrived at the reviewing ground. Oh, my! We weren't the only company to be inspected. The grounds were crowded with tens of thousands of soldiers going in all directions, looking for their designated spots.

"How many are there?" I asked our squad leader.

Shielding his eyes with his hand, he looked around.

"I'd say enough to make a division."

The sound of gathering soldiers was deafening as they kicked up enough dust to blot out the sky. But we took extra care of our bayonets, making sure they were dust-free. Our company commander, a pistol on his hip, was running around shouting, "Keep up the pace. Close up ranks."

We pressed up closer to each other and marched forward.

By seven thirty, nearly all the squads had found their spots. The area quieted down, with fewer feet moving about and fewer orders from their commanding officers. But that was quickly replaced by soldiers talking among themselves, some about what was happening that day, some about the reviewing stand. There were still others who were from the same hometown leaving their ranks to greet each other, since they seldom got to meet. To be expected, their platoon or company leaders yelled for them to return to their ranks.

Suddenly silence fell. Someone appeared on the reviewing stand; looking like a staff officer, he faced the microphone and announced the reviewing procedure. When the army commander walks by and says, "You comrades have worked hard," we must respond in unison, "The commander works hard."

"Have you all got that?"

"Yes!" we shouted in unison.

Then he told us to check our weapons, which immediately submerged the area in the deafening noise of soldiers checking their rifle bolts.

That was followed by closing up ranks, with the leader at each level reporting when it was done: after a company checked its soldiers, the company commander reported to the battalion, the battalion to the regiment, and from the regiment to the reviewing stand. The sound of crisp reports rose and fell.

Silence fell again when that was done, as a gray-headed old man appeared on the stand and swept his eyes over the soldiers.

"Who's that?" I quietly poked at our squad leader.

"The division commander."

At seven fifty, the old man looked at his watch and began calling out adjustments to the formations. It was awesome to see an old man call out the commands in a thick, gravelly voice: "Attention!" "At ease." We stood on tiptoes looking right and left to square up and create a perfect formation even with thousands of soldiers. It looked perfect from every angle, an orderly and magnificent array of troops. The grounds were so quiet that only the sound of army flags flapping in the cold air was audible.

It was 0800, time for the army commander to appear.

Time ticked away, and fifteen minutes elapsed, but no sign of the army commander. The division commander kept checking his watch up on the stand, while down below the soldiers were getting restless.

"Could he have forgotten about the inspection?" Fatty ventured a guess.

"Not likely. Maybe he's been detained," Chief said.

We were on edge as another fifteen minutes went by.

"I guess there'll be no inspection today," Wang Di said.

Before he finished, a motorcade of long, black sedans, shining brightly under the sun, emerged at the far end of the main road.

"He's here!"

We perked up. The area buzzed excitedly, but quickly quieted down again, so quiet this time we could have heard a pin drop. We heard the sound of car doors opening and saw people emerging from the vehicles. Among them were several heavyset old men, a few young ones, and a female soldier so beautiful she reminded me of a flower. The old men stood with their hands behind them while the younger men spread out and looked all around. The division commander, who was still up on the reviewing stand, nervously smoothed his uniform before turning to the soldiers down below.

"Listen up. Attention—"

"Eyes to the right—"

"Eyes forward—"

"At ease—"

"Attention!"

His voice cracked with the last shout as he put everything he had into it. Then he ran off the stand and saluted one of the old men who had just arrived.

"Army Chief of Staff, we await your command."

"At ease."

"Yes, sir." The division commander ran back up onto the reviewing stand, panting hard as he went.

"At ease," he shouted.

And we did.

The chief of staff made his laborious way up to the reviewing stand, where he stopped to look at the soldiers.

"Comrades."

We snapped to attention, sending the sounds of our clicking heels echoing across the grounds.

"At ease," he said. "Today the army commander will conduct a review and I hope you will all . . ." He jogged down the stand to report to another old man with sagging jowls and bags under his eyes.

"The troops await your inspection."

"Good, very good." The old man smiled, making the bags under his eyes quiver.

The reviewing commenced formally, though in fact it was just him walking past the ranks. We were, naturally, happy to see him walk by and we stood stock-still, our eyes fixed on a spot straight ahead. Row upon row of bayonets glinted impressively in the sunlight. We had melted into a collective and become part of the reviewing grounds itself. The commander seemed affected by the gravity of the occasion as he raised his hand to his cap. To me, however, he seemed not to know how to salute, for his hand was at a crooked angle; I noticed a sparkle in his eyes. Halfway through the review he said, "How's everyone, comrades?"

We panicked, because his greeting was different from the way we'd been briefed. We quickly recovered and shouted at the top of our lungs, "How do you do, sir!"

That sounded orderly enough to put our minds at ease, all but Fatty, who stuck to "The Commander has also worked hard." We heard him, but luckily, his was the only voice and the commander likely didn't hear him. Our company commander heard it, though, and shot Fatty an angry look.

Soon the commander arrived before our regiment. Holding our rifles at present arms, we made three, loud snapping sounds against the stocks as we moved to order arms. It was beautiful. But Chief had a mishap, scratching his forehead with the tip of his bayonet during the drill. Blood trickled down his face. Few people noticed what had happened and he didn't make a sound or move. The commander, however, was sharp-eyed enough to see and stopped to walk up to Chief. Knowing he was in trouble, Chief remained motionless. The commander stared at the blood on his face.

"Who's his company commander?" he asked.

"Me, sir." Our company commander ran over and snapped off a salute. He was scared witless by the sight and that sent a fright through the rest of us. The commander was going to give us hell, we were sure, and our squad leader glared at Chief, barely able to contain his anger. To everyone's surprise, the commander smiled as he patted Chief on the shoulder.

"This is a good solider," he said to our company commander.

We breathed a sigh a relief. Chief was elated, while our company commander gave a spirited salute and said, "Yes, sir. He is a good soldier, sir."

The commander mumbled a response, nodded, and waved at someone behind him. The flower-like female soldier came up and dressed the wound on Chief's head, revealing to us her identity as the commander's personal physician. Chief was so moved the corners of his mouth wouldn't stop twitching; tears slid down his face and merged with the blood.

We dispersed when the army commander finished with the review, and, singing a military march, marched in formation to the trucks for our respective barracks. The commander stood up there the whole time watching us.

An overview of our performance got under way the moment we returned to our barracks. Fatty was severely criticized for saying the wrong thing while Chief was commended for remaining motionless with a head wound. We were told to emulate him. A squad meeting followed, during which a change of key cadre was conducted to switch Chief with Fatty. After they changed sleeping spots, Fatty threw himself down on his new bunk and cried.

"What are you crying about?" The squad leader was unhappy. "You think this isn't called for?"

Fatty sat up and dried his eyes, fully aware of the implication of his behavior.

Chief, on the other hand, was beside himself with joy, as he sprawled on his bunk by the door to write a letter home. Wang Di walked up and turned Chief's head to check his bandage.

"Dumb people have dumb luck, as they say."

At lights out that night, I lay on my bunk and recalled the day's events. The army commander looked like a decent man. So, the higher the rank, the more a commander cares about the soldiers, I said to myself. Some time around midnight, I got up to use the toilet and ran into the platoon leader.

"Pretty impressive today." I tried some small talk.

"It was no big deal." The man buttoned his fly with a look of indifference typical of a veteran soldier.

"The army commander really cares about the soldiers," I added as we walked out.

I was surprised to hear him snort as he walked away.

"You have no idea," he turned to say. "The man's a real bastard. No one knows how many nurses he got his hands on at the hospital."

I froze. It took me a while to recover and return to the barracks, but I tossed and turned, unable to go back to sleep. I didn't believe what the platoon leader had said. How could a nice old man like that be a bastard? How could that impressive spectacle end this way? I was so disappointed I nearly cried.

4

A round of political study started to criticize Lin Biao and Confucius. Our squad leader received a telegram informing him that his father had died, so he packed up and left for home.

Without a leader, our squad had to stop the political study. The company commander moved Li Shangjin out of the boiler room to fill the position, welcome news to us all, because we knew that Li was a hardworking man with a good heart. When I went to the boiler room to help him move, he was, however, sitting on his bed with one leg under him, looking peeved.

"I'm here to help you move your stuff, Banzhang."

"Help me figure this out first, Banfu."

"What do you need to figure out?" I sat down next to him.

"Is this promotion good or bad for me?"

"Of course it's good."

He shook his head and sighed. "But I've been working in the boiler room for two months and nothing has happened with my party membership."

I had no answer for that. "Maybe they need more time to test you."

"Maybe." He nodded, before getting started packing.

The company was mobilized to participate in the anti-Confucius, anti-Lin Biao campaign. We weren't well educated enough to know much more about Confucius than his name. As for Lin Biao, all we knew was that he had been a time bomb by Chairman Mao's side that could have gone off at any time. We did our best, but higher-ups thought our criticisms did not go far enough, so a propaganda team was sent down to broaden our knowledge through a play. It helped when we saw the old man in the play relating how Lin Biao, as a landlord, had exploited the poor.

"But that was so careless. Lin was a landlord and yet was able to join the Politburo? How could they be so careless?" Fatty offered his view.

Chief was emotional and began to cough as he told us how his grandfather had been exploited by a landlord. Keyed up, everyone in the squad started writing pledges.

Wang Di was the only one in low spirits. He has been doing well since the first day, because he was one of the key cadres, good at painting and writing. But he was too smart for his own good, and stumbled on his way to advancement. Instead of criticizing Lin and Confucius, he put his intelligence to work on a personal scheme, setting his eye on the position of company clerk; being a mere key cadre was not enough for him. He sent the company commander a notebook with a plastic cover, in which he wrote a passage as a "mutual encouragement" with the commander. Instead of "mutually encouraging each other," the company commander sent the notebook to our platoon leader, who was annoyed that Wang had gone over his head to curry favor with the company commander. Yet the platoon leader didn't say anything to Wang; he simply gave the notebook to Li Shangjin with the comment, "This soldier has some problems."

Wang's face turned red and then white when Li gave him back his notebook. "It's just a notebook left over from some time ago."

Wang's second blunder had to do with his "lifestyle." Among the propaganda team was a female soldier who played a dulcimer. Wearing a small, brimless cap and form-fitting uniform, she was quite pretty, with downy hair on her face and arms. We all had our eye on her, including Wang, who said when we returned from the play, "She looks like an old flame of mine from school."

Someone reported his comment and he was summoned by our political instructor, who questioned him. We heard that Wang's face blanched as he swore he hadn't said anything that wasn't permitted, only that she looked like an old classmate. The political instructor let him off the hook by telling him to watch what he said in the future. But something like that was much the same as getting stove dust on your clothes, which stays with you no matter how hard you try. We knew nothing had happened to him and yet we all felt he did have "lifestyle issues."

"Which bastard reported me?" he fumed when he returned from his meeting.

These two incidents caused a major decline in Wang's status, and he lost most of his shine. No longer asked to help out with wall newspapers, he had to pick up his rifle to drill with the rest of us. But he was no good at it. By then we were practicing grenade throwing. The heaving distance was thirty meters, which we mastered easily, but not Wang, who could only manage twenty meters no matter how much he practiced. He burst into tears at one point, a rare sight, since we were used to seeing him mock others. He was good at crying actually.

"Damn, it's so hard!" he sniffled.

All this added up until the platoon leader decided to strip Wang of his title of key cadre, with Fatty as his replacement. After his misstep during the review, Fatty worked hard to make up for it and was looking pretty good, with active participation in the anti-Lin, anti-Confucius campaign. It turned out his family had suffered tremendously—his grandfather had died at the hands of their landlord. He wasn't satisfied with the required thirty-meter goal for grenade throwing either; he continued to practice every day after dinner. So he got his old title back. As for Wang Di, he committed a grave petty bourgeois error by glaring at Fatty when he lost his title, and saying, "You can have it. I don't want it. What's the big deal anyway? All you can do is throw a grenade."

The rebuke had Fatty tongue-tied; he opened his mouth but couldn't say a word as his eyes moistened. A meeting on daily life was held at noon that day, when the platoon leader came personally to "promote positive attitudes to rectify negative trends."

"You have only yourself to blame when you go downhill. But it becomes a character flaw when you mock those who are better than you."

Wang hung his head and kept quiet. He looked visibly thinner.

Fatty was feeling pretty good about his promotion and the praise from the platoon leader, but knew enough to hide his satisfaction when he noticed the look on Wang's face, especially since we'd all arrived together.

"I'm not entirely qualified to be a key cadre. I'll work harder."

Spring came, melting the ice and snow so the planting season could begin. We had to clear the desert floor of rocks, and then dig up and loosen the soil. We worked so hard our hands were covered with blood blisters. Wang Di was with us, but in lackluster fashion. Li Shangjin told me to have a talk with him, so I went out into the field with Wang one night after dinner.

"We get along well so I'm going to be frank with you, and don't be upset with me. You have to pull yourself together. Our training will be over in a month and you have to maintain a good record. Otherwise, you could be assigned to a terrible company."

"I know I'm finished, Banfu," he said with a bleak look.

I told him that wasn't true; he just had to get his act together and make noticeable progress.

"I'll give it try," he said, with little conviction.

It was late by the time we returned to the barracks.

"Did you talk to him?" Li asked.

"I did."

"Did he get a good sense of what he needs to do?"

"I think so."

"That's good." Li lit a cigarette. "He's too young to go downhill so fast. He has to toe the party line." Then he stood up. "Come, let's you and me have a talk."

I walked out again under the starry night sky.

"What do you want to talk about, Banzhang?"

"I've got something to show you." He giggled.

"What is it?"

He looked around to make sure we were alone before leading me over to a spot behind a sand dune, where he took a piece of paper out of his pocket. He handed it to me before turning on his flashlight for me to take a look. Oh, it was a photo of a young woman, heavy-set with a swarthy face framed by thick, rope-like braids. Her smile revealed a pair of big teeth. Puzzled, I looked up at him.

"What do you think?"

"Not bad."

"That's my girlfriend."

"How long have you been together?"

"I met her last time, when I went home to see my parents."

Now I knew; it was the girl for whom he'd risked his career by wearing his uniform and bayonet.

"Pretty good, Banzhang. You should keep seeing her," I said, thinking he wanted my view.

"I don't need to do that anymore. It's all settled. She's all for advancement. She asks me about my party membership every time she writes. She puts so much pressure on me I have trouble sleeping at night."

"No need for that, Banzhang," I said. "It'll come any day now."

He chuckled before murmuring cryptically, "Yes, I got some reliable info this afternoon. The company is going to grant party membership to a few squad leaders and I heard I'm one of them. That's why I'm showing you the photo."

Now I finally got it. I was happy for him. "Remember how you weren't sure about your promotion to squad leader? And remember I told you it was a test? See what happened."

He chuckled again. "I'm telling you because you and I are bud-dies. Don't tell anyone, all right? It's not a done deal yet."

"Don't worry. I won't."

He lay down on the desert and, with his hands behind his head, sighed. "Everything is fine now. I'll be okay even if I'm discharged. Now I can face those back home."

He was like a new person over the next few days, running around in unusually high spirits, as he made sure we all did our job well. Even his commands on the drill ground were loud and crisp.

At a meeting a few days later the political instructor announced the names of those comrades who had met all prerequisites for party membership. Each squad was told to discuss the results and offer our views to the party branch. He read out the names: "Wang Jianshe," "Zhang Gaochao," "Zhao Chenglong," and so on. But no Li Shangjin.

Stunned, I glanced at Li, who had looked cheerful at the beginning of the meeting, but now was ashen-faced and shaking uncontrollably, his eyes fixed on the instructor's lips. But the man was done reading names and had moved on to something else.

Li was nowhere to be seen when we returned to hold our squad meeting about the candidates. I asked if anyone had seen him.

"He's always saying that so-and-so lacks motivation for improvement," Wang said in his usual mocking tone, as he lay on his bedroll with his hands behind his head. "He must be off somewhere crying, since he didn't get selected."

"You saw him crying?" I glared at him.

"Don't listen to him," Fatty said. "Banzhang went to company headquarters."

"Why are you sucking up to him now that you're a key cadre?" Wang turned his attack onto Fatty.

"I'm not." Fatty's face reddened as he pounced on Wang.

I pulled them apart and pointed an angry finger at Wang. "What kind of backward talk is that? Are you itching for another lifestyle meeting from the platoon leader?" I walked out to look for Li.

He was standing blankly outside company headquarters, oblivious of all the people going in and out of the office. I ran up to drag him away to a quiet spot behind the toilet.

"Why were you standing there, Banzhang? It looked really bad."

He was still in a daze, as if he had lost his mind. "I went to ask the political instructor if he had missed a name, and he said no." Li began to sob.

"Don't do that, Banzhang. People can hear you when they come to use the toilet."

He ignored me and continued to sob. "The political instructor criticized me for having impure motives to join the party. But a few days ago . . . why did it change?"

"Don't be in such a hurry. Maybe you'll be picked after they test you a while longer."

"When will the testing be over? Probably not till I'm discharged."

"Let's put that aside, all right? You have to hold a squad meeting."

I managed to get him back to the squad, only to be greeted by the sight of the political instructor holding the meeting himself. He frowned when he saw Li and me walk in.

"Where have you been? The squad leader and the deputy squad leader are supposed to be present for the meeting to get everyone to share their views on the candidates."

He gave Li another look before walking out.

Li sat down and said in a flat tone, "Go ahead and say what you think. The banfu will take notes."

Li was a different person over the next few days; gone were his morale and attention to squad matters. He stopped getting us to work hard and could not care less about what we did during military training. The weekend evaluation put our squad in last place for daily routines, worrying everyone except Wang Di, who gloated over the poor rating and sang "Socialism is great" whenever he could. The others thought he was mean-spirited; they asked me to talk to Li again.

It was another starlit night when I took him to the same spot behind a sand dune.

"We know each other well enough that I'll be frank with you, Banzhang. Please don't be like Wang Di. Won't it be hopeless for you in the future if you let yourself go now because you didn't make the list this time?"

He had clearly lost weight. "You're right. But I simply don't understand why. I was as good as any of them."

"We all know that, and you spent a long time at the boiler room."

"Even not counting that, I've done my best since becoming squad leader and we were never behind."

"You're right, but you shouldn't dwell on these unhappy thoughts. Keep at it and see what happens when the training is over."

"I know that's the right thing to do," he said with a sigh. "I'd have wasted these past few years if I don't pull myself together."

"You have to have faith in the army and the party." I tried to make him feel better.

"You have no idea," he nodded, "but there's another thing that bothers me."

"What is it?" I was surprised.

"I shouldn't have been in such a hurry." He sighed again. "After I showed you the picture the other night, I wrote the girl a letter to tell her I'd be a party member soon. She wrote back to congratulate me. After what just happened, what am I going to say to her now?"

"That's tough, I agree. Here's what I think. Don't write her for now. Wait till next month, when the training is over and you become a member."

"I guess that's all I can do now." He nodded.

He did pull himself together after that and went all out with squad matters again. Soon our squad performance shone again.

One day, when Fatty, Chief, and I were out gathering pig waste, Li came running up to me. "Banfu," he shouted to me. He was smiling.

"What's up?" I put down my shovel.

"Come with me."

When I walked over, he led me to a spot behind the pigpen. "Good news."

"What is it?"

"I was in the bath house with the deputy company commander. It was just the two of us. As I was scrubbing his back, he told me that I as long as I held up under the testing, sooner or later I'd gain admission."

"That's good." I was happy for him. "I didn't think the army was blind to your performance. You'll be a party member sooner or later. Even a month is no big deal."

"You're right. I should have known better. It's a good thing I didn't act like Wang Di and let myself go." He jumped into the pigpen to help us.

"We're almost done." The three of us tried to stop him. "Don't get your hands dirty."

"One more person will get it done faster. We're all key cadres, so it's a good opportunity for us to talk about how to improve our squad performance."

That was what we ended up doing, squatting in the pigpen talking about our squad.

5

Our platoon leader was an eccentric who liked to do things his own way. Like sleeping. He preferred to sleep during the day and get busy at night. He was capable of snoring away in broad daylight, but tossed and turned when it turned dark. Being farm boys, none of us were used to afternoon naps, since we'd had to go out to cut grass after lunch. He, on the other hand, loved to nap and made everyone lie quietly in our beds along with him. After a day of training, we would be so exhausted we wanted nothing more than sleep, while he, full of energy, rested against his bedroll to read. When he read at night, he preferred a candle over a reading lamp, claiming that the candle was better at creating a feel of studious reading. But the bright candle flickered and lit up the whole room.

"Just like my grannie spinning cotton at night," Wang Di commented once.

Sometimes the platoon leader sacrificed his noon naps to write letters or lecture us. It put us on edge whenever he started writing, because it usually took him five or six tries to finish one letter. He'd write a page, read it, crumple it up, and toss it way with a frown. Then he'd start over again, only to repeat the process. That would go on for a while, until his mood soured and we knew better than to make a noise. If he wasn't interested in letter writing, then he'd give us a lecture or hold a meeting, like the one criticizing Wang Di earlier. We all agreed that we'd prefer that the platoon leader turn nights into days, for that would mean less trouble. We'd watch him after lunch and were relieved at the sight of him climbing into bed.

Tender shoots sprouted on the willow trees as a rare spring rain fell on the Gobi. The company commander gave us the day off since we couldn't train outdoors. Rainy days were made for sleeping, perfect for resting up. We were all yawning after lunch and spread out our bedrolls when the platoon commander raced in.

"No nap today. We're having a meeting."

That announcement made us uneasy, for that probably meant another lecture, though the gleeful look on his face said something else was up. Puzzled, we rolled up our bedding and sat in a circle to wait for him to start.

First he poured a cup of tea and blew on it noisily, then he settled into a chair and took out a notebook. "I went to a meeting at company headquarters," he said, flipping through his notebook. "Basic training will be over in three weeks, so we talked about your assignments. I'm going to give you a hint."

We tensed up and inched forward, our sleepiness vanishing instantly. Wang Di, who had been acting indifferent, grew suddenly attentive. With assignments pending after three months of training, we were eager to know what our future looked like.

"Relax. Your performance will decide which company you'll be assigned to. Do you want to join a good company?"

"Yes, sir," we shouted in unison.

"Good. Then you have to show it. Actual assessments will begin soon. You must work hard on your performance. It's all up to you."

He went on with his lecture for a while. "Are you confident you can do it?"

"Yes, sir," we shouted together again.

He lit a cigarette and continued with a squint.

"Why don't you talk about what you'd like to do?"

So we did. Some wanted to be assigned to the company, some to the firing range, some to the warehouse. The platoon leader then turned to Fatty, who was sitting next to him.

"How about you?"

Fatty was so emotional his face was beet red. "I'd like to drive for the army commander."

That made us laugh.

"You?" someone said. "

"Why do you want to be his driver?" the platoon leader asked.

"He looked like a good guy."

"Then you have to work hard." The platoon leader patted the back of Fatty's head. "There's hope for you."

Fatty looked pleased.

We were raring to go after the meeting, as we sat down to write pledges.

The pace of basic training picked up, with assessments of our grenade throwing and target shooting skills. It was hard on us, since we felt we were beyond that, but we threw ourselves into the training because our future depended on it. The assignment process was a competition: if one got a good one, another might not. Understandably, that strained our relationships, and the scheming began. We had once enjoyed throwing grenades and marksmanship, but no longer. Everyone was now given to finding a secret place to practice before lights-out, and no one said a word about how they were doing.

Li Shangjin called a meeting with Fatty, Chief, and me.

"We need more teamwork. If everyone just looks out for himself, squad unity will suffer, and so will our performance," Li said.

He held a squad meeting, at which he impressed upon everyone the importance of collaboration. After dinner that night, he got everyone to line up and march to the drill ground. We ran into the deputy company commander on the way.

"What are you up to?" he asked.

"Some extra practice during our rest period."

"Good." The deputy company commander nodded.

But it was still every man for himself; we did our best to throw the grenades but tried to hide the results. Li Shangjin was the only exception, as he ran around announcing distances.

The company commander gave us less time to fall out at night, reducing it from ten minutes to five. We were, however, seasoned enough to make it, and Chief no longer mixed up his shoes. Fatty was the only one who had trouble. He panicked, either because he was too tense from training earlier in the day or because he had trouble sleeping at night. He would hurry out after the whole company had lined up, sometimes carrying his backpack the wrong way, and once even wearing his pants backward.

"You're a key cadre, Li Sheng'er," Li Shangjin said, "so don't drag us down in our squad performance."

"That's the last thing I'd do," Fatty said tearfully. "I just slow down when I'm nervous."

"But you were able to do it in the past."

"That was then. I don't know what's happening to me, but I just don't have the energy."

Wang Di, who slept next to Fatty, said privately, "Fatty must be sick. He breathes hard at night and even foams at the mouth."

When I overheard the comment, I mentioned that to Li Shangjin.

"Did he have any health problems before?"

"I don't think so."

Fatty did even worse later. He was still fumbling in the barracks when we left to catch spies; he tried to catch up with us, but we didn't see him even after we returned to camp.

"Looks like he's really sick," Li Shangjin said.

"He must have epilepsy." That was Wang Di's diagnosis. "Why else would he foam at the mouth? He stiffens when he hears the whistle. It must be epilepsy."

Li Shangjin took me aside. "That would be a big problem," he said. "They would send him home, since the army can't take anyone with that kind of health issue. A recruit who came with me was discharged because of the same problem."

I looked around. "We have to keep it a secret, Banzhang. He wouldn't be able to face anyone back home if he was discharged after two months."

Li rubbed his chin, lost in thought.

"Besides, his epilepsy doesn't seem too bad," I said. "He didn't show any symptoms during our first two months, and it only acts up once in a while. So it's obviously an intermittent problem. We have to cover for him."

"Well, I guess that's all we can do," Li said. "You help him out when we have another emergency muster, all right?"

I nodded.

Fatty was dripping wet. Even his backpack was wet when he finally emerged in the dark.

"So you made it back," Li said.

"And you did it all on your own," Wang said sarcastically.

Still panting hard, Fatty couldn't respond.

I sought him out the next day around noon. "Do you have epilepsy?"

"We grew up in the same village, so you know I don't."

"But I remember your father did."

He looked down without a word.

"The army will send you home if you show any symptoms."

"I didn't mean for it to happen." He began to weep. "I wanted to do my best."

"Don't worry." I looked around before telling him what Li Shangjin had said the day before. I told him to make sure it didn't happen too often and offered my help during night fall-outs.

"You and the squad leader are good men." He gave me a grateful look. "I'll never forget you. If I become the army commander's driver—"

"Just be a good person, no matter what you do, and that's enough."

He nodded.

I then talked to every soldier in the squad to make sure they kept his secret. When we fell out at night, I told him to focus on getting dressed while I helped him with his backpack, and we walked out with him in the middle so he wouldn't stand out.

Two weeks went by and nothing happened. Li Shangjin and I were relieved. To show his gratitude to everyone in the squad, Fatty worked doubly hard, keeping the floor clean during rest periods and bringing in water for everyone to wash up, even going so far as to squeeze out toothpaste for us. He worked up a sweat, a pitiful sight to behold.

"Take a break, Fatty," I said to him.

"I'm not tired." He pretended to look energetic.

We thought everything was going well, but then a snitch in the squad reported Fatty's problem to company headquarters. Ordered to conduct an investigation, our platoon leader gave up his nap that day and sprawled on his desk to write a letter. After crumpling up a few sheets of paper, he called Li Shangjin and me over to the Ping-Pong room.

"Are you aware that Li Sheng'er has epilepsy?"

Li and I exchanged a knowing look, but we gave a vague answer. "We haven't heard that."

"You haven't?" He slammed his letter down on the table. "Someone reported that to company headquarters."

"Who?" I asked

"So you want to know who did it, eh?" He glared at me.

I looked down without saying a word.

"Well, well. I thought everything was fine in your squad, but you're hiding an epileptic from me to get me into trouble. Why didn't you tell me before?"

"We never saw him having any problem." Li made a courageous attempt.

"We're from the same village," I added.

"You're still not going to come clean, is that it?" The platoon leader said. "We'll know when I send him for an examination at the hospital tomorrow. I'll deal with you after that."

Having been lectured to, when we left the room, we wondered, "Who's that snitch? Why did he sell out a comrade like that?"

Neither of us said it but we both guessed it had to be Wang Di, who hadn't gotten along with Fatty to begin with. Wang was likely to bear a grudge after Fatty replaced him as a key cadre. Besides, as the "backward element" in the squad, he loved to stir up trouble, so he would not likely pass up a ready-made opportunity to add fuel to the fire. He had to be our snitch, a feeling that was reinforced when we went back and saw him laughing and singing.

"We'll deal with him later," I said to Li, knowing we couldn't do anything to him, because his action was considered progressive at company headquarters. We could only feel sorry for the gaunt, sallow-faced Fatty, who was worried sick as he waited for his fate to be determined the next day.

A three-wheeled motorcycle took him to the field hospital early the next morning, and he didn't return until the evening. We knew he'd be discharged the moment we saw his sad face; he would no longer be a key cadre and could never drive for the army commander.

He began to cry when he got off the motorcycle. "We're from the same village, aren't we?" He took my hand and continued. "I don't know who ratted on me. We came here like brothers. What turned us into enemies?"

"Fatty." That was all I could say.

"How am I going to face people back home?"

"What's the big deal if you have to go home? You'd only be throwing grenades if you stayed," Wang said before swaggering off.

We shook with anger. As if it weren't enough to rat on Fatty, he had to make that kind of remark to Fatty's face. I was so outraged I could only point at Wang's back and say, "Why you—Wang Di!"

"I'm so sorry, Fatty," Chief said as he went up to take Fatty's hand. "We're both key cadres and all we want is for the squad to look good. We never imagined something like this could happen." He too started to cry.

We sat around Fatty that night, as a sort of farewell. He stared blankly ahead; gone were his collar and cap badges.

"Comrade Li Sheng'er hasn't been in the army long, but we all witnessed how hard he worked. He was even a key cadre," Li Shangjin said.

"Comrade Li Sheng'er is an upright person with a broad mind, unlike some people who like to scheme behind others' backs," I said, casting Wang Di a glance. He was lying on his bunk.

"I'm leaving tomorrow, and I'd like to ask your forgiveness for anything I did wrong in the past," Fatty said.

Some of the soldiers began to cry, when the platoon leader walked in to join us. He took out a pack of Daqianmen cigarettes and gave one to Fatty, something he'd never done before.

"Don't blame me, Sheng'er. It was an order from headquarters and I had no choice." The platoon leader handed him a pair of rubber-soled shoes. "Here, for you to wear at home."

"I'm sorry I peed on you, sir." Fatty wept again with the shoes in his arms.

He left the next morning with the cook, who was going to buy pork. "Want me to take a message back to your family?" he asked before getting on the truck.

"No, thanks," I said. "Go learn to be a bricklayer with my father if life is too hard in the village. I'll write to him."

He nodded and tearfully climbed onto the truck.

The truck drove off, but we didn't turn to leave until it had disappeared from view. We had to practice grenade-throwing, but we weren't in the mood. Looking around, I found them all despicable. Back home we had slept on the wheat thrashing ground together, but they turned rotten once we arrived. How could eighteen-year-olds change so fast?

The call for another muster sounded.

6

Skill assessment got under way the day after Fatty left, to be followed by assignments, in which the skill assessment was a major component.

I had a talk with Wang Di before the grenade-throwing assessment. I told him that, according to the squad leader, he wasn't qualified for this assessment, since he was never able to throw thirty meters. Then I gave him a serious tongue-lashing, as a way to avenge Fatty.

"The platoon and squad leaders both hold the view that you're a loafer. You're dragging down the performance of the whole squad and platoon. What are you going to do?"

"How come I'm not qualified?" He was sweating. "How is that possible? And how do you know I'd fail?"

"You failed with dummy grenades, so how do you expect to pass with the real thing? A live grenade will explode and who will take the blame if you're killed?"

"I didn't feel any pressure with the dummies, but I might pass when throwing a real one."

"You think you'll pass? You won't, even if you do it twice. The squad leader and I have decided that you will not take the grenade test yet. First write a self-examination and analyze the ideological reason behind your half-hearted practice. You need to probe why you didn't practice more."

"What do you mean I didn't practice more? Look at that arm!" He threw his arm out before me and continued with a choking voice, "You're just trying to torment me."

"What did you say?" I gave him a searing look. "That's the problem with you. You don't work hard, and when we ask you to reflect upon it because we care, you say we're tormenting you. Do you expect us to give you a medal for failing grenade throwing?"

He began crying so hard that snot flew.

"If you have problems with me, tell me straight out. Don't put tight shoes on me like that. We came here in the same van and you know me well. I know I've got a big mouth, but I've never made any major errors."

"I don't know if you have or haven't. The squad and platoon leaders told me to talk to you, and that's what I'm doing. I'm not going to say anything else. I don't want anyone to snitch on me at company headquarters. What if they kick me out too?"

He stopped crying and glared at me. "What do you mean?" he demanded as he jumped to his feet and drew up close to me. "Do you think I had something to do with Fatty?"

"Did I say that? Besides, it was considered progressive to report."

"Well, well. Now I see you do suspect me." He pointed at me, his face crimson. "I don't care if you do, now that our friendship means nothing to you. So this is what you think. I wouldn't take the grenade throwing test now even if you asked me to." He ran off.

I was left standing there, confused. I told Li Shangjin what had happened when I returned to the barracks. "What if it wasn't him?" I said.

"Who else could it have been?" Li rubbed his chin. "There are only so many of us. I look around and he seems to be the likely one."

I went through them all, and Wang did seem the most logical one.

"That's it, then. Don't listen to his excuses. He's always been a bad egg, so it must have been him."

So that was that.

"I want to talk to you about something else," Li added.

"What's that?"

"Do you think they'll grant me party membership after basic training?"

What was I supposed to say? "Don't worry about it. Didn't the deputy company commander say they would?"

He nodded, but then said, "I'm just worried that the incident with Fatty will affect my chances."

"Fatty's problem was his alone. Besides, they've discharged him, so how could it affect anyone else?"

He nodded again but still looked worried. "I guess it's all up to me. I must find a way to improve squad performance." He got up from the bed and said, "Maybe we ought to let Wang Di take the grenade throwing test."

That surprised me. "But, didn't you decide against it?"

"He'll get a zero if we don't let hm. The squad will be affected if he gets a goose egg. Won't the company commander want to know why someone in our squad got a zero?"

Now I saw what he meant. "But it could be dangerous if he can't make it past thirty meters."

"The live grenades are a few ounces lighter than the dummies, so he might make it."

"Then we'll let him try."

"Yeah, that's what we'll do. We'll tell the others to move back when he comes up."

So I went to tell Wang, but couldn't find him anywhere. He must have gone off somewhere to mope. I went to the sand dune behind the drill ground, but he wasn't there. I'd only said a few words about his performance, and now he was off somewhere sulking. Not a real soldier, I grumbled, when I noticed a dark shadow running in the distant open field, as I turned to head back. Under the crescent moon, it looked like Wang, so I walked over and called out to him. He didn't respond. Now it was clear: he was running back and forth, practicing throwing a grenade. I was moved.

"That's enough, Wang Di. It's late."

He continued, without a word.

"That's enough. The squad leader said you could take the test with live grenades." I went up to drag him back and saw that he was drenched. One of his arms was so swollen it looked like rising dough.

He shook off my hand, as if pouting, and continued to practice. Then he threw himself on the ground and cried his eyes out.

"I wouldn't have joined the army if I'd known it would be like this."

"No one is trying to bully you." I felt terrible.

It was time for the real thing, which would take place at the hill behind the firing range. With the pin ring looped through our pinkie, we'd run down the hill and throw the grenade, the ring still on our finger. A loud explosion would sound in the valley. We had to hit the ground right away, so as not to get hit by shrapnel. That would not be fun. The testing standard was thirty meters to pass, thirty-five for good, and over forty as excellent.

Li Shangjin was first. A veteran soldier, he went up to do a demo and would not receive a score. As expected, his grenade went far, earning applause from everyone after it went off.

"I'm out of practice." He shook his arm. "I did fifty back when I was a boot."

"I want to be like you," Chief said. "I want to do fifty."

I was second up and managed thirty-eight. "You'd have been excellent if you'd thrown it harder," someone said, speaking for everyone else.

"That was very good. We'll be in fine shape if everyone does that well," Li said.

If everyone made it to "good," the overall grade for the squad would be excellent.

"All we have to manage is thirty-five. That shouldn't be hard," someone said.

Two soldiers went up next, one good and one excellent, earning applause from us all.

Then it was Wang Di's turn.

"Are you nervous, Wang Di? Take a break if you are," Li said.

Without a word, Wang held down the safety lever and looped the pin over his finger.

"Be careful, Wang Di!" Li backed off in fright.

Still without a word, Wang ran forward and tossed the grenade. We all flattened out on the ground.

"My God! Is he suicidal or what?"

An explosion sounded. We stood up and spotted Wang lying ahead of us.

"Are you all right?" someone asked him.

He didn't reply; instead he got up, picked up a tape to measure the distance. Thirty-six! Impressive. We were happy for him.

"That was good, Wang Di." Li went up and thumped him on the arm. "So you're cut out to throw live grenades!"

"That was no big deal," Wang said without looking pleased. "And you didn't want me to do it." He spun around and walked off.

"I was worried about him," Li said, feeling euphoric. "Who'd have thought he actually got a 'good.' Our squad will surely get excellent now."

The soldiers after Wang all got "good" or better, making Li so happy he took out a pack of cigarettes to share with everyone. The last one up was Chief, who had thrown farther than anyone at practice. He looked fully confident.

"I'll go over fifty," he said with a cough.

He went up after finishing his cigarette. We stuck our heads up from the bunker to watch him. While uncapping the grenade to put the ring over his finger, he suddenly spoke up,

"Do I put the ring over my finger?"

"That's right," Li said from the bunker.

"But the fuse looks shorter." Chief sounded worried. "It won't go off too soon, will it?"

"Don't worry. The grenades are the all same."

We laughed. "So Chief is only good at the dummies," someone jeered, as he ran forward. He raised his arm after a few steps and then we heard him shout, "Oh no. The fuse is too short. I can hear it ready to explode."

I stuck my head up and saw his arm go limp as the grenade left his hand. Oh no! It didn't even travel twenty meters before there was smoke. Chief froze at the sight. Li Shangji leaped out of the bunker.

"Hit the deck!" Li shouted as he threw himself on Chief. They fell in a heap when the grenade went off. We ran out after the explosion.

"Are you all right?"

Li rolled up and spat out dirt, his eyes glaring at Chief.

"Did you have a death wish?"

Chief sat up on the ground, still dazed, gazing blankly at the crater in front of him.

"My fuse was too short," he finally managed to say.

"Nonsense! You think the armory made one just for you?"

The tape showed fifteen meters.

We all felt sorry for him, particularly because he'd worked so hard. He rolled around the ground and sobbed.

"I didn't mean it. I wanted to do better. You all saw what I could do during practice, didn't you?"

Utterly deflated, Li waved and said, "That's enough. I didn't expect you to do worse than Wang Di. You panicked when handling the real thing."

That only made Chief cry harder.

The test ended with that unhappy episode. We walked listlessly back to camp in single file. Wang Di was the only one in high spirits back at the barracks. He was humming a tune as he walked out with his rifle, saying he was going to practice for the next test.

Chief didn't sleep that night, for he had dark circles under his eyes the next morning. He stopped me by the toilet.

"Will they take away my title as key cadre because of the incident?"

"Don't worry so much, just get ready for the next test," I said. "They'll keep you on as a key cadre."

He nodded before adding, "But what about my post assignment?"

I had nothing to say about that. "I don't know. I can't tell you anything."

"I've let you down," he said tearfully. "I'm a key cadre and I only managed fifteen meters."

"Don't let that affect your marksmanship test."

"I'll show you I'm not totally worthless." He dried his tears and said with determination, "I'll do better in the next test."

"That's the right attitude. I believe you will."

He worked harder than anyone during target practice, lying there aiming his rifle even when the others were taking a break.

Target shooting had three parts: two hundred meters prone, one hundred and fifty meters kneeling, and one hundred meters standing. Sixty was a passing grade, seventy was good, and anything above eighty was excellent. After a demo from Li Shangjin, three soldiers came up and all made it over seventy. One of them, however, cut his finger when it was caught in the safety. Li wrapped the man's hand with a towel.

"Very good," he said. "That was good shooting. Go take care of that hand."

Wang Di was one of the next threesome. One of them got a passing grade while Wang and the other man both made it to excellent. It was dumb luck that Wang got exactly seventy, nearly missing one shot. The squad leader would have liked all three to get seventy, but he'd learned a lesson from the grenade throwing.

"Passing is good enough, better than failing."

Carrying his rifle upside down, Wang took out a pack of cigarettes, picked one out, and lit it, without offering to share. But then, to our surprise, he crouched down and began to sob.

"That's enough, Wang Di," I told him.

"Don't cry. You did well," Li said.

Three more came up, including Chief; Li and I were both nervous for his sake.

"Be calm, Chief," I said. "Pull the trigger slowly."

"Go ahead, do your best," Li said. "You can take the credit if you do well, but it will be on me if you don't."

Chief nodded gratefully, but his lips and hands were trembling.

"Relax, Chief, take your time."

The platoon leader, who was watching us from a distance, shouted angrily, "What's going on there? What are you waiting for?"

The three soldiers got down for the first round, drawing cheers when they were done. Chief did well, hitting two nines and a ten.

"Great, Chief. Keep it up." Li and I were happy for him.

Chief looked grim and said nothing. He got up, moved fifty meters forward with his rifle and knelt to shoot. Again he did well, getting an eight, a seven, and a ten. Another cheer erupted among us while we moved forward with him to the hundred meter mark. By then he was bathed in sweat.

"I can't see very well," he said.

"Only three more left. Just try to focus."

"The target is filled with holes. What if I hit someone else's holes?"

"Don't worry. Even a crack shot couldn't do that."

"The target doesn't look straight. The ones ahead of me must have made it cockeyed."

"Are you losing your head again, like when you were throwing grenades?" Li was losing his patience.

The platoon leader ran over with a flag and lashed out at Chief.

"What's matter with you? Why are you taking so much time? My arm's getting sore holding the flag."

Chief and the other soldiers raised their rifles and began shooting. Li Shangjin and I were stunned to see that Chief missed two altogether and the third shot only got a six. When he recovered, Li got down to add up Chief's score with a twig on the ground and came up with fifty-nine, a point shy of passing. Forgetting his promise, Li yelled at Chief, "Couldn't you have tried harder and gotten the extra point?"

When Chief finally came out of a daze, he said woodenly, "Didn't I say I couldn't see very well? But you didn't believe me. See what happened?"

"Enough!" the platoon leader said with irritation. "I knew you weren't cut out for this. I bet you couldn't see well when you were throwing the grenade either."

Chief opened his mouth, but a searing look from the platoon leader forced him to swallow his tears as he stared at the target with his rifle in hand.

Our squad did not look very good when the two live-ammo tests were over. We didn't pass because of Chief's low scores, which made Li Shangjin sigh repeatedly.

"We're finished. It's all over."

"We did pretty well with daily work and in our formations."

"We'll have to wait and see how the other squads did."

All the squads in the company finished the tests two days later. Lucky for us, three other squads failed also, and Li and I could finally be a bit more at ease, though we couldn't feel good about ourselves, since we hadn't passed.

Things began to change in the squad. With his low scores, Chief's status as a key cadre was in jeopardy and others treated him differently, as had happened to Wang before. He felt bad and behaved like a maligned little mouse. He wrote a letter of resolution to show he would pick himself up, but there wasn't much he could do, since basic training would be over in two weeks. Wang, on the other hand, was looking smug again after his performance with the grenade throwing and target shooting; he was forever humming a tune and constantly spewing sarcastic remarks about everyone else. Sometimes he sounded so blustery he didn't seem to think much about Li or me. Offended by his insolence, Li and I had a talk about him, and concluded:

"He did well with the tests but deep down he's a bad character."

Under normal circumstances, Chief had to be replaced by Wang Di as a key cadre, but Li and I decided to speak to the platoon leader on Chief's behalf.

"There's no need to change the key cadre now that basic training will be over in two weeks. Besides, Wang Di is so arrogant he'd revert to his petty bourgeois ways if he got to be a key cadre again. Remember last time, when he sent a notebook to the company commander? The others in the squad weren't too happy about that. And he's always badmouthing the platoon."

The platoon leader, who had been writing a letter, frowned as he read it before crumpling the sheet up and tossing it away.

"What?" He turned to look at us. "What did you just say?"

We repeated what we'd said, which he thought over with a frown.

"Do what you want then." He waved us away.

Hence, no adjustment was made regarding the key cadre. After waiting a few days, Chief's spirits rose when he realized he wouldn't be replaced, and got active again; pulling out all the stops, he ran around all day, sweeping the floor, bringing in water for everyone to wash up, cleaning the toilet, and raking the pigpen. Wang Di, in contrast, lost some of his swagger when nothing had changed.

Then came time for postings, a tense moment for everyone. Our hearts were in our throats, as we wondered where we would be sent, though, of course, it was pointless to think about it. One morning we were all called over to the drill ground to await an announcement for job assignments. Standing in formation, I could almost hear everyone's heart beating wildly in their chests, as we craned our necks for the moment when we'd learn our fate. Before reading off his list, the political instructor gave a speech that could hardly get our attention; we began to whisper among ourselves the moment he finished, but immediately quieted down when he gave us a dirty look.

We got terrible assignments because of our failing scores. Several were sent to man a boiler room, some to guard a warehouse, while some others were sent to a combat unit. Wang did better than any of us; he'd be going to army headquarters. He'd likely be sweeping floors and bringing water for his superiors, but it was, after all, a position at headquarters. In a way, he'd gotten Fatty's dream job, which bugged us all. He'd done well on the tests, but he was a terrible soldier. When we were dismissed, someone asked the platoon leader about Wang's assignment.

"He has qualifications the rest of you don't."

"Why?"

"Headquarters wants someone who's at least five-ten, and he's the only one in our platoon."

That knocked us for a loop. There really was no telling how life would turn out for every one.

Chief was the cause of the lousy assignments in our squad, and no one could bring himself to forgive him even though he'd worked so hard. In fact, Chief would be growing vegetables in the field, the worst assignment of all; he looked about to cry when he heard, but knew better and swallowed his tears.

Wang was grinning broadly when we returned to the barracks, packing up his stuff and commenting to Chief, "Growing vegetables is pretty good. You'll be close to the source of the good stuff."

Chief gave him a wordless look. Being assigned to the training corps, I didn't do badly, but I felt bad for the others and Wang's self-satisfaction only aggravated me even more.

"You'll be close to the source of good stuff too. You'll be seeing the commander all the time, with plenty of opportunities to make reports."

"Why you—" Wang's face turned bright red as he pointed a finger at me, looking to be on the verge of tears.

A movie was shown that night, so we lined up to go to company headquarters to watch it. Chief sat on his bed as we were filing out.

"Come see the movie, Chief."

He gave me a glazed look before saying. "I'd like to be excused." Then he lay down with a blanket over him.

"Chief is acting weird." Li Shangjin took me outside. "Why don't you stay and talk to him?"

After everyone left, I dragged Chief out to have a talk in the desert.

Spring was in full force, and there wasn't a hint of chill in the wind blowing in our faces. A few rare blades of grass were struggling to sprout on the barren land.

He looked lifeless and I couldn't find the right thing to say, except to resort to cliché: "Your life is just beginning, Chief, so don't lose your will to fight over a couple of setbacks."

He sighed and said, "The only thing that worries me is I signed up to be soldier but am ending as a vegetable farmer for the army."

"Ignore what Wang Di said. His assignment may look good, but he'll be doing chores and running errands. It's not that much better. Besides, he's a damned snitch. It won't take long for people to see through him."

He looked up at me wordlessly.

"To be sure, your assignment isn't the best, but you still fared better than Fatty. No one can forgive Wang Di when you think about how Fatty was discharged."

Out of the blue he put his arms around me, to my utter surprise.

"I want to tell you something." He was choking on tears. "But you must promise you won't be upset with me."

"What is it?"

"It wasn't Wang Di who ratted on Fatty."

"Who else could it be if not him?"

"It was me," he said flatly.

"You?!" Stunned, I struggled out of his arms and stared at him. "You? How could it be? Why did you do that?"

He began to wail. "Fatty had his mind set on being the army commander's driver. It sounded great to me, so I wanted that job. Back then, he and I were the key cadres and I thought I'd be the one if he wasn't chosen. I snitched on him to eliminate the competition."

I could only stare at him.

"Now I'm suffering retribution for my action." He continued to sob. "Growing vegetables! What was the point of being a key cadre then?"

"You, you . . ." I pointed a finger at him, struggling for words. "You're so—that was really vile."

He burst into loud wails, sitting on his haunches.

Neither of us said a word when he finally stopped.

From the base in the distance came the sound of people talking, a sign that the movie was over.

"Let's go back," I said to him.

"Please don't tell anyone," he said timidly. "I told you because I trust you."

"So you wouldn't have told anyone if you'd been selected to be the commander's driver, is that it?" I glared at him.

"I'd have felt really bad if I hadn't told you." He began to sob again.

"You ought to feel bad; you're a snitch." I was relentless. "So we blamed the wrong person. Wang Di isn't too bad after all." I walked off without waiting for him.

"Banfu!" he shouted after me, with a hint of despair in his voice.

7

On a Sunday shortly before the end of boot camp, we went shopping in Dadian, a market town that had sprung up near the army base. It had shops, a restaurant, and a few willows; everything else was desert. We bought notebooks as gifts for each other to commemorate the three months we'd spent together. On the cover page we wrote things that turned out to be pretty similar: "May our friendship last forever," or "Best wishes for further advancement in life," or "Here's to mutual encouragement." Then we exchanged notebooks. Chief, who was in a funk, walked around with his head down; he'd obviously been crying, for his eyes were puffy. But he bought a pile of notebooks, one for each member of the squad. On mine he wrote in his squiggly handwriting, "The road in life is not as even as Changan Avenue—a mutual encouragement with Banfu." I knew what he meant as I recalled our conversation on the way back from Dadian.

"I'll be tending fields soon, Banfu," he said after we'd walked in silence for a while.

"Drop me a note when you can, all right?" I felt a sudden pang of sadness.

He took a deep breath and said, "I have a favor to ask."

"What is it? I'll do what I can."

"Please keep this between us. It'd be the end of me if others knew."

"You have my word." I nodded.

"I'm not going to give Wang Di a notebook," he said after a pause.

"It's up to you who you give them to. Besides, I don't think he's giving anyone anything."

That was true; Wang Di returned from Dadian empty-handed, buying only some toffees that he put in his pocket. I saw him pop them into his mouth.

"Wang Di is really weird. He was all about mutual encouragement with the company commander when he shouldn't have been, but he refuses when everyone else is doing it. I guess we're not good enough for him anymore now that he's been assigned to army headquarters," someone observed.

"Encouraging my ass!" When he heard the comment, Wang Di spat out phlegm and toffee. "Everyone has treated me like an enemy during our three months together. What's the encouragement for?" He took off running.

No one knew how to respond to his outburst.

We began packing that night, washing everything that needed to be cleaned. Li Shangjin walked in and out, looking agitated. I knew it was still about his party membership. Basic training was coming to an end but he hadn't heard anything. He grabbed my hand while pacing the room when we were alone.

"Basic training is nearly over, so how come I haven't heard anything?"

"Yes, it's about time." I had to agree with him. "I don't know why either."

"Could the deputy company commander have lied to me?"

I gave that question some thought. "A deputy company commander must mean what he says."

"I'm sick from all this waiting," he said with a sigh.

I went out with several squad members to do some cleanup the following morning. When we were done, I returned to the barracks and saw Li lying on his bunk. He was staring silently at the ceiling, which told me he was thinking about the same thing again.

"Time to eat, Banzhang," I said to him.

Imagine my surprise when he jumped up, took my hand, and said, "It's done. It's a done deal."

"What's done?"

"You know."

"So they told you to fill out your application?" I was happy for him when I realized what he was talking about.

But he gave me a disapproving look. "I can't believe you don't know. They want to talk to me before it happens. A headquarters messenger came to tell me the P.I. wants to see me after lunch. It has to be about that, doesn't it? Why else would he want to talk to me if not for my admission to the party?"

"That's true."

He led me to a spot behind the door and opened his palm.

"Take another look. What do you think? Look again."

It was the girl's photo, of course. I had to take another look at the plump girl for his sake. "Not bad."

"It's been a month since I last wrote her." He sighed.

"Now you can write her again."

"Later. I'll do that tonight."

He pretty much inhaled his lunch at noon. When he finished, he wiped his mouth and smoothed his uniform at a mirror, before giving me a shy smile and taking off. He tiptoed back inside about twenty minutes later, during our afternoon nap.

"That was fast." I sat up.

He waved before getting onto his bed, where he lay quietly. I thought everything was settled and that he was happily focused on the contents of the letter he'd write that night, when we suddenly heard him sob.

"What's wrong?" I went over to touch him.

He started howling.

"What's the matter, Banzhang?" Everyone got up and crowded around.

Forgetting his concerns about his image and the people around him, he shouted, "Fuck the political instructor!"

"What happened?" We were stunned and puzzled.

"It's not right, Banfu!" he said between sobs.

"What's not right?"

"The deputy company commander said I could join, but the political instructor told me I can't."

"Did he say that?" I was taken aback.

"And that's not all. He also said I'll be discharged. Just think, how can I go home and face people like this?"

"Ai-ya!" I sucked in cold air. "That's so unexpected."

He began to cry again.

We were told to fall out. Everyone else in the squad walked out with their rifles, leaving the two of us in the room. By then he had stopped crying; he was squatting motionlessly on the bed, while I sighed to show my sympathy.

"How do you think I've done since joining the squad?" he asked, his head down.

"Pretty good."

"Do I get along with the comrades?"

"You do."

"Have I said or done anything unbefitting my position?"

"No."

"How was our squad's performance?"

"We did as well as any others, except for the grenade throwing and the shooting range."

"So why did the political instructor do this to me?"

"I can't even guess."

"He must have something against me." He gnashed his teeth and stood up to pace again. His eyes began to glaze over.

"Don't let that bother you too much, Banzhang."

He continued to pace without replying before squatting down again with his hands around his head. "I'd rather die than go home like this." He got to his feet and shouted at the window, "Fuck the political instructor!"

"Someone could hear you." I dragged him away from the window.

"So what?" He gave me a fierce look. "I'd rather die anyway."

He didn't calm down until that evening. We sat around trying to make him feel better shortly before lights-out.

"You all go to sleep, all right?" He said.

We thought he was still in a bad mood, so we went to our spots quietly. Even Wang Di was feeling sorry him and went back to his spot with a sigh, but he crawled over to Li's spot after taking off his pants.

"Here's some candy for you, Banzhang." He pushed his leftover candy into Li's hands.

The lights went out and we shut up. I stared at the ceiling, unable to fall asleep. This was the worst night since I'd joined the army, worse than the night after Fatty was discharged. People kept tiptoeing out to use the toilet and everyone was tossing and turning until after midnight, when we dozed off. Soon, however, we were roused by the sound of a rifle being fired. It was loud and crisp, so startling us that we got up and looked around,

"What was that? What just happened?"

That was followed by the whistle for emergency fall-out. We raced outside, not bothering to get dressed properly.

"What happened?" we asked each other.

Someone said there were enemy spies while someone else guessed that one of the sentry guards must have discharged his rifle by accident. The company commander, who ran up with his pistol to calm the scene, panted as he told us someone had fired a shot at the political instructor. Chaos erupted before he finished and my heart skipped a beat, just as the deputy company commander ran up to say that the P.I. thought the person looked like Li Shangjin. He added that the shot hit the P.I. in the arm, but it was not a serious injury. We were told to line up and arm ourselves to catch Li and stop him from defecting, as we were only several hundred kilometers away from the border.

Another commotion broke out as we lined up and loaded our rifles to go after Li. Since he was our squad leader, soldiers in other squads all gave us the eye, making us lower our heads. A jumble of thoughts ran through my head as I raced forward. I spotted our platoon leader up ahead, armed with a pistol, and went to ask him, "What's going on, sir?"

Wiping the sweat from his face, he shook his head and sighed. "He couldn't take the test. But no one expected him to do this."

"It must have something to do with his party membership."

"He had no idea that the party branch had begun discussing his case and would admit him fairly soon." He sighed again.

"Then why was he called in for a talk? Why tell him he'd be discharged?"

"It was just a test." He shook his head again. "The P.I. said Li looked odd when he was left out last time, so he came up with this idea to test him. See what happened?"

A loud buzz went off in my head.

"Why couldn't he use his head? This was clearly a test, because a basic training company doesn't have the authority to discharge soldiers."

Another loud clap sounded in my head; I was on the verge of tears.

"You were wronged, Banzhang, you were screwed."

We spread out to form a skirmish line after covering ten kilometers. The deputy company commander stationed us ten meters apart. Rifles in hand, we were to crawl forward on our stomachs on the cold ground to catch Li Shangjin. The deputy political instructor gave the order of no talking and no coughing. We must try to catch him alive, but we were allowed to fire and take him down if he ignored a warning or resisted arrest. Immediately the field was filled with the sound of bullets being pushing into rifle chambers.

I did what the soldiers beside me did, but with a silent prayer: "Don't run this way, Banzhang. Avoid the skirmish line."

The eastern sky was showing a fish-belly gray as it brightened up enough for me to see the other soldiers in the line. There was no sign of Li. So the deputy company commander called us back to the base for breakfast, after which we would search for him again. Our squad was given the task of checking every nettle bush, with me as the leader. We went about it in silence, even Wang Di, who only made one comment: "It'll be a tragedy whether we find him or not."

I gave him a look to shut him up.

We didn't find him after searching all day.

A skirmish line was formed again that night.

Li remained at large for three days.

News of his escape reached command headquarters, which issued an order that we must find him in three days or everyone, from the regiment, the battalion, and the company would be held responsible. It frightened everyone into action, including the political instructor, who joined the search with his bandaged arm.

Another day went by and still no sign of Li.

Lights were ablaze at company headquarters each night.

Finally on the third day he was caught. We didn't find him, however; he came out on his own with raised hands. Turned out he was hiding in a haystack by the river, not far from the base. He emerged from the stack and surrendered, bringing a collective sigh of relief and energizing us all. Covered in hay, he looked gaunt and sallow-faced, his army uniform in tatters. He was still wearing his collar and cap insignias, but they were snatched off the moment he was arrested. They took him to company headquarters for interrogation right away.

"Why did you shoot the political instructor?" the deputy company commander asked an exhausted Li.

"He hates me."

"How so?"

"He blocked my party application."

They both went quiet, before the deputy company commander resumed questioning:

"So you shot him?"

Li began to sob. "You told me I'd become a member when I rubbed your back in the bath, sir. But the political instructor said no. Why would he do that if he didn't hate me?"

The deputy company commander's face turned red as he banged on his desk.

"You've gone too far, Li Shangjin, and the nature of your problem has changed. You shot a political instructor. Were you going to defect after that? Why didn't you?"

"I never thought of defecting. I just wanted to kill myself in the river."

"What?" Unprepared for the answer, he looked at Li for a while before continuing, "Then why didn't you?"

"I, I thought about my father back home—"

More silence.

After the interrogation, the company commander told us to conduct an in-depth criticism of Li Shangjin. Standing before the soldiers, he said, "This is the same thing Lin Biao did. He plotted to kill Chairman Mao and Li Shangjin tried to kill the political instructor. Lin Biao was going to defect, so was Li Shangjin."

Li was taken to a small room by the pigpen after the meeting; Chief and I were sent to guard him. When we got there, the very spot where we'd worked hard to make the squad look better, he looked at us, both armed, with a sigh before walking into the room with his head down. A squad leader had become a despondent, demoralized prisoner. Everyone else slowly walked away, and finally there were just the three of us left.

"Please find me something to eat, Banfu." Li said. "I haven't had much to eat for nearly a week."

I was reminded of the earlier days, when he shared his meat buns when I went to the boiler room during my guard shift. I took Chief to the side and said, "I don't care what the rules say, Chief. I'm going to get him some food. You can report me if you want."

Chief's face turned bright red as he snapped the bayonet off his rifle and handed it to me.

"Put this in me if I do that again."

"Good. I trust you." I nodded, before sneaking into the kitchen for a bowl of leftover noodles. The moment I stole back into the room, Li grabbed the bowl and began to stuff the noodles into his mouth with his hands. He got food all over his face and at some point even choked on the noodles to the point that he stretched his neck trying to breathe. I quickly went up to thump him on the back. Chief and I both were saddened by Li's sorry state.

Li sat against the wall that night while Chief and I sat outside.

"You shouldn't have done that, Banzhang," I said, but I realized he was fast asleep when I looked over.

"Wake up, Banzhang," Chief shouted.

We couldn't wake him no matter what we did, which brought tears to our eyes again.

"I have an idea, Banfu."

"What is it?"

"We let him go."

Stunned, I took a quick around us before covering his mouth with a hand.

"Not so loud."

"We'll let him go. What do you say?" Chief was whispering.

"What for?"

"He can run away." He blinked.

"Where can he run to?" I sighed. "Do you honestly expect him to cross the border?"

Falling silent, he just kept sucking in air.

"You're a good pal, Chief."

The night passed amid Li's snores.

A prisoner transport arrived from division headquarters to pick up Li Shangjin the next morning. He was only half awake when he was pushed on board and didn't even turn to look at us as he was driven away.

Chief and I stood blankly in front of the room.

"What's that?" Chief shouted. Looking in the direction he was pointing, I spotted a piece of paper inside. We went in to pick it up. It was the photo of Li's fiancée, a plump girl with thick braids, smiling back at us.

8

We heard, three days later, that Li was given a fifteen-year sentence.

The news didn't cause much of a stir at the company level, not after a thorough criticism was conducted over those three days. We were given a task and we all spoke up, taking our job seriously, just as before, when we had criticized Lin Biao. And the criticism was as comprehensive as the one against Lin Biao.

Everyone was looking out for himself during the criticism sessions, doing their best so as not to affect their job assignments. Li was one of us, so our squad was considered the "worst-hit area," which brought the political instructor and the company commander to our criticism sessions. Hesitant at first, we were soon vying with each other to come up with the most damning criticism, dredging up issues big and small, in Li's daily life to create the image of a most despicable criminal. It seemed the more we said against Li the more distance we could put between him and us. Wang, who had been sympathetic to Li with his reference of a tragedy, was the first to speak up, clearly hoping to avoid any adverse affects on his job assignment. He even offered something analytical, saying that Li's defection had its ideological roots in when he was disciplined for taking a bayonet home with him few years before. The P.I. nodded repeatedly in agreement. The others spoke up after Wang. Chief began to waver and sought me out during break and said with a red face,

"I'm going to have to do it too, Banfu."

"Go ahead." I gave him a look of contempt. "Did I tell you not to?"

"It would look terrible if I was the only who didn't." His face was even redder now. "I have to put on a show."

So he did when the meeting resumed. Although he had said it was for show, he went into detail, saying that Li Shangjin was depraved, always carrying the picture of a woman. He kept looking at the picture, Chief added, even after he was arrested. The company commander and the political instructor pricked up their ears; that was too much for me so I cut in, "It was a photo of his fiancée."

"If that's the case, then it was all right for him to look at it," the political instructor said.

"Of course he wouldn't be looking at it now. The girl wouldn't want him now that he's in prison," I added.

Everyone laughed, but we all felt terrible, so the criticism session ended.

Chief sought me out again at lunch.

"I probably shouldn't have done that, should I?"

"What are you saying, Chief?" I was irritated. "Did I told you not to? Did you know you'd get me into trouble when you said that?"

He covered his face with his hands and began to cry.

We were cleared after criticizing Li Shangjin and our job prospects were unaffected; we all got to keep our original assignments. The soldiers would begin to leave for their assigned company after a meal of braised pork.

Wang Di was the first to leave, in grand style; a Jeep was sent from army headquarters for him. No one in the squad had ever ridden in one of those before, so we all went out to watch him leave. He shook everyone's hand without looking pleased, saying simply, "Come see me at headquarters."

The platoon leader, who had been writing a letter in the barracks, crumpled two sheets of paper and came out to see Wang off. Wang actually ignored him and didn't shake his hand until the very end.

"I've caused you a great deal of trouble over the past three months, sir. I know I should have done better to keep my status as a key cadre. Please come look up me whenever you're in Dadian."

For some reason that turned the platoon leader's face red.

Wang walked up to me when the driver started the Jeep.

"I'm off now, Banfu."

"So long, Wang Di."

He took me to the side and, with his eyes reddening, said, "Do you know what they want me to do there?"

"Aren't you going to be a clerk?"

"I was assigned to be a clerk, but the driver told me just now that I'm there to wipe the butt of the army commander's invalid father."

"Really!"

"I was such a screw-up." He sighed. "You'll forgive me, won't you?"

"Wang Di!" I held his hands, lost for words.

"My grannie has been laid up for three years now, and I haven't been able to care for her."

"No matter what, do your job well when you get there."

"You're right, of course." He nodded and sighed again. "Please don't tell anyone, or they'll laugh their heads off."

I gave him a vigorous nod.

The Jeep went off with Wang Di on board, trailed by puffs of exhaust.

The political instructor from the army farm was next to come pick up their new member. A stumpy, swarthy man from Henan, Chief's superior sounded like a straight shooter. Chief, who had been in a funk over his job assignment, perked up when his political instructor gave him the good news. Having been a key cadre, Chief stood out among all the other soldiers assigned to the farm, so he was promoted as deputy squad leader even before reporting for duty. A blessing in disguise put him in a great mood, as he offered a cigarette to his superior while peppering the man with questions.

"You don't get many perks at the farm except for a fast track to party membership," the man said with the cigarette in his mouth.

Beside himself with joy, Chief nearly broke out in a dance, while the rest of us looked on with envy, as if growing vegetables were better than working at army headquarters.

Chief cleared his throat a couple of times and, looking at us, said to his political instructor, "I'll go wherever you tell me to, sir. I'll do it even if it's to take the comrades in the squad to feed pigs."

"We'll talk about work when we get back," The man laughed heartily.

That afternoon, the future deputy squad leader, Chief, got on the truck that the farm used to transport sheep droppings and left in high spirits to grow vegetables.

One by one, the other soldiers were picked up.

I waited until everyone was gone before leaving with my pack on my back. Being assigned to a training unit, I did better than the others in the squad. The camp for my new unit was a ways off, and I had to board a train at a small military station to get there. The platoon leader, who had to take the train back to his old company, was my traveling companion. No longer acting like a platoon leader, he chatted away, but I wasn't in the mood to join in the conversation.

"What's the matter?" he asked.

"I feel bad, sir."

"What for? Because of Li Shangjin?"

I shook my head.

"Wang Di?"

I shook my head again.

"Chief?"

More head shaking from me.

"For the others in the squad?"

I kept shaking my head.

"Then what for?"

"I got a letter from my father today."

"Something happened in the family?"

I had to shake my head again.

"Then what?" He fixed his eyes on me.

"He told me Fatty is dead."

"What?" He jumped in disbelief. "How could that be?"

I handed him the letter from my father.

It had arrived that afternoon. After he was discharged, my father said, Fatty didn't learn to be a bricklayer with him. Instead he stayed home to work the land. At some point he disappeared and, after three days, his family was so worried, a search was conducted. In the end they found him in a well northeast of the village, his body so bloated it looked like risen bread dough. He must have suffered a bout of epilepsy while drawing water.

"His epilepsy acted up again." He thumped the letter. "There was nothing anyone could do about it."

"I knew him well, sir." I couldn't hold back my tears. "It couldn't have been his epilepsy."

"Then what?"

"He was clearly a suicide."

"No!" He stared wide-eyed.

We walked in silence for a long time until we were near the train station.

"How long ago was that?"

"Didn't my father say it was two weeks ago?"

"Have you told anyone else in the squad?"

I shook my head.

It was dark by then, but the night sky of the Gobi Desert had an unusually bluish tint, as an enormous silvery moon appeared on the horizon.

The train whistled its way into the station.

"Let's go," he said.

So off we went, with our backpacks over our shoulders.

Remembering 1942

1

In 1942, Henan province experienced a catastrophic famine. A friend I respected sent me off to 1942 with a plate of bean sprouts and two stewed pig's feet. To be sure, this farewell dinner, had it been offered in 1942, would have been considered a gourmet meal, but at the same time, it might not have been all that impressive. In February 1943, when Theodore White, a reporter for *Time* magazine, and Harrison Forman, of the *Times of London*, went to investigate the Henan famine, where mothers cooked and ate their own babies, the provincial officials of my hometown hosted a banquet for the two foreign visitors with the following menu: thick soup with lotus seeds, spicy chicken, beef stewed with chestnuts, tofu, fish, fried spring rolls, hot steamed buns, rice, and two soups, plus three stuffed flatbreads sprinkled with sugar crystals. Even today, uncultured citizens like us can only read about such food in books or on the menus of fancy restaurants. White said it was one of the best meals he'd ever had; I say it was the one of best meals I'd ever read about. But then he added that he could not bring himself to finish it. In my view, the provincial officials of my hometown would never have been so shy. In a word, food was a big problem back home in 1942 and 1943, but it was likely an issue only for the common people. I imagine that in this ancient Eastern civilization, no government officials above the

county level would, under any circumstance, ever suffer a food shortage any more than they would face a dearth of sexual gratification.

For me there was another problem. As I traveled back to 1942
through a boring tunnel smelling of urine and mildew, I realized that
my friend had greatly exaggerated the importance of the mission he
gave me. After polishing off the bean sprouts and pig's feet, he told
me about 1942 in a tone befitting a commanding officer.

From the summer of 1942 to the spring of 1943, the catastrophic
drought ravaged the province, virtually wiping out both the summer
and fall harvests. The drought was followed by a scourge of locusts
that affected five million peasants, about twenty percent of the province's population. The shortage of water and the hordes of locusts
wrought havoc in a hundred and eleven counties.

Impacted peasants ate grass roots and tree bark, and the fields
were littered with the bodies of those who starved. The going rate
for women dropped by ninety percent, while the price of a young
man was reduced by two thirds. A vast area of the Central Plains was
affected and more than three million starved.

Three million dead. The somber look on his face sent chills through
me, but I had to laugh when I actually returned to 1942. True, three
million had died, but that was a trifling matter when examined in the
historical context. As three million people were dying, this is what was
happening at the time: Madame Chiang Kai-shek visited the United
States, Gandhi waged a hunger strike, a bloody battle took place in
Stalingrad, and Churchill caught a cold. In the global context of 1942,
any one of these incidents was more important than the death of three
million. Five decades later, we all know about Churchill, Gandhi,
the charming Madame Chiang, and Stalingrad, but who is aware that
three million people died in my home province from a drought? Back
then, the Nationalist party, the Communist party, the Japanese army,
the Americans, and the British were all embroiled in wars in Southeast Asia and inside China, including the border regions of Shaanxi,

Gansu, and Ningxia. The commander-in-chief, Generalissimo Chiang, was faced with a delicate political quandary, a jumbled mess that would have forced anyone, not just him, to push the three millions aside to deal with other problems. The three million was their own problem. So the mission my friend gave me dealt with details, not the big picture, as negligible as a sesame seed, not as weighty as a watermelon. The world's centers of action were the White House, 10 Downing Street, the Kremlin, Hitler's underground bunker, Tokyo, and the Huangshan Residence in Chongqing, China. In these luxuriously decorated sites, a select few, who dressed in clean clothes, drank coffee, and enjoyed hot baths, would determine the fate of the majority of the world's population. But these pivotal places and people were a long way from me, as I traveled, dirty and disheveled, back to a Hunanese disaster area littered with the bodies of those who had died of starvation. The explanation for this, the only explanation, is that I was destined to be the descendant, beginning in 1942, of those muddled, lowly disaster victims. The final problem: my friend had bought two pig's feet to see me off, but was in such a hurry he forgot to remove the hooves, so I was rushed off onto my journey after eating still-hooved pig's feet. You can see how reckless we were.

2

My maternal grandmother had no memory of the catastrophic drought of fifty years before.

"Grannie, fifty years ago there was a drought, and many people starved," I said to her.

"People starved during lots of years. Which year are you talking about?"

Grandma, who was ninety-two, had seen pretty much everything that happened to China during the twentieth century. An ordinary woman from the countryside, she worked for a landlord before 1949 and became a commune member after Liberation. She experienced ninety-two years of Chinese history. Without many thousands of common, dirty Chinese, the surging waves of revolution and counterrevolution would have been for naught, for they are the ones who, in the end, always suffer from disasters and pay for successes. But they have no role to play in history, for history is a stroll through magnificent halls. Which is why Grandma felt no shame in professing her forgetfulness. But the drought affected her countrymen, her own people, and it felt somehow wrong for her not to remember. She once saved my life, but that involved another disaster, one in 1960. A gentle woman, she was illiterate but possessed a great understanding of the world. I have always thought that China owes its development and confidence to these gentle, reasonable people, not to the lives of its sinister, cruel citizens. I take great comfort in the fact that, thanks to the care of a country doctor, she enjoyed good health and an infallible memory; in fact, she remembered the tiniest details from all our childhoods—my mother, my siblings, and me. I am convinced that she forgot 1942 not because of it wasn't tragic, but because people died so often in her past. It is fruitless to reproach those in power over those ninety-two years, but any official who saw people starve in his district should feel greater shame than my Grandma if he, his clan, and his children did not suffer. Doesn't being ruled by people like that bother and scare us? But her commonplace tone softened my agitation and anger, prompting me to laugh at myself. History focuses on the big picture; history is selective and easily forgotten. Who is in charge of the sieve with all its holes?

In 1942, after the drought came locusts that blanketed the sky and blotted out the sun. This special sign spurred Grandma to recall the connection between locusts and deaths.

"That one I know. So you were referring to the year of the locusts. Many people died that year, when locusts wiped out all the crops. Niu Jinbao's aunt set up an altar, and I went there to burn incense."

"Did the locusts come after a major drought?"

"Yes, there was a drought." She nodded. "Without a drought there would have been no locusts."

"Did many people die?"

"A few dozen, I think."

She was right. A few dozen in her village, or three million throughout the province. "What happened to those who didn't die?"

"Turned into refugees, of course. Your second great aunt was with one group and your third great aunt another group, and they all fled to Shanxi."

Neither great aunt is still alive. I can vaguely recall second great aunt's death and her black-lacquered coffin. I was in my twenties when third great aunt died; she was blind, her hair was gray, and she was curled up on a straw mat in the kitchen like a dog. Her son, Uncle Huazhua to me, had been a village party secretary for twenty-four years, from 1948 to 1972, but he had not managed to get himself a decent house and had become a village laughingstock. Putting Second Great Aunt and Third Great Aunt aside, I said,

"What about you, Grandma?"

"I didn't flee. The master was nice to me, so I worked the fields for him."

"Was the drought really bad?"

"Of course it was. The land cracked like a child's mouth and sizzled when you poured water on it."

She was right. After checking with her, I went to see Uncle Huazhua, who was, after all, the village party secretary, and recalled all the important things. The moment I brought up 1942, he said,

"A serious drought that year."

"How bad?"

Puffing on an Ashima cigarette I gave him, he said,

"Not a single drop of rain in the spring and less than thirty percent of the wheat was harvested. Some people got nothing out of their fields. Most of the wheat seedlings didn't survive, and even if they had, they couldn't produce any wheat."

"Did people die of starvation?"

"A few dozen did."

"But thirty percent of the harvest was saved, so how did they starve?"

He glared at me. "They had to pay rent for the land, didn't they? And grain for the army, and taxes. They couldn't pay the taxes even if they sold the land, so if they had survived the famine, they'd have been beaten to death by yamen officials."

Now I understood. "How old were you?" I asked.

He blinked and said, "Fifteen or sixteen."

"What did you do?"

"I didn't want to starve, so I fled to Shanxi with my ma."

I left him to seek out Uncle Fan Kejian, who, in 1942, was head of the richest family in the area. My grandma and grandpa worked for them; master and workers were very close. He became my Grandma's adopted son when he was only a few months old. Grandma told me that his mother turned the boy over to her at mealtime and she carried him around on her hip. After 1949, their status changed; Grandma was labeled a poor peasant, while his father was shot during a counterrevolutionary suppression campaign. He himself was considered a landlord and was kept under public surveillance until 1978. His wife, Aunt Jin Yinhua complained to me that she hadn't enjoyed a single good day after marrying him—only decades of suffering. Why had she done that? Well, they had married at the end of 1948. Over the years, my family maintained close ties with the Fan family. Uncle Fan greeted Grandma with "Ma" when they met. I witnessed with my own eyes how Grandma, like her master of the old days, generously handed a moon cake to the man who called her Ma, and he showed his gratitude with a smile.

So Uncle Fan Kejian and I sat under a dead scholar tree (it had probably been alive in 1942) and recalled the year together. He didn't know what 1942 was at first.

"Nineteen forty-two? What year was that?"

I was reminded that he was a privileged member of the ancien régime, so I should not have used the Western system, which has been in use only since 1949. So I said it was the thirty-first year of the Republic. To my surprise, the mention of the year really set him off.

"Don't talk to me about Republican year thirty-one. It was a terrible year."

"Why is that?"

"One of our small buildings burned down."

"Why?" I was puzzled.

"There was a drought that year, wasn't there?"

"Yes," I agreed, "a terrible drought."

"Locusts came after the drought."

"That's right, there were locusts."

"Many people died of hunger."

"Yes. They did."

He flicked the cigarette away.

"Many people died, and those who didn't stirred up trouble. Led by Wu De'an and armed with hay choppers and red-tasseled spears, they occupied one of our buildings. They killed the livestock, saying they were starting an uprising. At one point over a thousand people came to eat for free at our house."

I tried to defend the poor. "They had no choice. They were hungry."

"I know they were hungry and they had no choice, but they shouldn't have pillaged people."

"Yes, that was wrong. What happened next?"

He responded with an enigmatic smile. "Then a fire broke out. The sesame stalks were soaked in oil, so Wu De'an and his men were burned alive. The others fled."

"I see."

So that was what happened. A drought brought famine, causing people to die from hunger or turn to plundering and worse.

After bidding him good-bye, I sat down with a CCP representative of the county consultative congress who had been county party secretary before 1949. A tall, declining old man, he had an uncontrollable shake of the head, due to Parkinson's disease. Congress member or not, his clothes were old and tattered, the lapels covered with rice and oil stains. He lived in a compound with a courtyard, a tumbledown house with brittle yellow weeds growing on the roof. Before I had a chance to bring up 1942, he grumbled about his current situation, though I was not convinced he had a right to complain. His most powerful moment had been as party secretary before 1949, a position that differed from that of the current county party secretary, an official who served the interests of a county with hundreds of thousands of people. The county secretary of the old days was just a scribe, and back then the county population was only about two hundred thousand. He stopped complaining when I asked about 1942, and seemed to have returned to the days when he was young and powerful. His eyes lit up, even his head stopped shaking.

"I was the youngest county secretary in all the counties in the area, only eighteen."

I nodded. "Old Mr. Han, I heard there was a severe drought in 1942."

He managed to keep his head still.

"Yes," he said. "There was a charity performance by Chang Xiangyu and I was in charge of that."

I nodded again as a sign of respect. In 1991, the south was ravaged by a flood, and I saw a charity performance on TV. To me it was no simple matter to bring together all the performers, with their various backgrounds and talents. Imagine my surprise when I heard that he had organized one years before. He followed that revelation up with detailed descriptions of the successful performance and his spur-of-the-moment solutions to problems that cropped up in the process. He talked and laughed heartily.

"How bad was the drought?" I asked after he finished.

"Bad, of course. Why else would we have put on a performance?"

Skirting the performance, I persisted:

"I've heard that many people died of hunger. How many in our county?"

His head began to shake, from left to right, in rhythmic, quick movements, before he finally said,

"Twenty thousand or more, I think."

He couldn't recall. More than twenty thousand hadn't left much of an impression on a scribe. As I said good-bye to him and his charity performance, I heaved a sigh, shaking my head along with him.

This is what I've discovered about the Henan drought. According to the provincial gazette, Yanjin was one of the counties that suffered the most, but my interviews were fragmentary, incomplete, and inaccurate. After fifty years, flawed memories and personal additions or deletions by people I interviewed eliminated the need to take them at face value. What I needed to pay attention to was a report by Zhang Gaofeng, a war correspondent sent to Henan by the Chongqing edition of the *Ta Kung Pao*. Written and published in 1942, it was far more credible than personal memories. "The Truth about the Henan Disaster" not only described the drought and famine, but also what the starving people ate, which convinced me that perusing old newspapers was much more rewarding than interviewing people about the old days. It maintained a distance between the calamity and me and allowed me to sympathize with the people who suffered, while I remained well fed and warm.

The report was published on January 17, 1942.

△   This reporter must first tell the reader that today in Henan tens of thousands of people maintain a pitiful existence with tree bark (they have eaten all the leaves) and weeds. No one mentions the glory of "Army First" any longer, and "starving people fill the land" is but an inadequately sad phrase used to describe the disaster in Henan by those who are well fed and warm.

△   I need not dwell on the drought in Henan. The lofty phrase, "Save the people of Henan," has not only appeared in Chinese newspapers, but in Allied papers as well. I once felt "comforted" by those words, imagining three million people looking around desperately, the light of hope re-emerging in their eyes. But it was merely hope, and as time went by, all hope was once again buried in their sunken eyes.

Δ   One hundred and ten counties (including those under enemy control) were affected, with varying degrees of severity that can be marked by rivers. The areas near the Yellow River and Funiu Mountain were worst hit, followed by the regions along the Hong, Ru, and Luo rivers, and by the area around the Tang and Huai rivers.

Δ   Henan is a province of barren lands and poverty-stricken residents. Since the opening of war with Japan, the populace has faced the enemy on three sides. Then, when the war was at its most savage, a natural disaster struck. In the third and fourth months, western Henan experienced hail and frost, southern and central Henan suffered high winds, and eastern Henan was struck by locust attacks. Once summer arrived, not a drop of rain fell anywhere in the province for three straight months; rain in the early fall brought only a brief respite. A drought of disastrous proportions occurred. Before buckwheat in western Henan could be harvested, a heavy frost prevented the wheat berries from forming and the crop froze. In the eighth and ninth months, riverfront counties suffered a flood that turned the fields into oceans. A flood on the heels of a drought turned Henan into hell on earth.

Δ   Now they have eaten all the leaves on the trees. Every day, people go to the public mortars at village entrances to grind peanut shells and elm bark (the only edible bark) before steaming it for food. A child in Ye County said to me, "Mister, that stuff scratches my throat."

Δ   At every meal, dozens of refugees come to our door begging and crying for help. We cannot bear to look into their sallow faces and lusterless eyes, because we have nothing for them to eat.

Δ   Xiaosi died today, followed by Youlai, who was killed by a toxic weed, followed by Xiaobao on the outskirts of the village. Wretched, once lively members of the next generation are dying off.

Δ Recently I've noticed that the refugees' faces are puffy and that dark patches have appeared around their nostrils and in the corners of their eyes. At first I thought that was caused by hunger, but then I was told that it was a result of eating a toxic plant called moldy flower, a dry weed with no juice that turns green when ground up. I tried it and detected a putrid, musty smell. Even the legs of pigs grow numb after eating the weed, so what makes people eat it? The refugees know it is bad for them, but they say to me, "Mister, some people can't even get this. Now we have this stinging pain in our teeth and gums, our faces and limbs." Yes, the people in Ye county cannot find this weed, so they eat a type of kindling, which cannot be pounded into powder; but at least they do not have puffy faces and numb limbs. An old man said to me, "In my worst nightmare I never dreamed I'd be eating firewood one day. It's worse than death."

Δ All the livestock was slaughtered long ago. The pigs are nothing but skin and bones, the chicken's eyes droop from hunger.

Δ One jin of wheat fetches two jin of pork or three and half jin of beef.

Δ Primitive trade is in practice once again in Henan. No one wants the children. Men put their young wives or teenage daughters on mules and take them to Tuohe in eastern Hunan, Zhoujiakou and Jieshou, where they are sold into prostitution. Yet the price of a person is not enough to buy four bushels of wheat. A bushel of wheat costs nine hundred yuan, six hundred and forty-nine yuan for a bushel of sorghum, seven hundred for a bushel of corn, ten yuan for a jin of millet, eight yuan for a jin of steamed bread, fifteen yuan for a jin of salt, and the same for sesame oil. Without a solution to the famine, the price of food stays high, and the people have given up on finding food. The old, the weak, the women and children can only wait to be claimed by death. Young, strong men often take risks out of desperation. If the situation continues, instead of disaster relief, Henan will have to fight bandits to safeguard peace and maintain order.

Δ   With the arrival of winter, snowflakes have begun to fall. With no firewood, rice, or clothes, the people suffer both hunger and cold. The flimsy snowflakes are a vivid symbol of their fate. Time is running out to save these people.

3

Signs of life appeared in the fresh air at the Huangshan residence in Chongqing, where the mountains are blanketed with red peach blossoms and fiery camellia flowers each spring. After the fall of Nanjing, the Republican government moved its capital to Chongqing, where the Huangshan residence became the Generalissimo's official home. One of his four official houses, it was not affected by the nation's peril or its strengths and weaknesses; it compared well with the residence in Nanjing, and was no worse than the White House or 10 Downing Street. Chiang was, after all, the leader of a nation. No matter what your skin color, once you become the leader of a nation, you enjoy world-class food and housing, even when the people under your rule live altogether different lives. That is why I have always been a proponent of world leaders shaking hands and chatting among themselves, for they are the true class brothers. People of the world's nations need not unite nor have anything to do with each other. Even war is nothing to fear, because the leaders will not be hit until the last bomb falls, if then. If a nuclear war does break out, the few who remain standing will be the leaders of nations, for they will live above the earth with great views of the world below, their fingers on the buttons. The ones controlling the buttons will never be harmed.

The two centers of the Huangshan residence were Yunxiu Tower and Song Hall, where Chiang and the alluring Madame

Chiang stayed separately; hard to say what the arrangement was at night, if they felt like some activity. Air-raid shelters beneath the two structures afforded them the opportunity to escape air attacks by their class brother, the Emperor of Japan. How they lived day to day is difficult to ascertain, but they probably ate and drank as often as they wished, faring much better than one-point-nine-nine billion of the two billion Chinese living in the nation fifty years later. Anything beyond that is hard to imagine. Chiang could be assured that the Chinese and Western food served him was perfectly edible, but not elm bark and moldy flower; he drank water, not alcohol, did not smoke, had false teeth, and believed in Jesus. In 1942, Chiang had an argument with his advisor, an American named Stilwell. When they were about to part in anger, Madame Chiang tried to save the day with a pretty smile:

"You're an old friend, General, please don't be upset. Come to my villa for a cup of delicious coffee."

I read that somewhere. I wasn't interested in the argument, since both men were no longer with us. What caught my attention was that "delicious coffee" was still available in China in 1942, while people in my hometown were eating bark, firewood, straw, and toxic, moldy flowers that caused dropsy. Three million starved to death. Of course, contrasts like that show only that I was into something meaningless, vulgarizing everything. I also knew that for the head of a major state, the issue was not that his wife had coffee, just as long as they did not drink human blood (I heard that the emperor of the Central African Republic did that every day). No matter what they drank, he would be a national hero and a great historical figure as long as he managed the country well. I read somewhere else that, in order to get on the good side of the local militia, Chiang once said to Dai Li, the head of the secret service,

"Go take care of the problem. Remember, you can spend as much as you need."

Where did the money come from?

What I want to say is, he should not have disregarded the news of a famine in Henan when it reached the official residence in 1942. Of course he probably believed it, just not entirely. He said, "There may be a famine, but it can't be that bad." He even suspected the local officials of embellishing the crisis in order to get more relief money, like the army inflating the number of soldiers to get more supplies. Several decades later, his attitude was criticized in books whose authors condemned him for ignoring the people's suffering, for not caring enough, or for being obstinate. I was affected by how the authors wrote about the people as if they were their own children, and by their scathing comments about a heartless dictator. But I had to laugh when I calmed down, for it dawned on me that it was not he who deserved to be condemned, but these presumptuous authors who wrote decades later. Who had his head in the clouds, the attendant or the prime minister? The attendant, for sure. How could anyone understand what he was thinking without putting himself in his shoes, a man in an exalted position? Weren't all these authors useless scholars? How could he not be smarter than scholars—he was the Generalissimo! Who was the leader, a scholar or the Generalissimo? Who was more knowledgeable? Once again, the Generalissimo, naturally. It all rested with him—he cared about everything in the world, including the billions of people who inhabited it. Back then his thought processes were profound, far-reaching, and intricately complex, making it impossible for us to understand. Would he really dismiss news of drought and famine in Henan out of hand? Of course not. Unlike Madame Chiang, he came from an impoverished background. As he once wrote:

"My father died when I was nine. It is impossible to describe the miserable situation of my family at the time. Left completely alone, with no support, we were the targets of insults and abuse."

Someone with that sort of background had to know the hardships facing the masses on the lowest rungs of society. He could not possibly have been ignorant of the severity of the drought in any of the provinces. The scholars were mistaken in thinking that he was only a bureaucrat, while in fact they were the ones with their heads in the clouds. He knew what was happening. Then why did he not say what he was thinking? Why did he say it was not serious when he knew it was? Because before him lay many more serious and more complex issues that he had to solve carefully so as not to commit a grave historical error. We must realize that history will not be affected by the starving deaths of three millions; the Generalissimo was no longer a country bumpkin, but the leader of a nation. As a leader, he knew his priorities.

Here were some of the factors that could have changed the direction of history at the time:

First, China's status within the Alled forces, which included the United States, Great Britain, France, Russia, and China. Chiang might have been the leader of China, but when sitting down for a meeting with these leaders, he was reduced to the status of an ordinary person, a little brother, someone of no importance. None of them— Roosevelt, Churchill, or Stalin—thought much of him. If he meant nothing to them, that was a sign that China meant nothing to them. As a result, China was often the victim of aggression on the world's battlefields. As the poorest nation, it needed foreign aid to fight the war, and that was controlled by others; he could not complain about ill treatment. Chiang suffered insults and abuse, a loathing that roiled him deep down.

Second, the war with Japan. Chiang's army engaged most of the Japanese forces within its borders. Though losses of territory were substantial, by slowing the Japanese advances he delivered an incalculable edge to the other Allied nations, in terms of global strategies. But the leaders of those nations either did not note his contributions or decided to humiliate him in spite of them. The task of containment demanded far more from the Chinese Nationalist army than the aid it received. Most of the Nationalist army was engaged in a fight with Japan, giving the Communists respite in their base area; this influenced Chiang's policy toward the Communists. He was convinced that internal peace must be achieved before one can fight an external enemy. In terms of national interests, that concept was too narrow and could easily infuriate the populace. But from the perspective of a leader, it was essential. Focusing on fighting off invaders would make it easier for an internal enemy to grow strong enough to deal a fatal blow. He suffered tremendous international and domestic pressure over this policy.

Third, the Nationalist Party and the government were plagued by serious factional infighting. Chiang had once said ruefully that he should not have taken in so many warlord armies after the Northern Expedition of 1926. After 1949 he said, "My defeat was dealt not by the Communists, but by the Nationalists."

Fourth, serious strategic and personal conflicts arose between Chiang and his chief-of-staff, the American General Joseph Stilwell, which problematized American aid and Chiang's credibility in the US. Stilwell had already begun to refer to the Chinese leader behind his back as a "peanut."

These issues, as well as some that only Chiang knew as a result of his position, could easily have changed the direction of history and the way it was to be written. At a moment like this, drought in one province (there were more than thirty provinces at the time) must have seemed insignificant. Those who perished were mainly useless individuals, burdens on society, and could not possibly change the direction of history. By contrast, if Chiang dealt carelessly with his major political issues, history could very well have developed in a direction detrimental to him. What happened between 1945 and 1949 proves that that is what happened. For a national leader, any one of these issues would have a more direct and more consequential impact on him and his leadership position than three million people. From the perspective of historical importance, three million people were indeed of less consequence than a Peanut. So he was aware of the drought, but said it wasn't as severe as people said. As a result, he hated those who treated him as a fool or a bureaucrat and tirelessly provided him with data while mistakenly believing that he did not know what was happening, especially those meddling foreigners who were given to interfering in the internal affairs of other nations. This is what was going through Chiang's mind, how he saw the situation. But viewed from the perspective of the millions of drought victims, we cannot help but feel that he was a heartless, cruel dictator who did not care about the people's livelihood. One rule of thumb in this world has it that we common people will always suffer if we somehow get tangled up with a national leader. Owing to Chiang's attitude, thousands of victims were reduced to eating bark and other inedible, even toxic things, with no aid, no relief, and no assistance from the government. And so, a huge portion of the population died of hunger. But this was not the most important aspect of the situation; what made it worse were the taxes and provisions for the army exacted by the government while people were dying of hunger.

Chen Bulei said,

"Generalissimo Chiang does not for a minute believe there is a famine in Henan, claiming it has been faked by the provincial government. Chairman Li Peiji (of the Henan provincial government) said in a telegram that death was everywhere, that people were crying out for help, and so on. The Generalissimo condemned this as a fake report and ordered the collection of taxes from Henan as usual."

It was as if the government had picked up a knife to assist the famine by slaughtering people who, like dumb animals, stumbled around with glazed-over eyes. As a result, many died, while those who managed to survive formed a mass migration out of the area. Fifty years later, we can share the Generalissimo's view that the situation could not have been so bad, for that is the nature of the things. When we view a problem years after it has occurred, we are usually more broad-minded and wonder just how severe it could have been. But as the event unfolded, history was not so forgiving. In order to prove my point, once again I have to cite reference material, as I am convinced that it is more scientific to cite information trawled from historical reportage than for a writer to fabricate a story. To be sure, the latter can give a reader the feel of firsthand experience, but it is not factual and the data can be inaccurate; fifty-year-old material is more trustworthy than something conjured up through our imagination five decades later. In 1942, the American diplomat John S. Service wrote in a report to the US government:

> The greatest burden on the Henan farmer has been steadily increasingly in kind and requisitioning of military grain. This burden has been made heavier by the requirement that the province help to feed armies in South Shanxi (before the loss of the Zhongtiaoshan), where the main task of some 400,000 troops is to 'guard' the Communists.
>
> From numerous sources I was given estimates that total imposts are from 30-50 of a farmer's crop. These include a local government tax, the national land in kind (collected through the provincial government), and military demands which are varying and unpredictable. The taxation rates are based on the normal crop, rather than the actual yield for the year. Therefore, the poorer the crop, the larger the proportion which is taken from the farmer. And as the farmer does not devote all his land to wheat, which is demanded for the tax, the percentage of this crop which he must turn over is much higher.
>
> There is considerable evidence that the amount of military grain taken from the people is unnecessarily large. The time-honored custom of Chinese military, of reporting a larger strength than their units actually have, still holds good. By drawing full rations for his supposed strength the commander has a surplus to be disposed of for his profit. A large part of the grain on the open market in Luoyang comes from this source . . .
>
> There is a common complaint, also, that the impositions are not evenly and fairly distributed. Collections are made through the baojia [public security] officials, who are themselves the gentry and landlords, and who often see that they, and their friends, do not suffer too heavily. Influence is still based on wealth and

property; the poorer farmer sees a larger proportion of his grain taken—just as he sees his sons, rather than those of the jiazhang [village leaders] and landlord, taken for the army drafted.

Conditions in Henan have been so bad that for several years there has been a flow of population into Shaanxi, Gansu, and north Sichuan . . . The result is a partial depopulation of Henan and relatively greater imposition on those who remain behind. This movement has been heaviest from the 'front-line area,' where life for the farmer was hardest and which is now hardest hit by famine. A missionary from Zhengzhou says that many farms in that district had already been abandoned last year—before the present famine.

The culmination of these conditions has come this year. That there would be a serious grain shortage was known to the blindest government official in the early spring after the failure of the wheat crop. As early as July, refugees estimated at 1,000 a day were leaving the province. But the grain collection program remained unchanged. In many districts the entire crop was insufficient to meet the demands of the collectors. There were gestures of agrarian protest: all weak, scattered and ineffectual. Apparently, in a few places, troops were used against the people.[1]

Famine victims, already reduced to eating elm bark and dry leaves, were forced to turn over the last of their seeds to the tax collectors. The farmers, so weak they could barely walk, also had to provide feed for the army's horses, grain that was more nutritious than what they stuffed into their mouths.

Why cite a dispatch by Service and not by someone else? He was not Chinese and, not being part of the complex situation, he could be more objective. Yet what he reported, that the famine victims

---

1 John S. Service, "The Famine in Honan [Henan] Province," in Joseph W. Esherick, ed., *Lost Chance in China: The World War II Despatches of John S. Service*, (New York: Random House, 1974), 13–14.

actually had their taxes increased, was not the most serious. Worse was that officials took advantage of the victims and profited at their expense. According to an eyewitness account by Theodore White, some army commanders made fortunes selling surplus provisions to the famine victims. Frenzied merchants from Xi'an and Zhengzhou, petty government functionaries, army officers, and landlords who still had grain snapped up land passed down through generations at criminally low prices. A concentration and a loss of land took place simultaneously, the intensity matching the impact of hunger.

When the Generalissimo, petty functionaries, and landlords ruled over us, they controlled our fate, so how could we trust them?

In the end, large numbers of victims left their land and formed a westward exodus. That included the families of my second and third great aunt, along with many residents of Yanjin County. They had never once laid eyes on the Generalissimo, but the younger men stood at attention when they heard his name, while in his Huangshan residence, the Generalissimo's every gesture controlled and determined their fate. He was wondering: Where is China heading? And where is the world heading? The victims were thinking: Where can we flee to?

4

To this day, Uncle Huazhua rues the fact that he ran away after being conscripted into the army. Why hadn't he simply stuck it out?

"Who took you?" I asked.

"The Nationalist Army."

"I know it was the Nationalist Army, but which unit?"

"Our squad leader was Li Gousheng, the platoon leader was Ruan Zhidong," he said.

"Who were their superiors?" I persisted.

"I don't know."

Later when I looked it up, I learned that the Nationalist army stationed in the Luoyang area was under the command of General Hu Zongnan.

"What did you do after you were press ganged?"

"We were taken to Zhongtiaoshan and sent to the front line, where Japanese bombers killed the deputy squad leader and two soldiers on my first day there. I was so scared I took off that night, a stupid thing to do, now that I think of it."

"You ought to feel bad about it. You ran away at a moment of great national crisis, when the country faced a formidable enemy and your comrades sacrificed their lives. That was shameful."

He glared at me. "I don't feel bad about that."

Taken back, I asked, "Then what?"

"If I hadn't run away, I could have gone to Taiwan and would be a Taiwanese compatriot, a Taibao, now. A guy in Tong Village, Wang Mingqin, whose nickname was Stubborn Mule, was taken two years after me and he went to Taiwan. Last year he came back as a Taibao, with his second wife. He was wearing a big gold watch and even has gold crowns on his teeth. The county chief sent a car to pick him up. A big deal, wouldn't you say? I've got no one to blame but myself. I was too young and couldn't see the big picture. I was only fifteen and survival was all I knew."

Finally seeing what he meant, I tried to console him, "You're right to regret it now, but you were also right to run away back then. Just think. It was 1943, two years before the war was over, which was followed by five years of civil war. Who could say that you wouldn't have been killed like your comrades in one of the many battles? Of course, you could have become a Taibao like Stubborn Mule if you'd survived, but you wouldn't be here if you hadn't."

He gave my comments some thought. "You have a point there. Bullets have no eyes. My fate. I wasn't born to be a Taibao."

"You didn't become a Taibao, but you didn't do too badly either. You were a party secretary and have had a pretty good life."

That perked him up. "You're right. I was in that position for twenty-four years." Then his mood changed abruptly. He sighed. "But ten party secretaries can't hold a candle to one Taibao. And now that I've stepped down, I'm a nobody. The county chief doesn't know who I am."

"So what? Stubborn Mule knows the county chief, and he's still a stubborn mule. But let's not talk about him, Uncle. Tell me how Second Great Aunt and Third Great Aunt fled the famine with their families. You were with them, so you must have had lots of personal experiences."

Uncle Huazhua turned indifferent once we changed the subject, giving me a simple, dry narration.

"We fled, that's it," he said, rubbing his hands.

"How? How did you do it?"

"My Pa pushed a wheelbarrow filled with pots, pans, bowls, and other utensils. My second uncle carried children in baskets. We begged for food along the way, but mostly we ate bark and wild grass. I was press ganged when we got to Luoyang."

"That's all?" I complained. "Don't you remember anything from the journey?"

"I remember I was freezing at night when we slept by the road." He blinked. "I woke up from the cold but didn't make a sound when I saw my parents still fast asleep."

"How did you get press ganged?"

"There was a charity kitchen set up by the Catholic church in Luoyang. I went to get some congee and got caught on the way back."

"Did your parents know?"

"How could they?" He shook his head. "They thought I was kidnapped. I didn't see them again for years."

"How did they manage after you were taken?"

"A few years later my Ma told me that they hopped a train to Shaanxi and my Pa nearly got crushed by it."

"What about Second Great Aunt and her family?"

"They did the same thing, but the train left the station before they were able to get the youngest girl, your aunt, onto the train. They never found her."

I nodded. "Did a lot of people die along the way?"

"Lots of them! There were corpses everywhere and graves too. People were killed when they tried to hop the train."

"Did anyone in our family die of hunger?"

"Of course! Your second great uncle and third aunt. They starved on the road."

"Can't you give me more details?"

Visibly impatient, he gave me an angry glare. "They're all dead. What kind of details do you want?" With that, he limped away. Feeling awkward, I suddenly sensed how ill-intentioned my friend was when he sent me back to 1942. I was picking at my relatives' scabs, which had healed for fifty years, opening up bloody wounds. The thick scabs had turned into helmets by time and dust, as difficult to remove as moving a mountain. It was a windless day; I crouched down by wheat stalks warmed by the sun, struggling to speak with a deaf, mute, virtually incoherent old man with a runny nose. His name was Guo Youyun, who, according to political congress member, Mr. Han, had suffered greater losses than anyone else in the exodus of 1943—his wife, his mother, and three children. Five years later he returned from Shaanxi alone to start a new family. The look of the place he had rebuilt behind the stacks and lived in the past four decades showed that he was more capable than most, for it was a two-story building, uncommon in my hometown at the time, a mixture of Western and Chinese styles. But the contrast between his advanced age and the new house suggested that it was the work of his son, who was now serving as our interpreter. The forty-year-old man, who wore his hair parted in the middle and a watch featuring Gorbachev's face, was not particularly welcoming at first, though his attitude changed when he heard that the deputy police chief and I were childhood classmates. His attitude changed again, this time to impatience, after learning that my arrival had nothing to do with him, and that I wanted only for his father to return with me to the past, fifty years earlier, when he himself was still in the clouds awaiting his arrival on earth. With missing teeth, the old man was hard to understand, making his interpreter son even more impatient and giving me fragmented and uninteresting information about the past. Once again I was reminded of the difficulty of salvaging for the past among the living. But here is more or less what happened to Guo Youyun during his flight: His mother fell ill along the way, so he sold his younger daughter to take care of his mother, which led to a fight with his wife. For her it was not merely a matter of selling off the girl, but that she did not want to sell her own flesh and blood to save a mother-in-law she loathed. The mother died by the Yellow River despite the sale of the girl, and he buried her in a cave, since he could not afford a coffin. When they reached Luoyang, his older daughter contracted smallpox and died in a charity hospital. They were trying to catch a train to Tongguan when his son fell and was crushed beneath a wheel. He and his wife, the only two survivors, reached Shaanxi, where he herded sheep for the locals; his wife, fed up with the tough life, ran away with a human trafficker, leaving him all alone. Sniffling in front of the haystack, he spread his hands and said, "Why did I flee? So everyone could have a fighting chance to live. Who'd have thought that I would be the only one left after all that? What was the point? If I'd known that, I wouldn't have left. At least we would all be together till the very end, not dying along the road like that."

His son did a fine job translating this portion, which sounded as if the old man had been caught up in a vicious cycle. What puzzled me was why he was in tattered clothes, as if still fleeing for his life when he owned a two-story house. He was probably too frugal or he felt that nothing in his life had ever belonged to him. Apparently, this family, with all its material abundance, was not a happy one. It would be impossible to sort out their family relationships, so I turned to his son and said, "It was hard on him, the flight and all."

"He was worthless," he said. "I wouldn't have done it the way he did."

Imagine my surprise. "How would you have done it?"

"I wouldn't have gone to Shaanxi."

"Where would you have gone?"

"I'd definitely have gone to Guandong, a better place than Shaanxi."

I nodded. Guandong was more prosperous and offered an easier life. But my search of hometown histories showed that my kinsmen were never in the habit of fleeing to Guandong, something those from Shandong and Hebei did. Whenever disaster hit, people from my hometown always headed west, not east, even though the area to the west was as poor as the place they were leaving. Obviously, the situation was different in 1942 and 1943; the Japanese had taken Northeast China, which meant they would become a conquered people if they had gone that way. I reminded the son of this fact. He waved me off, flashing his Gorbachev watch, and made a shocking statement.

"When you're talking about survival, who cares who owns the place? So you head west to avoid being a conquered people and starve to death. What would you choose, being conquered or starving? Avoiding the Japanese meant that no one would give a damn about you."

I smiled silently, for I couldn't answer his questions. A miscalculation by the Generalissimo was the fundamental reason he had to flee to Taiwan in 1949. If I had been there in 1942, would I have turned to the Generalissimo, who did not worry or care one bit about me, or would I head for a Japanese occupied area, where I'd have a chance to live?

After saying good-bye to Guo Youyun and his son, I went to see an old woman, Mrs. Cai, in Shili Village. It turned out to be an even worse interview, for I nearly suffered a beating from her son before I had a chance to state the purpose of my visit. Mrs. Cai was seventy years old, making her twenty fifty years before. One night on her westward flight with her parents and two younger brothers, their clothes, money, food, and all their personal belongings were stolen while they slept. They could only wail when they discovered the theft. With no hope of making it to their destination, her parents sold her to save her brothers. At first she'd thought she'd been sold to a family, but then the trafficker took her away and sold her to a brothel, where she spent the next five years as a prostitute. It was not until 1948, during the civil war, that she managed to escape from the brothel and return home. Like Guo Youyun, she had a new family, and the unspeakable five years were a deeply buried secret, until some neighbor women brought it up again during a fight. But in the late 1980s, the uniqueness of her experience during the famine regained its significance as best-selling writers, seizing on the special importance of her life over those five years, came to interview her, with the express intent of turning her brothel experience into an autobiographical best-seller with a title like *My Life as a Prostitute*, which would guarantee its popularity. At first, the family was excited over the interest from so many interviewers, for they realized that their mother's experience was actually valuable and she deserved to be interviewed by well-dressed writers; they even felt honored. Yet as time passed, her children sensed that the writers did not really care about them, and were intent on making money out of their mother's sordid past. Suddenly, her children, all common peasants, felt they had been cheated and insulted and began giving the interviewers the cold shoulder. They even gave their mother, who was still smugly and happily reliving her past, a serious tongue-lashing, forcing her to clam up about her experiences. She recanted everything she'd told the writers, who were understandably put in an awkward position after they had written about her. *My Life as a Prostitute* thus suffered a premature death. Several years had passed by the time I got to their place, but her son thought I was yet another writer here to profit from his mother's sad past by resurrecting *My Life as a Prostitute*. As a result, I failed to speak with the old lady and barely escaped her son's attack; I have never been a courageous person. Besides, it was unseemly of me to pick at people's scabs, particularly an unsightly one on an old lady, just so I could write an article. I went back to tell my former elementary school classmate, the deputy chief of police. To my surprise, he did not side with me and, instead, criticized my approach. Swishing the belt in his hand, he said,

"You should have talked to me first."

"Why? You knew about her?"

"Not really, but I could bring her in for questioning, and that should answer your questions."

I flailed my arms in astonishment.

"No, please don't do that. I'd rather not interview her. Besides, she hasn't committed any crime, so you can't just bring her in for questioning."

He glared at me. "She was a prostitute and I'm in charge of cracking down on prostitution. So I have every right to bring her in."

"That was fifty years ago." I flailed my arms again. "If she was be brought in, it would have been the job of the police in the Nationalist government, not you, and certainly not after five decades."

"Fifty years or not, it's my jurisdiction." He refused to relent. "You wait and see. I'll bring her in."

I changed the subject to stop him; it took a long while to calm him down. When I took leave, I reminded myself of our days in school together.

We now must turn to Theodore White's article in *Time* magazine to continue the narrative of the flight. By now it was clear to me that he would be the protagonist of my essay, for the simple reason that by then no one had cared about the famine, not the leader nor the government whose officials were happily fattening their own pockets by selling relief grain. A great number of people died in 1942, and those who survived treat the disaster with indifference fifty years on. Only one person, a *Time* magazine reporter, a non-Chinese, was concerned about the three million who were dying on land ravished by famine. My face burned from embarrassment when I thought about how we Chinese had no concern for our own and left it to someone from outside to worry about the suffering masses. To be sure, he set out not to show sympathy for the starving Chinese but, based on his reporter's instinct, to find something to write about during the great famine. It was during his search for a news topic that he came face to face with the deplorable situation, which shocked him into speaking out for the victims out of a sense of sympathy and righteousness common among ordinary people. That later led to his confrontation with Chiang Kai-shek. It should come as no surprise to anyone that an American could get to see the Generalissimo so easily, while few Chinese could do that, not even his ministers, who would surely require an appointment prior to the meeting. The refugees could not depend on officials who had traditionally been considered the "parents" of the commoners, so their only hope was a foreign correspondent with little power, particularly toward the end, when he was able to bring some relief, a fact that dumbfounded me five decades after the event.

Theodore White related his trip in February 1943 to Henan, along with Harrison Forman, in his *In Search of History*. I mentioned at the beginning that they had enjoyed one of the best meals ever when they got to Zhengzhou. They made the trip by flying to Baoji from Chongqing, then transferring to a railroad handcar at Tongguan and arriving in Luoyang after a day-long journey, going in the opposite direction of the fleeing refugees. Switching to horses after entering Henan province, they rode to Zhengzhou, where they would then return to Chongqing by postal train. The route meant they could not have taken in much along the way. They wrote mainly bits and pieces of what they saw and heard; the views they expressed were thus highly personal. Since China was so different from America, his personal understanding was likely different from the actual implications of facts. But we can disregard the differences and focus on the details, on what he saw, for what appeared before his eyes along the way had to be true. Based on these factual accounts, we can experience the flight of 1943. Following is the result of my best attempt to sort out his fragmentary witness accounts:

1. What the refugees were wearing and carrying: "They had fled in their best clothes, and the old bridal costumes of middle-aged women, red and green, smeared with filth, flecked the huddle with color. They had fled carrying of their best only what they could—black kettles, bedrolls,

now and then a grandfather clock."[2] All this was a sign that they had lost faith in their hometown, as they left without a backward glance, even packing up time—their clocks. White and his traveling companion spent a night in the Tongguan railroad station, which, according to his records, stank of urine, feces, and body odors. To ward off the cold, many people wound towels around their heads, while those with hats covered their ears with the flaps. They were all waiting for westbound trains, even though the wait was aimless and pointless.

2. Their methods—mainly train hopping and walking. Obviously the former was highly risky, and White said he saw many bloody corpses along the way. Some managed to get on trains but died when Japanese bombs blew them up. Some climbed on to the top of a train and fell off at night when they lost their grip in the freezing air. Others were crushed to death by the moving train, but that was not the worst that could happen. The most horrifying was those who survived the fall. White said he once saw someone lying by the tracks, screaming in pain, with a broken leg, the bones exposed like a white corn stalk. The crushed hip of another person, still alive, was a bloody mess. The blood didn't bother him, White confessed; he was troubled by the incomprehension of the scenes he witnessed. What was going on in such a disorderly, undisciplined migration, and where were the government officials? Obviously White knew nothing about China.

Those who could not get on the train or lost hope on the train put their faith in their own legs and aimlessly, blindly moved westward. All day, White said, along the tracks "I saw nothing but endless lines of people traveling in groups

---

2 This and subsequent citations are from Theodore H. White, *In Search of History: A Personal Adventure* (New York: HarperCollins, 1978).

comprised of family members." It was spontaneous and unorganized, prompted by the famine and the desire to survive. It takes little imagination to see that they showed no emotion, for they had no inkling of what awaited them. The only faith they had was a hope that whatever lay ahead could be better and that things would be fine once they managed to get to the next stop. That is the philosophy of Chinese, something White could not understand. The column of refugees trudged, and if they fell from cold, hunger, or exhaustion they did not get up again. Fathers pushed and mothers pulled handcarts containing all they owned, followed by their children. Old women with bound feet stumbled along. Men carrying their mothers on their back struggled along, but no one stopped. If they came upon children crying atop the bodies of their parents, they quietly walked on, for no one would give a thought to adopting the children.

3. Human trafficking. The refugees quickly went through the little food they carried and were reduced to eating bark, weeds, and kindling. White saw people stripping trees with knives, scythes, and cleavers. It was rumored that the trees had been planted by Wu Peifu, a warlord who loved trees. The elms died after the bark was gone. When there was no more bark, weeds, or kindling to eat, people sold their children, family members with say-so selling off those over whom they had control. At times like this, compassion, kinship, customs, and morality no longer mattered, as the only thing on the people's mind was food. Hunger reigned supreme. A nine-year-old boy could fetch four hundred yuan, two hundred for a four-year-old boy. Young women were sold into brothels and young men like my uncle were press ganged, which they welcomed, since that meant they would eat.

4. Dogs feasting on dead bodies. So many people died on freezing days that the starving survivors were too weak to

dig graves, leaving a vast quantity of corpses out in the wild, food for hungry dogs. You could even say that dogs fared better than humans in the disaster areas of Henan during 1943. Dogs ruled. With his own eyes, White saw a woman's corpse on snow-covered ground less than an hour from Luoyang. Dogs and vultures were about to devour what appeared to be the body of a young woman. As many refugees as dogs slowly regained their wolfish nature, fattening up on the ever-present corpses in the wild, the source of their survival and reproduction. The dogs even dug up corpses buried in sandy soil, and they became picky, choosing only young and tender bodies, especially women. Some were half eaten, while others had been gnawed clean, including the flesh on the heads, leaving only a skeleton behind. White took many pictures, which later worked to help those who managed to escape the maws of the dogs.

5.   Cannibalism. People were turning into wolves. With nothing left to eat, they ate other people, just like the dogs. White said he had never seen anyone kill another human for food before then; his trip to Henan was an eye-opener. Now he was convinced of the existence of cannibalism. It was understandable if they were eating a dead person's flesh, since that was no different from dogs consuming corpses. But there were increasingly more instances of people killing others for their flesh or people feasting on family members. White saw a mother boil her two-year-old to eat, and a father who strangled his two children before cooking them for food. An eight-year-old boy who had lost his parents to hunger during the flight bumped into Tang Enbo's army, which forced a peasant family to adopt him. He later disappeared. An investigation exposed the boy's bones, gnawed clean, in a vat by the peasant's thatched hut. People swapped children or wives to eat. As I wrote, I felt that it would be a waste of their cannibalistic courage if they did not turn into

bandits, commit murder, or join murderous gangs. Seen this way, I felt relief and admiration for those starving people who, instead of fleeing for their lives, took over one of my landowner uncle's buildings, where they raised an army and slaughtered his pigs and sheep. A nation who ate their own instead of raising a fighting force to plan for revolt was a hopeless nation. These rebels, led by Wu De-an, eventually were burned to death by sorghum stalks doused in gasoline, but they formed the backbone of the nation and heralded hope.

5

The *Ta Kung-pao* was suspended for three days. That was the fault not of the newspaper's, but of the failings of the thirty million famine victims, including the families of my grannies and aunts, those who fled and those who stayed, those who starved to death and those who rebelled, as well as those who were eaten by dogs and those who were consumed by other humans. None of them had ever seen a copy of the *Ta Kung-pao*, whose Chongqing edition published their sufferings on February 1, 1943. The story so enraged the Generalissimo that he ordered the three-day suspension. Granted, the paper took its action partly because it was a newsworthy item, and partly out of the compassion that Chinese intellectuals traditionally feel for suffering masses. There might also have been some political intrigue involved, but this we will never know. The reporter sent by the paper to the disaster area was Zhang Gaofeng, whose personal history, experience, emotions, personality, and social connections greatly interest me, though I could learn nothing from the material at hand. The only thing I know about him is the portrait I gathered from his stories, which show him to be a well educated, decent, middle-aged man. After traveling to many places in Henan, he wrote the story, "A factual account of famine in Henan," which I cited earlier. Roughly six thousand words long, it raised a huge outcry in China. Every one of thirty million victims deserved tens of thousands of words to recount their suffering; Zhang used only six thousand, which, divided by thirty million, meant that each victim received an average of 0.0002 words, virtually zero. But it outraged the Generalissimo, who ruled over hundreds of millions of people, because many of them blamed the disaster on his bureaucracy. As I said earlier, Chiang did believe the news, but he simply had more urgent and important foreign and domestic problems to deal with. He could not let the thirty million victims influence his thinking, for they would not affect his rule over China, while he could lose his grip on power, even lose his position if he mishandled even minor details of these important issues. He was clear on what was serious and what was not, and that is not comprehensible to bookworms or ordinary people like us. Three million deaths out of thirty million meant only one death in ten. Besides, more would be born anyway; why should he worry when the cycle of birth and death was irreversible? That was what so fundamentally displeased him about the newspaper and what skewed the story. They misunderstood each other, and that was the cause of the tragedy. The author of the article held on to the belief that the Generalissimo, still in the dark about the severity of the problem, refused to investigate. Since the Generalissimo could not divulge the true reason behind his outrage, he took the simplest step to deal with a complex matter by ordering the three-day suspension.

Zhang's report, in addition to describing the suffering of famine victims, also recorded what the refugees experienced during their flight, much like Theodore White's *Time* article. By comparing the two, we gain a true picture of the famine and of the victims. Zhang wrote about the thousands of people trying to getting on trains heading to Shaanxi along the Shanghai-Shaanxi line; the daily stories of parents abandoning their children; the common occurrences of people falling to their death by losing their footing. In attempting to board trains, people were often severed in half and thus eternally separated from their family. It seemed just about everyone was turned into a cadaver for an anatomy class. Some chose to walk, with old and young stumbling along, or father and son pushing and pulling a handcart, or old couples in their sixties or seventies panting to keep up. "I haven't had a thing to eat for five days, Master."

He wrote, "I kept my eyes tightly shut, quietly listening to the creaking sounds of the handcart, which seemed to roll over my body."

He also wrote about dogs devouring people and people eating each other.

What he reported was all true, but the *Ta-Kung Pao* would not have been suspended if it had carried only true stories. The trouble came when, after publishing the "true account" on February 1, the editor-in-chief, Wang Yunsheng, used the "true account" to summarize the government's attitude to write a commentary titled "Looking toward Chongqing and thinking about the Central Plain." That disrupted Chiang's reasoning; put another way, it hit a sore spot, and he was livid.

From the commentary:

Δ Our readers have read "A factual account of famine in Henan" published in this paper yesterday. After reading it, even a hard-hearted person would shed compassionate tears. By now, everyone knows of the severity of the famine and the people's suffering, but readers probably do not have a clear sense of exactly how terrible it is. Few know about the thirty million people who have been plunged into the abyss of hunger and death. The bones of the dead litter the fields, their flesh picked clean. Those who fled have to care for the old and the young, but often ended up losing family members. They squeeze into a crowd and suffer a beating, but not all manage to get a registration card from the relief committee. Some die from eating poisonous weeds while others suffer throat and stomach pain after gnawing on bark. Taking their wives or daughters to a distant meat market does not guarantee that they receive a few bushels of grain. Who can finish reading such ghastly descriptions?

Δ Worse is that, even with the rampaging famine, the people still have to pay grain taxes. The Yamen continues to arrest people to extract taxes, so they starve and then sell their land to pay up. I recall how I had to keep closing my book and sigh when I read Du Fu's poem "The Clerk of Shihao." Who could have imagined that I would be witnessing a similar situation today? The teletype from the Central News Agency in Lushan reported that "the taxation and requisition of grain in Henan has been going well even during the ongoing, severe famine." And, "according to the head of the Provincial Land Management Bureau, the requisition has progressed nicely, as people everywhere offer everything they have to serve the nation." Blood and tears must have been shed in order for them to write about "offering everything they have."

The commentary continues with details on skyrocketing prices in Chongqing, where people are in a buying frenzy in the midst of price fixing, and the rich continue to live in luxury.

Δ   In Henan, victims of the famine have to sell their land and their family members, even starve to death, with no tax exemption. Why doesn't the government confiscate the property of the super rich and limit the purchasing power of the wealthy, who could care less about prices? When looking at Chongqing and thinking about the Central Plain, one will surely be besieged by painful emotions.

The Generalissimo read the commentary on the day it was published. That evening, the order to suspend the paper for three days was issued by the KMT's military committee and sent from the news inspection center. *Tao-kung Pao* did not print anything on February third, fourth, and fifth.

There is little available material on Wang Yunsheng, as with Zhang Gaofeng. Judging from the limited material, I sensed that he had a fairly good relationship with authorities and socialized with Chen Bulei, Chiang's close ally, even knew Chiang himself.

But I am sure that he was just a journalist who was clueless regarding the Generalissimo's situation and frame of mind. On the other hand, even by today's standards, we must admire his naïve courage in writing the piece. He was puzzled by the suspension, for he thought that writing commentaries was one of his many responsibilities, so why would it have angered the Generalissimo? As a promoter of democracy and freedom, wouldn't the Generalissimo be violating his own beliefs in openly suppressing public opinion? Wang put the question to Chen Bulei, whose response I quoted earlier. Since Chen was close to Chiang (the head of one of his guard units), this response is worth quoting in full to illustrate the Generalissimo's loneliness and quandary:

"The Generalissimo does not believe there is a famine in Henan . . . the provincial report of one is a fraud, one with exaggerated claims, and has ordered that taxes are to be collected as usual."

So it would seem that even Chen was in the dark, stunning Wang, who could not believe that the Generalissimo would not care about the people. As mentioned earlier, it was not really his fault; Wang was to blame for not understanding what was going on in the Generalissimo's mind. On the other hand, Chiang likely despised Wang, and had nothing but contempt for the journalist's naiveté and inexperience. At the end of 1942, before the piece was published, the OSS of the American State Department extended an invitation for Wang to visit the US. With the consent of the KMT government, Wang was issued a passport and bought US dollars, even enjoyed a farewell dinner hosted by Chiang and his wife. Then, after his flight schedule was settled, Wang read Zhang Gaofeng's report and wrote his commentary. Two days before his departure, Wang received a call from Zhang Daofan, the propaganda chief of the KMT central committee:

"The Generalissimo would like you to cancel your trip to America."

Wang did not go. Given the difference in understanding and ideas, as well as the unequal power status, Wang and Chiang waged an outrageous, yet laughable and senseless battle that might have appeared quite animated to an outsider.

One thing is certain: the report and commentary did nothing to alter Chiang's entrenched views and carefully formulated approach. He solved the problem through criticism and an order to stop publication, a long-standing and highly effective means of dealing with intellectuals. It is easy to break their spirit. Now that the criticism had been made, the newspaper had been suspended, and Wang's American trip canceled, there would be no serious repercussions, except that these intellectuals would learn to behave themselves. As a result, neither I nor the countless victims of famine would express any gratitude toward Zhang's report or Wang's commentary, since the noise they made had absolutely no effect. On the contrary, provoking the Generalissimo could lead to adverse consequences. So we must dispense with Zhang and Wang; instead we should thank the foreigner, Theodore White, who aided the poor during the famine of 1942–1943. His help made a difference, while the "aid" that produced no real effect could only put everyone through another cycle of torment as high hopes again turned to despair. That was why the Generalissimo adopted different approaches with different people. He was not excessively obstinate; in fact, he knew when and how to be flexible. With the numerous Chinese under his rule, he could upset a few, even execute a couple without affecting the larger picture. Chinese intellectuals considered themselves above the victims of famine, but in fact they were not that much higher in the mind of the supreme leader, who treated the foreigners differently. Every foreigner counted; he could upset a government if he mistreated one of its citizens, so he trod carefully. Such was the intricacy of foreign relations, where dealings between the people and their government was concerned. As an American intellectual, Theodore White felt the same compassion and outrage as his Chinese counterparts at the sight of the rampant suffering; he, too, published articles, not in China but in the US. And that was where the difference lay. The Generalissimo could order a paper suspended if it was published in China but *Time* magazine was beyond the reach of his authority. As White pointed out, the anarchistic situation would have continued in Henan if it not for actions taken by the American press. In a word, the Americans lent us considerable assistance, so I don't think we ought to have forgotten this page of our history when we later shouted "Down with American Imperialism," at least not for those two years.

After a tour of the disaster area, White was eager to send his dispatch, so he stopped at the first telegram office on his return trip and rushed a report out. Back then the government in Chongqing required that every news report be examined by the Central Propaganda Office. White's report would never have gone out if it had been inspected. His cable was sent to New York from Luoyang through a commercial radio station in Chengdu; that might have been a result of the lax regulations of this particular station (not a bad situation in an authoritarian country) or it could have been someone at the telegram office who had a conscience. In any case it flashed through to New York without inspection, and the news quickly spread via *Time* magazine. Madame Chiang, who was at the time making her world-famous visit to the US, was incensed after reading the report. Consumed by anger and prompted by recklessness, she hastily adopted the Chinese way by asking Henry Luce, the publisher of *Time*, to fire White. Unsurprisingly, Luce turned her down. America was, after all, a country that enjoyed freedom of the press. Even if a scandal involving President Roosevelt were exposed and Mrs. Roosevelt demanded that the reporter be fired, *Time* would not necessarily comply. Just consider how long Roosevelt had been a president and how long *Time* had been published. Naturally, Mrs. Roosevelt would not be that foolish; nor would she so easily succumb to the tempting thought of interfering with the press.

Theodore White became a controversial figure overnight in Chongqing. Some officials denounced him for evading the censors while others accused him of colluding with Communist party members inside the cable office. But no matter what they said, they could do nothing about him, and that was the key. By then, the information from White had gotten, through the Army intelligence service, to Stilwell, the American Embassy, and the Chinese Minister of Defense. White even met with the head of China's Legislative Yuan, the Governor of Sichuan, and Madame Song Qingling, the widow of Dr. Sun Yat-sen. No Chinese reporter or newspaper editor could possibly have mobilized such a broad swath of society.

The attitude of the Chinese Minister of Defense was:

"Either you're lying or someone has lied to you, Mr. White."

Both the head of the Legislature and the governor of Sichuan told White that it was useless to talk to them because only Chiang's word could spur action.

But getting to see Chiang was not easy; it took White five days. Without the help of Madame Song Qingling, Chiang's sister-in-law, it would not have occurred. (In an authoritarian system, family connections are not always a bad thing, for they sometimes work to the people's advantage.)

Based on White's recollection, "Madame Sun Yat-sen was physically a dainty woman." She said she was told "that he [Chiang] was very weary after his long tedious inspection tour and needed a few days rest. But I insisted that the matter involved the lives of many millions . . . May I suggest that you report conditions as frankly and fearlessly as you did to me. If heads must come off, don't be squeamish about it . . . otherwise there would be no change in the situation."

Chiang received White in his dark office, standing erect and slim, taut, offering a stiff hand in greeting, then he sat in his high-backed chair and listening to White with visible distaste. White interpreted Chiang's demeanor as an unwillingness to believe the report, which showed that White had made the same mistake as the Chinese intellectuals, and that they were not talking about the famine on the same level. They had a superficial understanding of Chiang. How could he possibly not believe them? Chiang surely knew more than White and had more details about the famine in Henan, but it simply was not the most important task at hand. Now some low-ranking

officials, Chinese intellectuals, and foreign correspondents were pil-
ing on him matters that were important to them but not to him. Put
differently, they turned a matter that was urgent on a regional scale
into an all-consuming major crisis and would not let go of it unless he
dealt with them. Worse yet, news reports had traveled outside China
and brought popular opinion down on Chiang. He had to put aside
more serious matters and listen to a meddling foreigner tell him what
was going on in China. How ridiculous was that! Infuriating and yet
laughable. Chiang wondered why so many hands of different colors
and shapes were being thrust into a pile of dog shit, which was the
true reason for the distasteful look on his face; that eluded White
for fifty years. A true proof that communications between peoples is
terribly difficult.

Bored and uninterested, Chiang turned to one of his aides and
said,

"They [the famine victims] see a foreigner and tell him everything."

White continued in his memoir, "It was obvious he did not
know what was going on."

White was wrong in his reading of Chiang; but matters in China
can be quite serendipitous, for without his misreading, White would
not have felt the outrage, which led him in turn to confront Chiang so
forcefully. White's sentiment and actions cornered Chiang, a highly
intelligent strategist who concerned himself only with major matters.
Chiang knew about the famine, but as an important figure, a head of
state, he could not refer to the thirty million lives as a trivial event.
How would that have made him look? That was something Chiang
could not disclose, and yet White's confrontation forced him to deal
with it. There was nothing Chiang could say or do, which only reinforced White's perception of Chiang's ignorance of the severity of
the famine. So White "tried to break through by telling him about
the cannibalism." Chiang did not believe that an American like
White, who did not know what it was to suffer, would have paid a
personal visit to the disaster areas and witness so many things. At

most, White had just made a cursory trip and heard some rumors. Chiang responded with a denial:

"Cannibalism could not have occurred in China, Mr. White."

"I saw dogs eating humans with my own eyes," White said.

"Impossible!" Chiang persisted.

White then called Forman, the reporter for the London *Times*, who was waiting in the anteroom, to come in and show the Generalissimo the photos they had taken in Henan. Forman's pictures "clearly showed dogs standing over dug-out corpses, which shocked the Generalissimo. The Generalissimo's knee began to jiggle slightly, in a nervous tic." I believe that the Generalissimo was angry at White and Forman, at the disaster zones, at his officials, at this unimportant matter, and at other urgent affairs of the world, which had rendered the equally serious issue of famine insignificant. If not for the geopolitical situation, he could have mobilized people all over China to help the famine victims; he could have made a trip to the disaster areas to comfort the people and polish his image as a caring leader. However incensed he felt inside, he could not let on, particularly not in front of a foreign correspondent. All he could do was jiggle his knee in a nervous tic over the pictures of a dog eating a human corpse. Like all Chinese rulers, Chiang made a strategic calculation and negotiated an about-face. With a serious look on his face, he appeared to have finally learned the truth and showed gratitude to those who made him see the light. "He took out his little pad and brush pen and began to make notes. He asked for names of officials" who failed at famine efforts. That is also typical of a Chinese ruler in dealing with problems—start with organizational policies. Then he wanted more names; he wanted them to give him a complete report, before thanking them and saying that they were better investigators than "any of the investigators I [Chiang] sent out" himself. The twenty-minute meeting was brought to an end and White and Forman were ushered out.

I am convinced that Chiang must have smashed a cup after the two left and used a curse word that he has been portrayed as saying in the movies: "Bullshit!"

Soon, just as Madame Sun Yat-sen had predicted, heads began to roll, all because of a photo of a dog and a corpse; it began with those unfortunate people who had made it easier for White to send the telegram, for they helped reveal to the Americans the embarrassing news of starvation in Henan. But many lives were "saved by the power of the American press" White wrote in his memoir. I imagine he must have felt quite pleased with himself when he wrote that; I quote him because it made me laugh. But the source of the power did not matter; the Generalissimo was persuaded to take action, which saved millions of lives. So who was our savior? Who saved the peasants? Ultimately it was the Generalissimo, the head of state, even if his actions were taken under a strange combination of circumstances and through an extraordinary misunderstanding. White took all the credit because he did not understand China; it did not occur to him that the American press, no matter how powerful it might be, functioned as a cause, not a result. In China, the American press could never top the Generalissimo. White was smug and so were foreign priests posted in China, such as Father Thomas Megan, who sent White a letter from Loyang:

"After you got back and started the wires buzzing, the grain came rushing in from Shaanxi by trainloads. They just could not unload it fast enough here at Loyang. That was score No. 1, a four-bagger to say the least. The provincial government got busy and opened up soup kitchens all over the country. They really went to work and got something done. The military shelled out SOME of their MUCH surplus grain and that helped a lot. The whole country really got busy putting cash together for the famine-stricken and money poured into Henan.

"All four of the above points were bull's eyes as I see and confirmed my former opinion that the famine was entirely man-made and was at all times within the power of the authorities to control had they the inclination and desire to do so. Your visit and your jacking them up did the trick, jerked them out of their stupor, and put them on the job, and then things did GET DONE. In a word, more power

to Time & Life, and to Fortune Long Life. Peace! It's wonderful!
. . . You will be long remembered in Honan. Some remember you
in a very pleasant way, but there are others who grit their teeth and
they've got reason to do so."

6

Famine relief work got under way in Henan because the Generalissimo took action. He said to go to work and of course work was done.
Yet between 1942 and 1943, the foreigners were ahead of the Chinese
in lifting the first batch of famine victims out of their misery. Even
though we dislike foreigners and would rather not owe them a debt
of gratitude, they are always there to help us out at critical moments.
What are we to do? At a moment like that, the urgent matter was to fill
the stomachs of the dying to pull them back from the brink of death
rather than consider famine relief from a holistic, macro point of view
that included spiritual and material salvation. Before the Generalissimo's order was carried out, the foreign priests, who had come to
China for spiritual invasion, had already taken action, devoid of political motivation or government decree, prompted instead by religious
principles. Sent by Christ to China to spread the gospel, the priests,
who included Americans and Europeans, Catholics and Protestants,
were there to do charitable work. The Americans and the Italians
were enemies in the European theater, but their priests worked hand
in hand on an altruistic mission in my hometown, saving numerous
lives. They would have been enemies on the battlefield, but they
were of the same mind when facing the dying in my hometown. Seen
from this perspective, people in my hometown might not have died
in vain after all.

　　Soup kitchens were usually set up in American and European
churches, so cities like Zhengzhou and Loyang, where there were
churches, had places for my relatives to eat. As I said before, my
Uncle Huazhua was on his way to a soup kitchen in Loyang when
he was seized by General Hu Zongnan. But where did these char-

itable organizations get the rice to make congee? As their faith in Chiang was fading, the American government sent relief materials to the missionaries to distribute. Instinct told the fleeing victims of famine, though illiterate, that they could no longer trust their own government and that their only savior was the foreigner, the white people. As stated by White:

"Missionaries left their compounds only when necessary, for a white man walking in the street was the only agent of hope, and was assailed by wasted men, frail women, children, people head-knocking on the ground, groveling, kneeling, begging for food, wailing, 'K'o lien, k'o lien' ('Mercy, mercy'), but pleading really only for food."

I did not feel embarrassed for my relatives as I read this passage; I would have kowtowed to the foreigners too. Victims of famine, who besieged any priests they encountered, surrounded the churches. If a priest had raised his arm to call for action, I believe that the people gathering outside a church would have risen up, bravely forging ahead; they would not have feared death. Incidents of resisting foreigners during the Second Opium War would never reoccur. Women and children sat by the church daily, where every morning the priests found abandoned babies and sent them to temporary orphanages— even the next generation of Chinese was entrusted to the foreigners, the only ones who allowed my relatives to understand the value of life. From a yellowed page of a newspaper published fifty years ago, I read a Catholic priest's reason for setting up a soup kitchen:

"At least they must die with dignity."

The churches had their own hospitals, which were soon filled by patients with terrible intestinal diseases caused by the ingestion of filth. As extreme hunger got the best of them, the victims stuffed dirt into their mouths to fill their stomachs. To save them, the staff at the hospitals had to get the dirt out of their bodies first.

Orphanages were also set up by churches to take in children who had survived their parents, but that had to be done secretly, for the places would be immediately overtaken by countless orphans once the people learned of it. Some parents abandoned or sold their children for their own survival. There were too many orphans and too few foreigners to help them. In other words, too many Chinese children were looking for foreign parents but there were not enough foreign parents for them. I once read a report that went:

"Hunger even destroyed the basic emotional bond between people. A crazed couple tied their six children to trees to free them to search for food for themselves. A mother went begging for food with an infant and two older children. When they were exhausted, the mother sat down to care for the infant while the older children walked on to the next village for food. By the time they returned, their mother had died but the infant continued to suck on the dead women's nipple. A couple killed their two children so they did not have to hear them crying for food. The priests did their best to take in abandoned children, but only in secret, because they would have been overwhelmed by countless children left at their doors if people heard about their charitable act."

Children are the barometer of a country or a government. If the children are weighed down by a heavy book bag and cannot finish their assignment even after taking it home, then that country must be stumbling along as well. Likewise, a government might not last long if it allows its children to die of hunger, leaving only foreigners to help. In the foreigners' view, the Chinese children, when healthy, were all pretty, with beautiful natural luster on their hair and a clever sparkle in their almond eyes. But now these children were emaciated, like scarecrows; where their eyes should be were now two gaping holes filled with pus. Extreme hunger extended their bellies; the dry, cold air cracked their skin. Their voices were hoarse and feeble, barely loud enough for them to moan for food. Were these merely problems with the children? No, they signified problems with the Nationalist government. If the Generalissimo, at his villa in Huang-shan, were sitting atop these children, wouldn't his confidence be affected? Would Roosevelt and Churchill show him any respect?

Chiang was, after all, still a human being—it always makes me sad to hear such an expression from say, a wife about her husband or vice versa. How disdainful! Chiang was still human and had to shown concern for the thirty million victims after a foreign correspondent placed a photo of a dog eating a corpse before him. He launched a relief effort after heads rolled, which meant that China joined in to help the victims. The efforts by the Chinese and their foreign counterparts were different; the foreigners did it out of compassion and their Christian doctrine, not spurred by anger from Roosevelt, Churchill, or Mussolini. Absent compassion or religious teaching (why had Chiang converted to Christianity? Was it purely because of marriage and sex, or political connections?), China had only an order from Chiang. Herein lies another difference between China and the West.

So, how did the Chinese government go about helping the victims? Please allow me to cite some sources. Readers are probably tired of my incessant effort to cite sources, but I have no choice if historical veracity is to be maintained. I cannot help it if you are bored. I am not writing fiction, a break from my usual work and the task my friend gave me. Please do not think I enjoy citing historical documents; in fact they confine me, like shackles, stripping me of the freedom to create. I was apprehensive when my friend handed me a bundle of documents.

"Do I have to read all of these?" I asked.

"Yes, otherwise, you will let your imagination run wild and make up stories as you go along."

So I have no choice but to go back to the documents again and again. Please understand my situation and forgive me for inserting so much of them into my writing; it was all my friend's fault.

Records of Chinese government's famine relief effort in 1943:

Δ The Generalissimo ordered the effort to be carried out.

Δ The relief work was marked by stupidity and an extreme lack of efficiency; the local officials behaved abominably, further worsening a tragic situation.

Δ Shaanxi, a neighboring province of Henan, which had more grain in storage, should have been ordered to send food to Henan right away to prevent the famine. But that would have benefitted Henan while hurting Shaanxi, and in turn upset the delicate balance of power that was indispensible to the government. It would never be done.

(Traditionally politics trump the people in China. Who created politics? And what for?) Furthermore, food could also have been delivered from Hubei, but the commander of the Hubei battle zone was not allowed to do that.

Δ Relief funds reached Henan at an excruciatingly slow speed. (What was the use of paper money when there was no food to be bought? Could they eat the funds?) After several months, only eighty million of the two billion yuan allocated by the central government reached the disaster area, where it did not serve the purpose of relief at all. Provincial government officials deposited the money in banks to accrue interest, while they argued among themselves over how to use it most effectively. In some areas, the local officials first deducted tax owed by the victims, greatly reducing the amount to the villagers. Even the national banks benefitted in the process. Relief funds from the central government arrived in 100 yuan bills, a relatively small amount, since a pound of wheat cost between ten and eighteen yuan. But the grain hoarders refused to sell grain to people paying with 100 yuan bills, forcing the victims to exchange the money for smaller bills at the central banks. The banks took a steep cut when changing the money, with a 17 percent fee. What the people in Henan needed was food, but by March 1943 the government had offered them about ten thousand sacks of rice and twenty thousand sacks of other grains, which meant the victims, who had been starving since fall of the previous year, got about a pound of grain per person.

Δ   Once the relief work was finally under way, the villagers continued to die, on the road, in the mountains, by train stations, in their own mud huts, or in deserted fields.

Of course not all the officials were so hard-hearted as to exploit the people as they died. Some found their conscience to do good for the people or to have a commemorative stele built for them. I've always believed that, as ordinary people, we don't care about officials' motivation, so long as they serve the people. They could be doing something for career advancement and promotion, or to show someone they loved what they are made of. We don't care, as long as it helps us. Following the lead of the foreigners and their examples, the compassionate General Tang Enbo came forward and opened an orphanage to take in those overflowing from the Western orphanages. It was a good deed. General Tang was a good man. But what kind of orphanage was it? This was what Theodore White wrote:

"In my recollection, 'It stank worse than anything else I have ever smelled. Even the escorting officer could not stand the odor and, holding his handkerchief to his nose, asked to be excused. These were abandoned babies. They were inserted four to a crib. Those who could not fit in cribs were simply laid on the straw. I forget what they were fed. But they smelled of baby vomit and baby shit, and when they were dead, they were cleared out.'"

That is why we say that General Tang was a good man; he was the best among all the government officials and generals, for it was still better to have an orphanage like that than not have any at all.

Donations were collected and charity performances were put on, but the money was turned over to the government to distribute to the victims. In 1942, the November issues of the *Republican Daily* were filled with reports of performances, concerts, sales of calligraphy and paintings, all for charitable purposes. County secretary Han from my hometown hosted one performance himself. I'm convinced that the donors and performers were sincere and compassionate, and they shed sympathetic tears for us. But the problem was, the proceeds could not be distributed directly to the victims; instead they were turned over, in an organized manner, to the government, which then distributed them to the people, also in an organized manner. The money traveled through one government office after another—from the provincial level to the county, then to the township, before reaching the villages—a worrisome number of offices. How could we be sure that the relief funds from donations and charity performances would safely reach us, with so many rounds of exploitation and fees after they left the government's hand?

But let's not dwell on that. The government is like our parents; when they skimp on our share, we accept it silently, like swallowing bloody teeth when they knock them out. The problem was made worse, though, when some of those unique characters with special talents spoke up at a moment like this, but not for the victims—what good would that have done them? Aligning themselves with the government, they studied ways to deal with the famine, as in a story published in the *Henan Republican Daily* on February 14, 1943:

"Liu Daoji, a staff member in the finance section, has invented and produced famine food; a person need only eat the complex formula once a week or the simple formula one once a day."

Fifty years later, any Chinese who reads this brief report will find it impossible to believe. Obviously, not only was the government unreliable, but even a staff member, one of us, the working poor, could not be depended upon. It would have been fine if the invention had been real; the government would have welcomed it, as it would not have needed to undertake relief effort and we the people would have welcomed it with open arms, for it meant that no one would ever die of hunger again. It would have been a panacea not only to the Republican government, for people continued to starve to death in the decades that followed the famine. The Chinese would enjoy everlasting peaceful and a bountiful existence if there had been a man-made food that kept a person full for seven days.

But we have yet to see that formula, proof that it merely served a propaganda purpose to calm the populace; not a single life was saved by it. Mr. Liu Daoji might have been a kindhearted, compassionate man with great patience and circumspection; or he could simply have been hoping for a promotion. Whatever his personal motivation, his formula was useless. We continued to die day after day, on the road, in the field, and by train stations.

This was the relief effort under the guidance of Mr. Chiang Kai-shek in 1943, which can be summed up in one word: it was a "farce." It served only as propaganda, a show to the world and to the foreigners. The Generalissimo ordered the relief effort, but his heart was not in it; instead, he was thinking about the world and the national affairs, as well as the delicate balance among various political powers, which was the crux of the farce. It was a circus act with many actors, but the victims bore the results. It reminded me of a phrase by Mao Zedong—"I wonder who will take charge of the people's livelihood in this vast world," which could be modified to question who would care about whether we live or die.

How did the dying victims feel about all this? Zhang Gaofeng, the reporter for *Ta Kung Pao*, had this to say:

"The people of Henan are brave souls who boast at their dying moment that premature death brings early reincarnation."

What grand sounding words! Who dare says that the Chinese have no religion? Who dare says that the Chinese are like loose sand with no sense of unity? When even the Buddha was confronted by such a situation, I believe, he could only say something like that. Why did the Generalissimo convert to Christianity? What has Christianity done for him? It helped him find a wife; that was all. But he got a major political boost from Buddhist teaching that has bored deeply into the Chinese soul.

To be sure, not all the thirty million Henan residents died of hunger. In fact, only three million of them, one tenth, starved to death. Three million fled the area, with more than twenty million remaining.

What were those who stayed put hoping for, when the government and their own compatriots ignored them? They pinned their hopes on the land after the drought, the only thing they could depend on, even though it was burdened with heavy, countless taxes and exploitation. Records show that Henan had a heavy snowfall in the early spring of 1943 and rain in the seventh month. Good signs. We were hoping, under the care of the old man in the sky, for a good harvest in the summer and fall. Everything would be fine if we had something to fill our stomachs; we could put up with a government filled with darkness, ugliness, filth, and exploitation. On this point, we believed that the Nationalist government back then actually shared our hope that heaven would bring the disaster to an end with clement weather to give us a bumper crop. If not, where would the government be when every one of its citizens died of hunger? Who would provide warm houses and delicious food for the leaders and officials of the governments so that they could use their brain power to come up with more systematic means to deal with the people? Who would they rule when the people were all gone? But the old man was not kind enough to concern itself with the wishes of the government and the twenty million people. Another disaster hit in 1943; the drought was followed by a scourge of locusts, worsening the people's suffering.

7

The locusts came in the fall of 1943. My friend, the editor of *A Hundred Years of Disasters*, had a different plan for a portrayal of the locust scourge, so my current story will not go into the details. There have been other, more impressive, locust attacks in Chinese history, a tale being written by another friend of mine, someone I deeply respect. But that does not mean I cannot mention it, since we are writing about locusts from different time periods. His occurred in Shandong in 1927 and mine in Henan in 1943; the plagues were similar but with different locusts. My grannie told me that those in 1943 were big ones, some green (young locusts, I think), some yellow (their elders), coming in swarms so large they darkened the sky, almost like the bombers during the Pacific War or Normandy landing. Their buzzing was heard miles away as they dove down to blanket crops that were denuded within an hour. In the spring of 1943, gusts of strong wind blew away the kernels of wheat on the stalks, followed by the plague of locusts in the fall. You can imagine how tough the peasants, life was like. The locusts came and people died off. My parents told me that the locusts, instead of eating sweet potatoes, peanuts, and cowpeas, feasted on peas, corn, and sorghum. To keep from dying, the surviving victims fought the locusts. We could not do anything about the government, whose exploitation and oppression were carried out by an insane mechanism, aided by weapons. But with locusts, we could fight face to face, without suspicion of revolt or riot. And that was the difference between a government and locusts. How did we fight? There were three ways. One, waving a bamboo pole tied with bedsheets to chase them away, which was a method that hurt others to benefit only yourself. When the locusts were chased away, they simply went to someone else's field; beside, they would come back the next day anyway. Two, digging wide trenches between fields to stop them from advancing. After finishing off someone's crop, the locusts would have to pass the trenches before reaching the next field; the peasants used pestles to smash them into pulp or burned them, a cruel but more effective method. I think as many locusts were smashed as the peasants who starved to death. Three, praying. My grannie went to burn incense at the shrine set up by Niu Jinbao's aunt, hoping that the locusts would spare her employer's crop. Records show that nothing they did had any effect; there were simply too many locusts for the sheets, trenches, and deities. Most of the crops went into the bellies of the locusts and the victims of drought in 1942 suffered a similar fate in 1943.

The tyrant of Nature damaged the lifeline of the peasants of Henan: the drought scorched their wheat, the locusts denuded their sorghum, and hail destroyed their buckwheat. They lost hope when the fall sprouts dried up, pushing them onto the path of death. At the time, hunger afflicted nine of ten Henan residents.

If the situation had persisted, I think that every man, woman, and child in Henan would have starved to death, not an outcome we and our government would have liked to see. Luckily, that did not happen and many survived to bring the next generations of Henanese into the world. Fifty years later, Henan regained its status as the second most populous province in China. How were they saved? Did the government adopt effective measures? No. Did the locusts fly off? No. Then why? The answer is, the Japanese came. In 1943 the Japanese advanced into Henan and saved the lives of many villagers. They committed atrocities in China, slaughtering tens of thousands of Chinese; they were our mortal enemies. And yet from the winter of 1943 to the spring of 1944, it was these bloodthirsty invaders who saved many people by giving away their military rations to sustain and nourish the Chinese in Henan. Of course they harbored evil intentions as they shared the food; it was a strategic move and a political plot to bribe the people, occupy our country, seize our territory, and rape our women. But they saved our lives. On the other hand, was our government completely innocent of any strategic intention or political plot when dealing with its own people? They did nothing to help us. Under these circumstances, whoever gives you milk is your mother, as the saying goes. By eating the Japanese food, we became traitors, but was this country of ours worth our loyalty? What was there to keep us from betraying it? The government taxed us nearly to death in order to fight the Japanese and the Communists, as well as support the Allies, the battles in Southeast Asia, and Stilwell. So we supported the Japanese army, helping them invade our land. Countless villagers from Henan, including my relatives, served as guides for the Japanese, supported the front and carried stretchers; some even joined their army to disarm the Chinese. Five decades later, it was impossible to root out the traitors because there were so many of them; we are all descendants of traitors. My reading showed that, during the weeks of fighting in Henan, about fifty thousand Chinese soldiers were disarmed by their own people. Here is the record:

"In the Spring of 1944, the Japanese army launched a major offense in Henan to prepare for another, larger scale battle. The nominal commander in the Henan battlefield was Jiang Dingwen, an eagle-eyed man whose stock in trade in Henan was threatening the administrative officials under his jurisdiction. Once he devastated the governor or Henan, scaring him into a scheme to take the little bit of grain from the peasants.

Deploying sixty thousand soldiers to attack Henan, the Japanese began its offense in mid April and met with little resistance from the Chinese. Morale was low in the Chinese army, which consisted of sickly peasants who had suffered greatly during the famine, after years of a lethargic lifestyle. The army seized the peasants' cattle for transportation purpose to fill a need in the front line but also to serve the army officers' private gain. With wheat as a main staple crop, the Henan peasants relied on their cattle for subsistence; their lives would be unbearable without their farm animals.

The peasants had been biding their time. For months, they lived in extreme hardship from the famine and the inhumane extortion from their own army; now they refused to take it any longer. Arming themselves with hunting rifles, hatchets, and rakes, they disarmed soldiers one by one at first, but eventually were able to disarm a whole regiment. An estimate showed that, over a few weeks in Henan, about fifty thousand Chinese soldiers were disarmed by their own people. Under such conditions, it would have been a miracle if the Chinese army had survived for three months. With villages engaged in armed uprisings, the Chinese army was no match for the Japanese, who, in only three weeks, seized the southbound corridor and defeated China's three hundred thousand soldiers.

How did they do that with a scant sixty thousand troops? By sharing their rations with the Chinese peasants, the masses, who in turn helped them achieve their goal. From late 1943 to early 1944, we assisted the Japanese invaders. Were we traitors? Were we Chinese?

When Theodore White interviewed a Chinese officer before the battle, White condemned the Chinese army for its relentless taxation, to which the officer responded, "The land still belongs to China even if the people are dead, but Japan will take over China if the soldiers starve to death." I think the response mirrored the Generalissimo's mentality. Yet, when the issue was laid out before the dying victims of famine, it became a question of becoming a Chinese ghost or a living traitor. We chose the latter.

This is my conclusion from going back to 1942.

Postscript

As I looked back on 1942 and 1943, what piqued my interest, besides the famine, were trivial matters occurring during the time. And the most interesting ones were two divorce announcements in the *Henan Republican Daily,* which showed that the famine might have been the dominant theme among the people back then, but normalcy continued to exist, marked by a myriad of complex emotional entanglement and daily lives. We must not generalize from isolated events; a fallen leaf does not usher in autumn and a blind man cannot "see" an elephant by touching it. We cannot simply focus on the famine and ignore the complete picture of a human existence. Viewed from this angle, we might have been overly critical of the Generalissimo. Moreover, from the two announcements we can see how much progress has been made in our society. Here are the complete texts:

Urgent Announcement

My marriage to the woman from the Feng family has been marred by discord and we cannot grow old together. We have agreed to a divorce. From today on, we are each free to marry whomever we want.

Zhang Yinping and his wife, Ms. Feng.

Announcement

On the sixth day of the twelfth lunar month, when I delivered goods to Loyang, my wife, Liu Hua, from Xuchang, ran away, taking her clothes, bedding, and other personal effects. She has not been heard from for several days. If anything happens to her from now on, I will not be responsible, as I am hereby severing all ties with her. I make this important announcement to alert friends and family.

Tian Guangyan, of No. 5, Zhongzheng West Street, Huaimiao Village for Yanshi.